Praise for Victor LaValle and

BIG MACHINE

"Haunting and fresh . . . heroically strange . . . playful, entertaining and deadly serious . . . There's a touch of Pynchon [but LaValle has] a style all his own."
—*Los Angeles Times*

"Spectacular . . . sprawling, fantastical . . . and beautifully drawn . . . 'Doubt is the big machine [that] grinds up the delusions of men and women.' This novel ends not with a bang or a whimper, but with the sound of immense gears starting to turn." —*The Washington Post*

"This tale is peculiar, magnificent and—as books about cults often are—quite funny." —*Chicago Tribune*

"LaValle employs a sly wit and deadpan humor. . . . Draw[s] comparisons to the work of Ralph Ellison and Thomas Pynchon." —*The Wall Street Journal*

"Beautiful." —*Vanity Fair*

"Fractures all of our notions of how well-made fiction ought to behave . . . idea-hungry and haywire, too alive and abrasive to be missed. The multicultural novel has come of age—smashingly." —*Kirkus Reviews* (starred review)

"*Big Machine* transcends the boundaries of standard literary fiction and defies readers' expectations at every turn. Fantasy and reality constantly mingle, but the core issues—though messy and complicated—are undeniably human." —*BookPage*

"LaValle is as much wry fabulist as he is dogged allegorist, and his flights of grim fancy are tethered by acute observations. . . . He can be awfully funny, too. . . . [His] devilish fable render[s] the visible world—of science, social hierarchies, and *New York Times* headlines—a load of cultish hooey."   —*Bookforum*

"Sweeping and swashbuckling . . . genius."
                    —*The San Francisco Bay Guardian*

"Truly spellbinding."   —*Time Out New York*

"The tension between sci-fi and noir material and realist approach makes *Big Machine* crackle. . . . [This] big novel grinds up our delusions about reality, spirituality and the principles of fiction."   —*The Dallas Morning News*

BY VICTOR LAVALLE

FICTION

The Ecstatic

Big Machine

The Devil in Silver

The Changeling

NOVELLAS

The Ballad of Black Tom

Lucretia and the Kroons

SHORT STORY COLLECTION

Slapboxing with Jesus

BIG MACHINE

BIG MACHINE

A Novel

VICTOR LAVALLE

ONE WORLD
NEW YORK

2010 Trade Paperback Edition

Copyright © 2009 by Victor LaValle

Published in the United States by One World, an imprint of Random House, a division of Penguin Random House LLC, New York.

ONE WORLD and colophon are registered trademarks of Penguin Random House LLC.

Originally published in hardcover in the United States by Spiegel & Grau, an imprint of Random House, a division of Penguin Random House LLC, in 2009.

LIBRARY OF CONGRESS CATALOGING-IN-PUBLICATION DATA
LaValle, Victor
Big machine: a novel / Victor LaValle.
p. cm.
ISBN 978-0-385-52799-6
1. Ex-drug addicts—Fiction. 2. Parapsychologists—Fiction. 3. Belief and doubt—Fiction. 4. Psychological fiction. I. Title.
PS3562.A8458B54   2009   813'.54—dc22   2009000381

Printed in the United States of America on acid-free paper

oneworldlit.com
randomhousebooks.com

Book design by Christopher M. Zucker

FOR OAKLAND,
CITY FULL OF GOOD

"Nobody trusts anybody now, and we're all very tired."
—FROM JOHN CARPENTER'S *The Thing*

1

We Like Monsters

1

DON'T LOOK FOR DIGNITY in public bathrooms. The most you'll find is privacy and sticky floors. But when my boss gave me the glossy envelope, the bathroom was the first place I ran. What can I say? Lurking in toilets was my job.

I was a janitor at Union Station in Utica, New York. Specifically contracted through Trailways to keep their little ticket booth and nearby bathroom clean. I'd done the same job in other upstate towns, places so small their whole bus stations could've fit inside Union Station's marbled hall. A year in Kingston, six months in Elmira. Then Troy. Quit one and find the next. Sometimes I told them I was leaving, other times I just disappeared.

When I got the envelope, I went to the bathroom and shut the door. I couldn't lock it from the inside so I did the next best thing and pulled my cleaning cart in front of the door to block the way. My boss was a woman, but if the floors in front of the Trailways booth weren't shining she'd launch into the men's room with a fury. She had hopes for a promotion.

But even with the cart in the way I felt exposed. I went into the third stall, the last stall, so I could have my peace. Soon as I opened the door, though, I shut it again. Good God. Me and my eyes agreed that the second stall would be better. I don't know what to say about the hygiene of the male species. I can understand how a person misses the hole when he's standing, but how does he miss the hole while sitting down? My goodness, my goodness. So, it was decided, I entered stall number two.

The front of the envelope had my name, written by hand, and nothing else. No return address in the corner or on the back, and no mailing address. My boss just said the creamy yellow envelope had been sitting on her desk when she came in that morning. Propped against the green clay pen holder her son made in art class.

I held the envelope up to the fluorescent ceiling lights and saw two different papers inside. One a long rectangle and the other a small square. I tapped the envelope against my palm, then tore the top half slowly. I blew into the open envelope, turned it upside down, and dropped both pieces of paper into my hand.

"Ricky Rice!"

I heard my name and a slap against the bathroom door. Hit hard enough that the push broom fell right off my cleaning cart and clacked against the tile floor. You would've thought a grenade had gone off from the way I jumped. The little sheets of paper slipped from my palm and floated to that sticky toilet floor.

"Aw, Cheryl!" I shouted.

"Don't give me that," she yelled back.

I walked out the stall to my cleaning cart. Lifted the broom and pulled the cart aside. Didn't even have time to open the door for Cheryl, she just pushed at it any damn way. I flicked the ceiling lights off, like a kid who thinks the darkness will hide him.

I'm going to tell you something nice about my boss, Cheryl McGee. She could be sweet as baby's feet as long as she didn't think you were taking advantage. When I first moved to Utica, she and her son even took me out for Chicken Riggies. It was a date, but I pretended I didn't know. The stink of failure had followed my relationships for years, and I preferred keeping this job to trying for love again.

Now she stood at the bathroom door, trying to peek around me. A slim little redhead who'd grown her hair down to her waist and wore open-toed sandals in all but the worst of winter.

"Someone's in there?" she asked, looked up at the darkened lights.

"Me," I said.

She pointed her chin down, but her eyes up at me. She thought she looked like a mastermind, dominating with her glare, but I'd been shot at before. Once, I was thrown down a flight of stairs.

"I mean, is there anyone in there that I can't *fire?*"

Oop. I lifted the broom and shook it.

"I was just sweeping," I said.

Cheryl nodded and stepped back two paces.

"I don't mind breaks, Ricky, you know that." She took out her cell phone and flipped it open, looked at the face. "But I need this station looking crisp first thing in the morning."

"I'll be done in a minute," I said.

Cheryl nodded, reached back, and swept her hand through her waist-length hair. The gesture didn't look like flirtation, just hard work.

"Hey! What did that letter say?"

I looked back into the bathroom. "Don't know yet."

She nodded and squeezed her lips together. "Well, I'd love to know," she said, and smiled weakly.

"Me too," I told her, not unkindly.

Then, of all things, she gave me a limp salute with her right hand. After that she turned in her puffy gray boots and walked toward the ticket booth.

THE BATHROOM'S WINDOWS were a row of small frosted glass rectangles right near the ceiling. They let in light, but turned it green and murky. Now, as I crept back to the second toilet stall, I imagined I was walking underwater, and felt queasy. I opened the door to find the first piece of paper right where I'd dropped it. And I recognized it immediately.

A bus ticket.

I bent at the knees and braced one hand against the stall wall for balance. My right leg ached something awful. I even let out an old man's groan as I crouched, but that kind of ache was nothing new. I'd felt forty ever since I was fifteen.

I held the ticket at an angle so I could read it in the hazy light.

One way, from Union Station to Burlington, Vermont.

An eleven- or twelve-hour trip if you figured all the station stops between here and there. The date on the ticket read Thursday, the twenty-first of January, just three days off. The name of the company on the top was Greyhound. I worked for Trailways. It sounds silly, but the logo made the ticket feel like contraband. I leaned back, out of the stall, and peeked at the bathroom door to make sure I was still alone.

I checked the back of the ticket for something, a note, an explanation. Nothing. Then I remembered that I'd seen two silhouettes through the envelope.

I ducked my head to the left, looking to the floor of the sanitary first stall, but it hadn't landed there. Then I looked to my right and saw that little cream-colored sheet, not much bigger than a Post-it, flat on the floor of filthy old stall number three.

Let me be more precise.

Flat on the floor, in a gray puddle, in filthy old stall number three.

Forget it.

Better to leave it behind than dip fingers in the muck on that floor. Even wearing gloves didn't seem like enough protection. Maybe a haz-mat suit.

Leave it there. Make peace with a little mystery.

I stood and rubbed my bad knee, even turned to leave, but you know that old saying about curiosity: curiosity is a bastard.

I opened the door of stall number three and tried not to look at the bowl itself, or at all that had smeared and splashed along the seat and the back wall. I opened my mouth to breathe, but the faint whiff of filth, like a corrupted soul, haunted me. It made my eyes tear up. Even my ears seemed to ring. I bet I looked like a nerve gas victim.

So I used the toe of my boot to tug the sheet of paper toward me, but it wouldn't move. I had to use my hand.

I lurched my middle finger forward, even as I pulled my head back, and touched the corner of the soaked little sheet. I flicked at it and flicked at it, but the damned thing barely shifted. I had no choice.

I picked the paper up, right out of the muck. The gray liquid didn't even run down my fingers, it just clung, like jelly, to the tips. It was cold and lumpy. My skin went numb. The wet paper lay flat in my palm; I peeled it off with my left hand, then held it to the greenish light of the windows.

"Ricky Rice!"

"Aw, Cheryl!" I shouted.

"Enough of that! You get out here!"

I would, but not yet. I stepped out of the stall and rose onto my toes, getting the soaked sheet as close to the windows as possible. I could see black ink on the paper. Make out the same handwriting that had scribbled my name on the outside of that envelope.

"I mean it, Ricky."

Cheryl pushed and strained at the door, and the wheels of my cleaning cart squeaked as they rolled. I blew on the paper to dry it. The cursive was small, but neat, legible.

The wooden door swung open. I heard its steel handle clang against the stone wall.

I paid no more attention to Cheryl because now I could read the two lines of the note:

You made a promise in Cedar Rapids in 2002.
Time to honor it.

Without thinking, purely automatic, I walked back into that filthy toilet stall and flushed the note away.

But not the ticket.

2

THREE DAYS I thought about that note. Thought about it, repeated it in my mind, tried to forget it. But on the third day I showed up at my job with a packed duffel bag, which I stored in my locker, my mind not yet made up.

Cheryl kept to herself that morning, which was for the best. If she'd chatted with me like usual, I might've admitted what I was considering and she'd have convinced me to stay. It was stupid to do otherwise in 2005. Lots of people were already losing jobs down here in the lower sector. The rest of the country hadn't been sucker punched yet. The bad news hadn't trickled up, but it would. Cheryl would've pointed all this out, and I would've agreed, ripped up the ticket, and taken my duffel bag home at the end of the shift. But I wanted to make up my own mind about this, so my cleaning took on a meditative silence. The only sounds I heard as I wiped down her computer screen were the growling winds outside her office window.

The outdoor crew worked on the other side of the glass, shoveling in the storm. I knew the guys who were doing it, and I sympathized. The snow had been up to my shins when I came in at eight, and it hadn't let up for an hour.

I washed windows, emptied trash, dust mopped and wet mopped the Trailways area, and all the while I wondered what to do when the clock struck noon. The bus wasn't actually leaving until twelve twenty-five, but where's the poetry in that?

By eleven I'd done as much in three hours as I would've stretched to eight on a normal day. If I did split on that bus, at least Cheryl couldn't say I'd left her with a messy station.

But where was I going? Burlington, Vermont? What kind of black man accepts an unsigned invitation to the whitest state there is? There'd been that sting on television where police told deadbeat dads they'd won the lottery, and arrested the guys when they showed up to collect. Maybe that's what this ticket was about. I wasn't a father to anyone, but I'd sure made some bad plays in my life. I wondered if I had any open warrants floating around.

Or could something good be waiting for me there?

Before I could go into the bathroom and wipe down the counters for the tenth time, one of the guys from the grounds crew, a bald guy with a face like a turtle, asked me to go drop salt on the sidewalks. I might've argued with him if his skin hadn't been blue.

I went out into the bright white cold with a ten-pound bag. I tossed the salt, and when that wasn't enough, I grabbed another bag. I didn't bother with my gloves, and pretty soon my hands dried out. Digging into the salt made my fingertips bleed.

It only took me about fifteen minutes to do one side of the station. Then I moved out to the parking spaces, but when I looked back at the building, it had disappeared. The snow came down like a shroud and I couldn't see the cars behind me, and I stood alone in the storm.

You made a promise in Cedar Rapids in 2002.

Time to honor it.

How did they know?

Wind got into the hood of my parka and raked across my face, so I shut my eyes and moved with one hand out in front of me. I was so lost I might've been walking down the middle of the train tracks, wouldn't have known until the locomotive stomped me.

And who were they?

Then my fingers felt a hard surface, and before I could slow down, I walked into it, face-first into the brick wall of Union Station. The doors I'd come through stood only five feet to my left. When I walked back into the station, I felt embarrassed, like everyone had seen me bash my face, and I went straight for the bathroom. I passed the grounds crew drinking coffee on the long benches, and their slurps sounded like snickering. The station seemed unfamiliar and slightly hostile now. For a moment I wondered if I was in the wrong place.

That damn bathroom snapped me back to reality. I'd just cleaned the place at ten forty-five, and an hour later it was vile. Someone had dumped handfuls of paper towels into one sink, then wet the mess until it turned to mush. Why? What the hell joy did it bring? There's a specific kind of guy who does this gutless vandalism, either in sinks or toilet bowls. I always imagine he's got a weak chin and a crooked spine.

The floors were murky with slush, so I mopped. I cleared the paper towel mush from the sink and checked the stalls. When I reached stall three, I opened the door slowly, afraid to find someone had snuck in through a window and vomited across the tiles. Thankfully, no.

But someone had added new graffiti. Two sentences, scratched into the paint with a blue pen.

"Suck a dickrub."

"Buttsex happened here."

As I got on that twelve twenty-five P.M. Greyhound bus, I felt absolutely no regrets.

3

NO REGRETS until about fifteen minutes into the ride. We left on time, which was a surprise in the middle of a snowstorm, but the driver didn't seem like a time-waster. Not the friendliest dude you ever met, he snatched tickets from people's hands as they boarded, but better that kind than the one who'd laze around the station chatting with the other drivers. Soon as he pulled out the station, the driver became our concentrated captain, his entire focus on the snowy terrain.

We weren't a full busload, maybe three quarters. I had a small Hispanic woman next to me. Me the aisle, she the window. She'd fallen asleep before the driver started the engine, and I wondered what she might be escaping or what mystery she might be moving toward.

I became so curious I felt like shaking her awake and asking, because the insanity of my own choice became clearer with each block we left behind. I watched the streets I'd crossed every morning on my way to the station, Railroad Street, Broad Street, North Genesee, and felt as though I were saying good-bye to three of my coworkers. And that's when I really understood: I quit my job.

I quit my job.

I was screaming inside my skull, I quit my job! I am forty years old and I just quit my job! What the hell was I thinking? I grabbed the arm rests and squeezed them so hard the plastic should've cracked.

I just felt so damn scared.

But it had only been a few minutes. We weren't even on the highway yet, though I could see the on-ramp in the distance. Flurries of snow slapped against the windshield, and the driver turned the wipers on just as he approached a red light. The driver stopped at the crossroads, and I shook in my seat.

Just get out now and go back. Cheryl won't even have noticed. Tell her you left for lunch.

But then the bus moved again. We reached the on-ramp. But, even now, there was still time! The bus skulked at the top of the ramp as the driver waited to merge. The snow came down so thick it could've hidden an eighteen-wheeler.

So I had one last chance to escape. I could holler to be let off and go back to the safety of a regular paycheck. I found myself on my feet before realizing I'd even moved. I grabbed the headrest of the empty seat in front of me, stepped one foot into the aisle, but then a voice shouted behind me.

"Negro, sit down!"

Who else could the voice be talking to? There were other Negroes on the bus (if you want to use that term), but none were on their feet. And do you know the craziest part? The most shameful part? I listened. I sat down.

As soon as I did, I became angry, at myself really, and turned around to snap at the speaker, but lost my voice when I saw the Negro who'd done the shouting. (I refuse to say African-American, it just takes too damn long.)

"Sit down and hear some truth," the man said, squinting in my direction.

This guy. He was three-quarters bum and, unfortunately, one-quarter legal ticket holder. He stepped into the aisle, grabbing the headrests on either side of him for balance.

"We are at war, you people. America is in a fight!"

And with that, thirty-seven passengers groaned as one. Those of us who were awake looked toward the front of the bus, at the driver, for help.

But the driver had abandoned us. He leaned forward in his seat and held the steering wheel even tighter, as if to say, Can't you see how hard I'm working?

"I'm not talking about Iraq. I'm talking about the battle here! On our soil. In our souls. "

We were on our own. Just us.

Once this became clear, the hobo paced the aisle. When he passed me, I got to see him better. He stooped when he walked, even though he was clearly younger than me. A slim body, but a puffy face, the blown-out nose of a lifetime drinker. I'll bet you could get tipsy licking the sweat on his forehead. I'm sorry to say this, but the man looked like a goblin.

"What kind of fight am I talking about?" he continued. "I'm talking about faith, people. Faith and belief."

Oh, no. One of those.

I would've liked it better if he'd just panhandled. Give him a few dollars and he'd be satisfied, but the religious types required a different reward.

Dealing with such folks goes in recognizable stages. First you appeal to authority, but the driver had refused us. So next you try and ignore. Most of the passengers slipped into an imitation of sleep. It was our best defense. Row after row, eyes closed and arms crossed. Some even faked loud snoring.

"Y'all think you can ignore me, but you're proving my point! Our nation is at war, but we're fighting in our sleep. How do you know whose side you're on if your eyes is shut?"

"I wish my ears was shut!" a man shouted from the front.

The last stage, in such situations, is when folks just lose their patience.

"Who said it?" the bum asked, stamping forward.

"I'm at war with your big mouth!" another passenger, a boy, shouted from the back.

The bum stalked the aisle now, looking for one set of open eyes. I saw him through the cracks in mine. As he bopped down the aisle, he became more aggressive. He never hit anyone, but bumped every chair in the row, throwing his one hundred fifty pounds like a round of haymakers.

"To be an American is to be a believer!" he shouted. "But y'all don't even understand what you believe in."

Now the brakes on the bus huffed and groaned. We were on the highway, but hadn't traveled too far. The driver brought us to a full stop on the shoulder, then got out of his seat.

That woke us up. Even the loudmouth got quiet. The Hispanic lady next to me craned her neck so she could see over the seat, then looked back at the bum with a smirk. She'd heard everything.

The driver pressed a button on the dashboard, which opened the bus door. Wind rushed in like water floods a sinking ship. People snatched their coats on. Snowflakes shot into the cabin, a blast of confetti that melted on the floor.

The driver clomped down the few steps and walked outside. Maybe he wasn't responding to the bum at all. Did we have a flat? Next came the squawk of grinding metal. The driver had opened one of the luggage bays.

Now many of the passengers got out of their seats. Even one old woman whose snore had been louder than the bus engine. I'd thought for sure she was asleep, but she stopped in the middle of a snort and got up to take a peek.

Even the nut leaned over an empty seat to take a gander.

The old woman smiled at him. "I *believe* you're getting kicked off."

"It don't matter," he said. He sneered to seem defiant, but already his voice had weakened. It looked cold out there.

The bus driver disappeared inside the luggage bay. Only one foot stuck out, and it kicked around as he searched. As if the bus was devouring him. Then a brown suitcase flew out, onto the shoulder, like a bit of indigestible beef.

At that, the passengers applauded. Me too, I must admit. The bus driver shut the bay door, another grinding squawk, then made his way back inside.

The bum dragged himself toward the front right away. I thought he might protest the excommunication, but there was nowhere to appeal. On this bus the passengers were all archbishops and the bus driver was our pope.

The guy spoke as he moved. "Who gets God? That's all I'm asking. Who gets welcomed to the table?"

"Just get off," a raspy woman growled from the rear.

The driver climbed the three steps into the bus and stood there, saying nothing. The snowstorm outside was so white, so bright against the windshield, that it turned the driver into a dark blue silhouette. A silent shadow pointing toward the exit.

The bum stopped before he reached the driver. His knees dipped even though we weren't moving, and he grabbed at the luggage racks for balance. He sighed deeply, a little theatrically, as he turned back to survey us. His eyes were as yellow as masking tape.

"Human beings are no damn good," he said. "We even worse than animals. We like . . ."

He trailed off, cleared his throat, but his voice hardly reached a whisper.

"We like monsters," he said.

Then he stepped off the bus.

Our driver pressed the button on his console, and the door shut with a low hiss. Outside, the guy lumbered over to his suitcase and righted it, then buttoned his coat.

"He don't even have a hat," the Hispanic woman next to me said.

The bus idled there, as if the machine were making up its mind too. The bum walked anyway, back in the direction of the on-ramp. On a clear day he'd have been in Utica in twenty minutes, but it might take an hour to get there in the snow.

That old woman, the one who'd faked a good snore, got up from her seat and walked down the aisle. She bent forward and spoke into the driver's ear. The driver looked at her, then looked away, into his side mirror. Then he pressed the silver button and opened the door.

The old woman hopped down each step and went outside. The bum hadn't even walked the length of the bus yet. She reached him and slapped at his arm. When he turned, she gave him her scarf, a purple puffy snake, and took the matching knit hat right off her head.

Then she returned to the bus.

But I guess the guy felt underwhelmed by the gesture. Maybe he thought she'd invite him back in. I thought she might have too. I wouldn't have been happy about it, but I would've understood. Instead, all he got was some accessories. So the guy looked up at the bus, squeezed the knit hat and scarf into a ball, then threw both right over the side of the highway.

He looked at us and refused to move, even as the blizzard nearly tore the buttons off his coat. A showdown, a staring contest.

One we lost.

After the old woman got back to her seat, the bus driver hit his button and shut the door. He put the bus in gear and we moved. In all this drama I'd forgotten that this was my last chance to go back too, and returned to my seat. That shabby man remained, scowling from the shoulder. For all I know, he died right there.

4

YOU DON'T JUST BRUSH OFF an episode like that. In fact, you may feel pretty terrible about it for a good long while. When I went to use the bathroom on the bus, I walked with my eyes at the floorboards. Everyone moved through the bus that way. The only relief came when we reached a new station and some passengers disembarked. They ran off the bus so fast they nearly tripped one another. And those left behind changed seats a few times, as if our chairs caused the pain.

Albany, Worcester, Newton, Boston, Hanover, White River Junction, Montpelier, and finally Burlington. A twelve-hour trip that took sixteen with snow delays. I didn't recognize anyone else by the end. Even the driver was different. I can't say I felt less guilty, but there was no one left to remind me of my shame. This wasn't a resolution, but it was a relief.

When we arrived at the Vermont Transit bus station in Burlington, I recognized the place. Not that I'd been there before, but places like it. This wasn't Utica, with its marble columns and historic landmark status. More similar to the stations in Kingston, Elmira, and Troy. By which I mean sleazy, greasy, and small. *Sleazy* is a little harsh. The Burlington station was just a forest-green one-story not much bigger than the private homes across the street.

The bus pulled in, only a handful of us on board. I saw two cars parked in the lot, but the snow had piled so high there might've been more buried. I should've arrived at a little past midnight, instead it was four in the morning. When I stepped off the bus, it didn't seem as if the sun would ever rise, the sky frozen in blackness. I wondered who, if anyone, would still be there to meet me.

On the last mile of my trip I envisioned my arrival. I imagined balloons and streamers. Or cops with guns. I only found a quiet station
where a couple of white people waited to meet a couple of other white
people. That's it. And I was one black guy standing by the snack machines in a daze.

But I didn't want candy. I wanted a hit.

A hit, a hit, a hit.

Can't be scared when you're sedated. I leaned against the snack machine, pressed the clear plastic buttons helplessly.

"Ricky Rice?"

I heard a man's voice, but when I turned around, all I saw was his belt
buckle. Had to lean back, really curl my spine, to see the eyes far above
mine. Talk about a titan! Maybe my confusion added a few inches, but
not many. This white man stood about seven feet tall. And just as wide.
His mother must've been a polar bear.

"Are you Ricky Rice?" he asked again.

He was prepared for winter. Brown Carhartt jacket and matching
snow pants. Logger boots and padded gloves. Even his face came covered with a graying beard that flowed down to his collarbone. I'll bet you
could sleep in a snowdrift when you're outfitted like that. Me, I had on
a peacoat and skullcap.

"I'm Ricky," I admitted. I kept my back against the snack machine for
balance.

Now he stooped so we could look at each other directly. I hadn't felt
this small since I was a child. Was he my escort, or was I his meal? I
gripped my duffel bag tighter so I could use it as a weapon. Treat this
like a shark attack and bop him in the nose if I had to.

He said, "My name's Lake. I have orders to drive you north."

5

WE CLIMBED INSIDE his enormous silver pickup. Warmth filled the cabin when Lake started the engine. Heat blew through the vents so hard it sounded like rushing water. Lake put both hands on the wheel. His Gore-Tex gloves swished against the cold plastic. We pulled out of the station. Lake puckered his lips and jutted his chin, and I watched him.

"We're on Pine Street now," he said. "And we're headed to Williston Road. From there we take the interstate about an hour. In case you were wondering."

I realized I was carrying my bag in my lap, like a child, a vision that made me feel vulnerable. I dropped the duffel between my knees.

Lake inhaled deeply. His chest was so thick that the brassy buttons of his jacket brushed the horn. He exhaled and yawned, licking his lips. From this angle, the hair surrounding his face looked like a mane.

I said, "How did you know about Cedar Rapids?"

"Iowa?" he asked.

"Come on, boss."

Lake stared into his rearview mirror as another truck rolled up behind us. It practically chomped on our bumper, but Lake didn't accelerate. He drove steady.

"Mr. Rice, how many bosses pick people up from bus stations at four A.M.?"

He had me there.

I jammed my foot into my duffel bag on the floor of the cab, digging into its side.

"So you don't know anything about Cedar Rapids?" I asked.

Lake said, "I know they make a lot of cereal there."

I leaned back, rested my face against the cool window. I'd slept on that bus, but not well. It had been like napping inside a steamer trunk. Lake's truck felt more like a sleeper cabin, so I slipped into a quiet stupor. And in this way I watched us get on the highway.

Lake stayed as good as his word. One hour on the interstate. Then I figured we were there. But I was wrong. We had another half hour on Vermont's back roads. They weren't paved streets, just snow on top of ice and ice on top of mud, a three-layer cake.

Must've been five-thirty by the time we reached those roads, but the sun hadn't crept up an inch. The sky remained blue-black, and in places the stars hid behind cloud cover. Snow stopped falling, but the wind continued, blowing so berserk that the top of every tree shuddered.

Despite my weariness I got scared again. Or maybe because of it. It's one thing to get in the car with some burly mountain man when you're still in a city. But when he gets you out into the country, well, there's too many tales about this going badly for a guy like me, and I couldn't help but ponder the possibilities. Dragged to my death, hung from a tree, kept prisoner in a shed for days. So the nervousness charged me up again, though Lake hardly seemed to notice. How could he? He was too busy driving.

His pickup was the kind you see in television commercials, where they hitch a blue whale to the back and the truck hauls that Magilla up a hill. But even this truck had trouble on these roads. The ruts were so deep that Lake weaved from one side of the road to the other. We weren't driving at this point, just surfing. I bet we would've flipped over if it wasn't for the surrounding forest, which stopped the wind from smacking us directly.

Then my anxieties spilled over. I pulled at the handle of my door instinctively. Lucky for me the damn thing stayed locked.

"What are you doing?" Lake said, though he didn't look away from the road.

"I don't know who you are!" I shouted. "You're taking me out here for some wild shit, admit it!"

"Calm down, Mr. Rice."

"Cut all this 'Mr.' business. I'm from New York. You don't want to mess with me."

Lake tapped the gas with his foot, and the truck bucked forward, moving with all the grace of a horny bull. Outside, the trees sobbed and groaned. Some bent so far I thought they would snap, and in fact some had. I could see them deeper in the forest wherever the moonlight grasped through the cover. Trees that had crashed, from the wind or the weight of the snow, and landed at painful angles.

"I'm a black man, you hear me? We don't play! I will knock your ass out! Pull over, motherfucker. Pull over!"

Lake ignored me. I wondered if I sounded tough or terrified. I felt both. I worked at my door handle again. Reached down for my duffel bag so I could break the window open. I'm not saying that was a good idea, just my only one.

Before I could get the bag into my hands, there was an astounding scream, wailing carried on the wind, as a thirty-foot tree snapped and fell across the road.

It landed just ahead of us. So close that its limbs raked the hood. Bark sprayed the windshield hard enough to cause a crack. The front of the truck bucked, the wheels lifting from the road. That tree probably weighed more than Lake's pickup.

We could only gasp and stare.

As we idled, the strong lamps of the truck illuminated the midsection of the tree, and from this close it looked unrecognizable, monstrous. The needles on its limbs became poisoned quills, and its bark an invulnerable hide. What lived out there, hidden in the dark?

I recovered and looked at Lake triumphantly, as if I had orchestrated this.

"I told you not to fuck with me. It's bad luck."

Lake looked across the seat. His eyes were so red! It was the first moment I considered he must've sat in this truck for hours because of all my snow delays. But I didn't sympathize, not just then. I scrunched my mouth into a satisfied smile and said, "What you gonna do?"

Step outside, apparently. Lake left the truck, slammed his door, then went to the back. Heard him fussing around, but I didn't pay too much attention because the man had left the keys in the ignition like a fool.

I slid toward the driver's side slowly.

Then this big bastard stalked right past the window, didn't even look in at me. I was halfway across the bench when he did this, but stopped moving. He carried a hatchet, two wood blocks, and had a length of heavy chain wrapped around his right shoulder.

He walked to the tree. It was the first thing that made him look small. Nature asserting its own scale. And this wasn't even that big a tree. Not a redwood, just a black spruce.

Lake slapped the bark the way you affectionately slap a dog on its side. Then he got down on a knee and placed one wood block against the tree. Got up, lifted the hatchet, and used the blunt end to knock the wood block under the tree like a shim. He did this again, about a yard lower. Then he slid the length of chain under the tree and ran it all the way round.

This was my last chance. He'd attach the chain to the truck, then reverse until he'd nudged it far enough for the truck to get past. Then we'd be back on our journey to my demise.

So I slid the rest of the way, until I sat behind the steering wheel. All set to put the truck in reverse, but my feet couldn't touch the pedals. This guy had his seat back far. So I was looking for the button or the bar, whatever that damn truck used, when I saw Lake climb over the tree and drop down onto the far side.

Now I could only see the upper third of him. You could've mistaken the man for bigfoot at this angle. A beast of the wild. He didn't attach the chain to the truck. He wrapped it around himself. Then he stepped back a few feet. From the motion I could tell he was kicking at the ground, digging in.

Then he pulled.

This white man is insane. That's what I thought.

Boy was he straining. Enough to make my shoulders hurt. Lake's mouth snapped open, and he made this sound, like a long, low rumble. If I hadn't been looking at him, I would've checked for storm clouds.

He kept pulling. Leaning backward. Screaming with effort.

Until, yes, that tree shook.

Just slightly. Hardly anything. A quiver. It resisted, but Lake would not relent.

The spruce scraped toward Lake now, an inch or two this time. The tree limbs on his side snapped in sharp protest. The big man kept shouting, and, rather than drive off, I rolled the window down, I stuck my head out. I kept blinking, wiping the snow off my eyelids. In the heat of astonishment, I didn't even feel the cold.

That's some old mountain man trick, I thought. Maybe the road was at more of a slant than I knew. Plus, he'd used those wood blocks. I tried to come up with an explanation, anything to feel less awestruck. But I was really only thinking one thing: this bastard moved a tree.

Lake stepped farther back and finished.

When the tree had been moved enough, just enough, for us to get by, Lake stopped pulling and leaned against it, severely winded. He heaved so hard his face touched the bark. He looked like he was mourning.

After gathering his things and dropping them in the truck bed, he got back inside the cabin. I'd pushed his seat all the way back again and taken my place by the passenger window. I didn't look at him, only at the body by the side of the road. But Lake didn't start driving, so I finally turned.

To find him staring at me. A challenge in the tight set of his lips.

I said, "Well, if we're going to get there, let's just get there."

Lake nodded and drove deeper into the hushed woods.

6

"WAKE UP, Mr. Rice."

What had I been dreaming of? I had a picture of my older sister, Daphne, in my mind. From when we were children. She protected me when I was still too young to handle myself. I suppose that's why I'd been dreaming of her. Because I wasn't so sure I could handle myself now. Would've been nice to ring her up, but she stayed all the way out in Long Island, and I doubted my prepaid TracFone could reach that far.

"We're here, Ricky."

Lake had already parked. He stepped out of the truck, came around to my side, and grabbed the handle, but it was locked. He fussed with the handle for another moment before he realized, and I just watched him in a kind of daze. Then he leaned close to the glass, his enormous face filling the window, the hair of his beard flattened like a sample on a slide.

"Please open up," he said quietly. "I'm tired and I want to go to bed."

He let go of the door and waited for me to do it myself. I opened the door and got out.

We were in front of a small wooden cabin, as dark inside as the sky above. I couldn't even make out the full dimensions, only the outline against the snow behind it.

Lake pointed at it. "This is yours, Ricky."

"I own it?"

"Sure," he said. "And why don't we give you a jet plane too?"

Wind blew over the pickup truck, over the cabin, over Lake and me.

Lake rubbed his face with one gloved hand. "This is yours as long as you decide to stay."

"What if I want to leave tomorrow?"

"Then we won't monogram your doormat."

"There's a doormat?"

"It's a house, isn't it?"

And not the only one either. There were a few more lined up near mine. Six cabins, maybe more, in a cul-de-sac. A half circle of homes. Most were dark, but one had lights on.

"Most of the others are sleeping," Lake said.

The idea that there were other people filled me with both relief and sorrow. Nice to know I wasn't being thrown into an isolation tank, but maybe they'd been invited here just like me. Mysterious note, one-way ticket. Maybe I wasn't being singled out. This is the part that brought a little sorrow. How embarrassing. To be a grown man who still wishes the world would tell him he's special.

"What is this place, Lake?"

"We're in a part of Vermont called the Northeast Kingdom."

I waved at the cabins. "I mean all this. Who invited me here? Who do you work for?"

Lake turned to the pickup while I took a step toward my cabin. Mine. Imagine that. I still couldn't. I'd been living in this one-room efficiency, sharing a bathroom with four sour men. I expected the cabin to disappear as soon as I touched the door handle. An illusion. A trick. A game. Can you guess that I'm a bit of a skeptic? Doubt has a long history with me.

Lake returned with my duffel bag. Hanging from his index finger, it looked as small as a fanny pack. "This is the Washburn Library."

I reached the steps that led up to my cabin, just a few. I touched the wooden door. A brass number hung on the front: 9.

"This is a library?"

Lake set the bag down by my feet, went into his coat pocket, and gave me a set of keys. He got into the truck, started it, rolled down his window. All this while I looked at the keys in my cold hand. Lake shouted over the wind.

"Turn around!"

He drove away. Clearing my view.

There was the Washburn Library.

An enormous building. One long flat slab of sandstone set down in some of the most inhospitable sod America has to offer. It looked as long as a football field, but because of the snow, the low building was nearly buried. Maybe that's why I hadn't seen it right away. Maybe I hadn't been prepared. Or willing. Now I saw it. The interior lights smoldered, and the Library glowed bleakly in the great woods. It looked like God's gravestone.

7

YOU'D THINK I'D SLEEP for twenty-four hours after that long trip, but I only passed out for five. Awake by eleven, I strolled around my cabin as if its four rooms made it a manor. Bedroom, living room, bathroom, and kitchen. I felt pretty giddy about each one. Nothing too fancy. There weren't mink blankets or platinum faucets or whatever the wealthy buy with their loot. Instead, the cabin felt like a cozy place you rent for a romantic weekend. Since I was alone, that meant lavishing my affections on me. I began by making brunch. The fridge had been stocked.

I stood in the kitchen beating eggs in a bowl while the bread browned in the toaster. I turned on a small radio in the living room. Found a station that played classical music. Now, I have to admit, the only thing I know about classical music is that it doesn't have a beat, but strings and horns seemed like the proper accompaniment for my first morning. They helped to calm me down. My first instinct was to run outside screaming my questions to the wind, but I didn't want to make an ass of myself. No one respects a panicked man. So instead I made brunch to the sounds of calming music. Like I'd become cool simply by acting that way.

I dropped the eggs into the frying pan, and they sizzled in concert with the piccolo playing in the living room. Then, as I went to get some orange juice from the fridge, I saw this brother breaking into my house.

How should I describe him? I'll be nice. He was portly. A portly black dude, going bald at the top, lifted my living room window and climbed inside, headfirst. The kitchen was adjacent to the living room, so I could watch him even though he hadn't yet seen me. The classical music almost made his movements seem graceful.

As he pulled himself through the frame, I opened a drawer by the sink and found a carving knife. Then I waited for him to get all the way through.

The guy wheezed and huffed as the thickest part of him met with the unyielding frame. He tugged and strained. I turned off the flame under the frying pan as the eggs hardened into an omelet. His legs came through, and he crashed to the floor, then turned toward my closed bedroom door cautiously.

"I think he heard you," I said.

He looked at me, and his eyes fluttered nervously.

"Well, shit," he said. "How come you didn't answer the door?"

"You never knocked."

He nodded. "I guess I didn't."

He wore a blue sweat suit, top and bottom. The fabric snug around his thick legs and pudgy belly. Maybe this was his cat burglar's outfit. He wore heavy hiking boots on his feet, but no coat, no hat, no gloves. He couldn't have come from very far.

"I live next door," he said.

"What's your name?"

"Call me Peach Tree."

"I mean your real name."

"Why? You going to file a police report?" He sneered.

I held the knife by the handle, loosely, and wiggled it. "Man, get up off my floor."

He leaned back, on his hands, and looked at my kitchen counter, the things on it.

"Can I have some orange juice?" he asked.

"Pour it yourself."

As he lumbered to his feet, I closed the window. Then I went back to the kitchen, dropped my omelet onto a plate, and took the bread out of the toaster. The pieces were hardly warm now, but I didn't really mind. I'd found a jar of raspberry jam in the fridge too, so I spread some on the toast. I kept the carving knife with me and took my food to the living room. Meanwhile, Peach Tree poured himself a drink. He filled the tallest glass he could find in the cupboard.

The small living room had a love seat and a rocking chair. Just to be sure Peach Tree didn't try to stuff himself next to me, I sat in the middle of the love seat, plate balanced on my knees. A small wooden desk sat in the corner, but it had no matching chair. In the opposite corner was an empty bookshelf. It was as if the room had been decorated with donated furniture.

"You're the one who came in last night, that right?" Peach Tree asked as he settled onto the rocking chair. Before I could answer, he drank his entire glass of orange juice in a prolonged gulp, like a child, blowing air through his nose so he wouldn't have to pause. Once finished, he slammed the glass down on the floor with a thud.

"Had a real long trip because of the snowstorm," I said. I sighed dramatically.

Peach Tree shrugged his beefy shoulders. "We all got troubles."

I gestured to the window with my fork. "You had enough troubles getting through my window."

Peach Tree's face shined with either sweat or oil. He was clearly a few years older than me, despite how he acted. He had a round face that might have looked distinguished if he'd shaved off the last of his hair. Instead the top of his head looked like a bird's nest, the brown egg of his scalp poking through in the middle. He looked at my plate, the meal still mostly uneaten.

"It's skinny bastards like you that's always making fun."

I couldn't tell, at this moment, which way he and I were going to go. I had an inclination to be friends, but these early steps can be delicate, especially with black men. None of us wants to be disrespected. We can be pathological about this. Our skin's so thin it's a wonder the blood doesn't leak out our pores.

"I shouldn't have snuck in here," Peach Tree admitted, something like an apology.

"Well, why'd you do it?"

"I figured you'd still be asleep!" He leaned forward, laughing at his criminal logic.

Now I looked at him closely. "Damn," I said. "What kind of drugs you on?"

Peach Tree sat back and clutched his belly. "Nothing, man. None."

Then he looked over his shoulder, into my bedroom. "You holding?"

And that's how me and Peach Tree became friends.

8

IT TOOK ME THREE HOURS to get Peach Tree out of my place. During that time we traded rehab stories, criminal records, and the names of our hometowns (Queens, New York, and Kansas City, Kansas). We even came up with a plan to take Lake down if he turned out to be dangerous. It had two steps: (1) steal Lake's truck, and (2) run him over with it.

But Peach Tree kept coming back to drugs. He didn't believe I hadn't brought a little something with me. Even just a taste. I swore I'd been off for three years, ever since 2002, but he rightly pointed out that three years is a finger snap in the life of an addict. I even let him go through my coat pockets to be sure.

When I showed him out, I heard signs of life coming from the other cabins farther down. Music here, or some loud conversation from another, even the scuff of someone shoveling snow. But I wanted to get used to my cabin before I made more friends. Peach Tree told me there would be a banquet that night at seven, right inside the Washburn Library, to welcome us all officially. Who'd told him? One of the other newcomers who'd arrived before him. It was like a game of telephone.

I watched Peach Tree until he went into his cabin, then put the chain on my door. Locked all the windows and drew their blinds. Then I went into the bottom of my duffel bag and found the needle and six baggies of heroin that I'd brought.

In the bathroom I shut the door and sat with the kit in my lap. Almost three years without a kiss. That's a lot of love to lose. I felt a little heartsick looking at the stuff. But if I did it now I'd be no use at the banquet.

Probably miss the whole thing. So I put the needle and baggies back into their Ziploc bag and hid them in the kitchen, under the sink, behind a stack of pans. To forget the temptation I cleaned my whole house, but I still felt the urge, so I went back to bed.

WHEN I WOKE UP AGAIN, it was night. I found my clock radio and checked the time. Six eleven.

The hot shower felt good. So did the shave. They even had cocoa butter in the medicine cabinet, and I slathered it all over, legs especially. My mother, my father, my sister, and me—put us all together and I doubt we would have weighed four hundred pounds. One of my old friends, Wilfred, used to call our family the Boney Bunch. He'd sing our theme song to me. "The Boney Bunch, the Boney Bunch, that's the wayyyy they became the Boney Bunch, dah-dah, dah-dah, dah!"

But what do you wear to a banquet at the Washburn Library? I sure hadn't packed a suit. Had I ever owned one? Sure, as a boy, but not since. So I did the best I could, found the outfit I wore when applying for jobs. A pair of khaki slacks and a royal blue shirt. I found an iron and ironing board in the bedroom closet.

I must have pressed those clothes three times each. I hadn't brought dress shoes with me, so I had to wear my brown work boots, but I cleaned them off with a hand towel. Even brushed the dirt out of the soles. I could have used a touch-up, but I doubted there were any barbershops on the grounds, so I just patted my hair and hoped it looked even.

Last, I put on my tie. I remember I bought the tie and shirt together. Both royal blue. At the time, I thought this was a smooth look, but I couldn't remember why anymore. Maybe I'd hoped they made me look like a gangster, but really I looked like the manager of a copy shop.

I opened my cabin door at six fifty-five and saw figures walking in the snow. Paths had been dug for each of us, leading from our cabins toward the Washburn Library. A white carpet. I tried to see the others, how they'd dressed. But it was dark, and everyone wore such heavy coats and hats. I couldn't even tell which were men or women. So I just shut my door, made sure to lock it, and walked the path that had been cleared for me.

The cold didn't seem so bad, not for the first three or four steps. I didn't feel any wind, unlike the night before, so I didn't feel battered. Didn't bother to put on my skullcap because I didn't want to mess my hair. But by the fifth step the cold clamped down around my skull like a parasite. A vampire. I mean it. The life was being sucked out of me.

Through my ears, my suddenly dry eyes, my tingling nose, and of course my still-wet hair. Holy hell. What kind of human beings decide to settle down in a place like this? I hurried, but when I reached the building, I was awestruck before it.

Two tall lamps stood on either side of the entryway, a short flight of concrete stairs that led to a single metal door. That was the only underwhelming feature. I'd expected a bank of crystal doors. Maybe you couldn't have something like that in this kind of cold.

Anyway, the four lamps threw light upward rather than down. They weren't there so you could see a door. They were there so you could witness the Library.

From a distance it had looked buried, but the roof actually sat at a pitched angle, higher at this entrance and tilting backward. From here the roof loomed above me, thirty feet in the air. The building seemed like a great stone throat, and I balanced at its maw.

9

"WHAT A SURPRISE, the black guy's late."

This was Peach Tree, the man who'd done a B&E on me earlier, a black man himself, calling me out. He stood with the other invitees, clustered in a knot only inches inside the lobby. They hadn't even taken off their coats and scarves yet. I thought Peach Tree was cutting on me just to make himself look better, to show that he was the good Negro. But imagine my surprise when I looked at the group and realized they were all black folks.

Seven black people in the Northeast Kingdom. Sounds like the start of a gruesome old folktale. Seven black people baked in a pie . . .

One of the women, a bookish type, crossed her arms and said, "I'm gonna slap somebody if I don't get some answers soon."

The entryway was just a narrow hall. A front desk, like at a regular library, sat to my left, but the chair behind the desk was empty. A coatrack stood behind the desk, seven wooden hangers on it waiting to be used. There were seven of us standing in the entryway now, five women and two men including me, dripping water onto the gray slate tiles.

But this layout seemed a little off to me. A building this grand had nothing more than a wooden desk at its entryway? So I opened the metal door, looked outside, then let it swing shut.

"You all realize this is a side entrance?" I said.

The others looked around, stupefied.

"It was the only door I saw," the bookish woman said.

Peach Tree pointed at the women. "I was just following them."

The hallway ran another twenty feet and ended in a sharp right turn. I looked down the way and back at my new companions. They stamped their feet or rubbed their arms, blew into their hands, anything to make it seem as if they weren't just too scared to go forward.

My childhood had trained caution out of me, for better and worse. My mother and father had been missionaries, and their labors had taken them across the country, into the littlest towns you never heard of, and the roughest cities that blighted the nightly news, and I learned to put my foot forward because of them.

So I unzipped my jacket, slipped it on a hanger, and walked down the hall alone.

A part of me really expected to turn that corner and find Lake holding a gun. Ready to shoot me for sport and claim I'd been menacing him. Would the police up these ways even take him in for questioning, or just toss my body in a bin? I thought of that lunatic from the Greyhound bus. I could disappear just as easily as him.

My eyes were shut when I rounded the corner, but I could tell I'd entered a large space, because the echo of my boots sounded like bass drums. I reached for the wall with my right hand and shaded my eyes with the left. There, in the dim room, sat an enormous circular dining table with tall candles lit in its center. For a moment the table looked like a giant radio telescope, the kind scientists use to survey outer space, and the candles were its great antennae. I watched the flames flicker rhythmically as if messages were being received.

I walked around the table, but didn't touch. Wouldn't even brush the tops of the chairs. There was a plush gray tablecloth that draped all the way to the floor. And nine red place mats.

"Hey, Ricky!" I heard Peach Tree call from the hallway. "You dead in there, or what?"

The room wasn't lit by candles alone. There were recessed lamps in the ceiling, but they'd been turned low. There were framed pictures on the walls.

More black people. Men and women. Standing together for posed black-and-white photos, all on a set of concrete steps much wider and steeper, more majestic, than the one we'd just used. Behind them a bank of doors, all made of frosted glass. The numbers varied. Sometimes nine, other times seven. Once there were only three in the shot. But all these pictures seemed very old, at least judging by the clothes. The men in sharp suits and women in fine dresses. Most of the guys wore hats, that was the real clue. 1950? 1920? How old was the Washburn Library?

"Man," Peach Tree muttered. "You didn't hear me talking to you?"

I saw Peach Tree's bald head peeking around the wall. Five other heads gathered behind his. They looked as nervous as birds. I waved them in slowly so they wouldn't scatter.

"Come on," I said. "Look at all this."

So they entered, and I introduced myself to the women. Peach Tree walked away from these greetings because we'd already met. He looked at the framed photos, at the swanky clothes the figures wore, and said, "They look like a bunch of Black Muslims."

The bookish woman, whose name was Violet, said, "I guess they do."

This made Peach Tree unhappy. "They better not ask me to sell no bean pies!"

Another woman, taller than all of us, who stooped with a tall woman's shame, said, "They don't look like Muslims. They look like church folk."

"How's that better?" Peach Tree asked. "I didn't come to Vermont to get saved."

Violet said, "Just because they're well dressed doesn't mean they're religious. Can't black folks get done up for another reason?"

"Name one," the tall woman, Verdelle, said.

"Maybe they're rich," whispered a third woman.

Her name was Euphinia, and she'd made fast friends with the fourth woman, Grace. The two of them were the oldest of the bunch. Both must've been in their sixties. They held hands tightly, and this made them look like a pair of schoolgirls.

"Then maybe we'll get rich too," Grace added.

The last of us was Sunny. That's how she introduced herself, and that's all she wanted to be called. First name or last? I didn't ask. She was even burlier than Peach Tree, so I didn't push. Short, wide, and slow to speak, but her small eyes showed clear intelligence. She was the only one who went around the room and looked at every picture.

After Sunny had seen them all, she said, "These look like class photos."

"So what's that make us?" Peach Tree asked.

Sunny rubbed the glass of the frame closest to her. It was so clean it squeaked.

"New students," she said.

Violet and Verdelle looked to be the youngest, midtwenties maybe. Sunny and I floated around forty, while Peach Tree, Euphinia, and Grace were closest to retirement. I tried to see some pattern in this, but couldn't. We weren't from the same city or state or region, didn't seem to have family ties. We stood near the banquet table playing amateur sleuth, but the one thing we didn't do was sit down. It was as if I could read their minds.

I hate to say it, but we didn't sit down because we didn't believe we were the honored guests. Suspected we'd been brought all this way just to cater for the real invitees. And then it was impossible to imagine another explanation. We expected to be given waiters' outfits. All of us seemed to feel that same way. Folks like us were always the help.

When the footsteps started, we stopped talking. We stepped away from the banquet table and stood with our backs to one wall. Euphinia and Grace even let go of each other's hands. You'd have thought we were lined up for a firing squad. And worst of all, we'd volunteered.

The sound of footsteps came from a second doorway, opposite the entryway we'd used, the clip of hard shoes coming down a staircase. When they reached the bottom, a small man stepped into the room to greet us.

This guy was no bigger than a bunion. He had big jug ears and skin the color and texture of chunky peanut butter. He was a tiny, trim old man. But he wore a sharp pin-striped suit, and that made him appear important. Put a medal on a mailbox and most people will salute.

"Look at you," he said, and his voice was a surprise. Not friendly, not warm. It came out a raspy growl. "Standing around like a bunch of monkeys."

I dropped my eyes before I realized I'd done it. And it wasn't only me. We all looked at the floor. Beside me, Euphinia even shivered.

He spoke again. Just as vicious, but even louder.

"So I call you *monkeys* and all you do is scratch your heads? Did you rob and kill the folks sleeping in those cabins? I can't think of any other way you disgraces got in here!"

But here's the thing. There were a bunch of us and only one of him. I didn't see Lake standing around to even the sides. Doing that math helped return my nerve.

I said, "Do you talk to people like that because you're only two feet tall?"

Peach Tree reached out and smacked me on the shoulder. I wouldn't even look at him.

The little man sneered, showing his off-white teeth. He said, "So a junky is criticizing me, that right?" He paused and undid his jacket. "Excuse me, a junky and a murderer."

"You don't know me," I said.

"I know what happened in Cedar Rapids. Let's start with that."

A few of the others looked at me now, sidelong glances of judgment.

The little man walked to a chair and pulled it out for himself. "Oh, I know about all of you. Don't go acting like he's the only one. You bunch of crackheads and criminals. Sit down already! Sit down and take your rightful place."

10

THE DEAN KNOCKED HIS KNUCKLES against the table slowly. "You all have to excuse me," he said. "I know I can be a son of a bitch."

The hall had the silence of a temple, so quiet that the candles on the table seemed to whisper as they flicked. This made each of us move quietly too. Not one of us dragged our chairs when we sat. And once we took our places, Peach Tree, Violet, Verdelle, all of them really did look different, a little finer. I hoped I looked the same to them. At the table, no one could see the uneven soles of my worn old boots, and I kept my boney hands tucked under my napkin. You could really only make out our astonished faces. All looking toward our host. This is the guy who can tell me why I'm here, I thought. Why we're all here. So of course we forgave him the rudeness. We only waited to hear what he would say next.

"Percy and Beatrice, would you do me a favor?"

Peach Tree and Sunny stood, listened for the order.

Even as the Dean gave them a few instructions, I looked into Peach Tree's eyes and hoped he could make out my faint smirk. Percy! He and Beatrice pushed back from the table, and that made our plates and glasses rattle. The glasses were filled with water and slowly melting ice. I could've used a little red wine.

Those two brutes clomped through the darkened entryway, where the Dean had just come from. They disappeared around the turn.

"I was at the Library before any of you were ugly babies," the Dean said, "but before I came, I kited checks. Got run out of Kentucky, Rhode

Island, and Oklahoma. And that's not the worst I've done, believe me. All the bad that's been said about you was said about me once."

The Dean nodded to affirm the truth of his statement. It made me wonder about the photos on the wall, the people in them. I turned and scanned the frames.

"All of them too, Ricky."

I turned back to the Dean, and he smiled at me. Honestly, his smile didn't look all that different from his sneer. Only the width of his eyes distinguished wrath from warmth.

Verdelle, who slouched even while she sat, said, "I'm not no criminal."

The Dean said, "You were never caught." He took a sip of water, set the glass down hard, and when he spoke again, his eyes narrowed. "But I know what you've done."

Verdelle's lips parted, but not in protest, just surprise. I thought she might give a confession. Instead she shut her mouth again and dropped her face into her hand.

The Dean stared at her now, but he spoke loudly enough that even Peach Tree and Sunny could've heard him, no matter how far they'd gone.

"Folks like us get used to making up stories, just to live with ourselves. But you don't have to do that anymore. The Washburn Library doesn't care who you were, only who you want to be. Out here we don't call you cons. Out here you're Unlikely Scholars."

All that sounded good. While Verdelle refused to look at the Dean directly, I found myself staring straight on. Hell, I might even have been grinning. Violet, Euphinia, and Grace all looked pleased. We were welcome here. *We* were. "Unlikely Scholars" sounded just fine. Some people act like it's a sign of weakness if you want to belong, but I think most human beings yearn to find at least one open door in their lifetime.

Now the sound of creaking metal could be heard from the darkened entryway where Peach Tree and Sunny had gone. The Dean looked over his shoulder, toward the noise, and it broke his command over us for a moment.

Euphinia and Grace scooted chairs closer, until their shoulders nearly touched. And to my right Violet patted Verdelle's place mat, a soothing gesture that made Verdelle look up and grin faintly. That left me on my own at the large table, and I counted the place settings, all nine of them. The Dean, myself, Euphinia, and Grace. Violet and Verdelle. Peach Tree and Sunny. That was only eight. Where was the other guest?

The creaking noise continued from around the corner. It was the

sound of something being wheeled across a floor. I imagined the little
black tires of a supermarket shopping cart.

Then Grace said, "How?"

The word came out of her so quickly I thought it was a burp. The
Dean turned to her and tilted his head.

Euphinia explained, "She means how did you know about . . . ?"

Instead of finishing the sentence, Euphinia reached down the top of
her blouse. It had been as well ironed as my slacks and shirt.

Euphinia fished a finger into her bra and came out with a small
cream-colored sheet of paper, folded over itself a few times. She unfolded it and held it up. Two sentences written in black ink could clearly
be seen. I couldn't make out what hers said, but that was okay because
I still remembered what he'd written on mine.

Euphinia flapped the paper.

Grace repeated herself. "How?"

Peach Tree and Sunny finally entered the room. Peach Tree at the
front and Sunny at the rear. Peach Tree made a show of his effort. He
hadn't grimaced and grunted that much even as he'd crawled through
my cabin window, but Sunny was clearly doing the real work. Her wide,
flat face bright with sweat.

They were pushing a long, silver hot food table. Our banquet was a
buffet.

The Dean indicated a wall socket, and Peach Tree crouched to plug
the hot food table in.

I really wanted some wine, but we never saw anything besides H_2O.
It was easy to see why. I felt like I might've shot dope with any of these
people at one time or another, even Euphinia and Grace. There's a look
to people like us, no matter where you go. Like we've been pulled out of
a fire, but not quick enough. No wonder we weren't being served hard
stuff.

Verdelle sat up straight for the first time that evening. Now she
looked large enough to touch the high ceiling. She stabbed the tabletop
with one long, boney finger and stared at the Dean defiantly. "Answer
Miss Euphinia," she said.

The Dean smiled at her as if he was pleased by her boldness.

He spoke only once Peach Tree and Sunny sat down again.

He said, "There is a voice whispering in the darkness. I have heard it.
Everything it says is true. It's been talking to us, to all of us, but the
world is so noisy we can't make out the message. Not unless we go off
somewhere, someplace remote and undisturbed and quiet . . ."

We began calling him the Dean that night, though he never introduced himself that way. Who gave him that title, then? Hard to say. I

can't remember one of us starting it. It seemed as though the term just appeared, a murmur in my ear, soon after he'd walked into the room. We might've heard it from the candle flames or the sandstone walls. Even the ice in our glasses seemed to chatter that name.

"So what do we do now that we're here?" I asked.

The Dean said, "We listen."

2

The Damned
Unlikely Scholars

11

THE NEXT MORNING I could still hear the Dean. His gruff tone, the snarl at the end of his sentences, his hard little fist slamming against the wooden table. I heard that last sound so powerfully in my dreams that it pulled me out of sleep. But then I realized it was someone knocking at my front door.

Knocking hard enough to bring the walls down, but I didn't run to answer. I wasn't trying to be rude, I really couldn't get up. Couldn't pull myself out of the maple Victorian bed yet, couldn't brush aside the cotton duvet at this time, you understand me? Getting up just then would've been like pulling myself out of a fantasy.

By the time I got up, the knocking had stopped. I figured it hadn't been Peach Tree, because he preferred the window. Maybe it had been the Dean? Come to finish the explanation he'd begun the night before. Maybe the others were now learning the greater secrets of the Washburn Library and I'd missed the chance because I was too busy snuggling with my comforter.

Those thoughts made me panic, and that panic made me run out of the cabin in a T-shirt and underwear. No coat, no pants, no shoes. Not even socks. Huffing like I was about to miss a plane. And come to find the others, all dressed and showered, standing in the snow in the shadow of Lake.

Only Lake turned away. I stood ankle deep in the snow that had fallen on my walkway since the night before. Right away my feet hurt from the cold, but I didn't run back inside.

Finally, Peach Tree cleared his throat and said, "Grown men shouldn't wear tighty-whities."

SO I SHOWERED, dressed, skipped breakfast because I was hurrying, and ran the path to the Library entrance we'd used the night before. When I entered the lobby, I found a kid sitting at the front desk. He wore his guard's uniform like a costume, kept pulling at the collar as if he were embarrassed by it. Before I could ask where the others had gone, he waved me through. He hardly even looked up from his newspaper.

I looked back at him, slouched in his chair, head down as he snapped through the pages, and wondered how far he'd come to get this job. He had long brown hair that he pulled back into a ponytail, a teenager's idea of workplace etiquette. He looked a bit young, but what did I know? Maybe he'd been an arsonist back in Dubuque.

I came around the corner and found the others. They hadn't begun the tour yet, only stood around in the room where we'd had our banquet the night before. Each one drank coffee or tea.

Violet and Verdelle, the tallest and shortest of our group, stood together in front of a framed photo. Verdelle pointed to one of the faces under glass, and Violet went on her toes to look closer. She pushed her glasses up from the tip of her nose and raised her eyebrows at the same time, a look of study and surprise.

But before I might've asked what they saw, Lake returned to the room.

"I'm sorry," I said to Lake, but meant it for everyone.

Euphinia and Grace were standing exactly where they'd been sitting the night before. Absently they watched the spot where our table had been. It was difficult to make the transition this morning. And not just for me. Peach Tree and Sunny hovered near the socket where they'd plugged in the serving cart.

"Don't be afraid," Lake said. He kept his voice gentle, but I knew how loud it could get. He hadn't been so demure while pulling that tree.

Grace said, "Nobody here is scared."

But she held Euphinia's hand tightly.

Lake said, "Then let me show you the rest of the Library."

Lake turned and walked two steps, but we didn't move. He sensed this and turned back. He didn't need to ask the question, only waited for one of us to answer it.

Violet was the one who spoke for us. She cleared her throat, tilted her head away.

"Where's the Dean?"

Lake waved us toward him. The man's hand looked as big as a boogie

BIG MACHINE 41

board. I couldn't have been the only one who thought he was going to swat our heads off. But when we didn't move, he didn't beg, only waited, and soon each of us stepped closer. Violet and Verdelle first. Then Euphinia and Grace. I beat Peach Tree and Sunny over there, but it was only out of pride. I wasn't going to be the last one again.

Lake only seemed more enormous indoors. If it had started raining, we could've gathered under him for shelter. But instead of projecting menace the big man seemed serene. Another person might've been insulted by what Violet had said, but Lake smiled peaceably.

Now we all stood at the bottom of the stairs the Dean had used the night before. Wooden steps, simple and clean. At the top of the stairs, a closed door.

Lake pointed up. "Every year the new Scholars expect the Dean to step out that door and give them the tour himself. But let me tell you something about the Dean, he's . . . unavailable. You're not going to see him again."

Euphinia brought her hand to her neck. "Ever?"

She asked it like she suspected Lake had eaten the little man in the night, a morsel before bedding down.

"Not for some time," Lake said.

"How long?" I asked.

"That really depends on you. On how well you do your work."

Now we, as a group, moved toward the stairs, like we were going to run up there and turn the knob and just beg the Dean for answers. But Lake stuck his arm out, blocking the way between us and the ascent. I have to say, even with Sunny and Peach Tree on our side, I didn't think all seven of us could take him.

He said, "You do your work and do it well. The Dean takes notice. Then, when *he* decides the time is right, he calls you up to see him."

Verdelle came the closest to Lake's eye-line, though still a good nine inches shorter. She looked up at Lake, her shoulders pulled back in defiance. "And then what will he say?"

Lake snorted, and for the first time he didn't seem so composed.

"Think I know? I've *never* been invited up."

And that's what did it. Broke our trance. Lake wasn't lying. He'd been snubbed for who knows how many years. Decades? And you could hear the humiliation in his voice. Admitting this made it harder to treat Lake like an enemy.

He said, "Can we start the tour now?"

"How come you took us through a side entrance?" I asked. It came out sounding accusatory, I'm sure, but the others must've been wondering too.

Lake shrugged his enormous shoulders. "That door is just closest to your cabins."

Now he turned, and we followed. But before going, each of us stole one last look at the staircase and the closed door at the top. I made odds, in my head, about who would be "called up." In what order. And I wasn't the only one. Even Euphinia and Grace let go of each other's hands. You could see the calculations on every grave face.

Lake took us forward, but the day was kind of a loss. No matter where our bodies were led, we remained at the foot of those wooden stairs.

WE FINISHED with our first full day, an orientation that left us all disoriented, and then we gathered in front of our cabins in the evening light. I'm talking northeast Vermont in winter, cold enough to cause frostbite, but no one invited the others home. Too soon for that. So we stood in a close circle in the snow. Wind slapped our backs and shoulders, tore through our cheap coats and threadbare scarves, it scraped any exposed skin.

What were we discussing? The Dean, of course. His disappearance still bothered us. While we appreciated Lake's time, it didn't soothe the feeling that we'd been dismissed. Disrespected. But as I shivered, I could see we'd already changed a little, the seven of us that morning weren't quite the seven of us tonight. If the Dean showed up now, we would've barked our complaints, but earlier today, in the banquet room, we'd clung to the walls like frightened puppies. And suddenly I felt happy he hadn't showed up.

People like us, poor folks I mean, we're wise in some ways but in others we act like children. We can be a pretty docile bunch. I know you're not supposed to say that, but for proof just go to any hospital emergency room in a broke neighborhood, I'm talking anywhere. We slump and slouch for hours as we wait to be seen by a nurse practitioner, and a trained doctor is as rare as health benefits at our jobs. It might take us five or six hours just to get some antibiotics, and the only way we're going to get seen any faster is if we've been filled with bullets. Even then it's going to take an hour.

We sit through treatment like that in hospitals and banks, at supermarkets and check cashing stores. No matter where you go, the poor have the capacity to endure. Some people even compliment us on it, as if endurance is all we can achieve.

The picture of the poor is usually of one wild, chaotic lot. Loud, combative, quick to complain, but that isn't so, not in my experience. Just dip into that emergency room and watch every tired face; we've been there for half a day and have yet to receive treatment. Most will only heave and sigh, that's the extent of our rebellion. The poor are poor and we expect to stay that way. We don't like it, but what can you do? That's our attitude. The poor aren't defeated, we're domesticated. If the Dean had given us that tour, we simply would've become his pets. Disappearing was really the kindest thing he could've done. It forced us to face an important question. Would we flounder without his guidance, or would we step up?

12

I REFUSED to be the last one up and out for a second day. Lake had knocked on my door at eight, so the next morning I woke at six. Showered, fed myself, and ironed my clothes twice. I had to do it twice because, well, I hadn't brought that much with me and I was already recycling the pants I'd worn to the banquet. Even after two passes, I could see wrinkles here and there.

By seven-thirty I sat near the front door just waiting to hear Lake's boots clomping through the snow. I planned to pop the door open just as he arrived, surprise him with my punctuality. But as the hour approached, I didn't hear his heavy steps, only the chatter of birds and wind rapping at my walls. Finally I just opened the front door; it wasn't quite eight but close enough. I stepped out, and who should be doing the same thing? Violet. Coming out of cabin three. The others as well, only moments after.

WE PASSED THE FRONT DESK. Behind it sat a new young, disinterested white guard. He paid more attention to his acne than to us, picking at a mob of pimples on his forehead. Then we moved, as a pack, through the banquet room. The Dean's stairs still filled us with curiosity and a charge, but we didn't linger this time. We wouldn't reach his door with wishful thinking.

Now we walked a long hallway, fifty yards at least. These were the staff offices. Rooms filled with women we'd met the day before, em-

ployed to refill our office supplies, deal with the Library's daily opera-
tion. But they weren't Unlikely Scholars. Lake had made that clear.
They were folks hired out of the local pool, from towns like St. Johns-
bury, Littleton, or Haverhill. The guards and office staff didn't seem
quite as intoxicated with their roles as we already were with ours. While
this place offered resurrection to the Unlikely Scholars, it only provided
these white kids with a living wage.

We passed their offices quietly. All their doors were shut, and the office walls were made of opaque glass. We could see shapes behind
them, more like gray ghosts than human bodies. Even on Sunday a few
staff members worked. We were here, so they were here.

We continued on.

This long hallway finally ended at the bottom of a steep staircase. I'm
not talking about some understated wooden deal like the Dean's. These
marble stairs went up three stories high and were the color of oyster
shells. They reminded me of the Grand Staircase inside the Metropoli-
tan Museum of Art. And we had to climb them to reach our offices.

Some of us were better at it than others. Violet, Verdelle, Peach Tree,
and Sunny went fast, giddy as children. Their boot steps sounded like
the beating of a thousand drums. Euphinia, Grace, and I took longer.

My problem was my lower right leg. Climbing that many stairs made
my knee feel like it had expanded under the skin, grown as big as a soft-
ball. My shin felt so cold now, more frigid than a Vermont blizzard. And
last I dragged my foot up. It had gone completely numb. I only knew it
was there because of its weight pulling at my swollen knee. I hadn't always been crippled like this, only since 2002. After Cedar Rapids I
couldn't spend too much time on my feet. Soon into the climb I started
to limp.

Taking it so slow did allow me to really appreciate the staircase,
though. Marble, yes, and ten feet wide. The handrails were carved from
the same stone. There were speckles in it that caught the light so it
seemed to flicker and glow. The climb felt like an ascent into Valhalla.
At the top I rested my numb leg. No more steps up, so now my gaze
drew down.

Into Scholar's Hall.

The day before, Lake stopped us here to ask if the layout of the Library seemed familiar. The long passageway we'd walked through and
now Scholar's Hall, which was shaped like an oval. Another long wing
sat on the other side of Scholar's Hall. That's where our offices lay.

No one came up with the answer, so Lake finally just told us.

The Washburn Library was laid out like the White House.

Scholar's Hall sat where the Oval Office would be.

Now at the top I crossed over the rim. On the other side another set of grand marble stairs led into the Hall. We went down those steps like miners entering a quarry.

At the bottom we marched past row upon row of enormous cedar bookshelves. Most of them full. The notes of past Scholars, those men and women who'd posed for the photos in the lobby, were all filed here. These shelves contained more than two hundred years' worth of their learning. The smell of the wooden shelves blended with the thousands of pages, and it created a comforting mustiness.

We moved across the maroon tiled floor of Scholar's Hall, walking so lightly that our boots barely scuffed. There were enormous picture windows at the top of the chamber, but the sunlight didn't quite reach the ground, so it felt cold down where we were. If some of the records were more than two hundred years old, then many of the Scholars were long dead. Walking among the volumes felt like a trip through a mausoleum.

Grace said, "Forget what Lake said yesterday, all that White House mess. I'll tell you what the Library reminds me of. Eddie Anderson and Jack Benny."

A statement that left at least five of us thoroughly mystified. Grace had hardly said a damn word in two days, and this was how she chose to break her silence? With gibberish?

Euphinia tapped Grace's arm lightly and said, "I see."

Peach Tree said, "Well, we don't."

Euphinia frowned at Peach Tree. "There's a story about how Eddie Anderson got rich playing Rochester van Jones on the old *Jack Benny Program,* and with that money he built a mansion for him and his wife right in the middle of Compton."

"So?"

Euphinia wiggled her nose dismissively at Sunny. "*So* his mansion was an exact replica of the one Jack Benny owned in Beverly Hills."

Peach Tree laughed, and it echoed through Scholar's Hall. "So you're saying that old bootlicking Negro loved his *boss* that much?"

Grace balled both hands into small, soft fists and shook them at Peach Tree. "You think that's the point, you damn water-head?"

"Well, what's the point, then?" he shouted.

Euphinia whispered, "We can have what anyone else can have."

We reached the far stairs. I had one hand on the railing in case I wobbled. Euphinia and Grace helped each other move up, stepping ahead in tandem. Even the youngest of us, Violet and Verdelle, moved slowly now. I replayed Euphinia's words in my head as we hit the top and went over the other side. One more set of grand stairs down. Into the last long hallway. Our hallway. Where radiators hissed in our offices.

Our offices were in the storefront style, just like the staff's. But unlike theirs our glass walls were clear. As you walked along, you could peek inside each room. Sounds like a display at a museum or zoo, but I didn't take it that way. The glass walls looked elegant. And the real benefit of them was that you couldn't sit around your office digging your nose or taking a nap. Anyone who's ever held a job knows how much of your day gets wasted that way. But now those habits had to go. There are benefits to shame in small doses.

Before stepping into our offices, we completed our quiet walk, marching to the very end of the long hallway. An enormous print hung in a gold frame on the northernmost wall. The day before, Lake had suggested that our work would start today. He didn't tell us what that work would be. But he did tell us about the painting.

"This is by Caravaggio," Lake had explained. "Jerome. Patron saint of scholars."

In the painting Saint Jerome has no halo around his head. Only a cardinal's red hat in the background suggests his holiness. It's easy to miss. The old man wears a robe around his waist and legs, but his upper body is naked. He leans forward while writing at his desk, and for company there's only an unlit candle, a crucifix, and a bleached skull. Jerome sits on a bed while he works, and the brightest texture in the room is his robe, the color of fire apples. He looks exhausted but in a state of frenzy. The man is lost in the mania of his calling.

Violet, Verdelle, Peach Tree, and Sunny. Euphinia, Grace, and me. We stood under Jerome's portrait and studied our saint as intensely as he studied his page.

13

WE WERE SO SERIOUS! Examining that old man so closely that we might've stayed there all morning if the guards hadn't showed up with our work. Three teenagers came down the marble stairs carrying boxes in their outstretched arms. They moved with the same lazy disdain that I'd used when mopping bathroom floors. The sound of their shoes on the steps was what knocked us out of our dream state. They stamped and jostled. They cleared their throats. They sighed and rolled their eyes. The boys went into each office and set out the materials they'd brought. Then, just as casually, they wandered back down the hall and climbed the grand stairs. Up and away.

Our office numbers corresponded to our cabins. I entered mine, number nine, and Sunny entered hers, number one, across from me. Each Unlikely Scholar did the same. My office had an oak desk and one of those knockoff Aeron chairs, one empty oak bookshelf, and an easy chair in the corner. A big gray computer sat on the desk, but it wasn't new. I saw little white tags on the side of the monitor and the hard drive. Both read REFURBISHED. I didn't mind that much. How many computers had Trailways made available to me? Absolutely none. As soon as I sat down, I got up again and walked into the hall, just to see if the others were as unsure as me.

Violet went through all the drawers of her new desk—just curious, I guess—while Euphinia and Grace couldn't even turn their computers on.

Meanwhile Peach Tree sat in the office across from Verdelle's and flirted with her through the glass, smiling wide. She must've been two feet taller than him, but he didn't care. "I like a lean woman," he'd told me as we'd walked behind her the day before. And Verdelle? Well, she did keep finding excuses to get up and sashay across her room.

I looked at Sunny again. There wasn't any point in me casting charm her way. She must've made some woman a very nice boyfriend back in prison, and that's all I'm going to say on the subject.

The guard had left a stack of newspapers next to my keyboard. I set them in my lap and read each masthead. *Mohave Valley Daily News, Daily Dispatch, Arizona Daily Sun, The Kingman Daily Miner, Today's News-Herald, East Valley Tribune, The Daily Courier, Herald, Arizona Daily Star, Tucson Citizen,* and *Yuma Sun.* Seemed like every daily paper from the state of Arizona.

Here was my first real job as an Unlikely Scholar and I had no idea what to do.

I leafed through each paper, looking for some mention of the Washburn Library. When nothing appeared, I hunted around for mention of the Dean or Unlikely Scholars or even Lake. Maybe the Northeast Kingdom. But not a damn thing stood out. I knew there must be some reason I'd been given these papers, but I didn't understand the motive. I felt lost.

The day before, Lake had led us to these offices and explained that the guards would deliver newspapers in the morning. When we asked about the step after that, Lake said, "I can't tell you." We tried to wheedle clues out of the big man, but he just repeated those four words. He didn't take any pleasure in our confusion.

I assumed the Dean had instructed him to be so vague, part of this larger pattern of leaving us to our own devices. I appreciated the practice of throwing us into the deep end, but this felt more like having our heads held underwater.

Now me and the other six Scholars floundered and gasped. I spent the rest of the day at my desk. Hardly even got up to use the small and well-maintained bathroom. The others were as committed. The others were as confused. In the morning we leafed through our newspapers enthusiastically. The sound of seven people turning pages quickly snapped like rifle shots. But by afternoon we'd run out of energy. The squawk of seven bodies leaning back in their chairs, a creaking chorus of personal defeats, that's all you heard at the end of our second day.

BY THE NEXT MONDAY, day ten, well, we weren't racing for the Library's side door anymore. We still went over together each morning, but the march had lost its urgency. Another day of being vanquished by handfuls of paper? No thanks. This started to feel too much like a real job. Something you hate to do and you don't know why you're doing it. I'd even tried to quiz a guard and two members of the office staff about the secret of these newspapers, but if they knew, they weren't telling. They answered phones, they delivered more printer paper. At the end of each day one guard came to our offices asking if we had anything for him. All we offered were questions.

So I sat in my easy chair, holding a page of *The Daily Courier* to the overhead light as if a message lay hidden in the paper stock. That's the point I'd reached. I'd have tried reading tea leaves or conducting a séance if I'd known how to do either one. At least they didn't bring us new papers every morning. We were left to sniff through our original stack until we caught the scent.

I looked across the hall at Sunny, who sat at her desk. She had a newspaper rolled into a tube and kept bopping it against her forehead as if she could knock an idea loose. Sunny saw me and unfurled the paper, showing me the front page of the previous week's *Journal & Courier*, a paper out of Lafayette, Indiana. A headline about the war in Iraq. She rolled it up again and returned to tapping her forehead.

Then a crash came from down the hall.

It was so loud that the newspaper pages flapped from my hands to the stone floor of my office. Sunny jumped to her feet, and her rolled newspaper echoed against the ground like an empty cardboard tube.

Sunny ran into the hall, and I wasn't far behind. Peach Tree and Verdelle peeked out of her office while Euphinia and Grace came out of the break room, Styrofoam cups of coffee in their hands. And we all stopped at Violet's place. Her chair lay on the ground, two of the four wheels still spinning from when she'd knocked it over. Violet's glasses dangled off one ear, but she hardly noticed. She stood over her desk, paralyzed.

Finally Sunny knocked lightly on the glass wall of Violet's office.

She looked at us with surprise. "I got it," she said, pointing at her desk. "I figured it out."

All the papers Violet had been given came out of the northwest, Montana and Idaho. But those dozen or so papers were folded and piled in a messy stack on top of her keyboard. She'd torn through every page, just like us, but then she'd refolded the dailies and set them aside.

A single green folder sat on the left side of her desk, with a two-inch stack of papers inside it. Violet opened the folder for us and took out the contents. There were typed notes and handwritten memos, faded receipts for meals and travel, and a series of Polaroid photographs.

Snapshots of a small mountain, taken from a distance. Then closer. And closer still. Until the shots were taken on the mountain, moving up a vague, overgrown trail. At the base of the mountain the camera caught thin tufts of grass and clusters of trees on all sides. The next shot moved farther up, and the grass went from green to a dried brown. The trees became thinner, even sickly. And the last picture was taken at the summit, but low to the ground, as if the photographer were crouching. In the distance I made out the gables of a decaying home.

No more pictures after that.

Alongside the photos Violet showed us the notes of a woman named Merle Waters. "Pimentel Hill, off Hollow Road, Onondaga County, New York state." These words were printed in block letters on the back of each photo. As well as the date: 1992.

Now I understood where this file had come from, those shelves in Scholar's Hall. This woman, Merle Waters, must've been an Unlikely Scholar too. One who'd been sent out to take pictures and make notes about Pimentel Hill. Why hadn't I thought to go through those old files? As Violet spoke, I watched her with admiration, but envy too.

Violet said, "I used to be a librarian, *assistant* librarian, at East High in Cleveland. And while I was looking at these papers, I thought about when we helped some of the kids practice for the SATs. You don't score well by learning everything there is to learn. You score well by learning what the *test* expects you to have learned. And how did we teach that to the kids? We showed them the old tests. That's what the prep schools do."

Violet set her glasses back on her face. She turned the sheets of Merle Waters's file.

"Instead of sitting here trying to *guess* what the Dean expected of me, I figured I'd go back and see how the Unlikely Scholars before us did it."

She got to the very end of the file, and there, flattened and yellow, lay a small newspaper clipping. Violet held it up for us to read. We huddled around her like she'd just invented fire. Five words were written in ink at the top of the page: "Daily Star, Oneonta, NY, 1991."

The headline of the article read: FAMILY CLAIMS TO HEAR MOUNTAIN SING.

At the bottom of the page, in the same handwriting: "Filed by Andre Dupree."

Violet set the old clipping back into the file, then gathered all the loose pages back into a pile. She stacked the Polaroids on top and shut the folder again.

She said, "This guy, Andre Dupree, found an odd little item, a weird story they stuck in the back of *The Daily Star* on a slow news day. But he clipped it and he passed it on. To the Dean, I guess. Then this other Scholar, Merle Waters, is sent to check it. And she finds this house there."

I pointed to the file. "Did she make it back? Does it say what happened to Ms. Waters after that last photo?"

Violet dropped her eyes. "No."

Peach Tree said, "But *our* part is just finding the news, right?"

Violet pursed her lips, raised her eyebrows. What answer did she have to that?

Peach Tree crossed his arms. "I'm not climbing no singing mountain. That's all I'm saying."

Violet turned and lifted her chair. She said, "I think we're like the scouts, gathering information. Remember what the Dean told us at our dinner: there's a voice crying out in the darkness. Our job is to listen. I'm going to look through my stack of papers and see if I find any more news like that. And when those guards come by this evening, I'm going to pass it on to them."

"I like that," Verdelle said. "We're *scouts*."

This struck us dumb. I think we were just trying to process all that we'd been introduced to in the previous week. Voices and cabins and this god damn library in the woods. Was I frightened or excited? I felt overwhelmed, but rather than admit this, I just got sarcastic.

I said, "They brought us all this way to cut newspapers? That's your big theory?"

Violet sat and rolled toward her desk. "You'd be happier if they gave you a mop?"

Peach Tree pointed at me and smiled. He said, "Burnt."

I returned to my office, but I had trouble. Like, what constitutes weird? An article about the alarmingly high rate of peanut allergies in today's children? The profile of a local car dealer who went to and from work on a ten-speed bike? If I looked at any article long enough, I imagined an unwholesome angle. Maybe the kids weren't allergic to peanuts. They were just being poisoned by their parents. Maybe the car dealer preferred a ten-speed because he'd stripped all the cars on his lot to sell for meth. Neither scenario was supernatural, but they would both be creepy.

Things only got worse as I heard others—Sunny, then Euphinia, then even Peach Tree—hollering about what they'd found. I felt like a dupe. Maybe I just wasn't smart enough to do this. That fear only got stronger when Verdelle and Grace eventually cried out in triumph too.

My sister, Daphne, used to tell me to act like I was sure of myself and eventually I'd come to believe it. But she was wrong. It's hard to fake faith, in yourself or anything else. At the end of the day Violet handed her articles to the young guard who appeared. If she'd done anything right, he didn't show it, just took the pieces of paper and shuffled away. The others held on to theirs, hedging, just in case Violet got it wrong.

After that they all went back to their cabins, but I stayed, working through the night.

14

I WOKE UP at eight-thirty in my easy chair, six Unlikely Scholars staring down at me. A green Scholar's file sat in my lap. I'd gone into Scholar's Hall the night before and grabbed one as a study aide. Mine had the notes and photos and original article. Even audiocassettes. My ration of newspapers spread across the floor and my desk. The Unlikely Scholars gazed down at me and my mess.

I'd experienced those looks in the past, but back then it was because I'd nodded off in the middle of a subway train or nodded off in the middle of a supermarket or nodded off in . . . the middle of a sentence. In fact, their expressions were so familiar that, for a moment, I actually felt high. I couldn't get a sentence past my tingling jawline, and my eyes felt like they were sliding off my face.

Peach Tree leaned closer than all the others and said, "This boy is zooted."

I had to rethink my night in a millisecond. Had I gone back to my cabin, found my six bags of dope, shot them up, then come *back* to work? Stress certainly made it easier to relapse, but I felt sure I hadn't done it this time. And as soon as I felt sure, the drowsy memory of a dope high left my face.

"I'm not zooted," I said, trying to sit up, which only made the folder fall to the ground, its contents landing on the newspapers with a plop.

"I'm *not*," I said again.

Euphinia and Grace stepped back and watched me. They both squinted their left eyes, tilted their heads, and pronounced judgment.

"I believe him," they said, nearly in unison.

Peach Tree sighed because he'd been outvoted. "Well, if he's going to look this bad, he might as well shoot up."

Verdelle slapped Peach Tree's shoulder lightly. With her other hand she helped me stand. She took my left and Sunny took the right.

Violet had already gathered up the loose sheets from the file and set them back in the green folder. Now she crouched over the newspapers I'd spread on the floor. She looked at all the articles I'd cut out. I'd even snipped some ads.

Violet grabbed one of the papers, the *Arizona Daily Star*, and said, "You been busy."

I sighed. "I just can't seem to get it."

She said, "Maybe we can help."

And just like that, following her call, the other Unlikely Scholars gathered all my newspaper clippings. Rather than returning to her office, Violet just plopped down on the floor in mine and read through each article, looking to see which she'd choose to send along.

Then Verdelle sat beside her. Peach Tree wriggled his big butt in between Verdelle and the bookshelf. Sunny sat in the doorway, and Grace took the seat at my desk. Euphinia stood in front of me, and when I didn't step aside, she said, "Think you might offer that seat to a lady?"

Once I moved, Euphinia sat and opened her paper, the *Mohave Valley Daily News*.

Then we heard footsteps in the hall. A heavy tread on the grand stairs. None of the guards had ever caused such booming. So when Lake appeared in the hallway, we weren't surprised. It had to be him or a triceratops. Lake reached my office and leaned against the clear wall, his body so big I thought we'd see cracks form in the glass. His bushy head poked into the room. We looked up from our places on the floor. To him we must've looked like a kindergarten class.

"Violet?" he said.

She raised her right hand.

"The Dean sends congratulations." He paused. "The rest of you should follow her lead."

Lake pushed himself off the wall, waved once, and left. The rest of us watched Violet quietly. Violet indulged a proud smile as she picked up the *Arizona Daily Star* again.

EVEN WITH A TEAM of seven it took a while to go through my stack. Hours, I mean. There were bathroom breaks and trips to have coffee, and debates about whether an article should be disqualified or passed on. As the pile of excluded articles grew, I got better at recognizing the difference. So did the others. We made progress in small ways.

Finally, when we had two dozen likely contenders, the others had me go through each one and explain why it had made it to the semifinals. I got it wrong a few times, but not often. And together we pared the pieces down to three undeniable favorites. That night, when the guards arrived, I'd send the trio to the Dean. All the others still had the pieces they'd clipped the day before. Only Violet had nothing new to offer since she'd spent the day training us. But she was the star pupil, so no one thought it would hurt her much.

At six o'clock we heard footsteps in the hall. All seven of us were still inside my office, and the steps weren't seismic enough to be Lake's. They were faint, someone small. Not one of the guards, but smaller.

I knew it wasn't the Dean even before I rose up, like the other Unlikely Scholars, and pressed my face to the glass wall of my office. (Sunny had commandeered the doorway.) I knew because the Dean wouldn't wear shoes that squeaked like that. So loud I thought a duck had snuck into the Washburn Library.

It was a woman.

She came down the hallway, walked to office four, unlocked it, and went inside.

She couldn't have been older than me. Thirty-eight or thirty-nine. And her thighs were so thick that she wobbled when she walked. Now, let me say that I don't mean that part as an insult. In fact, I mean it as the highest compliment. She was shaped like a bowling pin. The kind of figure that makes a man like me feel vigorous. And if I hadn't seen her in the context of the Washburn Library, I would've asked that thick little woman on a date.

Her face reminded me of a pinecone, just as brown. And she had these little nicks and bumps on her neck, half a dozen. They were razor scars. The kind you get from fighting, not shaving.

She opened her desk drawers and removed a few spiral notebooks. She stepped into the hall again, shut her door, and locked it.

I went to my toes so I could see her over Peach Tree's head. I guess you might say I was ogling. Then I caught myself and relaxed. I hoped nobody had noticed.

Right then Violet whispered, "What is wrong with her *hair*?"

If the woman heard Violet, she didn't show it. Just squeaked herself away. We watched her climb to the top of the great marble stairway and cross over again, into Scholar's Hall.

She didn't even look at us once.

After she disappeared, we were left to imagine her story, but we didn't even know her name. Instead we made up tales for an hour. None of them were nice. We gathered in the break room and gossiped over coffee.

The only idea that persisted, and thus seemed true, was that that woman had arrived at the Washburn Library years before we had. She was an Unlikely Scholar, but not from our class. We thought this because Grace claimed to have seen her posed in one of the photos in the lobby. We tried to solve the mystery, but didn't have enough evidence.

Finally, Verdelle, who'd claimed she wasn't any type of criminal, used a nail file to shred the shoulder off the key to her own office. Within half an hour she'd made it into a decent bump key. Verdelle then worked her bump key into the lock of that lady's office, and after a few minutes of jiggling she got the door open.

We didn't find much inside. Those spiral notebooks must've been about the last item left behind. She probably did all her work in her cabin, tucked in there day and night. Who knew that was an option? Then Violet found the envelope. At the back of a bottom desk drawer. The name handwritten in a penmanship we recognized from our own envelopes.

Adele Henry.

We left her office and returned to the break room, and Violet asked her question again. What was wrong with that woman's hair? Of all the strange bits, her hair remained hardest to forget.

Entirely white. Like polished bone.

She kept it short, a close little Afro, so it looked like she wore a swimming cap. A strange sight on a woman so young. And on dry land! When we talked about her, it kept coming back to the hair. As if this summarized the trouble with Adele Henry.

Violet first gave her the nickname. By nighttime, as we left the Library, I doubted we'd ever refer to her in any other way. The Gray Lady, that's what we called her. The Gray Lady.

My future wife.

15

OVER THE NEXT TWO MONTHS the Unlikely Scholars became friends. Forget standing outside in the snow. Now we had one another over for dinner four nights a week. Verdelle and Peach Tree turned out to be admirable hosts; Peach Tree knew how to cook his meats, and Verdelle loved to entertain. They didn't have dinners, they held soirées.

Wasn't quite the same with the rest of us, but we did serviceable work. Each week the office staff accepted grocery lists from us, and the guards drove to some nearby town and stocked up. I wasn't the only one to put beer or wine on my list, but none of us ever got a can or bottle.

Once a week I had the Scholars over to my cabin, so I got into the practice of moving my stash before each meal. If I'd left the baggies and needle under the bathroom sink, then I shifted them to the bottom drawer of my bedroom dresser. The week after that I changed to the top shelf of my broom closet. I couldn't leave it in one place too long because addicts are better than bloodhounds when it comes to chemical scents.

Violet and I became close. She liked me. And it wasn't one-sided. She was exactly my type. A bookish little thing. In Cleveland she'd been an assistant librarian *and* a meth addict. She knew how to pack a pipe and carry a conversation. That is a well-rounded person.

And yet I didn't do more than make time with her. Verdelle and Peach Tree set up house. Euphinia and Grace might as well have been conjoined twins. And Sunny did just fine for herself. She was juggling two young ladies from the office pool. Me and Violet had to boil over eventually. We were isolated too long to avoid it.

Two months, that's how long it took. A Thursday evening when Violet and I made Hanky Pankies for a dinner at Sunny's place. Violet brought the recipe from Ohio. Sausage, ground beef, Velveeta cheese, some garlic salt, and Worcestershire sauce. All of that heated and stirred until it became this glorious gloop, which we spread on slices of pumpernickel bread. Then we put them in the oven until they toasted. In a fine restaurant they'd be called tartines.

Violet and I left her cabin. Me carrying the warm cookie sheet, no oven mitts, her twirling a spatula in one hand. The sun had gone down just enough for the snow to turn a faint blue. Our boots on the packed snow sounded like we were walking across cardboard. We were nearly at the cabin, and I could see Grace in the window, setting dishes on the table.

"I feel like an old couple visiting the in-laws," Violet said.

I nodded. "Well, they must be your relations. Peach Tree's too ugly to be from my side."

She slapped my arm with the spatula. "I hope your parents came to our wedding at least."

Violet's words, and my own, replayed in my head as we walked quietly. Then she looked up at me and I looked down, and I knew she expected me to kiss her. Our first kiss.

Instead I said, "There's not going to be no church service."

"We're going to elope!"

"Violet," I said, "I could never mess with a little girl like you."

Violet dropped the spatula. It landed with its handle upright, the rest lost in the snow.

She had a very wide mouth and such full lips. There were dark patches on her cheeks, which only made her more imperfect and endearing to me. She wore large silver hoop earrings that day, like every day. A truly beautiful woman, in other words.

"Don't include me in your little fantasies anymore," I said.

Her eyes bugged wide and her eyebrows arched for a moment before they settled, but then her nose flared and her lips pursed shut as she sucked them in. She looked to the right, down at the snow, shook her head and sneered. Then she reached down and pulled the spatula from the snow.

"Fuck you, Ricky," Violet said. "Nobody wants your shriveled old dick."

She snatched the cookie sheet off my palm. Violet walked to Sunny's cabin, knocked too hard with the bottom of her spatula handle, and when the door opened, she went in alone.

———————————

WHEN THE DEAN'S INVITATION FOUND ME in Utica, I'd been trying to have a child for years. Three years. I'd impregnated a whole series of women in that time, but not one of them ever gave me a child. Weeks into the process and every single woman had a miscarriage. I mean, it just wasn't working at all. Eventually sex produced so much tragedy that I stopped having it altogether. Hadn't even masturbated since after my date with Cheryl in Utica. Have you ever known failure so deep it feels biological? If I hadn't found something else to sustain me, if the Library hadn't sought me out, I would've eventually committed suicide.

People might hear that and say, Commit suicide over not having a child? Come on. To them the idea seems ridiculous. Or it seems ridiculous for a *man* to think that way.

But when Violet gave me that smitten look outside Sunny's cabin, I knew how it would end. Why do you think I'd kept switching towns over the last three years? I'd start dating some woman at work, we'd get all loved up, family plans followed, and then the miscarriage ruined it all. One of us always had to leave. Me. And where would I find another place like the Washburn Library if Violet and I followed the same path? I hated to hurt her feelings, but I'd rather be alone than expelled.

And I stuck to my cover story: Ricky Rice, asshole. I didn't admit the truth: that I wanted a child but couldn't produce one and the frustration about killed me. Why not tell them? Some men might be cool enough to admit such defects to others, but I'm not one.

Of course, I hadn't always felt this fatherhood desire. Only since 2002, when I made a promise in Cedar Rapids, Iowa. One I had yet to keep, no matter how I tried.

Long before that I had made one woman pregnant. A decade ago. Her name was Gayle.

But we didn't have the child.

16

I SKIPPED DINNER at Sunny's that night. Violet had stepped into that cabin and repeated our exchange. The group's reaction hadn't been hard to predict. To the women Violet was a grandchild, a niece, a little sister. The next morning Peach Tree came to my office pissed, repeated all that was said. Even he'd suffered because of me. Verdelle, hit by a wave of female solidarity, wouldn't be giving him any butt for weeks.

Still, I refused to disappear entirely. Instead of coming to dinner four nights a week, I only ate with the group a few times a month. No more chummy chatter. Both Violet and I were grumpy for reasons no one would address out loud. As a result the group conversations revolved around the Library, the notes from the field. We talked about work.

We tried to guess who, exactly, was funding the Washburn Library. Indulged a boatload of theories—the Ku Klux Klan, the Federal Government, the New World Order, Corporate America, and sundry Illuminati—but while some of them gave us shivers, none made a damn bit of sense. After two and a half months we gave up that ghost. We asked Lake, but the man remained mum.

So instead we tried to guess *what* we were really doing.

The Washburn Library held an inventory of impossible events, documented, recorded, and even photographed until they seemed to be more than just hearsay. Euphinia and Grace argued that if you read these reports together, you had a different picture of the world. That the field notes, the files, were like dispatches from an undiscovered country. An atlas of the afterlife. And by working together—those of us in Vermont, those in the field, and with the Dean as our captain—we had become a kind of crew, navigating the deep waters between this world and the next. We were sailing toward the shores of the dead.

But what was waiting to meet us?

There is a voice whispering in the darkness.

It wasn't all gloom and mystery, though. There was a kind of joy even just in saying the names of the Unlikely Scholars who had written these reports. Merle Waters and Avery Evans. Diana Green. Maxwell Kudjo. Aloysius Bomford and Patricia Morrissey. Some of these folks had filed dozens of reports about dozens of strange places or things, while others, like Maxwell Kudjo, only had one. We tried to suss out what the differences could mean. Had Maxwell quit, or had he died? We still hadn't found answers about Merle Waters.

One name came up more than all the rest. One man who'd submitted so many field reports that his output practically matched all the other Unlikely Scholars combined. His name was Solomon Clay. As far as we could tell, he'd been working for the Washburn Library since the forties. We made jokes about this, imagining some stooped and crotchety old black man climbing into a sewer with a notebook and a camera, cursing and spitting the whole way down.

Solomon Clay. Who climbed the Grand Teton to find a glyph scored into Exum Ridge.

Solomon Clay. Who traveled to Polk County, Wisconsin, and recorded a disembodied voice saying mass in Norwegian inside a deserted Lutheran church.

Did we really believe all these things? It's hard to say. Violet and I were the most skeptical, but mostly because we thought we were smarter than the others and we feared seeming gullible. Violet and I treated the work as a pseudoscience, like phrenology or investment banking. We understood what connections the Dean expected, and we found them. Euphinia and Grace were least skeptical, because of the experiences that had brought them to the Library. In between were Sunny, Verdelle, and Peach Tree, who, to be honest, were willing to believe as long as they got to keep their cabins, these new lives.

We'd get into long arguments after our dinners. The problem was that all this evidence in Scholar's Hall could disprove as much as it proved. Merle Waters's photographs might only confirm that some crazy bastard built a Gothic revival home in a very inconvenient place. Or Merle Waters's disappearance might endorse the belief that she'd been devoured by whatever crouched inside those ruins on Pimentel Hill.

Violet had the hardest time with these debates. She'd yell, she'd ball her fists, she'd pace the room. Sometimes she looked epileptic while trying to argue for rational explanations. And the more Euphinia or Grace held to her belief, the more irate Violet became. Until she'd curse the whole Washburn Library, put every aspect of it down, just so the rest of us would admit she was right. She'd rather claim the Library was a monument to ignorance and superstition than accept that someone had good reasons to disagree with her. I don't think anybody held it against her. She was young. If things truly got heated, Violet even used insults.

One night she lost her temper and shouted, "Y'all think the damned Unlikely Scholars are like spiritual X-Men!"

The cabin became colder and colder as each of us walked out. I guess Violet had made us feel silly and naïve.

But then, two weeks later, we received our costumes.

17

AND DURING THOSE TWO WEEKS I moved my needle and dope, like usual. Took them out from the top shelf of the broom closet and hid them in my bedroom closet, under the spare blankets. Then took them from the closet and popped them behind the toilet, right under the plunger. Does that sound a little nasty? Then you don't want to know some of the places I've hid dope.

Saturday morning, two and a half months into my tenure, two weeks after Violet's bitter joke, I woke with the urge to get supremely high. No. That's not quite true. I woke with the urge to cross a snowy field, kick in Violet's door, and grab her tight. Or maybe I just wanted to blot out Violet with a more familiar pain. Either way, I woke up with a yearning that felt like the need to shoot up again. The needle and the junk were sitting in my fridge, chilling. I'd hidden them in the butter dish.

For people who've never shot up or snorted or smoked heroin, it can be hard to understand the allure. Catch sight of a man or woman whose arms are purple from old needle bites, look at the sunken face of a long-time user, how could anyone want to end up that way? But that's like passing a car accident and wondering why anyone, anywhere, drives. Don't focus on the mishaps; consider the pleasures instead. Taking heroin is like sinking into a tapioca hammock. If that doesn't sound good, then congratulations, you will not enjoy heroin. May I suggest cocaine?

So I woke up with the desire, despite being off the stuff three years. Peach Tree had been right: the urge doesn't go away. You only learn to ignore it. But that morning I felt the tingling so strong it lifted me out of sleep, and I was at the fridge, opening the butter dish, even before I felt fully awake. Had the butter dish in my hand, the cold like a soft kiss on my palm. All I had to do was lift the top and swing.

But then two strangers came kicking at my door.

Two very well-dressed strangers.

Small men in green suits and brown checked ties. Their outfits were identical, and so were they. Not salt and pepper, but pepper and pepper. I peeked at them from my kitchen window, the butter dish still in hand. I pushed the fridge door shut with my foot and watched quietly.

The one closer to me kicked the door again. Their hands carried small but heavy-looking cases. I tried to figure if I could shoot up without them hearing me, but when I tried to lift the lid, the butter dish fell to the ground. It didn't shatter, but bounced loudly across the tiles. My needle rolled one way and the six packets of H went another, still held together by a red rubber band.

And as soon as that happened, the twins looked at me.

"I see you right there," one shouted. "Stop that reckless eyeballing and come open this door, dummy!"

Right then, from the tone, I knew who they were. What they were.

Sheriffs.

I'd been evicted enough times to recognize that style.

I ran to the front door and pressed my body against it. I held on to the top lock so it couldn't be turned. I peeked through the little glass panels at the upper end of the door, right down on their square heads.

"You can't serve that eviction notice if you can't get in!" I said.

They both looked up now, and the other twin said, "You are dumber than dirt, fool."

I knocked the door with my good knee. "Well, who's on the outside? You cold yet?"

"We been sent to do something for you, not to take anything from you, dummy."

"Uh-huh," I said. "You're not getting in that easy."

They looked at each other. Their hair had been straightened, in that old style, and then slicked down on their scalps with grease.

"I'm about through," one said to the other.

His brother shrugged wearily, then looked up at me. "What kind of proof you want, fool?"

"Open those cases," I said.

They set them down, four all together. Then one of the brothers, the guy who'd said he was through, lifted one, and his brother popped a little lock. I expected to see handcuffs and mace and extra ammunition.

Instead there were scissors and measuring tape, rolls of thread, square pieces of chalk.

The brother holding the case looked at me and sighed.

"We're not cops, you dummy. We're tailors."

NO ONE HOLDS A GRUDGE like an old black man. The Chinese have shorter memories for the misdeeds done against them. So when I finally let the little tailors inside, after hurriedly hiding my stash in the oven, I didn't expect any camaraderie.

They walked in single file and set their cases down on the kitchen table. The four packs were heavy enough that the table's legs shook.

"You got some heavy yarn in there," I said, trying to be friendly.

The first brother looked up at me. "Why don't we just get this over with."

The pair had faces like Boston terriers, somber eyes that were a little too large, and jowly cheeks that only emphasized their frowns. This made them seem vaguely disappointed, no matter the tone of voice. The two had better posture than an English gentleman, and because of this the tops of their pomaded heads were about level with my shoulder.

"I'm Fayard and this is Harold. Raise your arms."

I hesitated, but didn't fight them, even if the tone was bossier than I would've liked. I raised my hands, and the brothers pulled out their yellow measuring tape.

While one worked on my upper body, the other kneeled and checked my legs. That one, Harold, grabbed the bottom of my pants and snapped them hard.

"You ever had your pants hemmed, fool?"

Fayard had his tape wrapped around my chest, but stopped checking it long enough to look down and see where the bottom of my pants flopped against the floor.

Fayard sucked his teeth, then shook his head. He pulled on my shirt sleeve. I'd fallen asleep in the shirt the night before. Its cuff came down to my knuckles.

"What size is this shirt?" Fayard asked.

I shrugged. "Large?"

Harold shouted from the floor. "Large!"

Fayard pursed his lips and blew out, a whistle meant to shame me.

"What size are yours?" I asked them. "Juniors?"

Harold stood up, stepped back, and opened his coat. He spun around once, slowly. The sleeves of his jacket just reached his wrists, and the bottom of his slacks floated an inch above my tiled floor.

"At least ours fit," Fayard said.

I MADE THEM TEA after they'd taken all my measurements, and this seemed to make them happy. They hadn't asked for drinks, but appreciated the hospitality.

"Come over here," Harold said, tapping the kitchen table lightly. "Let that tea steep a minute."

Harold opened another of the cases and took out a series of photo albums. Inside, there were all these pictures of folks tricked out in elegant clothing. Teenage boys and girls, women and men. Many smiled, some didn't, but each person had this aura, this zest. They looked happy. These weren't recent shots. They were all in black and white, looked like they'd been fished out of an archive. Maybe Scholar's Hall? By now even the teens in these photos, the ones still alive, might be a hundred years old.

"These pictures were taken by a friend of the Library's named James. He had a studio in Harlem many decades ago, and he photographed all the Unlikelies in his time."

I pointed at the pages. "These people were all Scholars?"

Fayard said, "Couple of them *still* are."

I liked looking at the photos even more after hearing that, but felt distracted by Fayard, who opened my drawers looking for spoons. He didn't touch the oven, but he wasn't far from it, and I felt scared. Like he'd pull the door open and see my works right there on a rack.

I must've been staring hard, because Fayard stopped searching, leaned back against the oven door, and watched me. Had they seen me stash the heroin?

"The tea's coming," he said. He made a twirling gesture with his right hand. "You go on and listen to my brother."

I nodded and looked at the photos again, but felt as if my own fingertips were on fire. I wondered if my eyes were misting up. What if he turned the oven on? How quickly would the plastic parts of the syringe melt? How long before the plastic baggies bubbled?

I looked back at Fayard again and said, "That tea's gonna get cold."

Harold tapped the photo album, but I wouldn't look at the shots, so Fayard nodded and brought all three cups over. He came around the side of the table and pulled out his chair.

"Come on, now," Fayard said quietly. "Let's find you something nice."

The brothers went through every page with me and told me to point out the pieces I liked. Some suits, hats, shoes, even one guy's cane, and they put each item on a list. They told me the proper names of each piece and the types of fabrics. Said it all slowly, the way you do when teaching someone a new language. Harold and Fayard wore *gabardine suits* and *Wembley ties*.

And I listened. Tried to. For a while I still wanted to tear the oven door off its hinges and get that dope inside me. But by the time I could recognize the Borsalino Alessandria hat, the urge had ebbed.

When we were done, they told me to expect delivery of the wardrobe in two weeks.

Those exact clothes?

"We can copy anything," Harold said. "And it hardly costs a thing."

"But why these clothes?" I asked.

Why not parachute pants, for instance? I'd missed the trend when it first came around.

Fayard and Harold looked at each other ruefully. Finally Harold nodded, and Fayard opened a fourth album. He flipped through a few pages, found the picture he wanted, and turned the book to me.

It was the Dean.

A young man, but a man and not a child. He posed with a slim woman, who wore a fringed flapper's dress, her arms exposed. She sat, and he stood behind her. Both looked into the camera with concentrated gazes.

Harold said, "This is how grown folks used to dress. Want to be an adult again?"

SURE AS THEIR WORD, the clothes arrived two weeks later, to the day. I wasn't even there to receive the stuff. I'd crashed in my office again, and when I returned to my cabin, walked into my bedroom, I found the closet doors open. Suits and shirts and even ties swinging on hangers. Pairs of shoes on the closet floor. Socks and underwear in my dresser. Three hats in a row on my bed.

I felt myself floating between awe and apprehension. You'd think this life would feel real by now but this was the last step. I felt that when I put on those new outfits, I'd be changed. No longer treating it like just a job or a meal ticket, but moving deeper into mystery. This would mark my true conversion. I sat at the edge of my bed and looked into the closet, stared at the clothes as if I was reading the stars.

I felt overwhelmed, even scared, I admit that. But eventually I got off my bed.

I pulled a gray flannel jacket from the closet.

The fabric smelled of cigar smoke and history.

I put on my uniform.

18

SIX MONTHS LATER I barely remembered a time when I didn't dress in three-piece suits. When I didn't live in a cabin in the Vermont woods. Only nine months into my tenure, but it felt like ninety years since Utica.

I woke up without an alarm clock, woke up before the sunrise, and moved around my cabin in a frenzied funk. You know when you work real hard just to avoid thinking about something? My time there had become like that. Waking up early, getting to work early, leaving work late. Pretty soon I wasn't spending much time with the other Unlikely Scholars.

Violet and I had devolved into bland politeness. Not even enough feeling between us to start arguments anymore. Peach Tree and Sunny still made conversation sometimes, but I was little more than a coworker, even to them. I had become the new Adele Henry.

All this distance because of Violet's broken heart? Nah. Violet felt rejected, sure, but she recovered soon enough. Even the other women let it pass eventually. The distance between me and the others solidified because I never explained myself. People can put up with a jerk, but not some nut who might flip on them inexplicably. It's just not worth the hassle.

The Gray Lady was still around too, but she stayed solitary. I hadn't heard the squeak of her shoes in the Library hall for many months. I would've thought she was dead if I hadn't seen the small garbage bin next to her cabin fill up every week.

So that morning I woke up feeling sour. I wasn't having sex, wasn't even masturbating anymore. It had been well over a year without a climax now, not a single tug, and as a result I didn't need an alarm clock to wake me. Not since I had all this excess energy gobbed up inside. If you'd attached jumper cables to my fingers, I could've started a car.

I left for work alone at six, instead of at eight with the other Scholars. I felt wrecked. It was only October, but it had snowed heavily the night before, so me and the other Scholars had been out plowing our pathways at midnight. You had to do it that way. If you left the snow until morning, you wouldn't be able to open your door. The guards had all gone home. We only had one snowblower and two shovels between us, so we'd worked together clearing one path, then the next. It was the most time I'd spent with them in months.

Doing the shoveling ourselves taught us why the Dean never had the front steps of the Washburn Library cleared in winter. There was a grand entrance, with a set of wide stairs leading to a bank of frosted doors, but during a blizzard you could waste hours clearing that whole side, or just a half hour digging out paths to the modest side entrance. By summer we'd all become pretty used to coming and going through the metal door. I'd skipped up the front stairs a couple of times in May and June, but really just for the novelty.

I'D BEEN IN MY OFFICE for an hour when one of the Library's guards, a kid named Connor, brought me the day's newspapers. A stack of twelve. I felt more comfortable with all the Library routines. In recent months, we'd even been given access to the Library's trucks and finally been allowed to borrow the keys and drive ourselves around. A sign of trust. And do you know, to my knowledge, none of us broke the social contract? Folks might go down into Burlington for groceries or just to eat dinner in a town, around new people, but no one returned with anything toxic as far as I knew. This was a different life indeed.

I thanked Connor and took the newspapers, laid them on top of my computer monitor. Then I opened the top drawer of my desk. Do you know that in all those months I'd never returned that very first Scholar's file? The one I'd grabbed on my night alone after Violet had figured out our job. I liked to take it out every few weeks and go through the contents. Reading through it reminded me of how little I knew back then, and how much more confident I felt with the work now. That packet had become my most regular companion.

I took out a microcassette deck, used it to play and replay one of the cassettes that had been in the file. It was a stream of audible noises recorded in a South Bronx parking garage six years before. Most of the sounds were what you'd expect: a faint wind, outside traffic—maybe a car horn or children shouting as they walked by. At times a door slammed, indicating, I assumed, someone entering or leaving that floor of the garage.

But there, moments after the door, as if triggered by the door, a voice. Young, male, repeating himself. What did he say?

I had more than just the cassette to work with. There were extensive photos of the stairwell, and pages of handwritten notes. The pictures and sounds had been captured by an Unlikely Scholar named Gartrelle Meadows.

The original article, from the *New York Post*, read: CHILD'S CRIES HEARD IN PARKING GARAGE. The Scholar who'd clipped it had written a name at the bottom, but it was illegible.

Since I still hadn't met the Scholars in the field, I tended to read a lot into little things. Like how Mr. Meadows wrote in tiny script. Or that he tried to capture the sounds he heard on paper. "BAMM!" for the door. "SEEPSEEPSEEP" for some birds. This came across as half-conscientious and half-bonkers, and I liked him even more for it. I wondered what kind of life he'd led before coming to the Library. Arsonist? Strong-armed robber? I remember my surprise when it turned out both Euphinia and Grace had been in trouble for identity theft. The first in Texas and the second in Michigan. Those two old ladies! They'd acted like they couldn't turn on a computer. Come to find out they once sold credit card info to the same cartel in Estonia.

The slam of the door played on the tape again, and seconds later the voice croaked once more. A single word, not much louder than a whisper, but definitely there.

What did all this stuff really mean? At some point this file had gone up to the Dean's office, but I couldn't imagine what he'd done with it. Was there some secret code? What mattered and what didn't? I'd become tired of simply clipping articles. I wanted to understand the larger design.

The slam of the stairwell door played, and I leaned into the machine, my ear against the speaker the way one person listens to another's heartbeat.

And this time it seemed as though the voice was right there, in my office. Like there was a boy on the floor behind me. Gasping. His moldering hand stretched toward the cuff of my pants. Hoping to turn me around. To make me understand.

Electricity. That's what the voice said.

Electricity. I wrote that word on a scrap of paper for the hundredth time.

19

AFTER FLIPPING OFF THE CASSETTE TAPE, I scrutinized the morning's papers. Most people begin on page one, but I didn't read them that way anymore. I wasn't after dispatches about the big events. I began at the back end, reading the stuff some editor had crammed beside the classifieds. For us the greatest gain came from the smallest features. What others threw away, we savored.

As I reached the front page of *The Washington Post*, the news turned to the war in Iraq, as it must. Two and a half years of fighting and many more to go. And yet, even though I pawed through a dozen papers each day, it actually became easier to forget the war as I read more. Thirty-five casualties one day, and a bomb killed twenty-four the next. But I've never known a statistic that actually touched my heart.

I brushed my fingers over the latest headline.

Then the door to my office opened and I nearly fell out of my chair. I'd been concentrating a little too hard on the image of a charred van. Could I really see bodies inside? I was so startled by the noise at the door that the pages in my hand rose with me. I clutched them automatically. Spun around to see who it was and moved so quick that I tore the newspaper in two. One war in my left hand and another in my right. The snap sounded like a pistol had gone off in the little room.

Lake stood in the doorway.

Or I should say that he twisted so he could fit his shoulders through the door. I hadn't spoken to him much in the months since our tour. Hardly ever saw him around. He wasn't a security guard and wasn't staff.

The Scholars joked that he didn't actually work for the Library, he was really an ambassador from the woods all around us, a dignitary from that foreign land.

"Mr. Rice," Lake said, but nothing more.

Was he taking attendance?

The offices of the other Scholars were lit up brightly by now. I hadn't noticed, but they'd made it to their desks. They must all have stopped their work, though, must've been watching my door, because Lake hadn't come down our hall since the morning he'd congratulated Violet.

Lake's glassy eyes scanned the room.

"You've been called up," he said.

I turned and looked at the phone on my desk, but it hadn't rung once all day.

"Who called me?"

Lake stepped into the room entirely, and I moved five steps back, pressed against the far wall. The man was as wide as my desk.

"You don't understand," he said. "You've been called up. To see the Dean."

"How can that be?" I asked, without meaning to.

"Only the Dean can tell you," Lake said.

With those words my suit shrank and I felt warmer. The glass wall of my office seemed to bend in the light. Had I begun to glow? How else to explain the heat in my eyes? Tears? All six of my former friends stepped out into the hallway now. I didn't want them to watch, and I wanted them to see everything. I didn't know what to do, jump around or faint, so instead I shook Lake's hand.

Now, you have to understand, the man didn't have his hand out. Those big paws of his rested calmly at his sides. I wonder if Lake thought I was going to tackle him. He must've been a little shocked, because when I grabbed his hand, he burped. Just a little noise, out of his lungs, that he couldn't stop. I grabbed one of his meaty hands with both of mine and shook double extra hard.

"That's great," I said. "Just great."

Lake didn't smile exactly. His big red face stayed largely the same, but he didn't seem angry either. Not until he looked at his hand and saw the little gray splotches on his skin. I saw them too. The ink from the newspapers, all those headlines, had stained my fingertips, and now I'd dirtied his hand.

"Sorry," I said.

He raised one finger and shook it at me. "That's just the price of contact." He added, "Tomorrow morning I'll come for you."

Lake turned to leave the room, and the other Unlikely Scholars hopped back to their offices. Light doesn't travel as fast as they did. Instantly they were tapping at their keyboards and whiffling through newsprint. Lake knocked on the glass of my office as he strolled off.

"Wash your hands," he shouted, and then went on.

I MUST'VE BEEN LEFT ALONE for a little while, but I couldn't remember the passage of time. Lake went away, and then, next in my memory, the other Unlikely Scholars crowded round. But my hands were clean, so I'd gone down the hall to the coffee room and washed them, but when?

"He's still shaking," Verdelle said. She stooped a little to look into my face, but spoke to the others.

"His eyes are even shaking," Peach Tree said.

"Can I get his stapler when he leaves?" Euphinia asked. "They never gave me one."

"If she gets the stapler, I need the toner cartridge out his printer," Grace added.

Finally I got back to the ground floor.

"Hey," I whispered. "I'm right here."

"No you're not," Violet said.

Called up to meet the Dean.

Peach Tree said, "I guess you won."

At which point the women looked at Violet.

"Ain't that something," Grace muttered.

Verdelle whispered, "Yeah, the same old thing."

Things might've gone badly just then. Violet put her hand on the back of my neck. I waited for her to scratch the skin off.

Instead she said, "We're going to have a dinner tonight. A nice one. A real send-off. For our friend."

Verdelle and Sunny, Euphinia and Grace, they watched Violet's mouth.

"You sure?" Sunny asked.

Violet took off her glasses, rubbed her right eye, paused a moment. "I am."

Peach Tree hit my shoulder, as if he felt relieved.

"She's got the right idea. That's how they used to do it in the way back when."

"That's how who used to do it?" I asked, watching Violet cautiously.

"Human beings," Peach Tree said. "I'm talking about the first, first times."

A feast, I thought. Where you toast and ask the Heavens for luck.

"We should have it at my cabin," I told him.

"Well, where else we going to do it?" Peach Tree asked. "You think I'm going to clean up my place for you?"

Euphinia said, "We should all bring something."

Each Unlikely Scholar shook my hand and left.

I stood still for twenty minutes more.

With the rest of my afternoon I went over Gartrelle Meadows's file again, the sound on the stairs. *Electricity. Electricity.* I felt a bit of that myself. The next morning it would be my turn. At four o'clock I sent the last report of my life up to the Dean.

Then I borrowed a truck, drove up to Newport, and spent most of my money on a treat for the feast.

20

AS I CLEANED MY CABIN, a great wind bruised the walls. It made a steady stomp against the roof and threw snow at all my windows. Winter in Vermont. I already knew it well.

At seven the Unlikely Scholars arrived together.

Carrying dishes of this and that, the same old stuff as always, but it didn't look the same. Even a bowl of mashed potatoes became whipped ambrosia.

We had a tuna casserole, homemade buttermilk biscuits, sweet potatoes, and even lobsters. A wild mix of food, right? But it seemed appropriate. We were a wild mix of people. Most of us were missing a couple of teeth somewhere in our mouths. Our fingertips showed scars and hardened skin from the years of cradling hot glass pipes. We bumped around one another, elbows and hips, as we set the table. But there wasn't as much chatter as I remembered from months before.

When we finally sat for the meal, it felt like a wake. Knives and forks clacking, cups thumping as they were set back down on the dining table. Our utensils were louder than us. We ate like that until our plates were clean.

Before anyone considered seconds, I left the room. When I returned from the bedroom, the other Unlikely Scholars eyed me cautiously. But I didn't want them watching me so I shook what was in my hands.

We'd been there nine months. Nine months of water and juice, tea and coffee, all the soda you might like. But not this. Not one glass of wine. From the hush you would've thought I'd just returned from the top of Mount Sinai. I shook the bags, full of reds, again. They were as heavy as stone tablets.

"Ricky," Violet whispered. "Everything's forgiven."

TWO HOURS LATER and we were singing at the table. Humming at least. Peach Tree doing a little Al Green while I tapped my chair to give him a beat, but I was thinking of the wrong song and messed him up. He got angry, just a flare-up, a minute of shouting that passed. None of us held it against him.

We were down to the last two bottles of Shiraz. Most of the food gone. I'll say this about us. We looked silly.

Each of us wore these fine Washburn outfits. Verdelle a two-piece twill cord "tailleur" suit, and Peach Tree a herringbone tweed three-piece. Sunny came in a men's gray worsted wool suit and hadn't removed her jacket throughout the meal. Euphinia and Grace wore matching evening gowns of chenille brocaded crêpe. And Violet looked almost sporty in a three-piece knickers suit. And yet, with all this finery, we looked a little foolish because we'd tucked paper towels into our collars like bibs.

And I don't mean one paper towel either. I'm talking about three or four, hanging down to our waists. You'd have thought we were in barber's chairs. But what else were we going to do? I'm not the only one who thought the Library might ask us to return the duds one day. And I did not want to get charged on some cleaning fee.

I uncorked the last two bottles and moved around the table, a bit wobbly. I poured out generous doses, then returned to my seat. The kitchen clock read ten past ten, but it felt later. Liquor turns some folks giddy, while others get aggressive. And it makes some people reminisce.

Euphinia said, "I got caught up in some trouble down in Victoria, Texas, two years ago. Did an account takeover on a couple, the easiest kind of ID theft. But I guess they lost their house over the debts. By the time I got caught, they were living out of their car. They tracked me down on the morning I made bail."

She sipped her wine.

"I had my money tucked in a bank in Houston, so I stepped out my arraignment at the Victoria County Courthouse and got right on Route 59. I figured I'd close out the account in Houston, then disappear. Had to go do it in person because no ATM spits out that much cash. I'm not on the road more than a few miles when this couple I'd cheated rolls up alongside me. I didn't know them, never saw their faces before, but I could tell they knew who I was. I was the Devil, as far as they were concerned."

We were so used to snowstorms by this time that we hardly flinched when my cabin's windows rattled. Outside, it sounded as if the woods themselves were running headfirst into my house. The walls groaned from another tackle.

Euphinia said, "It's not the first time I got found. I pulled onto the shoulder, and they stopped just ahead. I'd offer them some money if they'd follow me to Houston, just enough to make us even. They climbed out the car, this Mexican couple, calm as clams. I rolled down my window to talk, and before I even open my mouth, that man lifts the lock and opens my door. Pushes right inside! So I scramble to the passenger side, best I could, but there's the wife. She's blocking the door with her hip. And while I'm looking at her, the man punches me in the back of the head. Kept hitting me until I just passed out."

Euphinia stopped and sighed, dropped her chin to her chest. She spoke quietly now.

"You ever been in the south Texas desert? I smelled salt water coming up from the gulf, but I saw desert scrub and twisted acacia. It was like my nose and eyes weren't in the same territory. I got confused. And then this heat, this dry, dry heat. That couple dumped me and ran. I didn't see them. No cars. I found tire tracks and tried to follow them, but pretty soon I couldn't see straight. I was just wandering to death.

"Then I look up and I see all these *birds*, different kinds, circling and circling a spot up ahead. I figured that meant water. By the time I got there, I was practically crawling. I didn't have much strength. And when I got there, the birds didn't even scatter like birds do. They kept circling, or they perched in the brush and they watched me stagger. They kept chirping. All of them. So many, and so loud, I covered my ears. And finally I found a deep ditch, but there wasn't any water in it. There was a body, lying on its back. It was my own grandson."

Euphinia's hand sat on the table, clenched into a fist. Grace set down her wineglass and rested her open hand over Euphinia's knuckles until the fingers uncurled, lay flat again.

"I tried to run, but I didn't have the power. I kneeled at the edge of the ditch trying to understand what I was seeing. My nine-year-old grandson—Trevor Lee, we called him—was lying in that ditch. Wearing the suit we buried him in. I figured this was a delusion. Hallucinating from the thirst. So I was able to stay calm. But then that boy opened his eyes.

"He looked right at me, started moving his lips, and I *knew* what he was saying. I fell right into the ditch, dragged myself to him, and I touched his legs. His body was *real*. I crawled up to his side and watched his lips moving. I heard him say it was my fault he died. And I cried because I knew he was right.

"I put my hands over my baby boy's mouth. I felt his lips brush against my palms. He wouldn't stop damning me. So finally I gave up, I dropped my hands. I leaned over Trevor Lee's body. It was time to reckon with the way I'd lived my life. I put my mouth to Trevor Lee's ear and I made my promise.

"As soon as I did, all those birds stopping singing. They flew right away. Their wings sounded like a thunder cloud. Seconds later a heavy rain started. And that's what saved my life. I wandered out the desert. Two years later, I'm sitting here."

I raised my glass. "To keeping our promises," I said quietly.

"Amen to that," Sunny said, knocking the table with one hand.

Everyone sipped from their cups.

"And to Gartrelle Meadows," I added.

Why did I mention him? Of all the things I might have said next? He must've sat through a moment just like this. The night before the Dean's door opened. And maybe Euphinia's story would've sounded as familiar to him as it did to me. To us. To all the Unlikely Scholars.

Peach Tree raised his glass and sniffed. "To Audrey Green."

Each of us raised a cup and chanted the name of a Scholar we'd come across in the Library's files. They'd become a little mythic to us.

Finally Grace said, "To the Gray Lady."

"Adele Henry?" I asked.

"Even her," Euphinia said.

We'd actually set out eight places at the table, on the off chance she might show. I'd slipped a note under her cabin door, for nothing. We gestured toward her empty chair.

"And to Solomon Clay." I saved his name for last.

I rose from the table after that and returned to my bedroom. Got on my knees and dug for the last bag, hidden underneath my bed. The others swayed in their seats. When I returned, I carried one last bottle.

"It's time for the bourbon," I said.

Everyone hopped up to wash out their glasses.

21

AND YET, for all that drinking, I couldn't fall asleep.

I sent the other Scholars home by two in the morning and spent the next hours uneasy. First, I drank a few gallons of water so I wouldn't have a hangover. Then I lay on the couch trying to trick myself into dozing. Posing like a sleeper: shoes off, body scrunched onto the cushions, eyes closed, mouth open, a pillow under my narrow head, but my body wouldn't buy it, and after an hour I sat up. What would I do with all this time? I felt so nervous that I could hardly sit down. By dawn, I'm sorry to say, I'd torn my cabin apart trying to find my dope.

But now I couldn't find the damn things! I'd hidden them too well. I'd wrapped them in tin foil, I remembered that much, then thrown the tin foil into a Ziploc bag. But what had I done after that? I checked behind the toilet again. In the butter dish. The oven. I'd started out moving my stash every week, but eventually I only needed to relocate it once a month. The Library's work became my habit instead.

For all I knew, I'd buried the stuff outside over the summer, maybe next to my front steps. If so, I wouldn't be able to dig it out of the frozen earth now. I checked behind the radiators and even in my overhead lamps. I looked and looked and looked.

When the sun rose, I didn't recognize my cabin. I'd kept it so neat all nine months before this. Had my friends snuck a hurricane inside while I was using the bathroom? Who'd torn open the couch cushions and pulled out every kitchen drawer? Not me. I felt sick and silly to see so much damage, but at least the time had passed. Nearly seven in the morning now, and I felt grateful for that. Spent forty-five minutes putting everything away, and suddenly my meeting with the Dean seemed too near. I had to hurry into the shower. Before getting in I finally found the dope, six baggies stuffed into one of the toilet rolls under the bathroom sink. Too late to shoot up now, but I didn't throw them out either. As the water ran in the tub, I left them right on top of my pillowcase. Then I washed and dressed. Put on my finest outfit, a three-button charcoal pin-striped suit.

I left the cabin, and as I tramped toward the Library, I saw Violet watching me from her cabin. I waved, but she didn't wave back. She watched me for another moment, then let the curtain swing closed.

The sun had risen high enough for me to see all the cabins. With their lights off it seemed as if they'd shut their eyes to me. I moved toward the Library alone.

Before I went inside, three wild turkeys appeared in the snow. Their bald heads bopped up and down as they walked. With a clumsy dash they leapt onto the roof of my cabin. They searched for food up there and found nothing and I watched them. Until they hopped down again and beat a graceless retreat into the woods.

Imagine me seeing a thing like that in a place like this. There are people who say life is dull. Just a series of mundane events. But I can't agree. Things happen. Bet on that.

I MADE IT TO MY OFFICE, but my office wasn't there. The basics were still in place, like a desk and file cabinet, but my work had been removed. Every last clip, even notes scribbled onto index cards. The only thing left was a small picture I had kept tucked in the top drawer of my desk. Me and my sister, Daphne. A shot from our childhood. The two of us on our living room couch. Daphne's five, and I'm only six months old and totally naked. I look like a big old Junior Mint in her arms.

"Mr. Rice."

I looked up and saw that Lake, the enormous bastard, had snuck up on me again.

"You're pretty quiet for a big guy."

"Don't be nervous," Lake said.

"I'm not."

I said this, but when I tried to stand, I couldn't do it. My mind gave two commands: get up, and put that picture in your pocket, but I didn't manage either one. When I tried to stand, my hand shook and the photo of Daphne slipped out of my fingers, into my lap. And my legs didn't respond except to quiver.

"Don't be nervous," Lake said again, but this time he walked into the office and his colossal head blotted out the lightbulb. He lifted me out of the chair by pulling on my arm, and then, just as casually, picked Daphne's photo up from the ground. He undid my jacket and slid the shot into my pocket. Then he redid the button.

"Do I look okay?" I finally asked.

But he didn't answer me. What was he going to do, fix my tie? Darn my socks? The man wasn't my personal valet. He left the office.

Whenever I'd gone off heroin before, the people who loved me had praised the change excessively. I mean they'd really cheer me on. But was it really my only success? You wouldn't have known it by the look of me back then, but I always worked. Even when I stole and scammed and pulled knives on junior high school children, I still showed up for my shift at the movie theater, the restaurant, the bookstore. I took some pride in that, but it's a small victory, I guess. Certainly nobody else ever noticed.

So when I went on methadone, or even tried to totally kick a few times, my friends and even coworkers praised me up through the ceiling. But the more they focused on this one achievement, the more I realized I'd never accomplished anything else. When I was twenty-two, I could convince myself that better things were coming, but by thirty-six their praise sounded like pity. As I left my office, I leaned against the doorway and I prayed for strength.

"WHAT DO YOU ALL THINK of us?" I asked Lake as we came down the far steps, at the other end of the Library. Lake had a longer stride than me, and I tried to keep up, but soon my right leg went cold. I didn't mention it, but the sound of my right foot dragging behind me made the statement, so we went pretty slowly as we moved past the staff offices.

"Who all?" he asked.

I pointed at the closed doors. I heard the squeaks of office chairs and the mumble of women on telephones.

"The staff and guards. How do you all feel about the Library? About having a bunch of black folks living up in your woods?"

Lake said, "Vermont has lots of poverty. Especially around here."

I nodded, but didn't see how this answered my question.

"The Washburn Library pays regular. And it's getting harder to find steady work. That's what *we* think about."

We'd reached the recessed staircase that led up to the Dean's office. I'd only seen that little man come out of the room that one time, for our banquet. At some point we all decided he must have had a back door so he could shimmy out on the sly. We said this, but I don't think anyone believed it. Speaking for myself, I felt convinced that the Dean *couldn't* leave the Library, the same way my brain can't abandon my body.

Lake looked up at the Dean's door. He touched the wall with his big bare hand. Rubbed the index finger along the groove of a stone, then tapped the surface slowly. It reminded me of gesture I'd seen years before.

His hand continued to slap against the stone, and I remembered the man who'd done it before. A cop, back in New York. Lying on his stomach, tapping the pavement with his right hand while I stood over him.

"You ought to go up now," Lake whispered.

How many times had I looked up at that door as I went to work? Me and the other Unlikely Scholars. Every weekday, for nine months. We'd turned a simple flight of steps into a holy mile. You'll see stairs like these in any office building, a small school, any old house. They weren't special. Nothing like the ones that led in and out of Scholar's Hall, that's for sure. And yet I felt a fire up through my legs as my foot touched the first small step.

IT WAS AN ODD DAY when I saw that New York cop facedown on the pavement, tapping the ground with his right hand. Sunny but cool out, and the sidewalks were dirty, but that wasn't unusual because it was 1983. I was only eighteen and a stubborn kid, but that's not unusual either. I hadn't slept in a couple of days and really needed to eat. Though I didn't feel hungry, my body refused to pretend anymore. My guts groaned because they'd been ignored for so long. I'd been on my way to St. Mark's Place because I knew a hot dog vendor who'd sell me three buns for fifty cents, enough filler to get my stomach back on my side so I could then focus on scoring more dope. But when I reached Astor Place, I found a parade standing between here and there.

I came up behind one group of people and expected to see balloons or a marching band or a waving mayor. Instead I heard police sirens. I turned away on instinct, and my feet got the notion to run. Two cops came down the street on motorcycles with their sirens going loud, clearing the road for a patrol car behind them. And behind that patrol car another two cops on bikes making just as much noise. They were in a big blue hurry.

Then this guy on a delivery bike just pedaled out into the road. I mean completely oblivious. The idiot was wearing headphones! Shot out into the road, and the patrol car swerved to miss him and went right into an empty newspaper stand.

It sounded worse than it was. The first noise was just this bump. Made me think they'd hit a person and not a pile of wood. Then the patrol car, moving too fast, flipped right over, upside down. Now, that was louder. The cops on the bikes behind them went flying too. But the two lead cops, who'd been clearing the road with their sirens, only stopped their motorcycles long enough to pick up a satchel from one of the guys in the patrol car, and then they were gone. Looked pretty heartless to me. I only found out later, from nighttime news, that four guys had hijacked one car of a 6 train at gunpoint. The patrol car had been carrying a satchel with the ransom for the hostages. No wonder those cops didn't wait around.

I didn't know that at the time, though. And I wouldn't have cared. The thing with heroin, if you take it long enough, is that you lose that natural sense of concern. Feelings for other people, even for yourself, chuck them out the door. So right after this big wreck I just strolled through the crowd and right into the street. A real saunter. Went straight over to this one cop lying on his stomach. I couldn't tell if he was tapping the sidewalk to prove he was alive or if it was a Morse code signal or simply a way to pass the time until an ambulance arrived. But what seemed obvious was that he couldn't get up. Easy pickings. I bent over his body, so casual about it I'll bet the crowd thought I was an undercover cop helping out his comrade. I put my hand on his holster, flipped the little button, pulled out his revolver, and ran like a fiend.

The human mind, it needs a moment to process such a thing. So by the time the crowd started screaming at me, I was far beyond them. I carried that gun just nine blocks before I found a friend who helped me sell it. I didn't spend the loot on hot dog buns. New York deserved its reputation back then.

22

THIS EPISODE STAYED with me as I reached the top of the stairs. The Dean's oak door was as understated as the staircase. I didn't knock. Just stood there with my chin at my chest. I wondered how I'd fooled the Dean into believing I deserved to be there. First at the Library and then at his door. Did he know me? Did he understand the things I'd done? I should just toss myself down these stairs, I thought. I should steal a truck, drive down to the airport, and fly myself back to wretchedness. I imagined myself forty years from this moment. Who would I be if I ran away?

I saw an old man, sweeping.

Then I knocked so hard I thought the walls would fall down.

The oak door didn't open, but I heard a buzz so I grabbed the handle and pushed. The office was so dark that even light from the stairway didn't penetrate it. My feet stayed at the threshold and I leaned my head in.

"Can you hear my voice?"

Months and months since that banquet, but I still recognized the Dean's croak. I pictured his sneer.

"Yes," I said.

"Then follow it."

"Can I get a flashlight at least?"

No answer to that and no flashlight. I stepped in slow, testing the darkness with my foot.

"Shut the door behind you."

And now, sealed off, I might've been floating through the deepest region of space. Fallen into a black hole. I closed my eyes, concentrated on my feet because at least they touched something solid.

When I opened them again, the room hadn't become any brighter, but the Dean's voice cut through the gloom. He'd been talking, but I hadn't heard a bit of it.

"What did you say?" I shouted. "You're gonna have to repeat yourself."

"I don't have to do a damn thing! You better show more manners than that."

I wanted to smack that gnome already, even reached out my left hand on instinct, but he wasn't close enough. So instead I felt for the door-knob, just to get my bearings. It should only have been inches away. I hadn't taken a step yet. But I couldn't find it. As if some current in the room had moved me, pulling my body farther from shore. So I went down on one knee and touched the ground with both hands, fighting against nausea.

"Do you hear my voice?" the Dean asked again.

"You know I do."

"Then get off your knees and follow it."

I stood, but moved slow. I put one foot in front of the other like I was walking on a balance beam. I bent at the knees and stooped my back, one arm in front of me and the other to the side. The Dean spoke to me in the dark. I struggled to listen and keep my balance.

"Judah Washburn is the founder of this Library. A Georgia slave who escaped bondage in 1775. He ran west, into the arms of the Spanish. With them he explored New Spain, all the way to the Pacific Ocean."

There'd been so little blocking my path that I thought the whole room was empty, that I could just follow a straight line to the Dean. Soon I was moving too fast to stop myself, and I hit a table, hard. The edge got me right in the thigh, and I slammed the tabletop angrily. The thump echoed.

"Brush yourself off now, Ricky. Keep going."

I used my right hand to find the top of the first chair alongside the table, and once I found that, I edged along to the next.

"Judah Washburn had reached Northern California. But he still wasn't content. He'd traded an American master for a Spanish master. Was that really the best he could hope for?"

No more chairs, but I kept moving. My head cocked to the left, listening, my hands out in front, my eyes closed.

"Judah escaped his Spanish masters and wandered into the marsh-lands. Slept under oak trees. Living a fugitive's life, but still a free man's life. And one morning, at dawn, he heard a voice calling to him."

I had my hands out in front, at about waist level, so I wouldn't bump
into another table. Instead I smacked into a lamp. The shade bashed me
right in the face, and we both fell over. As the lamp hit the ground, I
heard its bulb crack, shards clicking against the wooden floor. I put my
hands out so I wouldn't land on my face, and pieces of the bulb dug into
my palms.

The Dean's voice grew louder now.

"The Voice said 'Do you hear me?' And Judah felt too scared to answer. So it asked again, 'Do you hear my voice?' Finally Judah cried, 'Yes!'
And the Voice said, 'Follow it.' "

I got to my feet, brushed my hands against my pants. Brought my
palms up to my face, but my eyes had only adjusted enough to see their
outlines. I licked my skin and tasted blood.

"Judah Washburn stumbled. He searched. He lost his way. He cried
for help, but only heard the same command. 'Follow it.' Until he realized
the call wasn't coming from the woods or the sky, but the soil. Underground!"

When I dropped my hands again, I thought I saw the Dean's silhouette. Small and slim; as subtle as a whisper. It stood still. I moved toward
it. Then the figure stepped backward.

"Judah Washburn found a path, and ahead of him he saw a figure. Too
tall to be a man. It led him forward, though he never could quite reach
it. And as he followed, the Voice kept calling. 'Do you hear my voice?
Follow it!' "

I lunged for the Dean. I didn't know if I should choke him or hug him.
Really, I just wanted contact, a little help. Instead I ran into a chair,
heavy and immovable, and I stumbled to the ground a second time.

"Finally, Judah Washburn had gone well underground and reached a
cold chamber. He couldn't see a *got damn* thing. The man had been
struck blind. But he *heard*. The Voice spoke to him, saying, 'I am the father of the despised child.' And Judah Washburn shouted, 'Then I am
your son!' "

My knees hurt, my palms were raw. I hadn't moved that far, but I
couldn't catch my breath.

"The Voice said, 'I made this land for my children. And all my children will have their reward.' "

I cried. I felt ashamed, but couldn't stop myself. I wanted the Dean
to pull me to my feet. Just that would've been reward enough.

"I could use a hand," I whispered, snuffling like a panicked child.

The Dean said, "I hear you."

And just like that, the Dean turned on the lights. One light. A small
lamp sitting on his desk. He stood over me, smiling.

I would've kissed the Dean's hand if he'd set it in front of me then. I felt humiliated and grateful at the same time. I'd started sweating badly, and wiped my face with my coat sleeve. What a mess. My only relief, the slightest solace, was that we were the only witnesses.

"So what do you think?" the Dean said.

I looked up at him, opened my mouth, a garbled answer at the ready. But he wasn't looking at me. The Dean's head turned to the left.

There were two chairs on this side of his desk. The one I'd bumped into and a second.

And the Gray Lady sat in it.

Adele Henry looked at me straight, cold as the polar ice caps. She shrugged.

She said, "He'll do. I guess."

23

WHILE THE TWO OF THEM talked, I stewed. I looked off into the distant regions of the Dean's dark office and wondered how far I could get if I ran.

"Have Lake pack Ricky's clothes," the Dean said.

"I'll ask him," the Gray Lady answered. She spoke with a smoker's rasp. It sounded like a thunderstorm brewing in her throat.

They wouldn't stop talking around me, the way you might discuss taking your dog to the vet. Speaking quietly because you believe the stupid thing just might understand. I really wanted to knock the shit out of them. Both of them. So I popped off my knees and stood straight because the only thing I had over these two was my height. Once upright I felt like an adult again, and a grown man has the right to demand answers.

"What in the hell is going on here?" I yelled.

But they didn't even look at me.

The Gray Lady had a large green handbag swinging from her right forearm, big enough for a bowling ball. She unzipped it, reached one chubby hand inside, and a maroon scarf hung from her fingers when her hand reappeared. In a quick motion she wrapped the scarf around her head twice, until all of her white hair disappeared.

Then I truly saw her face—straight, no chaser: round and a bit flat. She had large, brilliant eyes and a tiny dimple in her chin. The Gray Lady looked eager, concentrated, damn near combustible. I was angry, but a little impressed.

"I'm sure the Dean has some tissues on his desk," she said to me. "In case you want to cry some more."

Then she just sauntered off into the darkness, her shoes squeaking steadily. And, not five yards away, the oak door opened and she stepped out.

I turned back to the Dean. "I'm not working with her," I said.

"No. You'll be working *for* her, Ricky."

I had to put my hands on something just then, so instead of grabbing him I lifted the chair I'd knocked over. Picked the damn thing up and slammed its four legs down hard.

"This isn't a crib," the Dean said. "Stop throwing tantrums."

In the lamplight he looked like a little black baron. Back when men made their fortunes from coal and not computer programs. He wore an upturned mustache and a tiny Vandyke beard, and his hair was gray. He had a soft face that sagged with age instead of wrinkling. At the banquet I'd pegged him for fifty, but of course the picture in the tailors' photo album meant he was much older. Not that he seemed tired or weak. In fact his eyes were lively, but his reddish skin looked thin as paper vellum. I'd owned a Bible printed on the stuff.

The Dean wore a black suit and vest, every button done up, and the jacket hung easily on his slim frame, so I could see every handmade button. Each one was almost a circle, but not quite, with white specks in their black irises. I'd put on my finest suit to meet this man, but it was a smock compared to his.

He snapped a handkerchief from his breast pocket and gave it to me. While I dabbed the spots of blood from my hands, he reached across his desk, to a laptop. He flipped the screen up, ran his finger on the mouse pad, tapped twice. And then a new sound began. Over to my right, where there weren't any lights, a regular and aggressive noise.

-*Thwip!*- -*Thwip!*- -*Thwip!*- -*Thwip!*-

With some concentration I saw four bulky shapes in the corner. Honestly, they looked like trolls to me. Working so hard their shoulders heaved. The sound of pages being torn out of books. But I had to be mistaken, I knew this, so I concentrated on the shadows until I realized the four figures were only printers, the large industrial kind. In a minute they were producing pages at a berserk rate. Going so fast and constant they trembled. What could they be printing?

-*Thwip!*- -*Thwip!*- -*Thwip!*- -*Thwip!*-

Six centuries earlier I might've found four monks in a room like this, working in a similar pose. Locked away in a remote monastery, hunched over their desks, transcribing holy books or great philosophy. I know it's ridiculous, but once I made this association, I couldn't help feeling—

I don't know—respectful of the printers too. Ridiculous! Just machines. They were probably only spitting out expense reports and maintenance logs, but once a thought like that arises, it's hard to put it down.

"Absorbing, aren't they?"

"Yes," I admitted, but laughed a little, just to show I knew this was foolish.

"You look at them long enough," the Dean said, "and almost believe they're alive."

"What are they printing?"

The Dean waved. "Come see."

We approached the machines, the Dean more casual than me. They snapped so loud I thought they could bite. We stood over them. All four vented heat up toward my face as they worked. They *breathed.* They spat out pages, each sheet covered in type. I read what I could.

"Field notes," I said, sounding disappointed.

The Dean touched the top sheet. "Gospel," he said. "When I finally collect these pages properly, the whole world will know they're Scripture."

I followed his eye, expecting the pages to have changed, but they looked the same to me.

The Dean said, "The Voice sent Judah Washburn out into the world again. Had him retrace his steps until he reached the surface. Told Judah to walk toward the sun. As long as he felt that warmth on his face, he was moving toward his reward. Then the Voice gave Judah a single commandment: *go forth and survive.*"

"How'd Judah retrace his steps if he was blind?"

"Do you know what a determined man can do? Impossible things. And on the surface Judah found his reward quickly, less than a hundred paces away. Two half-buried trunks of Spanish gold coin. The Spanish milled dollar."

I touched the side of a printer, practically petting it. I felt its body heat.

"Judah found that money and knew he was in trouble. Where's a black man going to hold on to his loot in 1778? Only one place where he could even try. Vermont had outlawed slavery in 1777."

" 'Go forth and survive'?" I repeated. "What kind of mission is that?"

"A blind, black escaped slave is dragging two trunks of gold from California to Vermont. You think survival wasn't an absolute miracle?"

It was an incredible story, unimaginable, and yet here was the Dean telling it to me in the crook of a snowbound Vermont valley.

The Dean slapped one of the printers, and I flinched, expected the machine to kick.

"But Judah makes it to Vermont, builds himself a life, and do you know what the Voice tells Judah next?"

The Dean raised his hands like a magician.

"Nothing. He doesn't hear one damn word. For *years.*"

-*Thwip!*- -*Thwip!*- -*Thwip!*- -*Thwip!*-

"The man was about to go batty, thought he did something wrong. Pissed the Voice off. What does a person do when faced with all that *silence*? In Judah's case he took action. Ventured back into the world, blind and all, following every wild story he could. This was early in the era of spiritualists and mediums. He went to séances. Knocked on the door of every 'haunted house.' And that's even after some home owners called the slave catchers on him. Just the *rumor* of a phantom got Judah out of bed. Lived like that for twenty-six years."

The printers stopped thumping now, but only long enough to change paper trays. A moment of quiet, a faint mechanical huff, then back to printing again.

"But the man never heard a thing. And eventually his body gave out. Too old to knock on doors anymore. Kept gathering news, though. Got papers delivered to Burlington. Had his oldest daughter, Clotel, read them to him. Saved all the strangest stories.

"Eventually Judah had a new idea. Send Clotel out in his place. He loved her very much, but she'd developed an affection for canned heat whiskey. And in the depths of her drunkenness she'd claimed to have seen one or two eerie things. She had reasons to believe her father's story. And maybe he hoped the work would give her a sense of purpose. That a mission would defeat an addiction.

"Clotel sent him detailed notes from the field, every encounter summarized. Judah never stopped hoping he might decipher some message in those reports. That he might discover the Voice's next commandment hidden in them. And like that the Washburn Library was born.

"As he died, Judah hoped he'd done as he'd been told. His body might not live to hear the Voice again, but through Clotel the *faith* would survive."

24

"I HAD A FRIEND NAMED BOTTLECAP** who said God spoke to *him*," I said. "Heard the Lord until 2003."

"Why did it stop?"

"Bottlecap died."

The Dean frowned. Maybe he thought I was joking. But I wasn't. He might not have cared about Bottlecap, but when my friend passed, I felt wrecked. Never saw the body, but read about the death in a local paper, the *Record*. He was in Troy then. I was cleaning toilets in Kingston.

The Dean took my elbow. His touch felt so strange, so unexpected, that I pulled my arm back, and he had to grab me again. I could see his fingers on my arm now, and they were as thin as fish bones. He turned me around and we walked together. The only light sat on his desk, behind us, so we headed into a dim expanse.

We passed a grand table made of rich but modest wood, maybe walnut, with tall matching chairs. This must've been what caught me in the thigh.

"I chose that painting of Saint Jerome that hangs near your offices because it says everything about the Washburn Library and the Unlikely Scholars."

"We're saints?"

"You wish! Remember the painting, Ricky. There's Jerome's ecstasy. His spare little room. A skull, an inkwell, and something in his right hand. As many times as you passed it, did you ever notice what he's holding?"

"Something to write with. A pen? No. A quill."

"That's good, Ricky. I'm impressed. Here, at the Library, that's what you embody."

"A quill?"

"An instrument."

The Dean and I finally reached the other end of the office. I saw a shape in front of me, but couldn't make out what it was. It wasn't the darkness of the room, just that I needed a minute to recognize what stood before us. To give this thing a name.

An enormous fireplace. The hearth alone stood taller than me.

The Dean went down on one knee and reached into the right sleeve of his jacket. He had a prop hidden there. One long-stemmed match. When he pulled that out, I started thinking this whole meeting might have been a routine. Scrambling through the dark, hearing the history, and now the fireplace. How many other Scholars had been through these stations?

"People like you, me, and Ms. Henry. The other Unlikely Scholars. What do we all have in common? What are we, Ricky?"

I didn't know what he wanted me to say at this point. Instruments? Quills? Featherbeds?

"We are the descendants of America's greatest losers. Black folks. The only population that *came* to America to be enslaved," the Dean said.

"You make it sound like we had a choice."

"But that's the whole point. Everyone else *did*. But plain old black folks? I swear, it's like we're cursed."

"Is this supposed to be a pep talk? Because . . ."

I shook my head. Had I really traveled all the way to Vermont just to hear some old man grumble? Did every story about black folks have to be such a downer?

While he crouched, the Dean waved the long, unlit match like a wand.

"I'm not here to spread bad news, Ricky. Listen to my words. The Voice called Judah. Of all the folks it might've picked, it picked a runaway slave. Do you understand what that means?"

The Dean tapped the wooden match against the stone fireplace.

"Means it's ours, Ricky. The Voice chose *us*. Despised by many, but not the Voice. The American Negro finally got its god."

"Negro?"

"Oh, I can't keep up. Negro was an *improvement* when I was a boy. What is it now?"

I shrugged. "I always just liked *black*."

"Fine, then. Black people finally get a god."

I said, "I thought we had one already."

The Dean snapped the long match against the strike plate on the floor and held the lit thing up to me. "Are you from a religious background?" he asked.

"No," I said.

Let me explain why I lied.

Go and tell someone the worst thing about yourself. Cheated on a husband. Abused your child. Or, like in my case, that you've been addicted to heroin for half your life. Just tell them that and nothing else. You find that people come up with an entire history based on that one fact. They assume the worst about you.

This is true if you have a criminal past, absolutely, but even if you just had an usual childhood, people will look at you crooked. Long before my drug problems, I'd learned not to admit my history to strangers. I used to go through all the rigmarole of explaining my background to anyone who'd listen. Really trying to make a case that I was normal. But when I got older, I realized I was basically begging others to think better of me, and you can't beg people to treat you with respect. Either they choose to do it or you go around them. Don't waste time dignifying fools. So when the Dean asked if I had a religious background, it triggered my old defenses. I'd learned long ago that you don't tell anyone you were raised in a cult.

The Dean reached the match below the grate in the fireplace, where balls of white paper had been set. A stack of logs sat above them. The Dean lit the paper, blew out the match, and jabbed the match into the ground.

Not to poor-mouth about my life. I'd seen some spectacular things, but never a pretty little exercise like lighting a fireplace. Just as I thought the paper would die out, the bottoms of the logs began to glow and feed and spread and thrive.

"How would you describe the promise you made in Iowa?" the Dean asked.

I stared deeper into the fire, until I saw two figures, two men, tied, beaten, and lying on their backs in a basement. It was Cedar Rapids. It was 2002. One of the men was dead. One of them was me.

"I promised to be brave."

The Dean grabbed a brass poker from its stand beside the fireplace. He didn't stick it into the fire. The Dean tapped the brass poker against the ground.

"And have you been?"

I crossed my arms and watched the fire. I didn't speak.

The Dean and I stood before that fire, and I felt the heat against my thighs and shins. He jabbed at the flames, playing with the logs, shifting them. The fire grew larger, and new light ran up along the mantel. And after that it spread along the walls. Until the light exposed a large painting hanging over the fireplace.

"This is a Caravaggio too," the Dean said.

I could tell right away. The colors here were nearly as vivid as in Saint Jerome's. Nearly luminous. What oil had the artist dipped his brush in? No matter how righteous the subject, Caravaggio painted images that glowed with the vitality of evil.

I reached to touch the painting, or even just the frame, but the Dean grabbed my sleeve and pulled my arm back down.

"The Voice didn't contact Clotel either. Judah died and she took over. Clipping unusual cases out of the papers, going out to investigate. But she figured she'd have better luck with increased numbers. Clotel looked up her old drinking buddies, the ones who swore they'd seen demons in the vapors of their whiskey. A sorry old lot. She offered them the chance to catch the spirit, to tear through the veil. Most couldn't keep their eyes open long enough to say no. But two said yes."

"Did *anybody* hear the Voice again?" I asked.

The Dean pressed the brass poker against the floor.

"I have."

The Dean set the poker back in its stand. The brass clanged like a small bell.

"When I took over, the Library had fallen on bad times. Folks lost hope. One hundred fifty years of failure will do that. The best you could say is that they dressed better than they felt. But when I took this office, I read through all the old field notes, going back to the first handwritten pages Clotel sent her dad. Judah had hoped these pages were more than just details, but he wasn't meant to learn how true that was.

"These eerie events, every shadow we investigate, these *are* the Voice's attempts to reach us again. It's just the messages get scrambled on the way from there to here. But I've come to find myself blessed with a sacred literacy. When I read these field reports, I see the meaning behind the words. Think of me like an oracle, Ricky. I can interpret the signs."

"But how do you know you're right?"

He said, "I can only assure you that over the years I've been right a lot more than I've been wrong."

The Dean touched my shoulder so I would look at him.

"And now I'm telling you the Washburn Library is under threat. From one of our own."

"You saw this in the field notes?"

"I did. And a big moment is coming. It's been two hundred twenty-seven years since the Voice spoke to Judah Washburn. Two hundred twenty-seven years of us groping around *surviving*. But is that all the Voice wants for us? I don't know about you, Ricky, but survival is just not enough anymore. Maybe Judah couldn't hope for more back in 1778, but times change. The era of mere survival is at an end. Now it's time for prosperity.

"The Voice will communicate as directly as it ever did to Mr. Washburn. A new commandment. A new reward. I want all of us to benefit from that blessing, but this *got damn* traitor plans to keep the miracle for himself."

"If things are so urgent, why are we wasting time looking at another picture?" I asked.

"Not a waste. The Voice heard your promise. I *know* this. Now it's giving you the chance to be brave. Look up."

In the painting a thin young man holds a small sword in his right hand and carries an older man's severed head in his left. The boy's fingers grip the dead man's long brown hair, and the head swings free. The head is gigantic. Its veins dangle and drip below the chin while the boy glares with disgust and wrath. He doesn't seem sickened by the blood, only hateful of his victim. In the middle of the dead man's forehead there's one red mark where he's been struck hard. And that's what killed the older, bigger man, not the sword. The sword was only for separating the head from its shoulders.

The Dean said, "This is 'David with the Head of Goliath.' You figure out what it means. What the Library needs from you."

"We weren't Jerome in the other painting, so I assume we're not David or Goliath here."

"That's right," he said.

I stepped back, trying hard to figure out the tiny little item that would correspond to the quill in Saint Jerome's hand, but this painting was even sparer than the first. Nothing in the empty black background. I wanted to get it right, but there seemed to be only one, obvious, choice.

"The sword?" I said.

"Think of how David beat Goliath," the Dean said. "At the *Library* you were the quill."

"But out in the field . . . ," I whispered.

"You'll be the stone."

3

Into the
Lungs of Hell

25

OKAY, so we were an organization that embodied the quill of Saint Jerome and the stone that killed Goliath. We might even have been the chosen tribe of a god. But if so, if all that was really true, why did they fly us out to California on JetBlue? I'd been expecting a private plane, but instead we had coach seats. Now, I don't want to sound ungrateful. They did pay for a whole row. At least that gave me and the Gray Lady a little room, but come on. You don't expect secret societies to operate on a budget.

Lake drove the Gray Lady and me to the airport, but there wasn't much conversation. What could I say to her? She'd watched me crawl to the Dean, seen me beg for his help, and when we finally looked at each other, she only shrugged. I didn't speak to her, out of embarrassment and pride. And she didn't speak because, well, she wasn't interested. Instead we heard a monologue from the driver's seat because Lake wouldn't stop talking. He and the Gray Lady seemed to be friends. What was Lake saying? I can't remember. I was too busy trying to think like a stone.

I only came out of my haze when the Gray Lady passed me plane tickets. I checked the destinations. First a quick plane ride down to JFK airport in New York and then, from there, a nonstop slingshot to Garland, California. The West Coast. Yet one more part of the world I'd never seen. I tapped the tickets hard against my leg in a quick beat, just a nervous habit.

"You're not Max Roach," she said. "Put those away."

I put the tickets in my coat, but moved slowly. The way a kid drags his feet when headed for a vaccination. And she watched me the whole time. She refused to look away until they were in my pocket. I made sure it took a while.

Once they were put away, she leaned toward me and said, "Tell me, Mr. Rice. What do you want to be when you grow up?"

Six hours from JFK to Garland, that's what they told us once we'd boarded the plane. Garland, a small city in the Bay area, Northern California. Imagine one man hauling two trunks of gold across this country. One escaped blind slave with a few hundred pounds of Spanish coins. I gave a silent nod to Judah Washburn's survival instinct.

Our seats were in the very last row of the plane, and the Gray Lady took the window, plopped her coat on the middle seat, which left me with the aisle. Good enough. I'd need to kick my right leg out or else the knee would start to cramp after an hour or two. As the stewardess gave us crash instructions, I stowed my fedora in the empty carriage rack above my head.

We taxied on the runway, and, right away, I went to work. I'd bought a couple of magazines, just fluffy stuff, women half out of their clothes and sliding off a car hood, for instance. But I'd bought newspapers too. *The New York Times, New York Post, Daily News, The New York Sun,* and before the plane took off, I'd started leafing through them. From back to front, searching for curious news. There was a kind of comfort in this.

"You don't have to . . . ," she whispered, pointing at the papers in my lap.

"Just a habit by now," I said.

"In the field we don't bury our noses in newspapers, Mr. Rice."

"I wouldn't take pride in that."

She looked at me and narrowed her eyes. "Have you ever worked for a woman before?"

"Plenty of times," I said.

"So then you won't be challenging me every step of the way, is that right?"

The Gray Lady didn't wait for an answer. She crossed her hands, set them in her empty lap, and as the plane took off, she snored.

In the quiet of the flight I thought about why I'd climbed into the van that morning and why I'd boarded the plane. But did I have any real answers? What had been clear in the Dean's office hours ago seemed murkier that night. I opened the first newspaper in my lap and searched its pages until the familiar routine put me at ease.

WE'D TRAVELED BACK in time. Three hours' difference between Garland and Vermont, of course, but also the bland blue walls of the Garland International Airport terminal hadn't been updated since the seventies. The faded graying carpet could've used a wash, and the seats at the gates needed stitching too. But instead of making the airport seem dingy, it only made the terminal feel like a comfy old living room. Which must've made the Gray Lady and me seem even more bizarre.

We looked like ambassadors from the Jazz Age.

We didn't even make it to the baggage carousels before other people gawked at us. A teenage girl strode up to the Gray Lady and pointed at the fur collar on her jacket.

"Is that real?" she asked.

The Gray Lady smiled and touched it with her fingers. "What do you think?"

"You don't have an ounce of compassion?" the girl asked. "You really need a fur in a place that's always eighty degrees?"

The Gray Lady wore that fur-lined jacket, black stockings leading out from the bottom of her frock, a cloche hat, and a pair of black leather bluchers pounding the ground. And I wore my tweed three-piece. My Yale Brown fedora tilted slightly over my left eye. To cool myself I'd taken off my tie and undone the soft collar of my shirt so it swung open, a Byron collar they used to call it. The pilots in their sharp blue uniforms were just bellhops compared to us, but this kid was less than impressed.

Having said what she wanted, the girl stalked off triumphantly. Her black flip-flops clicked louder than heels.

Both of us stood there mortified. Embarrassed, awkward, and sheepish. The Gray Lady had seemed so powerful back at the Library, in the van, even sleeping on the plane. And just like that, snap, the balance changed. It wasn't that I felt the teenager was right, but both the Gray Lady and I understood that she was right *here*.

The Gray Lady pulled the fur-lined jacket off. She tucked it under one arm.

When I was a kid, I made this same kind of mistake. I thought my family was pretty normal, but the outside world corrected me.

26

GENERALLY SPEAKING, you don't hear of too many religious cults operating out of an apartment building. It just doesn't happen. They usually live in compounds, or on a ranch, or at the very least they've got a private home on some nondescript block. But whoever heard of a cult operating out of a two-bedroom in Queens?

That's melodramatic, I'm sorry. The cult had a whole floor of the building. My mom and dad, older sister, Daphne, and me, we operated in a two-bedroom place. A cult within a cult. The other members were our neighbors on the fourth floor.

We had leases, gave security deposits when we moved in. The building's super knew what we were, as did many people in the neighborhood, but the owners didn't. They didn't live in Queens. And frankly, they wouldn't have cared anyway. Cult, coven, or think tank, we always paid the rent.

I'm willing to call it a cult, or a Christian cult, now because they're only words, but they help other people understand a few things about us quickly. Small. Tightly knit. Set apart.

We called ourselves the Washerwomen.

When people asked our religion, I'd explain that we were Christians, but Christianity filtered through the wisdom of three women, three sisters from Jacksonville, Florida. Being a Lutheran didn't mean you worshipped Martin Luther, and though we followed the Washerwomen, our God remained the same.

Now try explaining all that to a pack of boys who've caught you waiting for your building's elevator. The kind of boys they seem to make everywhere. Who love kicking the weird kid's ass. The skinny home-schooled Christian cultist who lives in their building. Imagine dealing with that every time you're caught in the lobby, and you'll understand why I always took the stairs.

Ten times a day if I was sent on a lot of errands. Up and down so often that I really came to love that crappy gray stairwell. Half the overhead lights didn't work, and sometimes garbage littered the landings. The perfume of urine often filled the air, and yet I knew the environment with sweet intimacy. How cold the handrail felt in the winter, the sound of my skin slipping along the metal in a low -*swiff*- whenever I went down. The chips of a cracked stair sprinkling the ones below it like rock salt on a winter road.

It seems impossible now, but at that time I thought of that stairwell as a kind of cloister. Where I could find a special quiet. You can't predict the places where you'll encounter the unknowable.

27

THE GRAY LADY AND I TURNED AWAY from each other after that girl's rebuke. We walked again but with much less sashay in our steps. I don't want to give the wrong impression, though. We did still sashay a little. We'd been rattled, but not crushed.

I passed a rumpled guy at the terminal exit. One of those private drivers holding a handwritten sign: ADELE & LARRY. That's what it read. Didn't mean much to me, but the Gray Lady stopped. She didn't call out to me, though, just coughed loudly a couple of times. When I still didn't stop, she snapped her fingers. That's the kind of nonsense you pull on a waiter when you want more bread. But she did it to me. Then just stood there with her arms crossed, waiting. Both she and the driver watched me. The driver waved his ratty cardboard sign at me. "Adele?" he asked as I walked back to them.

"I look like an Adele to you?"

"I thought maybe it was foreign," he said. "Like you'd be French or African."

"No," I said.

"Then you're Larry."

"Ricky."

"Maybe I've got the wrong two people."

The driver wore his belly with a sense of pride. He wasn't fat, average-size everywhere but the gut. He didn't stoop to hide it, though. He leaned back to show it off. In order to get inside his pants pocket he had to twist the paunch. He took out a sheet of blue paper and unfolded it.

"Ms. Henry?" he asked.

"Claude! Stop playing games with Mr. Rice."

That was the loudest I'd heard her get. It was sort of nice to see her irritated with someone other than me.

"Does that paper call me Larry?" I asked.

"Just says Ms. Henry plus one. That's what I mean. I called back as I drove over here and was told that the plus one was a 'Larry.' Which is you."

"My name is Ricky Rice," I said.

His answer? There wasn't any. He just looked at the Gray Lady and said, "I'll go and get your bags."

It was only when Claude returned, carrying hers alone, that I realized he'd meant the statement literally. I had to cast a line between the passengers crowding the baggage carousel and hook the handle of my suitcase with my finger. Felt better once I held it. I'd packed the heroin in my luggage, all six baggies. But I hadn't tried bringing the syringe through airport security.

CLAUDE'S BLACK LINCOLN TOWN CAR IDLED in the arrivals pickup lane, and I couldn't believe airport security hadn't called the bomb squad. But when he opened the trunk, one of the security guys walked over and shook Claude's hand. They were pals.

The cuffs of Claude's pants were frayed, bits of fabric dangling. The kind of thing I wouldn't have noticed a year before. And what was that suit fabric anyway? Not tweed, not flannel, not worsted wool. Not cotton or even polyester. Carpet fibers, that's what they looked like. A whole cheap suit made of the stuff.

We left the bright airport and rolled down Garland's side streets. Block after block of single-family homes, one or two stories tall, with pitched roofs and little front yards. Places that were worn down along the corners and front stairs. They all had a little dirt under their nails. Garland had working-class hands. I became calmer because I recognized this kind of place.

There were the flatlands, which was the center of the city, surrounded by hills on three sides. I saw slightly nicer, larger homes at the base of those hills. And the nicest houses climbed even higher, at the middle and nearly the top of the mountains, scrambling up the incline like animals escaping a flood.

I got drowsy as we reached the highway, I-580, going west. Leaned against the car door, my face on the glass, soothed by a light rain that pattered against the windshield. I listened to it and looked into the sky.

The Washburn Library is under threat.

I could hear the Dean's voice now, as sure as the hum of Claude's tires. It was like the Dean was whispering to me across the continent. *From one of our own.*

The Town Car rose and dipped as we took the West Street exit off the highway and coasted down a ramp. I saw a small flock of offices on the horizon, downtown Garland, the only buildings in the city that measured more than six stories. Downtown looked like a rogue wave on an otherwise calm sea.

Claude parked the Town Car in front of a hotel called By the Bay, its name in big letters spreading across the third floor. Claude turned in his seat and said, "This is your stop, Larry."

I looked at the Gray Lady. "Just me?"

Claude spoke again. "Ms. Henry has a place at the Washburn estate."

She looked at me, took off her hat. In the dark car her white hair looked phosphorescent.

The Gray Lady said, "I will fetch you first thing in the morning, Mr. Rice. There's no need to worry."

"I'm not worried," I told her. "I'm pissed."

"Don't get ugly now," Claude warned.

He liked bullying people out of their self-respect. That seemed obvious. I wondered what kind of job he'd done before this one. What line of work would suit that personality? Much as I hated it, though, the tone worked on me. I was already getting out of the car before I realized he'd said something that deserved a smack. Funny, but in a way I even recognized this back-and-forth between me and him. Felt as familiar as being fingerprinted.

"I'm not some dog you fetch," I told them. It's all I could muster in my defense.

"Oh, boo-hoo," Claude answered.

I held the door open.

"Is there anything I can start doing tonight, Ms. Henry? I don't want to just sit around guessing why I'm here."

"I sympathize, Mr. Rice," she said. "First time in the field can be overwhelming."

"I just don't like feeling left out."

She put her hat back on. "I know it feels that way now, but you might regret it more when we let you in."

Okay, I thought. What are you going to do now? Pout about it?

Yes.

I also slammed the door. When I went to the trunk, I pounded on it until Claude popped it open. After I got my luggage, I left the damn thing open so Claude had to get out and close it himself. What can I say? You take your revenge where you can get it.

While all this happened a half dozen men watched me from inside the lobby of the hotel. Not interest, just assessment. Town Car. Three-piece suit. Carrying a wardrobe trunk. Meanwhile they wore threadbare sweatpants and decaying T-shirts, shabby shoes and scruffy haircuts. Which is a kind of ensemble too. The vagabond. The pauper. The bum.

But despite these differences we recognized one another. Like knows like. It's in the hardened skin and haunted eyes. Those didn't change just because I wore a vest. The men saw beyond my costume.

And in return I recognized not just them, but their surroundings. Suddenly I understood this hotel. The smudged front windows. The clusters of cigarette butts on the sidewalk, a medley of mentholated brands. Pea-green lobby walls for that institutional feel. I'd stayed in SROs many times and saw what happened when they tried to privatize. The rooms were slightly refurbished, but the clientele stayed the same. By the Bay was just a flophouse that went pro.

The guys inside must've been wondering the same question I asked myself.

Why was a guy dressed like me staying there?

All of us watched as the only person with the answer had her driver put the Town Car in gear.

28

HEROIN, like I said before, robs you of your empathy. And that's a problem, because empathy is what separates human beings from teenage boys. A real heroin addict is as callous as your average fourteen-year-old, and even after you kick, there's a long period before your sense of mercy returns.

Once that's back, you feel the rest of yourself resurface too, including your libido. And that part doesn't thaw. It flashes from frozen to blazing. Your resting body temperature even goes up a few degrees. That's probably a fact. So all this recent abstinence had been an extra special trial. It made my body fussy, touchy, even a bit vengeful. Just caressing a keyboard could give me an erection. Without the proper outlet my head had even started to hurt sometimes. So when my room phone rang, I hardly noticed because my chastity headache had a ring to it.

When I finally realized the bell wasn't going between my eardrums, I rolled over, onto my stomach, so I could reach the phone. This was the closest thing to sexual contact I'd had in well over a year. When I picked up the receiver and tried to say "hello," all I managed was a deep, long, nearly orgasmic groan.

A distracted woman's voice replied, "You have a wake-up call."

I'm ashamed to admit this, but when I heard it was a woman, I nearly finished myself off right there. I humped my mattress on instinct. Nothing crazy, I wasn't thrashing around, but if anyone had been there, they'd have noticed the faintest tremor, side to side, going on around my groin. A breath escaped from deep in my lungs. Maybe lower.

"You there, Mr. Rice?" she asked.

"Almost," I muttered.

"What is going on?"

Clarity finally returned to me.

"Didn't ask for a wake-up call," I groaned.

I heard the air from her nostrils through the pinpoint end of my phone receiver.

"That's not what I mean, Mr. Rice. There's someone here in the lobby. They asked me to wake you. Understand?"

"Uuhhhh."

"What?"

Quiet.

"Hello . . . ," the woman said.

A little more quiet.

"Mr. Rice?"

"Tell her I'll be down in a few minutes," I said. I reached the first floor feeling relieved.

And I entered the lobby of the undead. There were four figures who'd gathered around a cheap big-screen television as if it were a trough full of brains. Occasionally they'd talk or clap and laugh while watching a basketball game, but they still seemed like zombies to me.

The tiled floors of the lobby were so scuffed I thought the streaks *were* the design.

And the walls gave off the perfume of stale beer. Even this early in the day.

What a palace. Thank you, Washburn Library, for helping me relive my twenties.

But I guess the real reason I suddenly felt pissy was because I thought I'd left places like this behind. I'd been an Unlikely Scholar for less than a year, but already felt entirely changed. Maybe I'd hoped that the Library had made me elegant. Like I'd become a viscount in Vermont.

"Surprise!" yelled one man in a wheelchair.

I thought, for a moment, that he was talking to me, but he pointed to a player on the TV screen. I stepped out of the elevator and passed that mad crowd. I expected a cross-looking Gray Lady to be waiting, but she wasn't.

The front desk would be familiar to anyone who's bought Chinese food in a ghetto. Inch-thick bulletproof sheets between you and the money.

Behind the Plexiglas shielding I found a beefy short-haired woman with her arms crossed, sitting at the front desk. She had wide little feet that she balanced against the desktop as she leaned backward in a chair. There were four textbooks set out on the counter, and her stubby toes curled over the pages as if it was them doing the studying while her hands and mouth went about the work of answering the hotel phone.

"I'm Ricky Rice," I said. "You called my room?"

She pulled her feet off the counter and slipped them into a pair of red flip-flops waiting on the floor. I wondered if she was a Samoan. I'd never seen one in person before, but her color looked right. That and her thick, curly brown hair. A wide face that spread into a soft chin.

"You said there was a woman waiting for me?"

She stood up. She shimmied to get a better view. She was a woman who really liked to dance, I knew this about her instantly. Her gestures showed a graceful pep.

"Where'd he go?" she asked.

"It was a man?"

"Sure was."

"What did he say?"

" 'Is Ricky Rice staying at this hotel?' And I checked, said you were up on the fourth floor. Then he asked me to call, so that's what I did. He walked around the lobby for a minute. But he's gone now."

"Did he have a big gut? Cheap suit. Face like a dog biscuit?"

She laughed. "He was thin enough."

Now I looked out those front doors, expecting the stranger to walk in. It couldn't have been Claude anyway. Since he'd dropped me off, he knew I was there. So who? The uncertainty made me twitch.

I asked, "Did he dress as well as me?"

This wasn't my finest outfit, but still a blue-ribbon winner when you consider how men dress today. Just a sports coat and a pair of gray flannel trousers, my white shirt from the plane trip, a tie, and a pair of black Derbys. She leaned forward, forehead against the spotty Plexiglas, inspecting my outfit.

"He dressed better," she said.

Not the answer I'd been expecting.

"Did he say anything else?" I asked.

"You in trouble with the cops?"

"Not in a long time."

I tried to make it sound casual, goofy, but I felt like she could hear snippets of my court appearances playing in the spaces between my words. The woman even cocked her head, as if listening. I felt ashamed, so I turned to go back upstairs and wait for the Gray Lady's arrival.

Then the woman at the front desk knocked on the glass.

"He said one more thing."

I walked closer again.

"Asked if there was a lady with you."

29

MY FATHER DIED ALONE. Died that way even though my mother lived in the same town and I was two hours away, down in New York City. My older sister, Daphne, was probably the farthest off, out in Long Island, and couldn't visit. But distance wasn't the issue. He wanted us to keep away, and we agreed.

Not that the rest of us were all that chummy. We weren't the family that gabs on the phone every Sunday. My mother, Carolyn, and I had a habit of sending birthday cards to each other a few weeks late. Sometimes we even misspelled each other's names. I felt closest to Daphne and visited her when the weather was nice. (Those Long Island buses leave you standing in the cold too damn long.) Maybe most families are closer than ours turned out to be, though I wouldn't bet money on that.

Sargent Rice—that was my father's given name—remembered how much he paid for a meal in a Spokane restaurant back in 1959. Could even tell you what he tipped, down to the cents. Absolutely rhapsodized about that meal: two eggs sunny-side up, four sausage links, two slices of toasted white bread, only one pat of butter but they gladly brought more, a cup of black coffee, and a glass of freshly squeezed orange juice. All for $3.01, including gratuity.

It wasn't the food that mattered, but the bargain. He bought zipperless jeans from the "defective" bins. Found my mother a ten-cent iron missing its cord, bought a cord for a nickel, and fixed it himself. The iron didn't actually work, but what a savings that would have been! More than practical. Not simply frugal either. While most people like to

dream or hope or fantasize, Sargent Rice never indulged. Instead he devoted all that human passion to finding cheap deals.

You don't exactly love a guy like that. Not because you don't want to,
but because his nit-picking frustrates that emotion. To love a guy you
have to think he'd run in front of a subway train to save you. My father
would've stopped at the turnstile, hesitating because the fare had been
increased.

And yet my father was the one who believed in the Washerwomen
most. He convinced my mother—a sixth-grade history teacher when
they met—to join. To raise their children in a "cult." And when my
mother and father went out proselytizing, other Christians called them
much worse things than cultists. That's dedication. That's faith. How
could a person like him make such a leap in one way, but in all others remain the model of prudence? As a boy I asked him about this all the
time. Why do you follow the Washerwomen? And his answer remained
the same: common sense. This was the mystery of Sargent Rice.

But a mystery only satisfies if there's an answer at the end, and he refused to offer one. He used to hold me close, so close I could see the life
behind his eyes, but his soul always scurried off to hide. I'd run my fingers across his cheeks as he read to me, thinking I could pluck at his
spirit as easily as an eyelash. But when my fingers got too close, he'd
shut his eyelids. Wouldn't open them again until I dropped my hands
into my lap. Even then I understood his irritation. No one wants to get
poked like that, but why couldn't he understand what I was really after?
How could a child be wiser than a grown man? Eventually I got exhausted, I'd done too much begging, and I gave up. I felt affection for
him, nothing more. Even our mother came to think of him as a reliable
friend, that's all.

For him this realization was slow in coming, though it did finally pop
in December of 1971. The Washerwomen didn't let us celebrate Christmas because of its pagan origins. Just more evidence that the world had
fallen into disrepair. You want to talk about a way to make yourself weird
in America? Skip Christmas. Jewish kids and Muslim kids know what
I'm talking about. Jehovah's Witnesses too. Where's your wreath? Your
window display? It was just one more thing that put the Washerwomen
in a bad light. We didn't realize it, but our neighbors were making a list.

But in private my family still gave one another little gifts. That's a
hard habit to kick. My dad sat on our living room couch, the one with a
cheetah-skin pattern. I was seven and Daphne, twelve. She danced
badly, showing our mother a few steps, and I tried to imitate Daphne so
our mom would watch me too. Meanwhile Carolyn Rice packed the
torn wrapping paper inside old newsprint so the Washerwomen

wouldn't know we'd traded presents. The other faithful families might've been doing the exact same thing, but we couldn't be sure. And in the midst of this my father reached a pretty obvious conclusion. He'd been watching us quietly for a while. His gift that year? We gave him a pocket mirror. When he unwrapped it, he held it up between two fingers like he was lifting a mouse by its tail.

He coughed once, and I peeked at him. He shook his head faintly. Sargent Rice was as skinny as a lamppost and looked even slimmer on our wide couch.

He said, "This family won't even visit my grave."

We turned our backs on Christmas, on public school. On private school and Catholic school too. We weren't allowed to play with "outside" kids. That's what we called them. The world had broken, all of it failing fast. The Washerwomen were trying to save as many of us as they could before God's last bell. My father took this seriously. "You all better be ready," he'd snarl at Daphne and me every time we talked back or tried having a little fun. You all better be ready. But for what, exactly? He wouldn't say.

30

I LEFT THE WOMAN at the front desk and went back up to my hotel room to put on some finer clothes. When the woman said my visitor had dressed better, I guessed that our target had found me. So much for surprise. This hotel provided no protection, and I already didn't trust the Gray Lady worth a damn. What could I rely on besides myself? Only the clothes. Wearing them felt like donning armor.

I started with my burgundy sock garters.

In my room I slipped out of the slacks, down to my boxers, and then pulled those sock garters up around my calves. Their contact endowed me with a feeling of renewed elegance and security. I just lounged in my rickety wooden room chair, wishing I had some money left so I could buy breakfast. I'd spent my cash on those newspapers and magazines in New York. But despite a little hunger I felt like a rajah. I didn't even put the socks on yet, so the garter buckles bounced lightly against my skin when I shifted my legs.

My own family, I don't want to say we grew up poor, because that wouldn't be exactly true. We *chose* poverty, made a bit of a vow. We weren't supposed to pay much attention to material things, though of course that only made my sister and me want them more. This was hard on me, but impossible for Daphne. She wasn't even allowed ribbons to tie her hair. Those gifts we gave one another for Christmas? Mostly books. Packs of flash cards. (Yay?) A plastic model of the human anatomy. (Our mother quizzed us about the names of organs.) Nothing fun, that's for damn sure. So we learned to sneak our pleasures up the back stairs.

Daphne, five years older than me, owned a yellow plastic ring that she only dared to wear in the shower. The rest of the time she kept it wrapped in a sock and tucked into one of her old shoes. I knew about it because younger siblings are born detectives. That same Christmas night, when my father came to his lonely revelation, my sister and I had a fight. She wouldn't stop mocking me for my bad dancing. It was about that, but it wasn't. We were brother and sister, destined for disputes. So she made fun of me and I showed the yellow plastic ring to my father. I thought he'd yell, maybe take it from her for a month, but he was already in a bad mood. He made Daphne melt the ring in a pan on our stove.

FINALLY, I decided to put on some gray socks. They stretched and held so nicely once I attached them to the clips of the sock garters. Then it was time for the suit, a gray pin-striped number that flattered my narrow shoulders but still showed off my tight waist. Black Church Chetwynd shoes, and last, my fedora. It had a mulberry-colored band that complemented the burgundy sock garters. Why did this matter? Who would even know they were there, since my pants hid the garters? Me, that's who. I knew.

I looked at myself in the long mirror that hung on the back of my room's door, and for a moment I felt sheepish about going outside looking so dandified. This outfit would've made my mother blush and my father grumble. They had rules against flashiness, and as I looked at myself, I understood them. You might focus on a man who primps himself, but it can be hard to trust him. When he's looking deep into your eyes, he may only be checking his reflection. Maybe I should just go back to the slacks and sports jacket, wear the same shirt I'd traveled in.

But no, I wasn't my parents' boy anymore and these decisions were mine alone. Funny that I was forty and still needed to remind myself of this.

After I'd dressed, there wasn't much to do but wait for the call. In that quiet time I pulled out the photo of my sister holding me as a baby. The one I'd dropped when Lake came to get me. I weighed it in my palm. She's five in the snapshot, which means it was 1965. Ten years later Daphne was murdered.

Eventually the room phone rang.

I reached the lobby once again expecting to find the Gray Lady standing there, but my only greeting was a toot from the Town Car parked out front. That guy in the wheelchair was still in front of the television in the lobby, still shouting at the players on the screen. He was one of those guys who can't grow a beard, just sprouts patches of desert brush along his neck and chin. He saw me step out of the elevator, and pointed so his friends would look at me.

"I didn't know this hotel had a maître d'," he said.

The other three men just about burst, laughing at my outfit as I rushed to the front doors. Before I got outside, the two-wheeled entertainer spoke again.

"Table for four!" he yelled.

I was in such a hurry to reach the sidewalk that I almost tripped on the raised doorjamb, and that didn't help my sense of dignity. Claude stepped out of the car and came around to open the Gray Lady's door. She hopped out quickly. If she heard those men giggling inside, she didn't associate it with me. Instead she only waved at Claude, who shut the passenger door, got back in, and drove away.

"We supposed to run after him?" I asked. " 'Cause I've got this bad leg."

"Claude's got other business," she said. "Garland's a small city. We walk."

Had she not heard what I'd said? In case she hadn't, I stood there and pointed at the right leg, but the Gray Lady had trouble seeing my point because she'd already marched a block ahead. I had to scramble to catch up.

San Pablo Avenue, the street we were on, had a booming spirits industry. Bars and liquor stores on every other block, and half-dead homeless people haunting all the corners. These men and women, mostly men, sat on benches or leaned against stores. They stretched and yawned, as if they'd only just been released from their crypts. When we passed them, I looked away.

It was still early, only ten o'clock. We moved fast at first, but got slower because it's tough to hurry in clothes like ours. Adele wore a knee-length gray checked wool coat, and she cinched the belt just above her waist so the coat looked a bit like a dress. She had on brown leather gloves that matched her brown brogues, and a pair of green knee-length socks. The cloche hat from the day before had been replaced by a brown cap. A bicycling costume, that's what they called it once. The Gray Lady looked stout, but capable. She moved like she assumed I would follow. And she was right. I did. I felt a little warm in my clothes, but it wasn't bad.

At one point she looked at me, and I took her attention as my opportunity. There were so many questions I might've asked just then, it didn't really matter which. An answer to just one would've satisfied me. But she cut me off before I formed the words.

Ms. Henry said, "The traitor is Solomon Clay."

I stopped walking and leaned against the side of a liquor store, its red brick hot against my palm. Or did my hand just heat up on its own?

"Mr. Clay?" I whispered. "But he's . . ."

Ms. Henry crossed her arms. "He's what?"

I'd practically memorized this man's handwriting, raised a toast to him two days before.

"He's the best," I said, sounding as certain as I probably ever have.

Ms. Henry spat on the sidewalk. "You've never met him, that's why you can treat him like a god."

I pushed off the wall. "Have *you*?"

She undid the belt of her jacket and retied it. She looked away from me and down San Pablo Avenue. "Solomon Clay may have been a good Scholar once, but he's a fanatic now."

She pointed at me. "And we are going to kill him."

TURNED OUT we were going fishing out by the San Francisco Bay. Had a good chance of catching Solomon Clay there. After telling me who the target was, the Gray Lady practically jogged ahead of me. I couldn't keep up, so I kept my eye on her backside. Which I enjoyed. Soon my knee puffed up under my skin and my shin went frosty cold. I dragged my right foot after me the best I could. I enjoyed that part much less.

We got down to the water to find that the mayor of Garland had decided to hold a press conference right at our destination. He'd drawn an audience.

Garland had a claim on the bit of the Bay that hadn't already been taken over by San Francisco, Berkeley, and Oakland. Not much left after those three cities took their share, but Garland had built a tiny marina and even a shopping court to capitalize on what remained. They called it Stone Mason Square. The crowd wasn't huge, but the square wasn't actually that big. It didn't take all that many bodies to make it seem full. Seventy-five folks maybe. The Gray Lady looked confused.

"*This* is a fly in the ointment," she said.

"Weren't expecting a crowd?"

The Gray Lady looked at me with surprise, as if I had just showed up too.

"Claude had reports that Solomon was down here plenty in the last few weeks."

We got as close to the center of Stone Mason Square as possible, but there were too many people to get far. I couldn't see past all their heads to the waters of the Bay. The stores of the square formed a perimeter, and the crowd filled the space in between them. I tried to push forward, but the Gray Lady had another idea. She tugged the sleeve of my jacket, just once and just the sleeve, then let go so quickly that my wrist didn't even graze her fingertips.

Behind us an enormous bookstore had a small café extension that rose above the throng. It had started filling but wasn't as tight as the square yet. She went up, and I followed. The Gray Lady shoved through the crowd by using her great green purse as a shield, her forearm braced against one side of the handbag as she bopped the public with the other. A pear-shaped battering ram. People yelped, some shouted, but all of them moved.

Okay, I thought. She's an asshole.

Once we were up top, pressed against the patio railing, I could see the speaker's lectern at the head of the crowd. Any one of the dozen men and women milling around up there could've been the mayor.

"*Why* has Mr. Clay been down here?" I asked.

"Solomon believes the Washburn Library is broken," the Gray Lady said. "Corrupted. He thinks the solution is to start fresh, start again."

I pointed down at the square. "Is he going to build a new one here?"

She waved her hand over the crowd. "I was so surprised when we got here because Stone Mason Square is usually pretty empty. Most days it's just bums, passed out everywhere."

"Homeless people."

Ms. Henry nodded. "Solomon Clay is recruiting them."

To do what? I wondered, but felt scared to ask.

31

AT THE FRONT of the crowd an older man approached the lectern.

The mayor played at the microphone, leaning toward it and then away so he could speak with an assistant. His bald scalp glowed red as a lobster's shell. His thick eyebrows hung over his eyelids. The only strong feature on his face was his arrowhead nose. And he knew it. The mayor gestured with it, poked it at his aides as he spoke. It was the essence of his authority. His ascendancy owed everything to a few ounces of cartilage.

Not that the nose worked on everyone. His assistants were charmed, but quite a few people in the crowd jeered. When he turned back to the microphone, they hissed. One lady actually howled. The mayor looked tired. He must've wanted the job once, but not anymore.

A camera crew taped the speech while reporters held little recorders.

Back at the Library the Unlikely Scholars pored over newspapers from every state, but could that tall reporter there, for instance, the one whose braids hung below her shoulders, the woman with a lovely smile, could she imagine the value her work held for us? And me now, acting for the benefit of the Dean. The Dean in service to the Washburn Library. The Washburn Library acting on cues sent by the Voice. One long chain. But can a link contemplate its limitations?

Behind the mayor, not more than twenty feet, an enormous blue tarp hung loosely. Covering something, but I couldn't guess what. A cord ran from one corner of the tarp to the mayor's right hand. He pulled at it absently as he spoke, and a section of the blue tarp bobbled.

"Hello, everyone," he began. "Thank you for coming. I can see a lot of upset faces, and I understand that. I really do. This is the last place you expected to see me, isn't that right?"

The crowd agreed with more hissing and boos and then, strangely, applause.

"Well, sure, you remember when I was accused of forgetting Stone Mason Square. Not just me, but the entire city government. 'Where's *our* mayor?' I remember the graffiti. The activists who held vigils here claimed that all our institutions had failed."

The mayor stopped to clear his throat and leaned so close to the microphone that his nose brushed the windscreen. He scratched the nose slowly. He tugged the gold cord, and the blue tarp fluttered.

"People used to call this Panhandler Plaza. You could barely park your car before ten guys were at your window asking for change. If you didn't give them something, they insisted. And they could be *convincing*. Let's be blunt. People despised them. And eventually people came to despise Stone Mason Square."

More people jammed onto the patio. Behind me, beside me, right on top of me.

But somehow a zone of protection had been erected around Ms. Henry. I don't mean that people magically gave the Gray Lady lots of space, there wasn't that much room to give, just an inch or two on every side of her body. She leaned forward against the rail, her purse safe between the metal and her belly, her arms crossed over her chest, and each hand stuck into the opposing coat sleeve. She even retracted her neck, bringing her head down into the lapels of her jacket. Consciously or not people picked up on her anxiety and gave her the buffer she needed. I thought of a few moments earlier, the way she'd grabbed my coat sleeve but never come in contact with me. I'd been around her two days now and realized I'd never seen her touch anyone.

I, on the other hand, must've sent out invitations to nest in my pockets. These people were all up in my zip code. The guy on my right had become my conjoined twin. But you know what? I didn't mind. As I scanned the square looking for Solomon Clay, a man I wouldn't recognize except by some aura, I took comfort in the contact of human beings.

The mayor said, "But now here we are. Will we stick around for only one afternoon, then just return it to them? Or can we reclaim this space? Make it *ours* again."

Now the mayor tugged the gold cord hard enough that the blue tarp swept away.

A pair of brass gates were revealed behind him. They looked fit for a driveway instead of a dock. A circular plaque dotted the double gates, half the plaque on one gate and half on the other. Together they bore the image of a great, gnarled tree. Garland's crest, no doubt.

A banner hanging on the gates read WELCOME HOME.

The mayor said, "Ferry service has served our neighbors in Oakland and Alameda quite well, bringing much needed tourist interest as well as an easier way for local residents to reach their jobs in San Francisco.

"When I became your mayor, I promised that I would work to make sure Garland shared in this prosperity. Well, these gates mark the future site of the Garland Ferry Terminal. We'll break ground within a month and have the terminal built in a year. That's record time."

The mayor paused for applause, but very little came. People weren't withholding it exactly. They just waited to hear more.

"You'll see that banner reads 'Welcome Home.' Wonder who we're welcoming? It's *you*. We surrendered Stone Mason Square long ago. Surrendered the land to people who used it as a toilet. But I'm telling you those days are over. We can make this whole city ours again. Ours, not theirs!"

The mayor stood at the lectern and leaned into the applause as if the sound alone would lift him. He propped his elbows on either side of the lectern and seemed less tired than before. Even the people who'd only showed up to hate him had been seduced, if not by the speech then by the sight of those brass gates. They didn't go loopy for the guy, weren't whistling and crying. The approval might have been cautious, but there were no more jeers.

The mayor's aides tried to lead him away from the crowd now. They must've been used to making escapes. But not this time. The mayor refused. He had his bodyguards open a path. He moved ahead and shook people's hands.

The crowd followed him out of Stone Mason Square. They were all dispersing east, up the corridor of Broadway. The mayor's car idled there. The freestanding gates already seemed forgotten, and they looked so much smaller now. The gates were odd there without a dock, like a man wearing nothing but a cummerbund. And the lectern, on its own, looked as out of place in that environment as a winter sled.

A breeze came off the Bay and shook the gates. They clacked loudly. The sunlight made them look silver and tacky, like discarded jewelry. The banner, still strung across them, flopped lazily.

Ms. Henry and I were some of the only people left on the patio, and Stone Mason Square, below us, had cleared in quick time. This place might've been famous for its beggars once, but I couldn't see any just now. We'd passed so many as we'd walked down San Pablo Avenue. That must have been where they'd all gone. They hadn't disappeared. They'd been ejected.

The ferry gates shook again, but this time I didn't feel a breeze.

They shook loudly. Fierce enough that the Gray Lady and I turned our heads.

Then the gates exploded. They cracked in two.

One gate flung backward into the Bay and landed in the water with a splash. The other was knocked flat and burned black on the ground.

The mayor's lectern was a woodpile.

And the half-incinerated banner blew into the air, snapping like a flag. When it floated back down, it had been reduced to a single singed word: "Welcome . . ."

32

POLICE INTERVIEWED THE GRAY LADY, myself, and the others who'd been near there. They couldn't possibly take us all to a police station so they just broke us into groups and took our statements across from Stone Mason Square.

The voices! So many of us yammering beside one another. It didn't sound like *a* foreign language but all of them playing at once. I found myself listening to the chorus as if I could find a buried meaning, but I'd be lying if I said the message was clear.

A squadron of EMT workers herded the witnesses to their ambulances, just looking in our eyes, asking about aches. There were a lot more tears than bruises. I saw a wine bar on one corner and felt like enjoying a few pints, quarts, gallons. After giving my report, I made for the bar, but the Gray Lady hissed at me.

"Ricky! This way."

She cut through the people here just like she had earlier, doing the bump. After we got through, she pulled out a big old cell phone, dialed a number, and spoke into it.

When she got off, she said, "I told you Solomon was dangerous!"

"He did that?" I asked.

"You think it was spontaneous combustion?"

"Just because you say he did it doesn't mean I believe it."

My right leg was cold again. My foot already dragging. Just a half mile had aggravated the condition. The Gray Lady turned to me, unhappy with my skepticism, but I refused to apologize. Her little round face, her large brown eyes, I'd never met a person who intimidated me more. Forget killing Solomon Clay, just then I thought she might murder me. But she ignored my challenge and looked at my leg.

"I've got aspirin in my purse," she said. "If you're in that much pain."

"This isn't an aspirin kind of problem, Ms. Henry."

"Well, what do you want me to do, carry you?"

"You wouldn't carry me even if I was dying."

We kept walking, but slower. People continued to move past us on either side of Broadway. Jogging, sprinting, skipping toward Stone Mason Square. We were some of the only people moving away from the disaster. Around us the great buildings of downtown Garland cast long shadows.

"He came to my hotel this morning," I blurted out. She didn't have to ask who.

"You saw him?"

"No, but a well-dressed man showed up and asked for me by name. They told him I was staying on the fourth floor. And he asked about you, too."

"It's no problem," she said. But then she bit her lip so hard I thought she'd draw blood.

The Gray Lady went into her purse and then tossed me the bottle of aspirin. A way of making peace. I knew they wouldn't work because I'd been dealing with this pain since 2002, but how would it look if I complained and then didn't accept help? So I opened the bottle, popped about five aspirin in my mouth, and swallowed. Closed the bottle and looked at the label out of habit.

ASPIRIN. That's all it said.

The Gray Lady was armed with generics.

A JetBlue flight, putting me up in a flophouse, now some no-name aspirin. How about some Tylenol? A Bufferin! And I haven't even focused on the ten-pound cell phone she carried. I thought about the one snowblower and two shovels that the Unlikely Scholars were forced to share in Vermont. Euphinia and Grace bartering for my office supplies. It was like trying to fund the CIA with a lemonade stand.

"Where are we going now? The Washburns?"

"Claude is coming for us. He'll drop you at the hotel so you can rest your leg. But be down in the lobby by ten."

"And then?"

She pointed behind us, to Stone Mason Square. "We're coming back."

"How are we going to get past all those cops? They'll have the National Guard out here by tomorrow morning. Homeland Security too."

"That's why we're going tonight. Claude will get us in. That's his job."

33

MY FATHER BOUGHT A NEW CAR in January of 1972. Only a few weeks after he realized our hearts were no longer close to his, and soon after he made my sister melt her ring. I think he just got it out of spite. You don't love me? Then I'm blowing *my* money. He'd been rebuffed and would have his revenge. He bought a 1972 Jeep Wagoneer, which was absolutely aberrant in New York at the time. You should've seen the way people came down out of their apartments if Sargent Rice tried parking that behemoth between their cars. Even an Oldsmobile or a Cadillac shrank when he pulled alongside to parallel park.

It was big, brown, and barely manageable on the tighter streets in Queens. It let in too much sunlight and the tan leather seats got so hot in the summer that we placed damp towels underneath us for even the shortest trips. He spent most of our money on that car, even the amounts he should've tithed to the Washerwomen. And every year afterward, 1973, '74, '75, he traded in the nearly new truck and bought a newer one. Not just Jeeps, but always a four-wheel drive. In the last year of his life he paid more on his car note than his mortgage. The new cars became his only extravagance, and no one could persuade him to stop.

You have to picture Sargent Rice. Slim and all, but with a little belly. He wore his hair cut close, which only served to outline his widow's peak. A skinny man with a fat face, a pleasant face, widest at the cheekbones, and small black eyes that rarely focused on you. He'd be going over my homework, but looking out at the skyline, the ceiling, the nightstand. This made him seem energetic, inquisitive, even cerebral. My mother's the one who introduced me to Manly Wade Wellman and Stephen Crane, but my father's the one I called wise. Isn't that always the way? A mother's reward for running away is hate, but a father's is adoration. So was Sargent Rice actually so thoughtful? I don't know, but the farther he drifted, the more I believed it.

As the first few years passed and these new trucks just kept coming, my dad did hear about it from the Washerwomen. The three sisters as well as the other adults. But the community had much bigger problems than the excesses of one man. Flushing, our neighborhood, was curious about us at first, then amused. Then they ignored us for a while. But their interest returned, as regular as yuletide, and this time they focused on the kids. Were we being mistreated? Were we loved? They could've just asked us, but they wouldn't do that. People used to snap on my father, how could he buy a new car when Daphne and I wore the same clothes for years? But were their hearts really bleeding for the kiddies? None of those concerned citizens ever slipped me a winter sweater.

Their worry for the children only masked a patient hostility. The more we proselytized in their streets, the less they could stand our presence. If there hadn't been girls and boys to worry about, they would've raised alarms about the way the Washerwomen treated their pets. In 1973 we began getting visits from social workers, children's services, that kind of thing. They were squeezing us. But that didn't stop my father and his fetish for new trucks.

Every time Sargent Rice went to his truck, he'd open the driver's door and brush two fingers against his headrest. Then bring those fingers to his fleshy nose and inhale the scent. He did it theatrically when we laughed or covered our faces in disgust, but that was just a pretense made for us. He meant it. When he was alone, he did the same thing, without shame. (I know because I used to watch him from our window.) Those fingers went under his nose and then he'd rub them against each other, the tip of his pointer finger going up and down along his thumb. It must have been a wonderful scent, reassuring maybe. Sargent Rice and his car. Himself and himself. Sometimes a man retreats so far inward he mistakes isolation for dominion.

34

AT NINE P.M. I woke up again in my hotel bed. Before I even opened my eyes I felt bedbug bites along my body. It was like waking up on a bed of pins. I shot out of the sheets. Scratching at my belly, I saw tiny, tiny brown spots speckling the side of the mattress. By the Bay had retained at least one of the essential flophouse ingredients.

Then it was time to dress. I took a shower, wiped down afterward with the dishrag they called a bath towel, and then, when that was soggy, stood nude by the open windows drying myself in the cool winds. I kept the lights off.

Did you notice, by the way, that the Gray Lady said nothing about my suit when I met her for the walk to Stone Mason Square? I sure did. And if she wasn't going to pay me a compliment on *that* outfit, I wasn't sure what I could use to dazzle her. Everything else was nice, but certainly not better. Not even quite as good. I spent a long while bringing a sports jacket up to myself and checking that look in the mirror, then exchanging it for a sweater and so forth. I did the same with the slacks and, finally, the shoes. It was a painstaking process, and I ended up wearing exactly what I'd had on in the morning. Nothing less would do. But my fedora looked ostentatious. My sock garters seemed foppish and vain. Thank goodness no one could see them.

Do you really want to kill Solomon Clay? I asked myself as I dressed.

Just because the Dean and Ms. Henry told you to?

When I reached the empty lobby, I saw the clock hanging inside the motel clerk's cage. It read ten-fifteen, and I assumed the Gray Lady had left without me. If there was anyone who would, it was her. Plus Claude sure wouldn't be the one convincing her to wait. And yet, when I stepped onto the street, there Claude stood, in front of the idling Town Car. He even opened the passenger door for me.

"I told her you were coming and we shouldn't leave," Claude said. His belly nearly bumped the car door closed again. He leaned toward my ear as I reached the curb.

"I told her 'Larry is just a criminal, and criminals are always late.' "

And then I entered the car, sitting down before my brain could translate Claude's words. Again, I tried to place him. Where had I dealt with someone like this before?

The Gray Lady was in the backseat. She had a way of seeming in control of our whole mission, but ignorant of the static between Claude and me. Maybe he never acted like a dick to her so she didn't realize he had it in him. Too bad for me. I would've liked the corroboration.

"You're overdressed," she said.

If her outfit was the proper uniform that night, then I had no choice but to agree. As far as I could tell, Ms. Henry wore a green scuba suit. Not flattering.

"You look like a Spanish olive," I said.

As the car moved, the Gray Lady pointed at the rubbery costume that came up to her armpits. "These are waders," she said. "I have a pair for you. If you pull them up tight and be a little careful, I don't think you'll ruin your clothes. Of course, you could go back up to your room and change."

I waved her cautions away with one hand. "No, thanks. This is actually the outfit I wear when I clean my cabin back at the Library."

"I see," she said.

"I wouldn't want to ruin any of my *really* nice clothes."

"Of course," she agreed. "But maybe you should leave your hat in the car?"

I shrugged and tossed the fedora down onto the floor. She looked at it, then at me, just waiting for me to snatch it up. So of course I forced myself to stay nonchalant.

"So what are we doing tonight exactly?" I asked, looking at the roof rather than my endangered headgear.

"We're going into the sewers," she said.

It was an East Bay winter outside. By which I mean a modest rainstorm had started and everyone drove infinitely worse. You never saw so many brake lights going off without a reason. Was there falling debris in front of that Subaru? No. Had black ice developed under the Oldsmobile? Not a chance. These folks just hit the brakes every time they changed their minds.

The legs of the waders spilled off my lap as I lifted them. I was careful not to let them crush the fedora, and then doubly careful not to let the Gray Lady catch me staring at my hat.

"Will I have somewhere to change into these?" I asked her.

"Oh, of course," she said. "I've got a makeup trailer waiting for you at the crime scene."

I had to tuck my legs up into my chest, balance the waders below my feet, and then point my toes directly down and spear a Chetwynd shoe into each leg hole. A trick made more difficult by my hat, just there to my left, in constant danger of being crushed. In fact, I couldn't pull it off until Ms. Henry grabbed the fedora from the floor.

"You're just being silly!" she said.

She placed the hat on the seat between us, and I slipped both feet inside my waders, pulled the waders up over my legs, over my stomach, and to the bottom of my armpits. There were two straps, one to sling over either shoulder, and then I was ready.

Ms. Henry said, "Garland's system is split in two, one for water and one for sewage."

"We're going into the sewage tunnel, aren't we?"

She slapped her own knee. "I knew you were bright."

The Gray Lady called me bright. Why the hell did that have to make me so happy? I grinned, even exulted, after she said that. My face got so warm it could've baked an apple.

A compliment she regretted right away. She looked off, out the window. Like she didn't even want to see that whiff of praise floating in the air. She looked at her hands after that. Then at the ashtray in the door. Anywhere but at me. The only person in the car who returned my glance was Claude, in the rearview mirror, and from the crinkle around his eyes, the scrunch of his nose, I knew he was only scowling.

"And why are we going into the sewage tunnel?"

"We have two jobs out here, Mr. Rice. Kill Solomon Clay and keep the Washburn Library's existence a secret."

"What would Mr. Clay leave behind?"

"If even one of the bomb's components was bought in northeast Vermont, that could lead authorities to us. A man like Solomon might even leave a map taped to a tunnel wall. We're here to erase any marks."

I pulled at the straps of my waders. Ms. Henry made these tasks—this mission—sound commonplace, like the only people who might object were either traitors or fools, so I didn't say any more.

"I have these for you too," she mumbled.

She had two black cases with her, one twice as large as the other, but both were big. She handed me the smaller one, and inside I found a bunch of papers, a flashlight, a small knife, a compass, rubber gloves. I was familiar with everything in there, but because I had no idea what I would do with them, the flashlight seemed as absurd as a magic wand.

"And this is your badge," she said.

It was gold, flimsy. The top had an eagle with wings spread wide like so many badges do. The letters *U.S.* in blue just beneath the eagle's talons, and below that, the words "National Wildlife Refuge Agency."

"I want you to pin it to the upper edge of your lapel."

"No one's going to believe this thing is real," I said.

It looked like a wafer! I was thinking of a New York detective's badge, the gold shield. That thing would hammer nails. A toddler could bend this fake badge.

"Everyone will believe it," she said. "Environmental agencies were allowed into Ground Zero and the Pentagon well before the full search-and-rescue units. No one wants to breathe in toxic fumes, especially after so many people got sick clearing the towers. And swamp gases are exactly what a blown sewage pipe releases. Those cops will be jumping out of our way."

"You really believe that?"

"I'm sure of it," she said.

I knocked lightly against the window. If the car had been going slower, I might've broken my way out.

Ms. Henry spoke again, quietly and slowly. "Everyone there will want to believe in these badges because they *need* to believe in them. They will act as though we're legitimate unless you give them a reason not to. If you believe that you're a representative of the National Wildlife Refuge Agency, you will become one. At least enough to get by. I promise you this."

So that's when I began preparing my speech to the cops.

About how I'd been kidnapped by the Gray Lady and Claude, that they'd drugged me and dragged me into this car, even put these waders on me. I'm just an innocent bystander, Officer.

But when I looked at hers, pinned to her waders just above her small right breast, the badge did look more official. Maybe because I wasn't touching it. Ms. Henry projected unfussy authority. She didn't keep checking or adjusting the little thing. Plus the car was dark. It would be just as dark at Stone Mason Square. And lots of people, lots of sounds, maybe enough for these cereal box prizes to pass inspection. I decided to believe that the badges were real. Walk like a bona fide wildlife agent. How much difference could there be between me and the genuine article? Except for the training, expertise, and government sanction.

We reached Stone Mason Square. Claude bullied his car down Broadway through the crowds who were so used to having the right of way they didn't even register the Town Car until Claude beeped the horn. That moved them. The row of police cars alongside the square had lengthened, going one after the next for a whole block. There's something ominous about a patrol car with its lights off. It reminds me of a power line that's come down in a storm.

"We're hunting nonnative *spartina* if anyone happens to stop you, okay?"

I nodded at her, but who knew what the hell she'd just said.

We crossed the tracks, the only private car to do so, and Claude pulled into a vacant parking lot. Four officers immediately approached the car, their hands floating toward their holsters. The Gray Lady and I stiffened in our seats, but Claude looked pleased, even giddy as they closed in. Now, what kind of black man has fun teasing police triggers? But that's exactly what Claude did. Then, to make it worse, he threw open the driver's door and jumped out. Pumped his two beefy fists in the air.

"This is a raid!" he yelled.

If I'd had a gun, *I* would've shot him.

Those police? They flinched, but to their credit they never drew their burners. As soon as they saw his face, they greeted Claude with smiles and hugs.

The Gray Lady said, "Claude worked alongside them for twenty-eight years."

A cop. Of course.

As soon as I saw him hug his brethren, I could imagine him in the uniform. I should have known from the second I met him, because I can tell you for sure that he'd recognized me.

Police don't believe in ambiguity. To them there are two kinds of people, the Guilty and the Good. After a few years on the job most of them truly think they've been blessed with the Lord's eyes and they can pick a criminal by sight. When I came down the walkway at Garland International Airport, Claude saw Adele Henry plus one ex-con. Cops around the world have so many terms for us, for criminals: hamburger, mutt, shithook, toe rag, cluckhead, customer, mope, scrote, toad. I wouldn't be surprised to find out that in Garland the cops called all crooks Larrys.

There was a time when I'd have recognized Claude as a cop from as far off as Vermont. That type of intuition had helped me survive countless threats. Now he'd barely triggered an alarm. The Washburn Library had changed me for the good in many ways, but what instincts had I lost?

35

I WATCHED CLAUDE through the windshield. The other cops looked over-joyed to see him. This wasn't a guy who'd worked his forty hours and gone home. He might've been the kind to risk his life for other officers, one who sacrificed for the good of the job. I think those cops would have had a hard time believing my impression of him.

"Was he police chief or something?" I asked.

"Claude? He never even made it to sergeant. Master patrol officer. I think that was his title up until they kicked him off."

"Was he dirty?" I asked.

"That would make you happy."

"What makes you say that?"

"You're smiling."

I guess she'd known the man longer than me, so it made sense she might protect his privacy. And yet she and I were Unlikely Scholars. Where was that camaraderie? Besides, I just wanted to talk shit, but she had to go and make it seem childish.

Claude returned to us and opened the door on Ms. Henry's side. After she got out, he ducked his head inside and stared at me.

"You ready to do some real work, Larry?"

As I got out, I said, "Couldn't even make sergeant!"

He shut the door so fast it nearly clipped my hip. He butted against me with that belly, but I didn't step back.

"What happened?" I asked. "Were you corrupt, or just stupid?"

"I retired," he said.

"Because you had a burning desire to drive a taxi?"

Claude patted the roof of his ride. "This is a private car."

"And my name is Ricky Rice."

The Gray Lady had already started toward the site of the explosion, but she came back.

"It would look suspicious if you two got into a fistfight."

Claude said, "You've been spreading rumors about me."

She looked at me, then at him. "I didn't tell Ricky one bad thing about you."

"I just looked at you and guessed," I said.

Claude raised his hand. I thought he was going to slap me. I was going to bite his nose off if he tried.

Instead Claude said, "You should hurry down there, Ms. Henry. It sounds like the federal arm will be here later tonight. I've got no influence over them."

"You've done enough already, Claude. Thank you."

He smiled, but not much, and not at me. Then he left us so he could go speak with the other police. He practically skipped as he returned to them. The cops waved at us, little gestures and a few nods, not like we should go over and make friends, but like the office staff acknowledging the janitors.

As we walked, the Gray Lady asked, "What are we looking for again?"

She was testing me for my own benefit, but damned if I remembered the term she'd used in the car. I was too busy feeling my wrists ache from phantom handcuffs as I slouched through the gathered forces of Garland's police. I guess all the criminal hadn't been knocked out of me. I still felt the paranoia.

"Nonnative *spartina*," she said. "It's cordgrass. I know it sounds a little silly, but if it's growing in that pipe, it could've reacted badly with the sewage and released a highly combustible gas. There have been three cases in the last five years in Northern California alone."

I stopped moving. "Is that true?"

The Gray Lady walked ahead two steps, quiet now. She touched her face absently. The hand roamed up and squeezed the black tam that hid her white hair.

"Yes, it is," she said.

We reached the shoreline, where the mayor had spoken only that morning. I looked back at the patio where the Gray Lady and I had been, and wondered if Mr. Clay could've been there too. Right behind us. Solomon Clay.

The actual site of the explosion, including the remains of the lectern, was surrounded by crime tape and guarded by two young cops hunched forward in the nighttime chill. They talked with each other and only peeked at me and Ms. Henry to be sure we didn't disturb the scene.

The Gray Lady kept going. It looked like she was about to hop right into the waters of the Bay. She opened a little gate at the very edge of the square and went down a ladder that led to a sandy shore. Down there we saw the rest of the damage done by the day's explosion, a hole about the size of a washing machine in the concrete base wall of the square. There was crime tape across this too.

"Take out your flashlight," she said, then peeled the tape off on one side.

We climbed in.

36

THE WADERS WERE A WONDERFUL IDEA because ten seconds in that muck would've eaten through the soles of our shoes. It wasn't that deep, about two feet of sludge. Even with our flashlights and with moonlight coming through the hole, I only knew the Gray Lady was with me because of the shallow breaths ahead. Don't get me wrong, there was a cone of light up there, but I couldn't make out the person in control of it. Like I said, just her little breaths—sniffles, really—through the nose, an effort to fight the smells.

I wonder what to call that color of goo. There was green in it, but a golden cream too. Plus these veins of reddish mud floating at the top. Ms. Henry breathed through her nose, but I opened my lips, catching the air in there because I didn't want to smell the stuff.

"Close your mouth," she whispered. "You don't want sewage going down your throat."

Mouth closed meant nose open.

I've described the color, but there's still the stench to explain. Imagine a dying mule vomiting a soiled diaper all over your sweaty feet. The pipe smelled worse than that. Plus rancid milk was in there somewhere. What a bouquet. Our sniffled breathing made us both sound panicked as our legs sloshed through this pancake batter.

The Gray Lady hesitated, stopped moving actually, and I took the opportunity to get as close to her as I could. Rudely, I popped the flashlight right in her face. She squinted and curled her lips and showed her uneven teeth. The little razor bumps on her neck looked like a bad rash.

We'd gone another hundred feet down the pipe before I felt calm enough to ask a question. "Why did Solomon Clay defect?"

"He's not running off to Russia, Mr. Rice."

"But why does he *think* the Library's corrupt?"

"He's a fanatic," she whispered.

"You said that earlier, Ms. Henry."

And how many times had people called my family exactly that?

"You think sensible people plant bombs in crowded places?" she asked loudly.

The Gray Lady wouldn't answer me, not directly, not honestly. This only made me want to ask more questions.

But she interrupted me. "I'm sorry, Mr. Rice. Just one second. I have to adjust my cap."

This time it wasn't me who turned the flashlight on her. She simply tucked hers into the top of her waders, and the light rose up against her neck and face. It flattered the woman. Capturing her eyes, large and somber. She wore those drab olive waders, yes, but sable eyeliner too, heavier above the eyelids and faint beneath each eye. Then she pulled the black tam from around her head, and that white hair gathered the light until it flared around her like a pearl headdress.

Just let me look at her.

She got the cap on again, moved her flashlight. "Now what were you saying, Mr. Rice?"

What had I asked again?

I really couldn't remember.

SOON WE WERE IN THE THROAT of that sewer, where the air was so thick it felt like drizzle, and I sweated my clothes three shades darker pretty quick. The air wasn't combustible, but it did make me feel light-headed. My legs moved in that slow, mechanical way I recognized from dreams, like I'd trespassed into someone else's hallucination.

The Gray Lady had a little easier time than me because she didn't have to stoop beneath the low ceiling of the tunnel, but it also meant the sewage floated as high as her thighs. The coldness in my right leg now had a challenger. The back of my head was scraped raw. I thought it was just decay that made the top of the sewer pipe feel so rough against my scalp, but when I finally trained my light up, I saw a layer of grease seven inches thick and hardened into jagged copper rock. Bits of glass, hair, stone, insects, even eggshells were buried in there. Seeing that, I tried to stoop even lower because my head really hurt, but it was impossible to stay that low and keep moving. I was forty years old! And not one of those jog-around-the-track-with-your-baby-in-a-stroller kinds of forty.

At first Ms. Henry and I tried to swish through the water quietly, but being stealthy takes the energy out of you, and the more tired you get, the more you just want to hurry. Pretty soon we were kicking our way through, churning the sewage so loudly I'll bet people heard us from the sidewalk. Though maybe there wasn't anyone up there. We'd passed Stone Mason Square a while back, I was sure of that, were probably halfway toward my hotel already. Tree roots cracked through the surface of the pipe here and there.

The Gray Lady stopped ahead of me, and I was thankful for the rest, but it wasn't me that made her pause. We'd finally reached two offshoot tunnels, one going left and another right. Both even smaller than the main pipe. My back filed a protest and my legs signed it too.

She put a hand over her mouth before speaking.

"You go left and I'll go right and we'll meet back here in ten minutes."

I said, "Lady, if you try to leave me, I'm going to climb on your back."

"You're afraid?" she asked.

"Terrified."

This was one benefit of being a grown man and not a kid: I wanted to impress this woman, but not to the point of getting myself killed.

"Me too," she whispered.

Then I pushed it. I said, "Maybe we should hold hands."

A line! I used a line on the Gray Lady as we stood knee-deep in filth. Her smile disappeared. No hand extended.

"We'll check the left tunnel first," she said, and went in ahead of me.

I'LL CALL THIS PIPE JUNKY ROW because there were a lot of used needles floating in the muck. Both the Gray Lady and I kept our black cases in front of us as we walked so we wouldn't get poked in the legs. Along with the needles there were sheets of wadded paper, razors, pens and pins, buttons, lots of rags. We even passed through a cloud of plastic straws. Above us there were small openings in the ceiling that fed waste down into the water.

"It's been sealed," she said. "Look around. See if there's anything un-usual."

"Besides *everything*?"

"Yes," she said sarcastically. "Besides that."

The passage ended abruptly, a smooth concrete slab cutting us off. A very new wall, its age obvious because it wasn't stained, nothing growing through or on it. I knocked the concrete with my flashlight, and it made a quiet sound, *-pock- -pock-*, that echoed. Up this close the Gray Lady's flashlight exposed some numbers, code, in orange paint. Nothing that made sense to me. Information for other sewer workers who knew the language. Maybe this was the first work being done for that ferry terminal. Reclaiming Panhandler Plaza. I wasn't quite ready to move yet, so I stood there, panting, but pretending to study the digits.

"Do you understand them?"

"Pretty standard municipal codes," I answered.

Sounded good to me, but what about to her? She looked at the wall again, passed her light over it once more. I felt stuck between mistrust and attraction as I watched her move. And I wondered how I appeared to her just now, touching the numbers with my fingertips. In her eyes was I dashing or dim?

37

WE BACKTRACKED to the main pipe and then went across, into the other offshoot tunnel. If the left tunnel was Junky Row, then we should call the right one Jelly Lane. The stray needles were replaced by bright multicolored muck, sticky as jam to get through. Looking up at the narrow drainpipes in the ceiling, I wondered if there was a marshmallow factory above us. There were pink globs, purple globs, blue violet, and hot pink globs. They looked like the heads of baby jellyfish bobbing at the top of the sewage. I even thought they might be some freaky marine life spawned in the chemical vat of the sewer. But when I pressed at them with my black case, they simply popped and oozed, like blisters, blending with the sewage that carried them. They weren't creatures. They were bubbles. They added to the overwhelming spice of the air down there, and I felt the edges of my perception turning fuzzy.

The globs actually grew bigger as we trekked down the tunnel, growing from baseball-size to softball-size. Each blob had a little weight to it, so when you walked through one, it pulled slightly. It felt like someone catching at your pants. That was bad, but worse was if you walked through a few at once. Then they all seemed to grab together. Swarms of them slowed us down.

"You doing okay?" I asked her, as if she was the one getting fidgety.

"Fine."

She said this, but my flashlight caught sweat on the back of her neck.

I looked behind me, just as a precaution, and when I did, I saw that the globs I'd been kicking off hadn't just floated away. They'd passed behind, but stuck together in my wake, one after the next clinging to the back of my waders. It trailed for yards. I'd grown a glowing tail.

And that was just about enough.

I didn't think, just reacted. Thrashed in the water because I needed to, absolutely got damn had to, get those glowing bubbles off my ass. I spun, but that only made the whole tail wrap around me. They wouldn't pop. They held. I was under attack by foam!

And losing.

I stamped my legs, swung my case, howled and coughed and splashed. Please just give me some space. That's what I would've said if I could've said anything. But I couldn't. Instead I growled as I fought them. And, finally, finally, I tore myself free.

To find the Gray Lady just watching me.

"You need a cigarette break," she said.

I pointed at her. "Check."

She turned her flashlight away from me, then back.

"I think they sealed this pipe up too. Looks like another new wall just a ways down. It's close enough that I can see the same orange numbers, but I want to make sure. The Dean would want me to be thorough. So I need you to stay cool for just a little longer, okay?"

What the hell did she call me? Was she speaking Spanish all of a sudden? Or Creole? It damn sure wasn't English, was it? I heaved and sighed and caught my breath while she repeated herself, but I still didn't understand. So she pointed at the spot where I stood and then held up her open hand, and I got it. Stay. At this point I was too exhausted to be scared.

She left me.

But wait, here's a little gift for Ricky while he recovers. The sudden and overwhelming smell of perfume.

I shined the light behind me and prayed the new scent wasn't coming from there. Thankfully, it wasn't. It came from above. I pointed the flashlight up and, just a few inches to my left, saw another small drainpipe. I moved closer. Stood as straight as I could. Pointed my nose at the opening and inhaled.

Laundry soap.

Sweet laundry soap.

Not that industrial kind either, which is mostly just ammonia. This was a combination of a dozen home detergents. We must've been underneath some neighborhood Laundromat. The pipe gave off an aroma of berries and lemon and rose and violet and vanilla and lavender and just a hint of ammonia. It was a welcome antidote to the poisonous stench of the sewer. I shut my eyes, and I'm sure I was smiling. Then I heard Adele Henry's lovely voice.

"This tunnel is sealed. I don't see anything that would expose the Library." I heard her sigh deeply. "I'm going to check under the waterline to be sure."

"Don't forget to hold your breath!"

I nearly sang the sentence.

She paused. "Is everything all right?"

"Don't I sound all right?"

"You sound *cheerful.*"

"Just smelling the roses," I said.

"I'm glad I wore gloves," she responded. Then I heard the rippling sound of her hand brushing through the sewage.

I enjoyed the outrageous moment, the ridiculous mental image of my nose pressed to a laundry pipe while the Gray Lady groped through sewage.

Then I felt a hand touch my arm.

I wanted it to be Ms. Henry's, needed it to be hers, but when had she ever touched me? Besides, she was still way down *there.*

As soon as I registered the touch, it became tighter. Gripping my left wrist. It did more than hold. It tried to drag me down. And I didn't fight, not exactly. Not at first. Instead I tried to see who it was. That was my stupid first reaction. Not fight or flight, but understand. But the flashlight was in my left hand, the one that had been grabbed, so I couldn't do more than wave it over the sewage. The dot of light flickered against the sewer walls.

Now a second hand touched me, wrapping around my left elbow.

"Mr. Clay," I whispered. "Solomon Clay."

He didn't answer. I could only see outlines in the dark. I wasn't fighting a man yet, only a shadow.

I jerked my forearm away from him as hard as I could now, and he fell forward, but held on. Then he squeezed my arm harder, and my fingers opened and I dropped the flashlight. It fell right into the muck. I saw even less after that.

I tried to punch with my right hand now, but without any light, I only swung at the air.

The silence only felt more powerful the longer it went. I'm not saying this was a quiet moment, not with all the splashing and my own heavy breaths. I mean his lack of words. His hush was worse than a threat.

I felt an insane pressure around my wrist and elbow. A squeeze like you wouldn't believe. Can bones turn to dust? I wondered. I was about to find out. But then I heard this ripping noise instead. I swore it was my skin, but it was only my jacket and shirt. He tore off my sleeves at the shoulder, and my whole left arm was exposed.

"I'm innocent," I whispered. "I've got no fight with you."

Then he stabbed me. Just above my left wrist.

"Adele!" I screamed. "Adele!"

I looked down, and now my eyes had adjusted so I saw the back of his head. Bald, sweating, sickly, almost green. I had to stop pretending. This wasn't Solomon Clay. This wasn't any man. I felt a heated pain in my wrist, as if this thing were digging the blade deeper, until it reached bone. I tried to pull away, but failed again.

Down the sewer line I heard the Gray Lady. "Mr. Rice?" she called.

How many minutes passed before she arrived to help? I couldn't count them, but finally she appeared.

Flinging road flares?

That wouldn't have been my first choice of weapons, but maybe that's all she had. Either way the pressure on my wrist and elbow weakened. Red sparks flashed around me, nearly hit me in the face. She was barely aiming. So what did I do? To get out of the fire lane? Yup. Plopped right down into the sewage. I didn't even get to take a breath.

The Gray Lady chased my attacker down the tunnel, but there weren't any more flares left. She came back as I stood up. I fished my flashlight out of the gunk with my right hand. She held her flashlight and looked at me with concern.

"Why didn't you have a gun?" I asked.

She crossed her arms. "And what were you doing? Besides panicking?"

"Blow it out your ass, Ms. Henry."

The Gray Lady trained her flashlight on my forearm and asked me to turn it round so she could see. There were red marks around my wrist, like rope burns. The same around my elbow. But no stab wound. Not like the gash I'd expected from all that fighting. No torn flesh. Not even blood. It seemed impossible.

She leaned closer to my arm. I did too. But when I moved in, she pulled back. Even down there, after all that, she couldn't relax. Close up I saw just a tiny little pinhole prick in my skin. Nothing more.

"What was that?" I asked her.

"Solomon Clay," she said. "Who else?"

"You're wrong," I said. "Or you're lying."

The Gray Lady looked behind us.

She said, "I wouldn't keep anything from you."

Of course I didn't believe her, no one with any sense would. I'd held some suspicions before this, but now I really wondered what I'd volunteered for. Why had I assumed the Gray Lady and the Dean and the whole Washburn Library were on my side? Or even on the right side? Just because I wanted to believe such a thing? And once I'd turned a little skeptical, why didn't I *do* anything differently? They told me to fly out here and I flew. They told me to climb into a dark tunnel and I dove in. A domesticated animal. Maybe Solomon Clay had come to my hotel to warn me, not to harm me. Imagine entering a fight without knowing the sides.

I used to hang around the dope spots trawling for exactly that kind of chump. White, black, yellow, or brown, it didn't matter. If they were on the block looking soft, then I played chummy. Just give me the money, I'd say after a little conversation. I'll go upstairs and score us that dope. It didn't always work, but worked much more often than you can guess. I'd go up, buy the bags, and sneak out a back way before those fellas ever knew they'd been played. So now I stood there in the sewer wondering at my role. Had the whole Washburn Library made me into a vic?

I replayed the feeling, something sharp piercing my skin. I raised my flashlight to see the cut more closely. The tiny little wound looked like a needle mark, honestly. I certainly recognized those. Had I been stabbed, or injected? Was it my imagination, the adrenaline, or just fear that made the spot feel like it was burning? No, it wasn't the wound, deeper than that. This pain was in my blood. What had just been done to me?

I stared at the spot. Ms. Henry did too.

It was as if we could see poison flooding my veins.

4

Big Machine

4

Big Machine

38

THE WASHERWOMEN WERE THREE SISTERS from Florida who escaped north before the Jacksonville police found what they'd left behind. All three women had husbands and children who would be discovered, six days later, tucked into blood-soaked beds.

The Washerwomen shot their families, plain and simple. And when it was over, they fled to New York. They'd been born Baptists, but the murders marked a change. They didn't lose their religion, they resurrected it. After those deaths they became *better* Christians. That's what the Washerwomen believed.

I wonder how that sounds to someone who wasn't there with them, firsthand. Crazy, no doubt. Terrible. Criminal. Even evil. I can't really argue. It comes across as pretty nuts to me too from a few decades away. But I was there then.

Years after our community fell apart, people still called the Washerwomen devils, and when my old apartment building went condo, they had a very hard time selling the places on our floor. As if the living rooms and kitchens and stairwells were still possessed.

So what could possibly make my parents stay and raise their children into such a thing? That's the funny part about the Washerwomen. Their doctrine fit my father well. Their main idea was pretty straightforward: the Church is broken. Which one? Take your pick. All choices were correct. The Church, that abiding institution, had stopped working. A new church had to take its place. Something small and defiant and renewed with concern. Which is about as traditional an idea as Christianity has.

This appealed to my father because, in his own life, certain institutions had failed him too, and he appreciated that the Washerwomen hadn't surrendered to despair.

To show how profoundly they distrusted every church, they even rewrote the Bible.

And why not? They wouldn't be the first. The King James Version (1611). The English Revised Edition (1881–85). The American Standard Version (1901). The Revised Standard Version (1952). Others include the Amplified Bible, the Contemporary English, the Darby Translation, the Douay-Rheims 1899 American Version, the Holman Christian Standard Bible, the New Life Version, the New Living Translation, the Wycliffe New Testament, and the Message. That's just a few examples written in English. So why couldn't the Washerwomen try?

And if it had been as simple as one more approximation of the original texts, maybe it would've been okay. If these three sisters from Jacksonville had been self-taught in Hebrew, Aramaic, and Greek, then pored over the available source documents and simply transcribed what they'd found, I doubt many people would've had trouble with them. The problem is that the Washerwomen's version wasn't about translating every line on what to do about stolen oxen or all the names in the priestly class. They deleted that business entirely. When African slaves came to the Americas, they identified with the bondage of the Jews in Exodus, and this, above all else, was why they embraced Christianity so firmly. So the Washerwomen's version of the Bible didn't take place in towns like Jericho or Judea. Instead the Israelites escaped out of Georgia and Tennessee. And, for that matter, in this book they weren't even called Israelites. They were called Negroes.

LET ME ALSO MAKE THIS CLEAR, the Washerwomen didn't *tell* anyone about the mass murder. They omitted that from the official record. Because that would, you know, drive sane people away before they had a chance to hear the message.

Our small community only found out about it after the news made it from Jacksonville to New York, and it's sad to say that this took quite a while. What does that have to do with me? New York seemed to say. I'm busy wit my own problems, ovah heah! While a womanhunt electrified northern Florida, and southern Georgia, it only rated grainy "Wanted" posters in the post offices of Queens. In the days before cable news and Internet searches, infamy had a good chance of remaining localized.

By the time those rumors did filter north, Sargent and Carolyn Rice knew the sisters too well to believe the rumors were true. The whole

Washerwomen community felt that way. Because of love they held no doubts.

This sounds like our great mistake, putting our trust in three women who'd been accused of a massacre. And yet, for all that, it wasn't the Washerwomen who killed my sister, Daphne.

It was me.

39

THE GRAY LADY AND I CLIMBED OUT of the sewer, and then I hid in my hotel. Never was I happier to see the ratty room at By the Bay than after I'd locked the door behind me. Riding back from the sewer in Claude's car, I was afraid Claude and Ms. Henry were going to lock me away for observation. But they didn't. Just left me off exactly as they had the night before. In fact, I'd say the Gray Lady looked more frightened of me. As if I might spread some sickness to her. She practically booted me out of the car that night. I got upstairs, shut the door, and stuck a chair under the doorknob. Had the Gray Lady set me up, or was I being paranoid? Should I search out Solomon Clay myself and hear his side?

But how could I track him down when I barely had the energy to tear off my soiled clothes? Funny that no one in the lobby knocked me for being saturated in sewage. The only time they noticed me was when my clothes gave off a snotty vibe. When I looked like a mess, they disregarded me. I piled the soggy suit on top of the bathroom sink, but I felt woozy before I could even get a shower going. Nearly passed out on the tile floor. I made it into bed, and there I lay, feverish and aching.

The Gray Lady didn't forget me. Phone calls began the next morning, right around eight A.M. That went on, every hour, until noon. Then the desk clerk rang, saying I had visitors. First Claude and then, when I wouldn't let him up, Ms. Adele Henry. But I denied her too. And, to my complete amazement, By the Bay wouldn't just let them up. Who expects tight security at an SRO? By late afternoon the desk clerk had been persuaded to come upstairs herself. She knocked at my door, but I refused to open up, and eventually she left.

For the rest of the night my mind returned to the shadows of the sewer. I thought of the laundry detergent flowing down from that pipe until a citrus scent returned to me. The splash of Ms. Henry and me marching through the sewage. The attack. Being stabbed. The poison.

As my mind gathered these impressions, my body throbbed. It felt as though each of my muscles was leaping out of my skin. They jittered and sparked so badly that eventually I couldn't shut my eyes. And finally, the next morning, I tried to rise.

Getting myself to sit up, then stand, that energy all came from the power of positive thought. But when I fell forward, face-first onto the floor, that was hard-core reality. My body couldn't think itself past its pain. So I lay on the dirty tiled floor, not because I liked it but because I didn't have a choice. If my mind had tried to rally the limbs just then, we would've fallen into civil war. So I lay there.

Being a reasonable diplomat, I decided on a series of concessions. We'll lie on the ground for five minutes. Okay, we'll stay here for ten.

Twenty minutes, but nothing more!

After thirty, my arms were willing to press me up, and my legs agreed to take the weight. See that, a little compromise lifts your spirit.

Like that, a model of statesmanship, peace between body and mind, we ran the shower. Got in and washed ourselves. The fever got worse, bad enough that even a steamy shower felt lukewarm when compared with the temperature in my skin. I came out and found it necessary to enter into a second set of negotiations.

This time as the body slumped stubbornly on the toilet seat while the mind wandered up along one of the walls. We were in danger of never coming together, but finally my soul mustered the others back around the bargaining table.

We need help. We have to get out of this place. Is everyone agreed?

I awaited their answer patiently.

BY NOON we'd decided to wear a Norfolk suit. It was no less formal than my pinstripes, but more rugged. Have you ever seen one? Probably not, unless you've been out shooting in the English countryside in the 1870s. All Harris Tweed and warmer than a bear's butt. Good for "hard wearing." It even had a strap that went around my middle, which helped to hold me straight up, like a truss. There weren't too many old Scholars rocking the Norfolk look, but there had been one guy in the photos, thankfully.

Add to the suit a pair of calfskin chukka boots and a black and white herringbone newsboy cap, and I looked like Ricky Rice, Gentleman Adventurer. But I felt like Ricky Rice, Terminally Ill. The last thing I did was take out my heroin. I put those baggies in my pocket, thinking of them almost like a talisman, an evil to ward off greater evil.

In a way, heroin had already protected me. While I felt feverish and achy, while my limbs shivered, I was still able to shower, to dress, to move. Kicking dope so many times had toughened me. All those withdrawal pains had weathered my body. Leather wasn't even as durable. Everything hurt, but I could still function.

I got on the creaky old elevator and rode down to the lobby. Leaned against one wall for support. I heard myself huffing even though I'd hardly moved. It sounded like the sigh of a dog when first setting itself down.

An older guy got on at the second floor, one of those grumpy-grandad types, wearing a green cardigan all buttoned up. A newspaper folded under one arm. He stared at me the whole slow way down. When the doors opened, he said, "Negro, you are a mess."

I pushed myself off the wall and stood straight.

"Blow it out your ass, Redd Foxx."

He took the paper from under his arm, tapped his leg with it a few times. He looked me over again. Then he said, "Mmm-hmmm."

We sort of raced for the elevator exit, only two feet, but Fred Sanford hit the lobby first. When you lose a footrace to a seventy-year-old, you know you are not in peak physical shape.

He met a few of his cronies out there, gathered to the television again. What were they watching? Not basketball. Maybe the news? That guy in the wheelchair held the most prominent position, only inches from the screen and directly in front. I suppose that if he was their leader, this counted as a place of prestige. The man in the cardigan walked over to the lame one and whispered in his ear. Then they both looked at me. Instinctively I clutched at the belt loop of my Norfolk jacket.

"Hey, Jeeves!" the man in the wheelchair shouted.

"Spot of tea?" he added in a bad British accent.

If I'd been feeling better, I might've given him a few lines back, but my pride couldn't overcome my palpitations. Maybe I should try to reach a hospital, I thought. I bet I could find a men's shelter closer by. Or a church.

I stumbled toward the front door. I looked back, but they weren't even watching me anymore. They were back to the big screen. And I misjudged how close I was to the hotel doors, so I bonked right into the glass. The front door opened and I tripped across the threshold, but before I fell, a pair of meaty hands caught me.

"Careful there, Larry."

Then my right hand twisted, Claude pulled my arm behind me, and in a moment he had me hemmed up in a police hold. His Town Car idled by the corner. I couldn't have seen it from the lobby. He guided me toward the car now, right arm bent hard behind my back.

"Fucking . . . !" I shouted, but didn't have the power to complete a sentence.

"Close your mouth," he whispered, "or I'll close it."

We reached the Town Car and he popped the back door open. Claude tossed me inside, really threw me, so I went into the back headfirst. I fought the best I could. This meant flailing around like a dying bird, which didn't help much. The only good thing is that my slacks glanced off his cheeks a few times and left a faint red mark, a little Norfolk burn.

Meanwhile, Claude put me in plastic handcuffs.

One loop tight around my left wrist and the other loop around the grip of the car door so I had to sit at an angle, the right side of my face pressed to the window. Claude slammed the door, which made my ears ring. Then he ran around to the driver's seat and got in. If he had taken me to a field right then and dumped my body, no one would have known.

THE CAR RIDE TURNED into a silent battle, like most of my time with Claude. I stopped myself from asking where we were going, and he restrained himself from shooting me in the head. Because he had to hold his anger in, Claude drove badly. He swept from one lane to another on the highway.

As we passed the Grand Avenue exit, the highway took a slight curve. In the distance I saw a hill with rows of deco homes in tangerine, taupe, or alabaster, three and four stories tall, chimes on a child's xylophone.

A large lake rippled below those homes. I saw the calm, green water. It was the color of a Granny Smith apple that's been left on the counter too long. I sat up higher in my seat, which made the handcuff cut into my skin, and saw a crowd down by the water. A few held signs with slogans, but I couldn't read them from where we were. My eyes were too blurry for that.

As we continued, I felt a new, more localized pain in my forearm. Right where I'd been jabbed. I'd thought it was the cuffs digging in, but even after I shifted my body, the burning sensation remained. I still felt feverish and achy all over, but now it was like someone had sewn a spark under my skin. I watched the wound, afraid blood or pus or something worse would leak out. But nothing did.

Claude finally got off on MacArthur Boulevard. To my right there were three small, lopsided apartment houses, all decorated in late twentieth-century Security Door. Battered cars lined the side streets. It wasn't a bad neighborhood, just distressed.

On the opposite side of MacArthur Boulevard, across from the moldy apartments, a big old park bloomed. At least that looked nice. Trees rose three stories high. A chain-link fence divided nature from the neighborhood. We drove alongside the park, stopped at the first traffic light, and then made a left. Into the park. I leaned forward, trying to understand.

Maybe Claude really did mean to shoot me in the woods. I tried to control my breathing.

There was a great stone entrance and we drove through its arch, up to a wooden guard station. Claude waved at the pair of guards inside, but they hardly looked at him. It would be a mistake to call the duo "security," they were too lackluster for that. They were working hard just to keep their eyes open. The threat of napping was the greatest danger they faced.

"Where . . . ?" I muttered.

Claude raised one hand triumphantly. "This is the Washburn estate."

40

CLAUDE DROVE SLOWLY along the main road of the estate. A few white pickups were parked along either side of the two-lane road. Each truck had a familiar *W* stamped on both doors. Why did that make me feel better? Nothing more than a letter, but it connected this place to the Washburn Library in Vermont. It was only as we passed them that I noticed one truck had two flat tires. Another was missing its windshield, and leaves had blown inside the cab. They littered the front seat and the dashboard.

Sycamore trees lined the main road, rising thirty feet high, their bark yellowed and flaking. The branches were bare. They leaned across the road, toward one another, and we drove below them. Their grasping, empty branches wove together and formed a ceiling of spiderwebs.

I had a hard time reconciling the magnificent trees with those broken-down trucks and the third-rate sentries at the gate. Things only became more confusing as we continued through the grounds. There was so much land, but large sections of the lawn had gone brown. Except for at the entrance, I didn't see a human being anywhere.

Claude made a right turn.

"That's where the Washburns live." Claude practically cooed when he said it.

The Washburn mansion. Fifty rooms, easily. Eggshell white. With a great circular driveway leading up to its front doors. Arched windows everywhere, all the curtains drawn. It was time to meet my makers. Through the fever, the pain of handcuffs, I also felt my pulse thump nervously.

But then Claude drove right by.

Claude passed the mansion gleefully. I could see him stifling laughter as he looked back in the rearview. It made him happy to confuse me. I twisted as far as I could while wearing those flex cuffs and watched the mansion recede.

He drove down a narrow gravel road and entered a tiny grove of trees. I saw a few scattered cabins that looked like the ones back in Vermont, except these had shingles missing on their Spanish roofs, and one's windows had been replaced with sheets of wood. At the end of the lane Claude pulled into a driveway. He stopped the car, popped the door locks, and turned around in his seat.

"Get out."

I flopped my numb left hand. "Want me to chew this off?"

Claude honked his horn at this cabin, the only one in decent shape. The Gray Lady stepped out. She wore a mustard-gold tam that covered most of her hair and cast a shadow across her eyes. Without makeup she looked oily, shiny on her forehead. A tan plaid gingham housedress covered every part of her except her hands and face. She looked exhausted, actually. And plain.

The Gray Lady smiled. She flapped both hands in the air as a greeting. I couldn't tell if she was excited or shooing me away. She looked halfway crazy.

"Come in," she said. "Come in."

But, of course, I couldn't. Claude stepped out of the car, came round to my door, and when he opened it, he had a small pair of precision cutters hidden in his palm. He grabbed my fingers and squeezed them tight, a boyhood torture, while he snipped me loose.

The Gray Lady stayed at the door. "What's the trouble?" she asked.

Claude slid the plastic line and the pliers into his jacket pocket without seeming to move at all. Then he straightened, smiled at Ms. Henry, and said, "The boy's a little tired, that's all."

"You must've been great at planting evidence," I said as I stepped out.

Claude slammed the door fast, trying to catch my fingers.

I reached Ms. Henry's cabin, and as I stepped forward, she stepped back, almost mindlessly. I'd have brushed against anyone else as I came in, but the Gray Lady moved too far, too fast. I'd missed her again. She didn't trust me, but that was okay. I didn't trust her much either now. Once I got in, she stepped around me, back into the doorway, and waved Claude off.

The Gray Lady shut the door, walked through the partially furnished living room and past the dining table. She went into the kitchen and poured me a cup of tea. I heard the trickle. She came back and set the cup and saucer on the dining table. I hadn't moved from beside the front door.

"I'm a hostage," I said.

The Gray Lady looked at the cup of hot tea again, touched the side with her pointer finger. "Is this about the other night? Because—"

"This is about twenty minutes ago when Claude *abducted* me from my hotel."

"Oh, come on, Mr. Rice."

"He put me in handcuffs!"

She approached me cautiously now, palms up to calm me.

"Let me see."

I opened my Norfolk jacket and pulled it off. As I stretched my wrist past my shirt sleeve, I peeked at this lovely cabin she had all to herself. Once inside, I realized it was twice as big as the ones in Vermont. One here and one there. She was doing quite well for herself.

I showed her the crease on my left wrist.

"He must've been frustrated. You wouldn't come out."

"It's my fault, then?"

"That's not what I mean. I mean we were both anxious to make sure you were all right."

"Well, I'm not," I said. I heard myself and wondered if I was pouting again.

"Let me see the wound," she said.

I unrolled the left sleeve, up to my elbow.

The red marks around my wrist and elbow, where I'd been grabbed, had blistered a bit but not too bad. I felt terrible, but refused to show it. Not to her. I'd have liked to sit and groan. Instead I kept my back straight and spoke slowly, but with volume. All Ms. Henry had to do was feel my forehead to realize I wasn't healthy, but of course that's something she wouldn't do. Instead she pulled a ballpoint pen from one of the pockets of her housedress and stabbed the cap into my forearm.

"Does that hurt?" she asked.

"Of course it hurts. You're jabbing me."

"Why are you snappy?" she asked, and jabbed me again, harder.

"I got attacked in a sewer pipe. A sewer pipe you led me into. Let's start there."

The Gray Lady tapped the same pen cap against her lips absently, then stopped, remembering it had just touched my wound. She wiped her mouth with the back of her hand.

"Drink your tea," she said. "You'll feel better."

But I doubted that. Instead I decided to be nosey and peeked into all the rooms in her cabin. I didn't even ask. I thought she'd yell at me, but she let me explore. Only her office looked genuinely inhabited. Two desks, both old, wooden, and kind of crappy. One made of pressboard while the other looked like it had been left out in the rain since the fifties. There were tall particle board bookshelves that leaned sloppily in one direction or another. The computer was big and bulky, and I saw a little white label stuck on the power cord: REFURBISHED EQUIPMENT. A hunter green throw rug lay on the floor between the two desks. A wooden picture frame hung on the office wall just above the older desk, with a single hand-painted word in red: Rigor.

"You've really made this place cozy."

"Oh, shut up," she said.

We went back into the living room, to her dining table. There were four chairs, but three of them had dust on the seats. Her cell phone lay on the table. I'd seen smaller car batteries. I picked it up without asking. It felt as heavy as a barbell in my right hand. It was one of those old numbers where you flip down a hinged mouthpiece to talk and raise the antenna to get a signal. If there'd been a handle on the side, so you could wind it up to charge, I wouldn't have been surprised.

"Where'd you get this?" I asked. "1987?"

She slapped the wooden table. "What's your problem?"

"I want to know what the hell happened to me."

She slipped her pen back into her pocket. She pushed the tea toward me, just one limp little gesture.

"Come look at this," she said quickly.

She walked around the table, away from me, to a set of books stacked up on the mantel of her dusty fireplace. It wasn't anywhere near as big as the one in the Dean's office, and the cobwebs in the corner told me this one had hardly been used. The Gray Lady grabbed one book from the stack and brought it to me.

I read the cover. It was a volume in the Time-Life Books series about the paranormal. Volume 34: *Angels & Demons.* She flipped from one page to the next. There were drawings and photos and paintings next to sections of text, but I couldn't concentrate on any of it because I thought she had to be joking.

"Why are you showing this to me?" I said.

She looked up, but when I held her gaze, she stared at the page again.

"I'm trying to prepare you," she said. "You might think you're ready for all the answers, right this second, but hearing too much too soon will just drive you away or drive you crazy. Neither one is any use to me."

"Fine, Ms. Henry. But *this* is really the best you can offer?" I asked. "What happened to me down there? At least tell me that."

"I really don't *know!*" The frustration in her voice was actually convincing.

Now she looked back at the other books on the mantel as if some grand power lay in one of them, the rest of the Time-Life Mysteries of the Unknown. But I doubted we'd find answers in Volume 12: *Mysterious Creatures* or Volume 16: *Phantom Encounters*.

We weren't part of a high-end organization. I just had to admit this. We had money, but not limitless amounts. Access to information, but not the top secret kind. These "research manuals" could be ordered by phone. We weren't calling in any special strike force for support. We faced the extraordinary armed with the subpar. I looked at Adele Henry and finally accepted an obvious fact. If she or I served up any heroics, we'd be baking them from scratch.

41

I WANT YOU TO PICTURE THIS: it's a lovely Sunday in your town or city. You've actually roused the family, put on the formal clothes, then sat through a service that lasted an hour, maybe more. Time served, you shamble out of your pew, open the front doors, and find a man or woman on your church steps reading the Bible aloud. You don't recognize this person and he or she is blocking your path, if not with her body then with the volume of her voice. You might even try to parse out which passages are being recited. They sound familiar enough, but the specifics escape you. It must be from one of the books you've hardly cracked. Maccabees or Hosea or Geritol.

You figure this is one of those super-Christians, here to tell you the good news that Christ died for you (as if you hadn't just heard).

Finally you actually listen and ask yourself, Was there really a woman named Josephine in the Bible? *Malik* and his coat of many colors? Luther parted the *Mississippi*?

Do you know who hated to hear this stuff? Everyone. White churches and black churches. Korean churches, Puerto Rican and Dominican churches. Presbyterians and Methodists, and any other denomination you might name, always chased the nutballs off. Those nutballs were my parents.

The Washerwomen directed their followers to go out into the world and preach that every church was broken. But we had the repair manual. This meant traveling. That was quite a shock, since most of their followers had been born and raised in the five boroughs. And you can fool yourself if you're raised in New York. Think that somehow your birthplace alone makes you cosmopolitan. But it isn't true. We're rubes too. For us a trip to Scarsdale is a safari.

Our parents were gone for eight months every year. Moms for three and dads for five. The Washerwomen were the only adults who lived with us all year long. Our parents traveled the continental United States delivering this cockeyed gospel.

Your church is broken! The Washerwomen are here to rebuild!

The Washerwomen didn't proselytize to people of other religions, or those without any beliefs. There were two billion Christians to reach first. Then we could move on to the rest of the planet. And they meant to do exactly that. Faiths aren't founded by modest types.

But none of this is why our folks remained loyal. Not really. The proselytizing was a task, and the ambitions a dream. So why, honestly, did we swear by the Washerwomen?

Gina, Karen, and Rose called themselves "priests without a parish." Local clergy discussed the Washerwomen the way you discuss a calf born with two heads. Like, Can you believe that? Isn't the world bizarre! The cult on Colden Street. Once, a visiting Anglican priest even gave the sisters a nickname: *episcopi vagantes*, the "wandering bishops."

It was a title the sisters liked (the English, not the Latin). They embraced it, whether it was intended spitefully or not. They used to call each other by that name. Even had fun with it. Once, I was in the hall and Gina waited at the elevator while Rose stood at the door of the apartment the sisters shared. Rose yelled, "Hey, bishop! Wander over to the store and bring me some mustard greens!" Gina had to come back to the apartment to get a few more dollars for the greens, but Rose wouldn't hardly move out of Gina's way. I bear witness. They stood there grappling, foreheads pressed against each other, two sisters, a lion and an ox. They seemed to shine like beasts of prophecy, their vitality more persuasive than any words.

That's why we believed.

42

THE GRAY LADY SET HER BOOK DOWN on the table, then warmed herself some tea. Once the water boiled, she came back with her cup and found me touching that silly book cover. All black, the words in silver lettering. Mysteries of the Unknown. *Angels & Demons*.

Below that title was a large illustration. An angel in silhouette, exactly as you'd imagine: bird wings extended and the body in flowing white robes. Light streamed from behind so you couldn't see its face.

"Well?" she asked, and sipped her tea.

"On the way over here, I saw they were holding some kind of rally," I said.

"What?" She gulped from her cup.

"There was a whole crowd over by the water."

"Probably Laguna Lake," the Gray Lady said. "What made you think of that?"

"I was thinking I'd probably feel safer around them than I do around you and Claude."

"Don't lump me in with him," Ms. Henry said. She took both teacups into the kitchen. I hadn't even sipped mine. She ran hot tap water, and it made a hurried splash against the sink. A gurgle came out of the drain.

"Well, what would you need?" she called out.

I went to the kitchen doorway.

"To cure all this mistrust," she continued.

"I could use a doctor," I said.

She dropped the teacup she'd been handling, then picked it back up and ran it under the water. Squeezed dish soap onto a sponge and started cleaning.

"You're feeling that bad? You don't seem like it."

"I don't *always* complain, Ms. Henry."

When she was done with the first, she started on the second. She smiled to herself. "No?"

She meant to be lighthearted, but I couldn't oblige.

"I need a doctor, Ms. Henry." I rolled down my shirt sleeve and redid the button.

I stepped into the living room, grabbed my jacket off a chair, and pulled it on, slid the belt loop back around my middle. I touched the back of my left hand to my forehead, but I couldn't be sure if my fever was worse or better, because all my skin felt hot.

"I can give you some medicine if you're feeling weak."

"More aspirin?"

The Gray Lady stopped running the water.

"There's a mobile health screening truck. Actually, they park it right by Laguna Lake on weekdays."

"You talking about one of those vans that check your blood pressure? Because I don't think that's the problem."

"No, Mr. Rice. There's a heavy homeless population near the lake, so the truck caters to them. It offers more comprehensive care."

I grabbed the back of one dining chair and squeezed the wood until my anger drained. Really, I wanted to kick over the table but didn't have the strength.

"So I tell you I need to see a doctor, and you tell me to get in line with a bunch of bums?"

"Claude and I have to go to Contra Costa County. It's urgent. But I'm sending you to Laguna Lake to get care. They'll look you over, help you out, then you take a cab and wait for me here. That's the best I can do on short notice. You've been getting your per diem?"

"Nobody told me there was one."

"Fifty dollars per day. I gave a hundred fifty to Claude this morning. He was supposed to put it in your hand when you finally came out."

"Claude and I have had trouble ever since we met. He hates convicts and I hate cocksuckers."

Ms. Henry opened a counter near her fridge. "He's not charming, but he works. Anyway, I've got some cash here. Take these phone cards too."

"Phone cards!" I laughed. This was only getting worse.

"How about food stamps?" I asked. "Can I apply through you?"

She laid the money, the cards, and her phone number on the countertop, and I picked them up. I walked back into the living room, and it seemed even larger than it had just minutes before, nearly empty, cavernous. Hollowed out.

I asked her, "What's the point of all this space if there's nothing inside?"

She ignored me, took up her cell phone, flipped down the mouthpiece, and extended the wiggly antenna. She said, "Claude and I will drop you off."

But I was already at the door. My pride wouldn't let me get into that Town Car just now.

"I'll walk," I said.

Even slammed her door as I left.

NOW, IT WAS QUITE DRAMATIC that I told the Gray Lady I'd walk all the way to Laguna Lake, but it was a bluff. Walk to Laguna Lake? With my knee? And a fever? Maybe even some kind of poison running through me? Forget that. I just said it because I'd seen a bus stop right in front of the Washburn estate when Claude first drove me in.

When I got to the bottom of the steep, winding perimeter road, I found the guard station and the stone front entrance. The guard on duty warned me that I'd have to wait, though, that buses around there ran slow.

Coal becomes a diamond in less time than it takes to catch a bus in Garland. I waited so long that I saw Claude and the Gray Lady leave in the Town Car. Felt so foolish that I stepped back and blended into the fence as best I could. Once the car reached the far bend of MacArthur Boulevard, I stepped out again. Still no bus on the horizon.

Well, damn.

I really *would* be walking.

43

I REACHED LAGUNA LAKE in about two hours. Yes, *hours*. Feeling both cold and feverish, dragging my right leg, and a fire running up my left arm. The burning sensation had traveled a little higher now, from the forearm to the upper half. A slow-moving toxin. I was practically crawling by the end. Leaning against walls, people's fences, cars, streetlamps. I wouldn't have blamed the police if they'd picked me up for public drunkenness. The idea of that screening truck only became more attractive as I moved. I'd scorned the thing when Ms. Henry mentioned it, but I'd curl up in its wheel well to get a shot for the pain. So I pushed on and pushed on.

Three buses passed me along the way, but I was never at a bus stop when they did. I'd figured I could hail a cab, but they didn't do that in Garland. You couldn't just wave and have them stop. You had to call their dispatchers or catch one idling at a train station, which was just the last aggravation for me. At that point I decided I'd walk all the way or die. That would really teach Garland a lesson. Needless to say I wasn't in a tender mood when I reached Laguna Lake.

Turned out those people I'd seen, the ones gathered at the base of Laguna Lake, were there for a protest. Their signs displayed words like *preserve* and *respect*. A small crowd of people, a multiethnic congregation, the kind of gathering you don't tend to see in real life, only in bad films.

We got to watch television in moderation when I was a kid. The Washerwomen didn't consider it unholy. For instance, they followed college football (Bethune-Cookman Wildcats!). And I remember all those

flicks from the eighties, like the Death Wish series, where you'd see
street gangs with members from every racial group. Asian and black and
Latino and white, maybe even a Native American guy. (You could tell because he wore a headband and had long, straight black hair.) Those
gangs were meant to be menacing on-screen, but they always made me
laugh. What crew was this? I'd wonder. Had gangs really figured out
racial unity as the rest of us failed to grasp it? Those were some very en-
lightened thugs! I guess the directors didn't want to offend anyone, but
as a result they told everyone a lie.

But here at the lake I'd finally come across a multiethnic crew in reality. A Bay area church led by a preacher who clearly emulated Mr. Jim
Brown. The preacher had that stern firmness you find in the brothers
who broke their backs in the sixties but survived. This preacher was all
shoulders. Bald as a stone. Wearing the kind of black leather trench coat
they stopped making in 1985. Somewhere in that man's wardrobe lay a
matching black leather baseball cap. For sure.

He spoke to his congregation under a colonnade at the base of the
lake. They held candles, raising palms over the flames when a strong
wind blew, and dropping their hands a moment later even as the wind
continued. But the lights never went out, which seemed like the kind of
tiny miracle that can fortify one's faith. They listened to the preacher,
and I walked closer to hear him, but reached a woman at a small folding
table first. She looked like she hadn't eaten in decades, but by choice.
Devoutly healthy, fervently fit.

"Want to buy a candle?" she asked. "The money goes to our food
bank."

"How much?"

"Whatever you've got. Most people are giving five."

I had one of those in my wallet now, and she handed the candle to me
after I paid. But when I tried to walk off, she grabbed my slacks near the
waist, and I hopped back because the only other touch I'd had in a
month was way down in that sewer.

"You'll need this," she said.

She handed me an AAA battery about as thin as one of her fingers.
The candle wouldn't work unless you popped a battery into the handle.
I looked back at the folks under the colonnade, reflexively cupping their
hands over the plastic flame when a breeze started. Then letting go
when they remembered the light was fake. Hard to tame certain instincts. I slipped the battery in my candle and it lit. I waved it at the lady.

"Electricity," I said.

Passing her, I reached the sermon. The preacher had a surprisingly
nasal voice. He spoke quickly, breathed heavily, and radiated the frantic
energy of a boxing coach.

"What you have to understand, see, is that this is the last straw. This is the last straw's last straw!"

"Yes!" a man in the crowd yelled.

The preacher said, "The success of any society must be judged by the life of its worst off. No other calculation will do."

"Yes!" a woman screamed.

"But what if the worst off are never even counted? I mean, how long do you put your faith in the census taker if the census taker never comes to your door?"

"Not long," another voice offered.

The preacher clasped his big hands and shook them.

"Now, on Tuesday the mayor spoke of better times coming to Garland."

"Hah!" someone called.

"Well, I'm going to surprise you because I agree. I want to feel welcome in Garland. I want you to feel welcome too. I want us *all* to step inside the tent. You remember what Luther said? 'A house is not a home when there's no one there . . .' I know. Please excuse my singing!"

He dropped one hand and rubbed the back of his neck with the other.

"But *that's* the real question, isn't it? Always has been. Who is welcome?"

The preacher turned, walked to the water's edge, reached down, but couldn't quite get his hand in there. The lake sat a little too low. So he stood and came back to us, looking at his dry hand as if it had disappointed him.

He spoke quietly.

"When our mayor made his plans to rejuvenate Stone Mason Square, he faced one big problem. All those folks sleeping on the sidewalks. Where do they go? Well, you and I know because we've been feeding more of them over the last three months. They've been relocated as far as Fresno. Our mayor treated the square like an anthill. Just kick it over and send those bugs on their way. Being treated like that, I can understand why someone would blow it all to pieces! And from all reports, Mayor Brandy plans to do the same here. To resurrect Laguna Lake. Which sounds fine, but will everybody be welcome in that paradise? Or will some of us, the worst off, be locked outside the gates?"

I looked around for journalists, but saw none and wondered if this congregation would really be able to inspire some interest. I admired the preacher's idealism, but so many people were struggling. Could a handful of homeless folks compete with a war or a weak dollar?

But then I felt a powerful guilt and remembered my trip to the Library months before. We sent that man off our bus. Drove away and left him in a snowstorm. The preacher and his congregation might as well have been protesting me. I dropped the electric candle into my coat pocket. I walked away, alongside the lake, on a concrete path that surrounded the greenish waters.

Finally the gray concrete of the path turned different colors, white and green. There was so much goose shit mashed into the ground that it discolored the pavement. A row of wooden benches ran alongside this path in an S shape. Parents sat with their children. The children threw food to the birds. Vagrant pigeons and ducks poked at everything. Bread, birdseed, or balls of paper.

I saw pelicans, cormorants, terns, and gulls. Angry geese moved in teams. I wandered forward. Couldn't lift my left arm because now my shoulder boiled. I was so exhausted that it helped me in a way. My mind stopped registering pain and fatigue. I entered a meditative state. As long as I didn't rest, I could walk all day.

And then, from a hundred yards off, I saw him. Sitting on a bench with his legs crossed at the knee. Though I'd never been given a picture, I had no problem recognizing the guy. The Unlikely Scholar we'd idolized. The enemy of the Washburn Library. The traitor. The fanatic.

Solomon Clay.

44

SATURDAY MORNING FOR A CHILD in a so-called cult was not that different from Saturday morning for most other kids. We wanted to watch cartoons too, we wanted to play. The difference is that we put on church clothes instead.

We weren't going far, not even to the other side of our apartment building, but the trip stressed me out anyway. Me and my sister both. Daphne took her longest showers on Saturdays, and I looked out the window of our fourth-floor bedroom to watch the boys in the street. They were doing what I wanted to do. Slinging jokes and kicking one another and dancing through those liberated weekends.

The morning I'm thinking about now, I was leaning at the windowsill, but didn't long to play with those boys quite as much as when I was younger. I was only ten but felt like a veteran. I'd survived an untold number of skirmishes with those kids. So it wasn't that I wanted to play with them, just that I wanted to play. And anyway, our whole community was feeling a bit sad and anxious because one of our own kids had been taken: Veronica Gibbons, a sixteen-year-old girl who liked to dye her hair crazy colors, no matter what her parents or the Washerwomen said.

A social worker had come by claiming she was taking Veronica for lunch and a simple interview, but Veronica never came back. She was put into foster care, and her parents were told that she wouldn't be returned. Child endangerment. That's what they called it. They took her on Tuesday. Her parents so scared they seemed crippled when we visited to show support. Sitting on the couch, watching a television that wasn't even on. Four days later, on Saturday, I leaned at the windowsill and wondered if Veronica felt scared out there.

I felt shocked, but I can't say Veronica's abduction (later, in the press, they called it "liberation") was a surprise. Renouncing Christmas, denigrating the Church, revising the Bible, even my father's new trucks added to the strain. Maybe the neighbors just had enough. All those grievances led, finally, to this Saturday. It's a famous date, at least locally. November 8, 1975. Neighborhood kids called it the Night of Thunder.

My mother came into the bedroom that morning and told me to get away from the windows. She pulled the curtains closed again and squeezed my shoulder too tightly. Carolyn Rice was as skinny as my dad. And she could never grow her nails very long. Not on her toes or her fingers. They were dry and brittle, and because of that she never wore nail polish. She didn't talk with her hands like me and Daphne did. She hated to show them to anyone, even us. So she squeezed my neck and let go just as quick and crossed her arms again. She tucked those hands into her armpits. She did this automatically, all the time, and never realized it made her seem perpetually angry. She had a good sense of humor, but you'd never know it from that stance.

"Put on your suit," is all she said.

Then she went to the bathroom door and nearly punched it off its hinges, so impatient with my sister's stalling. She went inside and pulled Daphne out the shower. My sister and I shared a bedroom, so I waited in the kitchen while Daphne dressed. I heard my father in their bedroom. He'd returned from the road on Thursday, two months earlier than scheduled.

Big band music played on his little alarm clock radio. I heard the opening and closing of drawers in there. I'd seen open suitcases the night before. He wasn't planning to leave us. For all his faults he'd never do that. This afternoon the Washerwomen were running, all of us I mean. We wouldn't lose one more child. Time for a mass migration. An exodus.

My mom left Daphne and came to me. She picked at my hair until it was a relatively round little Afro. Then she looked me over, tightened my tie, kissed my ear (going for the cheek, but I was fidgeting), then she went back into her bedroom. I felt warm air rush from under the door, and the big band music became louder. My mother was so anxious and distracted that she left the pick in my hair. But I didn't even have time to pull it out before my sister appeared.

Now that Daphne had been put in motion, she didn't even ask me to come with her. She just dragged me out by my wrist, while I fought to stay. The pick fell out along the way, its metal tines pinging against the tile floor. We bucked along through the kitchen, into the living room, and out of the apartment. I dragged back as best I could, but Daphne was fifteen and she had our father's strength. The rangy kind, which isn't about muscle. It's all starch. I weighed more than her (and I didn't weigh much), but if she'd wanted to, Daphne could've lifted me over her head. I believed that.

So the two of us walked out of apartment D23 in our duds. My little blue suit even had a blue vest. Daphne's white handbag matched her white lace socks, and she wore an aquamarine church dress. But she was proudest of her black kitten heels. They were the one thing of hers I never touched, and even as she dragged me down the hall, I wouldn't get near them.

In that hallway we found the other eleven children left in the Washerwomen's community. Fourteen of us had made this march just the week before. I've got to say that we were well trained. Leave that many kids on their own for even a minute, and you can bet six of them will put their lives at risk somehow. But I only remember two boys who ever skipped out of our Saturday services, and even they only missed it a few times. We weren't conscientious only out of fear of being punished, and that's the part that seemed hardest for outsiders to understand. When everything went bad and the police took our statements, when reporters tracked us down, there was only one thing they refused to believe: that we'd *liked* so much of this life.

So it wasn't a long trip to church. A walk of less than two hundred feet. From our apartment to the Washerwomen's. The floors of our apartment building were shaped like an uppercase *F*, so for me and Daphne it was a walk from the bottom of the letter up to that first tong, turn a right and walk to the end. Ring the doorbell of apartment D3 and enter holy ground.

If that's all it took to get there, then why did my sister and I get so stressed about the trip? It's because the walk was a bit of a gauntlet thanks to those same boys I'd been watching outside. They loved to creep up the stairway on Saturday mornings, crack open the heavy black door, and bother us as we marched to Saturday service.

If we were lucky, they might just heckle us. Open the door and shout things like, Paging Dr. Jesus! Or they might yell, Tiiiiiiiits! (The taunts weren't *always* about religion.) But worse was when they felt bold enough to step into the hallway and throw handfuls of pennies or gravel. Sometimes they just left bags of garbage in front of our apartment doors.

How'd those boys even find out about our Saturday morning ritual? I don't know. None of us was going to brag that at ten A.M., while regular kids were out playing tag, we suited up and spent the daylight hours kneeling in a living room. But children are clairvoyant about what makes other children squirm.

That morning Daphne and I met up with the other kids and walked toward the door of apartment D3. We kept looking back down the hallway as we moved, waiting for the neighborhood boys to appear. But they never showed up. We thought maybe they'd heard about Veronica and today they'd kept away out of sympathy. I don't know if this was true, but it's what we thought. And this only made us feel worse. Things must be really bad when teenage boys feel sorry for you.

For that reason I wanted to get inside the apartment. In the hallway my clothes felt like a clown suit, but inside they would return to vestments. My best friend, and pretend cousin, Wilfred, rang the bell. The Washerwomen opened the great door.

Obviously all three of them didn't answer. It was Gina, the oldest, who let us in that morning, but when I remember them, it's hard to think in singles or even pairs. They were a trio, from the first day to this, the very last.

"I'm so glad you could come," Gina said.

Like we had a choice!

Gina reminded me of a duck. The way its head leans back toward the tail so that it seems suspicious of all it sees. She was the one you didn't lie to, the oldest and least fun. Everything out of her had a lesson attached, even that greeting. "I'm so glad you could come" was meant to imply that *of course* we had a choice and we'd made the right one by appearing on time. Not a bad bit of wisdom, I guess, but I still preferred Rose's greeting. Rose was the youngest of the three sisters. Whenever Rose answered the door, she'd just look at all us kids gathered there and say, "Who are you people?"

But I don't want to downplay Gina's appeal, especially that morning. She watched us as we stood at the door and didn't say one thing to cheer us up. Instead, as we passed her in single file, she touched the top of each head, and it was a reassuring pressure. Kids like a firm hand. We'd been in danger of floating off into our fears, but Gina pulled us back down.

"Can I use the bathroom?" I asked Gina after she lifted her hand. I wanted to fix the dent she'd made in my Afro before I saw Rose.

"I don't know," Gina said. "Can you?"

"May I use the bathroom?" I corrected.

"Of course you may," she answered.

Quickly I popped past my sister and Wilfred. They'd already found the other kids in the kitchen, all crowding the third Washerwoman, Karen, as she prepared biscuits for the oven. I twisted the dirty silver bathroom knob only to find Rose inside. She yelled, "Shut that door!"

Which I did.

Jumping into the bathroom and closing us both inside.

"Usually people step *out* of a bathroom when they find it occupied," Rose said.

"Not me," I whispered.

"I guess not," she said. "Why are you covering your head?"

I dropped my hands.

"You need to run a pick through that hair," she said then. "I can't believe you left the house with it all dented like that."

I felt too embarrassed to speak.

But then I noticed that I hadn't caught Rose in the middle of a shower, though she was standing in the tub. On the rim of the tub, actually. With the small bathroom window up, her face to the opening, and in her right fist a lit cigarette. Nine more, smoked down to butts, were in an ashtray. She was as anxious as us children. Imagine catching Buddha biting his fingernails. *You're* nervous?

"Wave your hands or something," she said. "Kill the smell. Be useful."

I flapped my arms, but there wasn't much use in pretending I was getting rid of the smell. I kept hopping but only because it made Rose smile. Better to see her grinning than in fear. But I don't want to pretend I was all about cheerleading. I was ten, and Rose an easy fifty-five, but my feelings for her weren't entirely innocent. Where do crushes start? Close to home.

Rose had the kind of body that collected in the middle. Her skinny face and neck matched her skinny calves and ankles, but the parts in between were swollen. And not in a good way. She wasn't buxom, she had a belly. She wasn't pretty. None of the Washerwomen really were. Rose's thin eyebrows ran together in the middle, and I never saw droopier ears. And yet that woman captivated me all the same.

"You're not supposed to be smoking," I said. "Karen is sick."

"My sister's not sick. She's dying."

Rose went onto her toes, put her face against the mesh window screen, brought her right hand to her mouth, and pulled on that cigarette. She let the smoke sit in her cheeks so long it came out her nose first. She blew the last of it through her tightened lips.

"Have you kids been talking much about Veronica?" she asked.

I pointed at her and the cigarette. Strident as only a child can be.

"You shouldn't be doing that," I scolded.

It hung on Rose's lip as she leaned back against the wall.

"You're right, Ricky."

"Then why don't you stop?"

The cigarette dropped from her mouth, into the tub, and Rose stooped to get it. When she stood again, she sighed deeply. She said, "King Jesus is perfect. Not me."

45

HOW CAN I DESCRIBE what it felt like when I first saw Solomon Clay?

This way: there's only one train platform in Manhattan that looks like a missile silo, that's the 53rd and Lexington Avenue stop on the E line. Its low ceiling makes the space feel cramped, but the tunnel walls curve out in a way that plays with your depth perception. These crazy dimensions make the track look fantastically long. Instead of six hundred feet, it feels like six hundred miles. You see the headlights of a Queens-bound E approaching, but it's hours before the train reaches the platform. And you watch. There's a tremor in the ground as it charges forward, moving fast enough to kick up a hurricane. You lean out, and the wind snaps your clothes. It tries to pull you down onto the tracks. Then the lead car is so near you can see the motorman in his booth. If you don't step back, that train will turn you into paste. Your heart dips but you can't pull away. The metal wheels screech. Your teeth begin to ache. The silver thunder rushes closer. Threatening to detonate.

Solomon Clay marched toward me.

"Ricky Rice!" he shouted. "You black bastard."

Parents sitting at the benches looked shocked, a few covered their children's eyes by mistake instead of their ears so the kids still heard him. Solomon Clay clapped as he approached, applauding the way he'd scandalized the proper folk. He was his own best audience.

"I was starting to think we'd never meet," he said. "I figured I'd just stay in one place and let *you* catch up with me."

I'd been right about one thing: the man was old. He looked like he'd been around for centuries, but I don't mean shriveled or worn down. More like a cast-metal sculpture. He'd been dipped in bronze and left to dry. When he spoke, his cheeks resisted the movement and he had to strain to show his teeth. His features remained so stiff that his head seemed like a bust. When he clapped his hands, I swear I heard the faint clanging sound of a hammer striking a metal plate. But that's not how I knew who he was. What had I recognized from one hundred yards away?

Of course it was the clothes.

Solomon Clay wore a six-buttoned black wool double-breasted suit with a cream-colored tie peeking out the collar. A black Borsalino beaver fur fedora tilted to the side. A pair of black brogues on his feet, and over them, the final touch, white satin spats. Spats! He shimmered inside his platinum threads. A god in gods' clothing.

And I was just a tired junky in a knockoff Norfolk suit. All thoughts of the screening truck disappeared. "I'm here to kill you," I said.

"If you can make a fist, I'll be surprised, Ricky. You look terrible."

I looked down at my hands, both left and right, and couldn't manage much more than twitches. If he'd just let me sleep for about thirty hours, let my legs get the feeling back in them, I'd be able to do some damage. Maybe if I could have a nice spa day first.

Solomon said, "I knew the man who wore that suit before you."

I crossed my arms over the jacket as if he was going to snatch it off my back.

"His name was Dabney Reed, and he died in those clothes."

"This is a copy of the one I saw in the picture," I said. "Harold and Fayard showed me."

Solomon pointed at me and laughed, but it came through his stiffened lips like a hiss.

"Those are *the* clothes in the picture, Ricky. They aren't knockoffs. They're relics."

I found myself undoing the belt loop in my Norfolk suit without thinking. Dabney Reed had died in this coat. And who knew how many others before him? It was like finding out you're sleeping on your uncle's deathbed. I got the coat off, but then I couldn't drop it on the ground or throw it into Laguna Lake. My hand just wouldn't release it. I didn't want to wear it, but I didn't want to let it go. I looked to Solomon Clay, but he wasn't studying me.

"This here is Martin," Solomon Clay said, and a man stepped from behind him.

I say man, but it was a kid, one of the homeless teenagers I'd seen all over Garland. A white kid with long, unwashed hair and tattered clothes. His skin splotched red on the cheeks and forehead. His face looked like a piece of chewed bubble gum. The boy had an enormous backpack, which he dragged on the ground, probably carried everything he owned. This child, Martin, stood in the shadow of Solomon Clay.

"Spare anything?" Martin asked me, sounding both sad *and* antagonistic.

"You're hanging out with beggars now?" I asked.

Solomon Clay sniffed. "I wanted a better class of people in my life."

"Anything?" the kid insisted.

But I didn't answer him, I couldn't. I saw a brown splotch on one sleeve of my Norfolk coat and couldn't stop staring. It was only dirt, that's what I told myself, but another part of me became convinced it was Dabney Reed's blood.

Martin shook his head. Mr. Clay patted the boy.

"Ricky here was a heroin addict for almost twenty years, and somehow he thinks he's better than you, Martin. I told you that's how it would be, didn't I?"

Martin looked at me when he answered. "Yes, you did," he said.

"Now you ought to get on," Solomon said. "And do what you're meant to do."

Martin looked even younger now, with that mopey frown. His adult body hadn't grown in. Not more than fifteen, and a small fifteen at that. He lifted that backpack, swung it around, onto his shoulders, and nearly sent himself to the ground.

"This is for you," Solomon said, and handed the kid a folded hundred-dollar bill. He did this slowly, theatrically, so I wouldn't miss his generosity. It was the first thing to draw my attention from my coat.

Martin took the money. He stared at the bill in his palm. Finally Solomon Clay pushed Martin forward, and the boy stumbled off.

"You should've given him a few bucks," he said.

"I didn't want to."

Solomon Clay nodded. "I relied on that."

But, frankly, I wasn't bothered about Martin. Instead I found myself watching the way sunlight reflected off Solomon Clay's face. Or was it coming *from* his face? I'd never seen skin burn so brightly before.

There are ancient paintings and sculptures that depict Moses with small rams' horns. He wasn't born that way, of course. It was a transformation that occurred after Moses came down from Mount Sinai with the Ten Commandments, the effect of having seen the true face of his God. But the horn imagery came about because of a mistranslation from the Hebrew to the Latin Vulgate. It wasn't that Moses sported shofars. It's that the word for "horns" is the same for "send out rays." Our friend Saint Jerome made a translator's mistake. It can be tough to go from one language to another. The Washerwomen grappled with this problem as they wrote their holy book, what to update, approximate, or delete.

When Moses returned from the mountain, his skin glowed. It sent out rays. I remembered this as I watched Solomon Clay's gleaming face.

"Where have you been?" I whispered, though I didn't even mean to ask the question, to flatter the man with my curiosity. The words just came.

"You'll never get there," he said. "It's too late. You're already corrupted."

"Me *and* Ms. Henry are here to kill you."

"Is that supposed to scare me more?"

"It should," I said. "She's no joke."

He waved his right hand in the air.

"That's your team? A dopehead and a . . . Before she came to the Library, that woman sold for pennies. You understand me? Twenty dollars! That's what men paid to love her. You could love her in the mouth or right up the ass, but *she'd* have to pay *you* to go swimming up that funky tweeter. That's your Ms. Henry. A shitstain whore."

"I suppose you were born in a manger?" I asked.

Why defend her? She certainly hadn't done much to earn it. Not from me. I guess it was an instinctive reaction. Partly about Ms. Henry, sure, but even more because Solomon Clay seemed to think I was the kind of man who could be turned so easily. Adele Henry had been a prostitute. Was that supposed to make me wretch? Come on. He'd have to do better. I remember Gayle, the last woman I'd truly loved. She'd stabbed me right through my shoulder with a shish kebab skewer, and even still we'd almost had that baby.

Almost.

Solomon Clay sighed. "They give you an order to kill me, and you just snap to it?"

"I had my doubts," I said. "But now that we've met, I'm hoping to cap you in the chest."

I wasn't feeling brave exactly, but the way he'd spoken about Ms. Henry had sparked a tempest in my heart. I was as surprised by this reaction as Solomon Clay.

"This is the whole problem, Ricky. Right here. When you showed up at the Washburn Library, for all your problems, you were still your own man. That's my guess. But you spend a couple of months being coddled and you sign your soul away."

"My soul's my own," I said.

"That's what you think, but it isn't so. Remember what the Voice told Judah Washburn?"

I am the father of the despised child.

"But let me tell you what my years with the Library taught me. Oppression doesn't make people noble. Give any of us a little comfort, and we'll kill to keep it. The despised become despicable. The Unlikely Scholars aren't any different. Adele finally taught me that. I had to *leave* the Library to find the Voice's children."

I turned around then, a snap so fast it actually hurt my neck. Where had that boy with the backpack gone? Where did you get to, Martin? Solomon Clay saw me searching, so he grabbed my shoulder and pointed.

There were these big wet splotches, like dabs from a giant painter's brush, along the concrete path next to Laguna Lake. Already one hundred yards away, Martin lifted his heavy bag back onto his shoulders after having taken a moment's rest. And when he did, there was another splotch on the concrete.

Solomon said, "What if I told you the reason Judah never heard the Voice again is because it was disappointed in him?"

"A blind black dude got all the way across the country with two chests of gold," I said. "I think Judah did pretty good."

"And that's it? The Voice blessed Judah so he could sit on some money in the woods? Nah. The Voice stopped talking to Judah because Judah was selfish."

It was hard to follow Solomon Clay. My mind was on Martin over there. I meant to run in that direction, but I was bone-tired. And, I hate to admit it, I was scared.

"Now you've got that mutt, the Dean, giving orders. But he wants to hoard the blessings, just like Judah. Keep the Voice his secret out there in the woods. But that's exactly why he's never heard it directly. He doesn't deserve it. He's not deciphering the Voice in those field reports. He's only eavesdropping."

Martin really started moving. He'd basically retraced my steps. From the benches to the walking path, and now he'd reached the congregation under the colonnade.

Martin looked at the congregation ruefully. They'd built a fire under there. It burned in a small metal barrel. Battery-powered lights weren't going to keep those people warm. Flames rose out of the little drum. How long before they'd be forced to put it out? Not long probably, but they'd let it heat the air while they could.

"How can you know all this?" I asked. "It was two hundred years ago."

Solomon Clay squeezed my arm tight. "I know because the Voice found someone it could trust. Your team is too late. The Voice already spoke. Two years ago. To *me*."

Martin dropped his head, straining forward as the heavy weight of his bag resisted.

There were only a handful of folks under the colonnade now, the preacher in the leather coat among them. Now that Martin had started toward them, he really sped up fast. That's momentum for you. From a walk to a trot to a jog to a run. But the congregation stayed largely unaware because the minister was speaking to them again.

Martin's face lost all expression as he rushed toward the congregation. He looked blank, empty, void. I reached out with my right hand, clutching at the air.

I felt a cold touch across my heart.

"But those people are on *your* side," I whispered.

"Being sympathetic doesn't spare them. I'm here to sweep the board clean! Then the despised will inherit the earth."

The boy reached the barrel, and, as he did, he flipped the backpack off. He found a new strength. When he'd stood in front of me, he'd been a frail boy, but he'd aged.

Martin lifted the soaking backpack and dropped it inside the barrel.

The congregation had no time to run or even shout.

Their fire ignited the explosives inside.

Martin just stood over the little barrel. He didn't try to escape. Martin used his last moment to wipe his moist hands on the front of his jeans. I saw him do this.

Then there was a blast so loud it rocked everyone in the park. Children and adults went flat on the ground. Laid out and dazed. I went down. No one screamed, that's the amazing thing. Kids didn't cry. A row of ducks watched solemnly from the shore.

The roof of the colonnade went up directly, like a gentleman lifting his hat. Flames shot out from between the columns, and the congregation cooked in the blaze. I smelled it. Clouds of black smoke blotted out the sky, and the roof finally crashed down again, landing at an angle.

Mr. Clay stooped over me. "Do you want to know the order the Voice gave me? Just three words."

I could move my body, but the shock of the blast paralyzed my mind. I couldn't meld thoughts with actions. When I tried to hit him, grab him, I only found myself slapping the ground. My back stung sharply, between the shoulder blades, like I'd fallen on a stone.

Solomon said, "Vengeance is mine."

46

ROSE FINISHED HER LAST CIGARETTE and left me alone in the bathroom. I might've stayed until sunset if Karen, the middle sister, hadn't come to the door. She twisted the knob a few times, lightly, so I'd know someone was there, and then waited patiently until I unlocked the door and opened it. She was in the hallway, kneeling, pretending to sweep crumbs from the clean floor.

"Did you think we wouldn't miss you, Ricky?"

Because of her illness Karen had gone down to about a hundred pounds. She'd been nearly two hundred once. There were deep lines on either side of her mouth, and her eyebrows were falling out. They were only two black pecks above each eye.

"You can't come in here," I whispered.

"Why's that?"

"It smells."

"Did you have a BM?" she asked.

"No!" I shouted. Not only out of embarrassment, but because *BM* was a term reserved for three-year-olds. I was ten.

Karen leaned backward, resting her butt on her feet, and moved her head left to right trying to see inside, around me.

"It smells like cigarettes," I explained.

Karen put her hand over her mouth and nose.

"How many did Rose smoke?"

"I don't know," I said. "A lot."

Karen tapped the door with her pointer finger. "Let me in."

So I opened the door, and she lifted herself into a crouch and walked inside. Then she stood, sniffed, and smiled at me, for me.

"Can't hardly tell," she said.

Then she coughed like hell for more than a minute.

Her beige pantsuit flapped, loose around the legs and midsection, though they'd been snug only a year before. When she recovered, Karen said, "I don't want you telling Gina about Rose's smoking, okay? Even if she asks."

"That's lying."

"Yes it is, Ricky. I'm telling you to lie to my sister."

A kid is always confused by straight answers from adults. He's not taught to expect them. But, after thinking her answer through, I thought I understood so I said, "Okay."

Karen Robins, feeblest of the Washerwomen, but the one who actually kept our community's pulse. She touched the sink. Rubbed at water spots on the faucet.

"We're going," she whispered. "You've heard?"

"Yes, ma'am."

Now Karen held my cheek. "And are you ready?"

I didn't know the answer, so I didn't speak.

"I'm very tired," she said.

I put her hand on my shoulder, led Karen out into the living room.

It was a large space, as cold as a meat locker, chilly in the winter because the windows never sat evenly in their frames. We strove toward spiritual triumph, but we still lived in a tenement.

There were state maps on the walls and little red lines drawn over various routes. This was how we tracked the movements of our parents, the pilgrims. I felt I knew the back roads and highways of the United States intimately because of all the time I spent staring at the pathways of our folks. We'd get letters from them with detailed driving directions or bus routes, read them aloud on Saturdays and then draw the lines onto the maps with red pens. When our mother couldn't send letters, she'd mail me and Daphne local newspapers and we'd pore over them closely to guess at the routes between this town and the last. In this way Carolyn Rice educated us even from a thousand miles away.

I entered the living room to find the other kids already sitting on the floor. The state maps covered all four walls. America wrapped itself around us.

Gina and Rose sat on a yellow sofa pressed against one wall. Karen joined them while Rose gave me a suspicious eye. Gina poured iced tea from a green plastic pitcher into tall cups for herself and her sisters. I refused to look back at Rose and tried to find an open spot on the cut pile carpet.

There were a few spaces, one right beside Daphne, for instance, but forget that. I spent enough time with her. I went farther back, toward the windows, but not because I hoped to peek outside. That's just where I'd find Miss Annabelle Cuddy.

Annabelle Cuddy, I still remember you! With your mouth of crowded teeth and your enormous Puerto Rican Afro. You bit your nails until your fingers bled. We danced to Ohio Players' "Fire" at a party in your living room.

But despite what I might've wished, she was not my little girlfriend. She hadn't decided between me and Wilfred, my play-cousin. I wonder if everyone, everywhere, used that term, *play-cousin*. It means that we weren't related, but always close. Best of friends. Real road dogs. Right up until Annabelle Cuddy became beautiful.

So, my dawdling in the bathroom meant that Wilfred had enjoyed many minutes alone with Annabelle, and apparently he'd used them correctly. When I got there, she was leaning close as he spoke into her ear, and when she tipped over too far, she threw her arm around his shoulder.

And the thing about Wilfred is that he actually had shoulders to grab. Same age as me, but he looked twenty. How is that possible? He'd skipped six grades of puberty. What ten-year-old is big enough to dunk? This was happening in 1975, don't forget, not the modern era, when sixth graders look ready for the NBA.

But I had two things over Wilfred. The first is that he was big, but lumpy, and self-conscious about it. When Annabelle put her arm around him, I watched him shift, afraid she'd drop her hand and graze his gut.

The second thing I had over Wilfred Tanner? The boy had no game. Wilfred thought "Pssst!" was how you woo a woman.

I sat down on the other side of Annabelle quick, trying to think of something funny, but before I could speak, the oven bell rang in the kitchen and Gina left the room. We'd been going through this ceremony for years, so it was natural, nearly automatic, for all the kids to stop shifting or flirting and sit straight until Gina returned to the living room. We'd lived with the ritual too long to do otherwise.

The Washerwomen only brought three things with them from Florida: their guns, their love of college football, and any number of outstanding Southern recipes. Gina carried a plate of hot biscuits, a bowl of butter, a bowl of sugar, and a stack of napkins all on a tray. Combine the biscuits, butter, and sugar to make yourself some sugar bread. In the desert the Jews received manna. In Queens we were also blessed.

This might seem crazy, feeding so many young bodies that much sugar and then tucking them indoors until nighttime, but really we only bounced around for about half an hour, and after the rush we settled into a daze that lasted well past lunchtime, ready to listen quietly for hours. A truly prostrate audience. The Washerwomen weren't fools, not on their worst day. They knew how to hold on to our crowd.

"Before we eat," Gina said, covering the biscuits with a napkin.

The first thing, always, was to pray.

Karen stood slowly. Rose and Gina followed. Then all the children stood and bowed our heads and recited the Lord's Prayer in the traditional words. They didn't try to revise, improve, or modernize everything in the Bible. Some things were ideal already. We prayed for Veronica's safe return. We were thankful to find all our parents back with us. We asked for protection while our community moved.

"The peace of the Lord be with you always," Rose whispered at the end.

"And also with you," we responded. Then we moved around the room, shaking hands.

Annabelle stood between Wilfred and me. She waited to watch us wrestle for her touch. Wilfred even turned toward me, flexing his fat hands. I think he actually meant to fight, right in front of the Washerwomen. That boy was in love! But I turned my back on both of them and walked over to my sister.

"Peace be with you," I said as I shook Daphne's veiny hand.

"Peace be with you too, Ricky."

I looked back at Annabelle and Wilfred. They were so surprised by my exit they hadn't even touched each other yet. He looked confused. When she turned to him now, she didn't smile. It was one thing to choose Wilfred, another to be stuck with him.

Daphne smacked me in the back of the neck, just for jokes, and then moved on. I kneeled in front of a small girl, Altagracia Munoz, who already had her hand out.

She shouted, "Peace be with you, Ricky!"

"Peace be with you," I said.

I understood her excitement. The adults might have been preparing for our mass migration, but I couldn't be anxious right then. This was my favorite part of the day. Shuffling around and greeting one another. So much of our lives was spent memorizing the stories of the Bible (both the Washerwomen's version and the King James) or listening to a sermon, meditating on concepts like goodness or sin, that it was easy to forget the glory of simple affection. To look into another person's eyes and wish them peace. To have them do the same. The surprise is when you realize you both actually mean it.

Now the living room felt cozy despite the cold.

Those state maps along the walls had been put up so we could track our parents, the red lines illustrations of their commitment, but eventually the maps themselves became manifestations of our mothers and fathers. Here in Queens, with us, in their place. So it became a habit to even wish peace to these sheets of paper because then we were still touching our loved ones. And even though our folks were actually back in Queens that morning, we tapped the maps out of habit, moving from one wall to the next.

Peace be with you Maryland, Montana, North Carolina, and Utah.

Peace be with you Mississippi and New Mexico.

And so on, crossing the living room as if we were settlers traveling the Great Plains.

We treated the whole nation as our family.

The practice of shaking hands as part of the greeting was pretty much the standard in churches by that time. But it wasn't the only choice. There were congregations that only smiled and nodded to one another, nothing more. Some hugged. There's even something called the *holy kiss*; that one goes back to Saint Paul. But it wasn't used much. You know how people get about smooching just anybody, even somebody they know. But that afternoon I felt it was time for a return to Saint Paul's holy kiss and suggested it to Annabelle after Wilfred had no choice but to leave her side so he could shake hands with the other kids.

I saw my opportunity so I slid up beside her and explained the history of the greetings. Handshake, hug, and wave. And, of course, that holy kiss. A practice in need of revival. Did she feel holy enough, *Christian* enough, to bring it back? For instance, she could begin with me. . . .

Annabelle, I remember your exasperation!

But also, my lips blessed by yours.

47

WHEN I WOKE UP AGAIN, a paramedic and a cop stood on either side of me, but I wasn't lying on the ground anymore. I'd been propped up on a bench.

"I thought you weren't supposed to move an unconscious body," I said to the EMT.

"I didn't move you," she said.

The cop watched me. Was that a flash of recognition on his face? I'd been shifted one hundred yards farther back from where I'd fallen when the bomb went off. Solomon Clay must have dragged me to safety. That's what I thought first. But then, I'd been safe right where I was, so why pick me up, really? Then I figured that moving me made for perfect cover. He wasn't running from the scene, just helping a victim.

The cop asked, "Where were you before?"

"Way up there." I pointed, and my left arm throbbed. The whole thing, from fingertip to shoulder. Like I'd dipped it in boiling water.

"Do you feel any pain?"

The EMT leaned forward as she asked this, and her shirt hung away from her boney frame. I looked right down there and saw her bra, a robin's-egg-blue. I should've mentioned my forearm, but suddenly it wasn't my primary concern. Now my nipples stung real bad. I leaned forward to answer her question and flinched when my skin scratched my cotton shirt.

"Is it your chest?" she asked.

I nodded, pulled at the belt of my Norfolk jacket. Had Solomon put this back on me? It took me a couple tries to get it open, and while I flailed, the EMT and the cop just watched.

"That's some outfit," the EMT said.

The cop nodded, spoke louder than he had the first time. "Are you visiting from another country?"

I finally popped the belt, opened the jacket, undid the shirt, my chest stinging the whole time. Only to find there were no marks, no scratches, burns, or cuts. Just my two brown nipples.

The EMT leaned close, poked at me with a gloved hand, frowned a little.

"You can close that up now," she said. "I don't see anything wrong. Why don't you let us take you to the hospital?"

But she spoke without enthusiasm. I think I wasn't interesting enough. Weren't there some people out here who'd experienced real trauma? She hadn't become an EMT to give middle-aged men chest massages. And while I needed the help, I felt paranoid, like I'd been broken down to my very last compound, the part that's kin to a cornered rat. If they had me in a hospital, they could handcuff me to the bed. I know how it sounds, a little unrational, but I wanted to find a dark corner where I could curl up alone. Let me get my thoughts together. So I told the EMT I didn't want to go in for treatment, and she walked away before I finished the sentence. Leaving me with the policeman.

He asked for basic stuff, name and address. He asked to see some proof so I gave him my New York nondriver ID. After writing down that info, he asked why I'd come all the way to Garland since my ID still listed my home as Utica, New York. He waited for a suspicious answer. But I offered the blandest one instead. I came out here for love. I'm in this city because of a woman. This disappointed him so much that he returned my ID quickly.

Nearby a table with bottles of water was set up next to an ambulance, and I took a bottle. A pair of geese nipped at an EMT's jump kit as if it was a lunch box. Survivors with the worst injuries had already been evacuated, so only the lucky ones, like me, and the unlucky ones, the corpses under the colonnade, remained. Plus lots and lots of spectators, huddled in agitated crowds along the sidewalks across the street from Laguna Lake. First Stone Mason Square, and now this?

I walked the block toward downtown Garland and reached a pay phone. I moved with an awkward stoop so I wouldn't brush my nipples against my shirt fabric. Whenever I did, it felt as if I'd rubbed my chest with broken glass. I kept stopping and reaching into my shirt because I expected to see some blood. But there never was any. Finally, I stopped redoing the Norfolk jacket and let the front hang open.

At the pay phone I went through each of the calling cards the Gray Lady had given me. The first two barely had a nickel left on them, but the third had a whole dollar. I got Ms. Henry's voice mail and told her what happened at Laguna Lake. I didn't ask her to come find me.

As soon as I hung up, I felt the boiling feeling from my arm again, but this time it had moved up to the space between my left shoulder and my neck. It felt like a hand grabbing my scruff, and I turned expecting to find the cop from the lake, but I was alone. The throbbing near my neck threatened to knock me out. When's the last time you ate? I asked myself. Maybe all this could be solved with a little food.

But even after my third convenience store spicy tuna roll, I wasn't feeling any better. I went back in for a big bag of guacamole chips and even a pint of orange juice. When I finished those, I bought a cherry ice cream bar. Thank goodness for that per diem. I didn't eat this way normally, but this time I just passed through the aisle, and whatever I craved I ate.

I missed my rented room back in Utica, the one right over a barbershop where the owner sold weed back by the hair dryers. The closest thing I had to a home base in Garland was the By the Bay hotel. I used my last phone card to call a cab. Let them fight their war without me.

THE CAB LET ME OFF on the corner of 35th and San Pablo Avenue, but instead of using the front entrance of the hotel, going through the lobby, I went around back. Seeing that homeless boy, Martin, under Solomon Clay's influence made me a little suspicious of every vagabond I passed. Mr. Clay might've pushed the boy forward, but it was Martin who'd carried that explosive bag. He'd played a willing part. So now even a crowd of smokers in front of By the Bay might be more soldiers in Solomon Clay's indigent army. Using the service entrance seemed safer.

I went one block over, and was amazed by the new quiet. On San Pablo Avenue you heard the jabber of a hundred cars as they moved along the street, but the loudest sound on Chestnut Street was the wind thumping against the old houses across the road. It was so hushed that I even heard the window blinds snapping in one of the hotel rooms above me.

Looking up, I saw that loud old blind swinging out through one room's open window like a big gray flag. Those blinds probably hadn't been white in years. I didn't like seeing it slipping past the frame, though. What if someone tripped and went right through the opening? I looked at the ground, expecting to see a suicide, because, you know, this day hadn't yet been morbid enough. But I found nothing.

The blind snapped again up there. Once, twice.

It wasn't until I reached the back parking lot that I realized the sound of the blind had stopped. I looked up just because it made me feel better to know the window was safely shut. The sun flashed in my eyes. I point this out to admit I was squinting, not a perfect witness, in other words. But I still know what I saw: the big gray shape had slipped out of the window. It pressed against the brick wall of the hotel. But, rather than being carried off with the wind, the big gray shroud moved up.

It climbed.

48

NOW CAME THE HARD PART for the Washerwomen, giving a sermon in a storm.

We'd said our peaceful greetings, then pounced at the snacks set out by the Washerwomen. Within minutes the kids were all in fifth gear. I mean amped. Talk about getting high! Methamphetamine has nothing on sugar bread, and trust me, I know.

Thirteen live wires in their living room, and even the Washerwomen looked a little scared. I could tell because this whole morning they hadn't sat as close as they did now. We whooped and hopped, damn near hollered, and the living room floor bucked beneath us. Even the state maps on the walls began to flutter. We made the whole country shake.

I wonder if it wasn't this kind of thing that actually turned our neighbors against us. Not that they were religiously intolerant, but they didn't want to live above or below a juke joint that got loudest on Saturday mornings. Right when they meant to rest. Maybe the first few calls to child services only happened because the Washerwomen conducted riots in their living room.

"All right now," Karen said. "All right."

But it hardly registered. Not over all our noise.

Gina and Rose stayed seated, but clapped loudly. Hushing and shushing, but I don't believe they meant it. I think they *liked* the way we turned all wild. A preacher loves to channel the ecstatic much more than motivating the mild.

"You must control yourselves," Gina said, but her voice wavered.

Only Rose spoke loud enough just then.

"You all have been going on long enough!" she shouted. "If I have to get off this couch, I'm gonna whup every one a you."

Most of us had the good sense to heed her threat. We'd heard rumors about what the Washerwomen had done in Jacksonville, because parents hide the truth as well as sieves hold water. But we didn't believe those stories were true. Not Gina, Karen, and Rose. Still, a respectful fear remained. We quieted down.

Everyone but me.

I couldn't help myself. Most of the kids had restricted themselves to one or two pieces of sugar bread, but that morning I'd had three. Okay, four. This wasn't a cafeteria. The Washerwomen didn't keep track of how many times you got in line. And by the second piece of bread there were no lines, just a mob grabbing at the tray. I didn't always eat four pieces, but I'd been gluttonous this time. Let's say it was nerves. I might as well have poured the sugar from the container straight down my throat. I was plugged in. That's why I didn't listen. One hundred thousand watts.

Also, Annabelle Cuddy kissed me! It was my first kiss. And Wilfred saw it. It wasn't just the sugar.

And what was I doing with all that power? Imagining things. I guess that's what you could say. Not seeing hallucinations, but living in a daydream. While some of the kids had been dancing and hopping, a bunch of us boys wrestled in one corner of the living room. That's what boys do when we're excited. Or angry. Or nervous. Bored. Pretty much every occasion is a good occasion to get our fists up. And the Washerwomen encouraged this. They were Southern women who had no interest in raising punks. Both girls and boys were meant to be strong. You might fistfight or just argue, but you better not lose.

I'd squared off against some other boy at first, but Wilfred quickly stepped in. He'd basically bumped the other boy toward the stereo set and then come at me. Wilfred was only ten, but easily mistaken for a young man. And me? I might be mistaken for a stick of black licorice.

Nevertheless, I'd hopped on Wilfred's back. You could say I was choking him, but that's probably generous. I like to think I made a nice necklace, at least.

"Now, now . . . ," Karen wheezed, stooped over, as if she might collapse. "Be cool."

Wilfred had probably stopped being real angry after a few minutes of fighting. I sensed this because he hadn't pulled me off his shoulders and squeezed all the water out of me. He was really only giving me a piggyback ride at this point, but in my head I meted out hellish tortures.

I forgot to mention what I'd been daydreaming about, exactly. I was playing out a scene from my favorite book in the King James Bible. The book of Esther. That was my nectar. I never admitted it to anyone, but the Washerwomen's version of Esther just didn't compare. They couldn't match the bloodlust of the ancient world.

No surprise, of course. It's got to be the most mindlessly violent story in the whole book. The one where the Jews rise up against their enemies and, at one point, slay seventy-five thousand of them in one day. That's 3,125 people per hour! Talk about a valley of slaughter! Can you see why this would thrill a boy like me?

Also there's a great moment in the Second Book of Kings when the prophet Elisha is walking through a town called Bethel. Some small boys see him and start yelling, "Go away, baldhead! Go away, baldhead!" So what does Elisha do? Does he forgive? Nope. He curses them in the name of the Lord, and in the next moment two she-bears come out of the woods and maul forty-two children. I used to draw pictures of the she-bears chewing off boys' heads.

In the Washerwomen's version the same moment takes place on the south side of Chicago. The children all taunt the bald prophet, whose name is now Hampton. The kids shout, "Crackhead! Crackhead!" But instead of she-bears this prophet calls forth two rottweilers. The kids still get their heads bit off, so that was pretty good.

So when Rose made her threat to us kids, I didn't register it because I wasn't there. I was back with Esther. How could I, a Jew living in the land of King Ahasuerus, heed the cautions of a woman sitting on a couch in Queens? I was squeezing at evil Haman's neck! (Boo! Hiss!) I couldn't stop until I'd dragged him to the gallows once meant for my man Mordecai.

"That boy is getting on my last nerve," Rose said.

And in my manic state I shouted, "Go have another cigarette! The bathroom's free!"

You ever seen a black woman fly?

When I said those words, Rose launched off that couch. Rose. Object of my adoration. Fifty-five years old and a heavy smoker, but she changed, her every organ revitalized by rage.

She raced across the room, and children scurried from her way. Even Wilfred had the good sense to submit. He tapped my arm, the one still around his neck, and shouted my name. Finally he flung me off his back and fell to the floor, and Rose actually leapt over his big butt. That's when I fully returned to the present. To the Washerwomen's living room.

Rose's eyes were flat and blank, her mouth curled up into the kind of howl you find etched into gargoyles that guard monasteries. She wasn't. herself. Or she wasn't the woman I'd met just an hour before. In this state she might really throw me out the living room window. It was the first time I believed she really might've killed her family.

Had I really just been praising, even celebrating, violence?

Well, let me amend that. I am morally opposed to violence, anywhere and everywhere, if it's directed at me.

In the meantime, being only ten and unable to articulate my new-found respect for peace, I did the next best thing. I screamed.

"Daphne!"

Someone else might've beseeched Jesus, but my idol was already in the room. Daphne Rice. With her hair pulled back into a short ponytail, she had the silhouette of a claw hammer. And she could hit just as hard, let me tell you.

My big sister jumped to her feet.

Rose was nearly on top of me.

Daphne threw herself between us.

Then things got a little nuts.

49

I DIDN'T GO RUNNING into my hotel, but I couldn't exactly run away either. Where would I go? Instead, I stood in the parking lot and tried to convince my mind that my eyes had been lying. There had *never* been any blind flapping out through an open window, and so *nothing* had pulled itself up another two stories and then flopped over, onto the roof.

Somehow my brain wasn't convinced—it refused to let the rest of me move—but it couldn't come up with a better plan. We had to go inside because the outside was even less defensible. At least I had a key to my room. If I wandered the streets, I'd collapse, just one more bum, and there were plenty of those around San Pablo Avenue already.

Go inside, I thought. Let's just get to it.

So I opened the back entrance and found a squad of old men huddled in the service hallway. Three sat on a row of chairs, and the fourth held a video recorder, taping them. I thought I'd walked onto the set of a Sunday morning political chat show. But instead of three old white guys in bad suits, it was three old black guys in bad sweaters. They sat in a semicircle and spoke into the camera, slowly, though they stopped a moment after I opened the door. It was such a confusing sight that I stepped backward, even stammered an apology as the sunlight illuminated their faces.

"Step in or step out," said the guy doing the taping.

I didn't recognize him or the one seated closest to me, but the other two were more familiar. The man in the green sweater had ridden the elevator down to the lobby with me earlier that day. And, sitting in the middle, was that clown in the wheelchair. The guy with all the jokes. I stepped inside, slamming the door shut. Now the director stepped away from the recorder.

"You ruined our shot!" he said.

I slapped the corroded green walls. "I did you a favor."

I expected a louder response, especially from the one in the wheelchair. At the very least I thought he'd crack wise. If the guy in the sweater thought I had looked bad earlier, I must've seemed undead by now. But they didn't speak, none of them. They only seethed. This made them seem more serious. For the first time I actually looked at the cheap camera, noticed the low ceiling and dim lighting. They were filming themselves, but the image wouldn't come out too well. The three men would hardly be seen. The director went back to the camera, his face lost behind the machine.

"Get on now," one of them said. "This is grown folks' business."

What would they do to me if I stayed? The part of me that likes to argue wanted to find out, but my stomach pitched. I couldn't catch a break from my body. The throbbing and burning in my neck had stopped, but in their place I felt a powerful nausea. I left those men because I had to a find a toilet.

I floated from the ground floor to the fourth. Even before I stepped inside the elevator, I imagined myself ascending. As the elevator rose, I was already walking down the fourth-floor hallway. And as the elevator opened, I was already on my bed, comatose.

So I was halfway down the dark fourth-floor hallway before I noticed the broken lights.

Every bulb above my head had burst, and because of that every doorway was cloaked. When I'd left earlier that day, they'd been working fine. I turned around, confused by the change, and one foot ground into the shards of a lightbulb. I bent down to pick up one of the pieces, but dropped it right away. It was still too hot to hold.

I would've run right then, believe me, but I didn't have my balance. Buildings like By the Bay, poorly made and hardly maintained, were famous for falling apart. The uneven tiled floor rose and fell in both directions, and I felt like I was lost on a treacherous sea.

I pressed my left hand against one wall to steady myself. I felt some vomit coming. My nipples felt raw again. I pressed my right hand against the other wall to help me stand.

But it wasn't a wall, it was the door to a room. Not mine. I couldn't make out the room number because of the dark and my dizziness. I had to lean in nose-close to read the digits: 407. Only two doors down to mine. I could manage that. But when I pushed myself away, trying to get moving, the door to 407 popped open and I could see inside.

The room was decorated in a style I'll call Near-Bum, the distinction being that this mess was in a hotel and not on a cart in the street. Stockpiles of clothes and books and random small appliances. Hell, there might've been a time machine inside, who would know? But, for all this, it was the door itself that deserved the most attention.

It had been smashed in. The handle bent at an angle and chips of wood on the floor.

I turned and looked at room 408 on the other side of the hall and found the same evidence. A damaged door lock, the same easy access, a room as mute as a grave. Instead of following this ugly path toward my room, I traced it backward to the elevator because I am a man who *will* run away.

409, 410, 411, 412. All the same. I reached the elevator and pressed the call button. I stood very still while I waited for it to come, as if that would hide me somehow.

I looked back down the darkened hallway. The problem with shadows is what they hide. Because I couldn't see anything, I saw everything. I felt like I was down in the sewers again. Where was the elevator? I couldn't take the stairs for fear that my tired legs would give out. Imagine that: Ricky Rice escapes a monster but gets done in by some steps.

Finally the elevator arrived. As I stepped inside, I heard a sound in the hall. Wood creaking. I told myself it was one of the rooms I'd been in, just a breeze pushing a door open, but I didn't really believe that.

I stared down the dark hall, both hoping to see something materialize and praying that I wouldn't. Without meaning to I opened my mouth as if I was planning to speak, but I didn't know what to say. A shadow twisted in the hall. It rose so high it touched the ceiling.

I pressed the lobby button, but the elevator door wouldn't close. When I looked down, I saw I was pressing the button that read DOOR OPEN. Even after I realized this, I couldn't pull my finger back. Not right away. It was like when you know you're asleep, stuck in a nightmare, but can't make your body wake up. I didn't actually move my finger. It just fell away from the button.

I heard a wet slap in the hall. No mistaking it. Something dragging itself across the tiled floor. Once. Then again. Movement. Coming toward me.

Why hadn't Solomon Clay taken credit for my attack in the sewer? He didn't even mention it, and he wasn't the modest type. And though I didn't believe Ms. Henry about much, she did seem as unsure as me about what had gone on in the tunnel. So who knew what happened to me?

Now the elevator door slid. There wasn't much space left before it closed.

In the hallway the silhouette seemed to wriggle like an eel, not a man.

Something reached out of the darkness, a flash of puckered skin, all yellowish-green. It slapped against the wall and pulled the shadow forward. But that was the only noise, otherwise silence.

Then I found my voice. I pleaded with that shadow as the elevator shut.

"What did you do to me?" I shouted.

50

HOW MANY WARS HAVE BEEN STARTED over a little sugar rush? More than just the one in the Washerwomen's living room, I'm willing to bet.

Rose came at me, and Daphne jumped into her way. The two bodies tangled and went to the floor. Then Gina leapt off the couch and grabbed my sister by the shoulders. Gina was nearly seventy, but her grip made Daphne scream, and when I heard my sister's cry, I bit Gina on the leg, right through her polyester pants. That's when Rose kicked me in the cheek.

At which point Wilfred stopped the smackdown. He stood at the window, as did many of the other kids now. Must have been something quite dramatic on the sidewalk if it could draw attention from our grappling on the blue carpet.

Wilfred said, "It's a cop outside. Cops."

Gina and Rose let go of me and my sister. Daphne came over and touched my face. She had carpet fibers in her hair, and I picked them out one by one. I looked back to the window, where everyone else had gathered. Only Karen stayed on the couch, too weak to rise just yet.

Daphne looked outside too, but I couldn't motivate myself. I was too busy watching Wilfred use this opportunity to touch Annabelle. She stood at the window, tiny next to his great mass. And when he put an arm around her shoulder, she leaned her face against his chest.

Gina turned back to Karen. "There's two patrol cars parked out front."

Karen said, "They might not even be here for us."

"Well, who else, then?" Rose asked, tapping the glass.

Gina said, "Maybe that couple downstairs finally killed each other."

Rose nodded. "That would be lucky."

Karen cleared her throat and huffed as she stood. Gina hurried to her side to provide a little balance, while Rose stayed at the window, tapping the glass as if she wanted the police to take notice.

We, meaning most of the kids, turned back inside now and wondered what was going to happen next. Maybe the cops *were* here for the Beltrams on the second floor. A couple who fought so loudly they could be heard across the street. Some evenings you'd see faces across the way, elbows out on their concrete sills, gazes trained on the second-floor windows, waiting to hear gunshots.

But it seemed more likely the police had come for us. To take away every child, just like they'd done with Veronica Gibbons. This thought was the worst of all.

Karen said, "We'll send some people down to ask around."

She and Gina moved to the door, but Rose stayed with us. Rose lunged for me.

"Rose!" Gina yelled.

Finally Rose followed. But before she left the living room, she said, "You kids keep calm." Then she took a breath. "Calm as you can."

The Washerwomen left us alone, and we stayed at the window. There were two patrol cars, four cops in all, but they weren't parked directly in front of our building. One to the left and another to the right. They could've been responding to calls from our neighbors on either side. Their lights weren't on, though, and the cops stayed in the car. I watched one, in the driver's seat, take out a newspaper and flip the pages lazily.

Police cars generate interest, but not limitless amounts. Small pockets of people waited on the sidewalk, looking at our building with as much curiosity as to the buildings around us, hoping to see someone in handcuffs. But when the police didn't leap or grab or even mosey, those crowds lost interest, just as we did in the apartment. After half an hour the Washerwomen hadn't returned, but we'd stopped staring down. A few of us ate the last of the sugar bread, but not me. An hour after that the three sisters returned. The younger kids were half-asleep on the floor. The older ones, like Daphne, sat up like sentries just underneath the living room windows.

The Washerwomen cleaned while we watched them. They cleared the tray, the empty plates and bowls. Took their glasses back to the kitchen. Wiped the table of sugar and crumbs. This was normal, they always cleared, and seeing a return to the routine really calmed us. When they were done, Karen and Rose sat on the couch. Gina came to the windows and pulled the blinds down. She sat with her sisters again.

Even the Washerwomen became drowsy soon. This long period of quiet, the crash after the crest, was normal too. Call it prayer or meditation or transcendence (if you're feeling generous), but we spent the middle hours of every Saturday mute in the living room. All the surprises of the morning passed out of us, the big fight and the shock of those patrol cars, the loss of Veronica Gibbons and even the early return of all our parents from their missionary work. Most of all the looming threat of our impending move subsided. Not forgotten, but set down.

Finally, Altagracia, not more than seven years old, sat up and crossed her legs. She looked at us on the floor and back to the drowsy Washerwomen on the couch. Then Altagracia posed a burning question.

"How come *The Munsters* can't come on every day?"

That popped me right up. Most of the others too. My cheek hurt so I rubbed it. We didn't look at Altagracia, but at the Washerwomen, who rubbed their eyes. Rose bumped the end table, and its glass top rattled.

Gina asked, "How do you know it doesn't come on every day?"

" 'Cause I don't *see* it every day," Altagracia answered, exasperated.

Karen said, "But that doesn't mean it's not on, Altagracia. Just because *you* don't see it. How many days a week do you get to watch television?"

"Two."

Gina said, "Well, then, how can you be sure it doesn't come on the other five days? You're asking the wrong question, baby girl. You should be asking why you can't watch television seven days a week."

"Well, why can't I?"

"Because watching that much television will turn you into a straight fool," Rose answered. "You won't do anything else with your time."

Annabelle Cuddy raised her hand. "What if we only watched good shows?"

Rose asked, "And would you be willing to put your faith in the television producers to make that many good shows? Enough to keep you from seeing nonsense most of the time?"

"That's asking a lot of those producers," Karen added, almost sounding sympathetic.

Rose said, "We can barely fill one Saturday with you each week."

Altagracia hadn't done anything wrong by asking her question. She had good reason to look pleased with herself. She was so happy, in fact, that she stuck her stubby little thumb right into her mouth, too proud to be embarrassed of her habit.

We were meant to ask, and the Washerwomen had to answer. That was the next part of our Saturday service. And as they answered one question, we asked another. The point was to challenge them.

"So maybe you should just work harder," I said.

Rose nearly came up off the couch again. I covered my bruised cheek instinctively.

"What did that boy just say to me?" Rose asked.

"If you offered us more," Annabelle said, "we could visit here all week."

I smiled when Annabelle said that. It felt like she was defending me.

Karen leaned forward now, so far forward I thought she was about to vomit, and even her sisters moved their hands to catch her.

"Seven days a week with a houseful of kids will absolutely kill you," Karen said.

"Or them," Daphne muttered.

Had the sisters heard her? Most of us on the floor tensed, waiting for a reaction, but none came, and I felt so relieved for Daphne.

But even without hearing my sister, the Washerwomen went silent and sad. Karen's statement had them reminiscing, I guess. Maybe to the time before they'd put their families to bed. Gina got up and went into the bathroom for a while.

When she got back, I apologized a dozen times. Figured I'd started us down the path that had led to the anger in the room. Maybe I'd even started it hours before as I clung to Wilfred's fat neck. Better to just say sorry. So I did my apology routine, but Karen wouldn't have it. She didn't want a child's pity, so she snapped at me.

"Are those questions, Ricky? *That's* what this time is for."

But before I could respond, my sister raised her voice.

Daphne said, "Okay, *Karen.* Did you ever think that by keeping all of us out of school and locked away from other kids, you've turned us into a bunch of weirdos? You ever think this is all a mistake?"

How that's for a question?

Karen said, "The pride of your heart has deceived you, Daphne. I snapped at your brother just now, and you got angry. I see that. But your question, is it really what you want to know, or did you just mean to hurt my feelings?"

"Both," she said.

Karen sneered. "If you really envy those children outside so badly, then I'll get up and open the front door for you! You don't have to stay."

I said, "Aren't you just trying to hurt my sister's feelings now?"

Wilfred brought his big legs up to his chest. "Maybe you keep us all closed up so we'll only listen to you."

Rose nodded. "Well, that doesn't seem to be working."

Gina rubbed her right hand on the sofa arm. She said, "You could do a lot worse than honoring our example."

"The pride of your heart has deceived you," Annabelle Cuddy repeated to them.

There might've been a lot wrong with the way I was raised, or at least it was plenty strange, but I can't dismiss the parts that were right. Growing up in a deeply religious household, my mother and I started having conversations about war when I was five. By the age of seven I'd been introduced to the concepts of humility and sacrifice. I was expected to think about realities much larger than my own. Contemplation was considered a worthy pastime for a religious child, and I'm still grateful for that.

Rose punched her knuckles into her own leg.

"You go ahead and get on your knees in front of a television, then. Worship some show. Choose that instead of being devoted to *us.*"

I said, "So you want us to believe in God, or just in you?"

My sister turned to me. Wilfred and Annabelle too. Altagracia gawked.

I hadn't said the wrong thing. I'd just won this little game.

Rose said, "Ricky's right. We're elevating ourselves."

Karen nodded, agreeing with Rose. She smiled at us weakly.

Karen said, "I remember Gina, Rose, and I were sitting in church on a Wednesday evening in March 1961. We had a guest preacher that night, Reverend Cook. People called him 'Constant' Cook because he traveled the country giving sermons *every* night, had been on the circuit for two straight years. He had a nice way of talking, hardly ever raised his voice. And he had a lazy right eye. He called attention to it. Said he wasn't born that way. One summer morning, when he was twelve, he had a vision so powerful it just knocked the right one off center."

Karen patted her heart.

"A vision of a church as big as a football stadium, every seat filled. And down on the fifty-yard line Reverend Cook preached the gospel that had built this temple. That Jesus wanted us to be comfortable. The good Lord wasn't happy if we weren't rich. And why *not* us? Our people had sacrificed and died! Only an evil God would deny us our due. And our God wasn't evil, he was good. . . ."

Gina and Rose spoke together, "All the time!"

Karen continued, "When Reverend Cook said he'd build his first church right outside Jacksonville, my sisters and I volunteered to help. We'd worked as treasurers for our church and had a talent for managing money. Reverend Cook would send us what he'd collected as he traveled, and we kept the books. We started fund-raising around the city ourselves. We turned every stone. We shook out every coin purse. We knocked on every door. Even white folks'.

"But do you know that once we had the money, we just couldn't give it up? When Reverend Cook came asking to see the ledger, we showed him falsified notes. We knew he wouldn't catch on quick because Reverend Cook was illiterate. And he had a trusting heart. We didn't even feel ashamed of ourselves. We were protecting that money from Reverend Cook's hubris. He was going to build a Tower of Babel. That's how we justified our actions. And when he raised a stink with the local preachers, it wasn't hard to get those men on our side."

Gina said, "They appreciated a few small donations."

Rose added, "Minor offerings."

Karen sighed. "When it all fell apart, Reverend Cook carried the blame. So many people had given money, but the only one to prosper was him! That's the gossip that spread. Reverend Cook had become one more false idol. No one took this harder than Reverend Cook himself. He felt so terrible he shot himself in Missoula.

"And we actually felt lucky, you believe that? With him gone who could prove what we'd done with the money? And all those preachers we'd paid distanced themselves from Reverend Cook too. Painted him as a serpent from the safety of their pulpits."

We'd never heard any of this before. Usually the Washerwomen obscured their personal history, saying they'd arrived in New York with a mission, nothing more. As Karen told us this now, I looked at the carpet, not her. I felt shocked by her honesty, like I'd been by Rose's in the bathroom earlier. But I appreciated it as well. Today we were being spoken to like adults.

"Most Christians speak of doubt like it's blasphemy," Karen said. "But doubting God is like disbelieving oxygen. Thankfully neither needs our permission to sustain us."

At that a whole bunch of us inhaled a deep breath. It was as if we meant to test Karen's statement. When we exhaled, we were still alive.

Karen continued: "Doubt is an essential human trait. But why? If we really believe we're created by God, then nothing got dropped in by accident, right? So what purpose does doubt serve? If it's useless to disbelieve heaven, then maybe we should cast our eyes to earth.

"Who do you believe in and why? Do you see men wise in their own eyes? There's more hope for fools than for them. Jalen deceived Eric. Larry deceived Jalen, Saul fooled the astrologer in Birmingham. Half the Bible is folks getting tricked! So maybe we rethink doubt. Not as our enemy but our ally.

"Think of King Jesus as our greatest doubter. Who saw the order of society and taught us to defy it. Who saw the ugly urges in ourselves and taught us to resist them. As we navigate through the powerful tides, doubt is our rudder. If we'd questioned our motives, maybe Reverend Cook would be alive. So many others too . . ."

Karen clapped her hands. They were worn down to nothing but bones and veins because of her illness, hardly any flesh left on those fingers. And yet when had she seemed stronger, more vital, than right now?

Gina whispered, "Come up here, Ricky."

When I say I won the Washerwomen's game, it sounds a bit silly because the reward was just three hugs. Still, every child yearned for the privilege. We threw out those challenging questions to earn their praise, the question that would lead here, to the lesson. And to the wisdom the Washerwomen felt they *must* pass on.

I stepped over my sister's hand, bumped into Wilfred's knee with my thigh, came around the sofa table and into Gina's arms. She cradled me so tight I thought I'd turn into a diamond.

Then I moved on to Karen, who could hardly lift her arms now that her sermon was over. She rested her head on my shoulder and leaned her body against me. I held her up.

Last in line was Rose. Her thin arms kept me at a distance. "I'm sorry for hurting you, Ricky. I lost my temper. Will you forgive me?"

"Yes, ma'am," I said.

Rose pulled me down by the shoulder until her lips rested against my ear. The warmth of her breath, it nearly overcame me. Rose smelled like jasmine, a scent she loved to wear.

She said, "Doubt is the big machine. It grinds up the delusions of women and men."

51

AS I STUMBLED OUT of By the Bay, I wondered who I could call for help. Dear old Mom? No. Call the Dean and beg for camaraderie? Not likely. Why not try the police? That's what some people would do. But not me. I dialed the Gray Lady's cell phone.

Why? It was that moment when Claude drove me to her cabin on the Washburn estate. When she opened her front door looking like a hot mess. Wearing only a housedress and slippers. Lack of makeup making her face look uneven and old, and yet, when she saw me, all she did was wave her hands in the air. Had I met anyone else so willing to expose themselves? Look at me. I'd agonized over sock garters. A little style is a good thing, but you can't trust a person who won't be ugly in front of you. I wouldn't say I trusted her yet, but I was willing to try.

The Town Car arrived a few minutes later, and when they found me, I was crouched beside the pay phone. The heat in my neck had returned, but now it had spread to the middle of my back, right between my shoulder blades. The car pulled up, and I was doubled over, but I kept an eye on that hotel.

"You're hurt," Ms. Henry said, stepping out of the car so fast I thought she'd fall.

"Be careful." I pointed across the street. "There's something wrong."

"In the hotel? Your room?"

"Something is up there."

She stared across the street and up to the fourth floor. I followed her eyes but had no idea what she expected to see. It's not like the fourth looked any worse than the third or the fifth. Then I saw her scan the skies.

"You can't go back inside," she said.

"Why don't we send Claude in with it?"

She pointed at our ride. "Just get in the damn car!"

I tried to move with some dignity, but even ten steps felt impossible. I lifted my left foot, and my back burned. Lifted my right foot, and my nipples chafed. Each step aggravated one of my conditions. I felt dizzy. My headache returned. I'd nearly drowned in flop sweat by the time I reached the car door.

Claude didn't even turn around to look at me. Just turned his radio up.

After the explosion at Laguna Lake the National Guard had been mobilized. One nearby unit, anyway. And sent to protect . . . San Francisco?

They were talking about this on every local station. The Bay area was getting help, but somehow Garland *still* wasn't top priority, even after two explosions in three days. While the attacks had started in Garland, they'd obviously move on to San Francisco. That seemed to be the governmental logic. Or possibly Berkeley. At the very least the terrorists would upgrade to Oakland, right? Garland wasn't even the redheaded stepchild. It was the baby abandoned on a street.

Claude sped onto I-580 fast. I couldn't offer much more than a heaving sound to Claude and Ms. Henry's debate about where to go next. I felt flush and nauseated. My head throbbed, my chest hurt, my ankles even swelled.

Then I vomited, though there wasn't much to it, mostly bile.

"Did that boy just puke in here? This is a Lincoln Town Car!"

"Open the windows," the Gray Lady said.

I had my hands on my knees, and she reached into the space between my arms and chest, pressed the silver tab until the window scrolled all the way down, then pulled her arm backward again. That's the closest we'd been yet.

"Larry!" Claude yelled. "You're going to clean that up right now!"

He had one hand on the steering wheel, one hand in the glove compartment, and no eyes on the road. He merged onto the freeway with some sort of sixth sense as he threw a rag at me.

"His name is Ricky," Ms. Henry muttered.

Claude didn't hear her, but I did.

Claude drove down the highway for only a minute or two. He pulled onto the shoulder, clicked his hazard lights, and got out. Came around to my side so he could look at the mess himself. Was he cringing at the sight of my vomit or the sight of me?

"I need a hospital, Ms. Henry. Not some screening truck."

"Try to make it," she whispered.

Then I screamed, "Call me an ambulance!"

"You're an ambulance," Claude said.

"If we got one, they'd take you to Kaiser," the Gray Lady explained.

"Then meet me at Kaiser."

"No, no," she whispered. "That's not possible."

Claude dropped the rag on top of the little puddle between my chukka boots and pressed on it with the toe of his Florsheim shoe.

"He could go to Alta Bates," Claude said.

She shook her head. "We can't afford either one."

Claude must've realized he wasn't soaking the vomit with that rag, only pressing it even deeper into the carpet, so he pulled his foot off.

"Let's take him to Highground," she said. "They'll look at him for free."

Claude slammed the door shut, but opened it again. Now he leaned forward—head into the car—then stepped back and shut the door a second time. Walked around the bumper, but returned to my side, opened the door for a third time, and said, "Who's going to pay for this?"

With his chin he motioned toward my vomit stain.

"I don't know how much it would cost, Claude."

He stared at the Gray Lady. "Let's say seventy-five dollars."

She opened the green handbag. "I'll make out a voucher."

Claude slapped a hand down against the roof.

"No more vouchers. No promissory notes. No fucking IOUs! I've tried to get someone over at the Washburn place to cash these things like you said they would, but they tell me I have to wait until Mr. Washburn is around to sign off. Well, that man must spend every day of the week on his yacht because I've never seen him!"

Claude glared at Ms. Henry, and I looked at her too. She held two vouchers, a pair of red tickets, which she shuffled as if this was a card trick and now one of them would turn into cash.

Claude growled. "Well, your credit is no good. You're not qualifying for any loans from me. I get cash, right now. I don't care if it's five dollars, but I get it in my hand or I'm going to call my old friends on the force and turn the two of you right in. I don't even know what kind of bad shit you've got me into, but I better get paid to be in it at least."

The Gray Lady said, "You work for the Washburn Library. I know things have been a little tight, but that's got to count for something."

"Lady, I'm just a man with a car for rent and a few connections."

I turned to him. "Claude, I know you don't like me, but I'm really serious here. I need help. Something is *wrong*."

He didn't spit at me or mace my eyes or any of the meanness I expected. Instead he turned his head and stared down the highway.

"I'm not rich," he whispered. "I can't just be running around having adventures like I'm some fucking kid. Give me a little something and I'll get you there."

Claude had been a man of authority once, but life had reduced him to a scavenger now. It was hard, in that moment, not to sympathize.

"Do you have anything, Ricky?" the Gray Lady asked.

"Whatever's left in my jacket pocket."

Claude dug into my right pocket quickly, then tried to reach inside the left but had to roll me toward him so his hand would fit. He found two fifties. He snapped them. Stood outside and held the bills up to the sunlight, making sure he could find the little authenticating strips.

While he did that, Ms. Henry snuck her money out of her purse. Stuffed it down her shirt and tucked it safely into the bra. When Claude looked inside again, Ms. Henry held her purse up for him and he rummaged around, but found no money. Not even coins.

She was good.

52

MY HUG WITH ROSE was interrupted when my father knocked at the Washerwomen's apartment door. Well, not just *my* father. All our fathers. And mothers too. Every adult. Eleven couples in the hall. Rose pushed me back, stood up, and went to let them inside.

Because Sargent Rice was the first one into the living room, I blamed him for the end of my special moment. What a surprise! A son who's hard on his father. What's next? A daughter who won't cut her mother a break?

My father walked in, saw me standing by the couch. He knew I'd posed the winning question. "You did well," he whispered, but I turned away from him.

The other Washerwomen stood up as the rest of the adults entered the living room. This was so rare, parents in there on a Saturday, that Altagracia cried. Nothing yet, not even the story of Reverend Cook, had scared her more than this. She cried, and it spread to the littlest children. Their parents went over to console them.

But it didn't work. Being held was even worse than being seen. They'd stormed our sanctuary, and we hated them for it. Most of the older kids looked down, as if they were ashamed of their parents. Only Wilfred stood up and went to the window rather than stay with his surprisingly small mom and dad. He pulled at one of the blinds and peeked outside.

Karen spat, "Get back from there."

His mother and father each grabbed a hand and pulled Wilfred over to the rest of us.

Gina spoke to the kids. "We're going now. We're ready."

I thought we'd say a prayer together, but no one offered anything. Parents just held their children and led them toward the front door. The state maps on the walls showed their wrinkles now. Each one as rumpled as linen slacks. They weren't coming with us.

Good-bye, Texas, Indiana, Idaho.

My mother clapped for Daphne, and my sister went to her. My dad knelt down next to me.

"Ready to get?" he asked.

He smiled, and his round face actually looked excited.

"You're going to leave me behind," I said.

He sighed, stood up. "Why'd you have to say that?"

"You did it before."

He nodded and shut his eyes. It was an old story that I'd used against him plenty of times. A mistake my father once made. He'd dropped me someplace where he shouldn't have. He'd left me.

"Not really worth talking about right now, little man."

I frowned. He grabbed the top of my shoulder and squeezed it.

"I'm here," he said. "I'm here."

And this is really why I'd brought up Sargent Rice's old mistake. He'd drifted too far from us, from me, to share love, but pain travels greater distances.

"Okay," I said. "Let's go."

And he dropped his hand. Stooped down. Looked into my eyes. Found his smile again.

Then we left the apartment side by side.

EVERYONE HAD ASSEMBLED in the hallway. That's not quite true, makes it sound too organized. We'd just gathered into a little mob. Half the parents in front and half in back, and in between the two stood the Washerwomen and the children. I ended up next to Wilfred. I peeked ahead, searching for Annabelle.

"Where are we going?" I asked Wilfred. As if he knew. Sometimes even I mistook his size for maturity.

"We not going anywhere," he whispered. "It's cop cars outside."

"They were out there this afternoon."

He looked down at me.

"It's like ten of them now. Lights on and everything. Up and down the block. Even a truck."

I didn't believe him because I didn't want to believe him. How were we going to get past a roadblock like that? Our parents had filled small suitcases for each of us and handed them out. I was annoyed because my mother and father wouldn't know what I wanted to keep. They'd probably just packed a bunch of clothes.

They had their own bags lined up against a wall. Even less stuff than us. Just book bags. We were traveling light, which I thought might help. We could probably go down and out through the laundry room, into the weedy backyard. There was a fence to climb, and then we'd be in the backyard of a store that sold Indian ingredients and saris, both. We might have to break in, but we could just file out the front of the store and get free. Disappear into the night. The adventure of this idea actually made me feel better for our chances. How could we get caught if we did something so daring?

A few of the parents went to the stairwell door, and then I felt even better. Better that than the rickety elevator. One last trip down the sanctified steps. It would be so quiet inside the stairway that I could say my little prayers, and God would even hear them because I believed He dwelled there.

The first set of parents went down, and the Washerwomen next. We kids mingled in afterward. The last of the parents followed in the back. But the staircase got crowded quickly. The space could hardly hold us. I thought I only felt claustrophobic because Wilfred stood next to me, but it didn't take long to realize it was more than that. We weren't moving forward, we weren't going any farther down.

The parents in the lead stopped at the bottom of the landing.

Kids bobbed their heads trying to see the problem.

One parent broke off, went down to the third floor, but the others stayed and kept us from descending. And my own father, who was at the back, ran up the stairs, toward the fifth floor. For a moment we heard nothing, then this faint snap. It came from the top of the stairwell and from the bottom. Then the noise got closer.

The stairwell lights were going out.

Lightbulbs popped, and darkness came at us from both sides, a pair of rising waves.

My father finished first. Then the other dad, Mr. Ward, returned a little out of breath. Sweat ran down the front of his nose. I looked up, waiting for them to smash these last two lightbulbs so we could scurry away in the shadows. But they didn't do that.

The fourth-floor lights stayed on.

"Consider this our lifeboat," Karen said.

It wasn't just me, but all the children, who looked down at the stairs, confused.

Karen hushed us, as if our stares made sounds.

At the far bottom of the stairwell I heard the door groan as it opened. A man's voice shouted up at us from the lobby.

"Hello! Hello! Please be advised that the New York City Police Department has been ordered to enter your premises!"

We didn't speak, not the adults or the kids.

The man at the bottom shouted again. "We are sending units up. If you are armed, you will be shot. Do not fuck around!"

I turned toward my dad, expecting what? I don't know. An explanation. A solution. Even a wink. But he didn't offer any. He, my mother, and the other adults only locked their arms in a way that penned the children in. The parents at the bottom did the same. I watched my dad. His eyes were shaking so bad I thought they'd spin right out of his head. Sargent Rice seemed even more scared than me. I never understood him so much as I did just then.

"It's all right," I whispered to him, but I can't say if he heard me because Karen cleared her throat just then, and it drew our attention to the Washerwomen.

Rose spoke. "Get your backs up!" she shouted. "Stand straight!"

Which we did without thinking.

Gina smiled. She pointed down the stairwell, into the dark.

"They think we're shipwrecked, but we know the song of the sea."

Gina reached into her pants pocket and came out with her gun.

I lost my breath. I mean straight hyperventilated. I dropped my stupid little suitcase. Its clump echoed so it seemed like all the kids had dropped theirs too. The stairway seemed to get hotter, but it might've just been the fear inside me. I reached out for some hand, any hand, and found Wilfred's. He didn't pull away. He didn't push me back. Wilfred held on just as tight.

Karen said, "It was two years before Reverend Cook's death really hit me. Our part in it. The guilt became so strong my sisters and I, we about lost our minds."

"Yes," Gina said. The gray pistol looked feral in her veiny hand. Something that wouldn't be tamed.

"By that time we'd built three houses right near one another, on property we bought with Reverend Cook's money. I was sitting in my kitchen, snapping the ends off some green beans I'd just washed. I heard a woman's voice calling my name from the parlor room.

"But when I reached the parlor, it was empty. Then I heard her calling from the entryway, and when I got there, it was empty too. When she called for me again, I followed, but didn't expect to find anyone. That voice led me through whole house, all three floors. Every bathroom, every closet, every bedroom. It took me so long to pass through every room that when I ended up back in the kitchen, the beans I'd washed were bone-dry. I felt this shame come over me, so powerful and cold I thought my heart would give out. What was the point of all this space if there was nothing inside?"

Karen said, "I felt like I was standing on Reverend Cook's grave, and I finally faced the truth. We'd mistreated that man. Me, my sisters, those preachers we'd paid off. Their congregations. Even our families. We tore apart his church and used the timber in our hearth. Everyone who'd benefited shared the guilt. A guilt that would last for all their living days. That night we pardoned our families. But more was required of us. We were meant to build a new church. Save as many souls as we could from the corruptions of this world. The temptations we knew all too well."

Karen lost her breath. She inhaled slowly. She whispered, "I hoped to rescue so many more. But I won't be ungrateful."

Which of the kids cried first? None. It was our parents. Some were scared, but maybe others felt relieved. Escaping this hard world is number one on many wish lists. Some grown-ups yelped, and the kids followed.

"Stop that shrieking!" Rose demanded. But who could listen to her now?

The stairwell door creaked down below, and I imagined a mouth opening as wide as it could go. How many cops were they sending up there? The same sound came from the roof, a door moaning there. They must've climbed up the sides of the building. I heard the shuffle of boots on the steps, but they weren't coming too quickly. No one wants to run blind into a potential firefight.

Karen and Rose reached into their clothing now, maybe their pockets or their purses, I can't say. It really looked like they pulled those guns out of their sleeves. They looked calm. I mean their faces. Flat and empty eyes.

I didn't scream because it still seemed impossible. The Washerwomen weren't going to shoot anyone. No, no, no. But then each sister put a gun to a child's head, and those kids still didn't run. Bernard Hubbard. Greg Yarbrough. Altagracia Munoz. It sounds insane, I know, but we refused to accept that they'd pull the triggers.

Until they did.

The stairwell didn't get loud, like I would've expected. It got quiet instead. My ears went fuzzy, like I was nearly deaf, and I couldn't even make out my own voice. Not the voices of other children either. But I felt that we were screaming. I mean the vibrations of our cries hit my chest. The bodies of those three children slammed against the stairwell walls. I can't say I saw Altagracia die. I guess I refused to see.

My sneakers squished in blood. I knew that's what it was, but wouldn't look down. The walls of the stairway stank with it. I felt as if the hall had filled with steam, a new heat that wet my hair, the side of my face.

The Washerwomen put their guns to the heads of two more children, Keisha and Olivia Broom. And now one adult, Mr. Ward.

-Sssswump!- -Sssswump!- -Sssswump!-

The pulse of those muddy gunshots felt like an unearthly heartbeat to me.

Now our meekness was beat by our fear. The first six victims had basically fed themselves to the pistols, but the rest of us kids would have to be caught. We went crazy trying to escape. We clawed at each other, climbed over one another. Beat at each other with our little suitcases. We did anything to get away.

The police finally reached us and scuffled with the parents at either end. Were our folks defending the Washerwomen at this point? Hard to say. The cops couldn't be expected to differentiate. They wrestled anyone who'd hit puberty.

Then the last of the stairwell lights went out. I wasn't sure if the police knocked them out or if they broke in the struggles. Each cop came down with gun drawn, one hand on his pistol, the other underneath to steady his aim. And in that second hand each one held a flashlight. As they moved in the total darkness, their flashlights threw bright spots onto us, onto the walls, onto the ceilings.

I didn't register them as flashlights. Blame a boy's imagination, but in my frightened mind something of the dead had been released by the bullets. Those weren't lights. They were souls. The spots and flashes zoomed across our faces, and I felt I was being touched by holy kisses, my lost friends saying good-bye.

Rose stood right behind me suddenly. She pressed the muzzle of the gun against the left side of my neck. It was still hot from the previous shots. I felt that fiery bite and I knew what came next: bullet escapes the barrel, slug enters my head.

I kicked backward instinctively. Harder than I'd ever hit anything. And Rose fell back. Just a step, but it was enough. The lights continued to dance against the ceiling. It looked like a map of heaven. I moved hysterically. I didn't run, I climbed.

I never doubted that our parents could do this to us. Tackling and smashing the cops who'd finally arrived. Even offering up their own children to the guns. I never doubted they could do this because they adored the Washerwomen too.

You should've seen me all those times when I ran errands for my family. If the cashier at the supermarket told me the bill was $3.25, I'd ask her to go over the figures with me again, right there, even recalculating the tax on the back of the receipt. If the DON'T WALK sign flashed at me on the street, my first instinct was to ask, Why not?

Doubt is the big machine. That's what they told us. It grinds up the delusions of women and men. Well, we doubted every damn thing the world could offer.

Except them.

Even though us kids heard snippets about what they'd done to their families. Even though we'd guessed at the rest. We didn't want to believe it. That hadn't been Gina, Karen, and Rose. Those were the Robins sisters. Three women we'd never met. What happened in Jacksonville had been the nightmare, but our community was meant to be the dream.

But now I fled from Rose's pistol, practically flew over the girl in front of me. I grabbed at her hair and used that to pull myself over her. One of her hands tried to grip the railing, but the railing was slick with blood. I felt no remorse, only the grind to survive. But as I leapt forward, I looked down. The flashlights, those lost souls, illuminated this girl's face.

I'd grabbed the back of my own sister's head.

Daphne.

I didn't see her pupils because they'd rolled into her skull. She looked blind and helpless. She screamed, but everyone was screaming. She'd been moving forward, but now bent backward because I pulled myself over her. Then Rose's gun touched Daphne's temple.

-Sssswump!-

It's true that Rose squeezed the trigger, but I sacrificed my sister to save myself.

Our community ended that night. News of the gunfight spread so fast that everyone in Queens claimed to have heard the shots thundering.

A cult called the Washerwomen committed mass murder. That's how the papers reported it. That's the story that stuck. Every adult who survived got jail time, including Sargent and Carolyn. Group homes for the children. Daphne and the other victims were given to the grave.

No mention of the lights was ever made.

53

HIGHGROUND HOSPITAL SHOT UP before us, an off-white tower on a hill. It stood amid small, quiet, private homes and hovered just above busy 14th Avenue. Claude pulled into a curved driveway and stopped in front of glass admitting doors.

The Gray Lady leaned close to me so she could look at him around the headrest. "Why don't you just park in the garage?" she asked. "We might be here for a while."

"Parking on the sidewalk is free," he said.

He remained there, clinging to the steering wheel just to make clear he wouldn't be carrying me. I remembered that bus driver leaning forward as he drove us through the heavy snow. The Gray Lady would have to do the lifting, and I wondered how she'd manage the feat. I admit I felt a bit excited: we were finally going to touch! No getting out of it now. It wouldn't be skin, I understood that, but the idea of her hands cupped under my arms moved me.

I took so long fantasizing about the moment that I didn't notice the Gray Lady run into the waiting room without me. She returned moments later with a nurse pushing a wheelchair.

Ah, Ms. Henry, you got away from me again.

The nurse wheeled me inside the waiting room, and left me at a desk while she walked around to the other side. Asked for my name, my symptoms, a home address. Then she told me I'd have to wait. Wheeled me over to an empty chair and lifted me into it before I could protest. I looked worse than most others in the waiting room but better than a few.

You have to be catastrophically sick to pass to the front of a public hospital's line.

A large crowd was waiting there. Half of them were children of patients who just couldn't afford a babysitter. The kids tried their best to use the emergency room like a jungle gym, climbing onto end tables and hiding behind potted plants. Inventing fun is a child's true genius.

I sat in one chair, arms balanced on each arm rest, with the Gray Lady beside me, hands in her lap. I tried to meditate, concentrate on my aches. I located that hot pain sitting between my shoulder blades and talked to it as if it was alive. Just leave me alone, I thought. Why not get out of here? I know it can't be comfortable stuffed up in my narrow back. Wouldn't you be happier somewhere else? You know, Claude has a very roomy belly.

But it didn't work, of course. The fire in my spine smoldered.

I leaned back in my seat, pressing against my shoulder blades, and when I did that, my upper body twitched, nerves scrambling, all the way up to my neck. A jolt so powerful I jerked forward and took the pressure off. As soon as I did that, the harsh pain went away.

"What was that thing at my hotel?" I asked Ms. Henry.

That's what I said, but my sentence came out mumbled. I had a lot of saliva in my mouth now, and it took concentration to keep the drool from spilling past my lips. I thought I'd throw up again, right there. Ms. Henry looked at me and scrunched her eyebrows. Had she even understood what I said?

"I saw you look up at the sky," I explained once my mouth was dry.

The Gray Lady whispered, "I have to call the Dean and find out what to do about Claude. My phone won't work in here. I'll be right outside."

"No," I huffed. "You know what it was."

She bounced the phone on her right knee. It looked as big as a bike engine in her fat little hand. My mouth filled with saliva and I sucked it down again, a little louder than I meant to. People waiting in nearby chairs looked at me with disgust.

Ms. Henry spoke softly. "*They,*" she said. "They're called the Devils of the Marsh."

"Come on."

She looked at me calmly, like she wouldn't bother arguing.

In the sewer I'd been sure it wasn't Solomon Clay, wasn't any human, and felt the same in the elevator at my hotel, but I couldn't bear the idea now.

And yet. And yet. What had I *seen* in Cedar Rapids? Did "Devils of the Marsh" sound any more impossible?

"And what are they?" I asked.

"You know how we go out in the field and do the Library's will?"

"Yeah."

She said, "They do the will of the Voice."

"So they're good?"

She touched her neck, covering the small, healed scars.

"I wouldn't say that."

I sucked in again and didn't bother to register the loathing of those nearby. I wanted to know more. At least she was finally telling me something. But before I could ask, I coughed and couldn't stop. It got so bad my throat burned and my eyes watered and Ms. Henry's only reaction was to wiggle her big phone.

"I'm going to call the Dean. Find out how I should proceed. You heard what Claude said. He'll turn us in easy as that." She snapped her fingers.

The Gray Lady opened her green purse, rummaged around. Stared down into the bag. Meanwhile, I struggled to catch my breath.

"It's our job to keep the Library secret," she said, more to herself than to me.

She stood up. She looked at me. I'm sure I was a terrible sight, but she seemed unconcerned.

"Take care of yourself, Mr. Rice."

She took a breath.

She left me there.

54

I NEVER SAW A DOCTOR WALKING through the emergency room, and even once I was moved to the little examination stalls in back, it took a while for me to meet one. Nurses ran the show. Husky women in their forties who distinguished themselves with different sets of festive scrubs.

They wheeled me back before the Gray Lady returned, and even though I craned my neck to see through the big waiting room windows, I didn't see her outside. I thought of leaving a trail from my chair to the back room, but I didn't have any bread crumbs. Besides, how did I know she'd follow the path? Who was I kidding? That lady was gone. How could I have believed that nonsense about calling the Dean? She wasn't off to deal with Claude. She'd abandoned me. In this condition I was more trouble than I was worth.

The nurse helped me into a stall, then pulled the curtain shut and left me alone again. Ten minutes may have passed, but it felt longer, and I couldn't even lie down for fear of aggravating the sore spot between my shoulder blades. With each minute I imagined Claude and the Gray Lady driving another mile, another mile. By the time the nurse came back, they were far away. Even this stuff about the Devils of the Marsh seemed like part of the trick. A way to shock me into shutting up long enough for them to flee.

The nurse checked my blood pressure, asked questions about my pain. She took some blood. Left again and returned with a doctor some time later. Dr. Leonard France. White-haired and lean, his eyes as red as radishes. The kind of man who'd been tired for years, maybe even generations. I heard patients in other stalls calling out for attention, and after checking me, the doctor went to them.

This back-and-forth, the same nurse and doctor leaving and returning to my stall, went on for another hour. They gave me a paper robe and told me to change. I kept looking at the double doors that led out to the waiting room. When they swung open, I hoped to see Ms. Henry's round face there. But I never did.

My nurse might've gone on break, but Dr. France returned to me more often, even to the detriment of other patients. When he came to take my blood for the third time, one of the other patients, a muscular man, started yelling about why I got so much attention while he was left to sit there like a jerk. I wondered the same thing.

The doctor came again. This time he said, "Are you willing to go upstairs with me?"

"What's up there?" I asked. "The morgue?"

He laughed, and I realized I'd come to like this guy. Whenever he did something, he asked my permission first, rather than just doing it and explaining only when it was done. Even something as simple as checking my pulse for the fifth time.

"Nothing like that," he said. "I just want to rule a few things out."

"Okay, then."

I slid myself off the exam table.

He put me in a wheelchair, which I didn't mind, and took me up himself. That part scared me. These doctors only paid such close attention to the real crisis cases. We passed through the waiting room quickly, less than five seconds, and I made one last sweep for the Gray Lady, but she wasn't to be seen. That's when I felt the deepest fear. That I was truly alone, penniless, had no one to stand with me.

"Ricky Rice! I'm back!"

I heard Adele Henry clearly, loudly. A shout so unexpected she must've shocked everyone else in the waiting room too.

"And I'm staying!" she said, just as loudly.

I put one hand on my chest to trap her promise there.

THE DOCTOR AND I didn't speak in the elevator. Not as he rolled me down the hall.

He took me to a dark room and wheeled me to a mattress. Next to it a somber technician played with a large machine. It looked like a business-size copier with a little green display screen on top. When the technician turned to us, the light of the screen made him look sickly. I

lay down and felt the throbbing in my back again, just a little, so I didn't
go all the way flat.

"Ready?" the technician said.

But who did he ask? The man wasn't looking at me or the doctor.
Maybe he spoke to the machine.

Dr. France said, "Just lift your robe, if you would. Up to your chest."

This was the first procedure the doctor didn't explain, so I hesitated.

The technician said, "Let's go."

Once my gown was up, the tech squirted cold jelly across my stomach and then pressed a wand against my skin. He pushed the wand left
and right. Murky objects floated around on the display screen.

"Anything?" the doctor asked.

"No liver damage. No gallstones. Kidneys look okay. You want to
check his heart?"

As the technician spoke with the doctor, he smacked the keyboard,
and the image shifted. Watching a mechanic check your car engine is
just as mystifying, though at least you get to keep your clothes on. The
doctor leaned closer to the tech. I thought he wanted to see the screen,
but instead he spoke quietly into the man's ear.

"What about that other thing I mentioned? You see anything like
that?"

The tech turned and frowned at the doctor. "Of course not."

The way the wand pressed against my skin really hurt, but these guys
didn't notice.

I waved at the doctor. "You're going to have to tell me something."

Dr. France looked relieved, actually, smiled widely.

"I'll make this plain, Mr. Royce. Your blood volume has increased by
about twenty percent. Glucose levels are quite high. Your leukocyte
count has gone up to almost seven thousand milliliters."

"That's plain?"

The technician threw a few napkins in my direction and indicated
that I could wipe myself off, which I did, but my belly still felt sticky and
cold. I wanted to say something about it, but the question of my comfort
seemed utterly irrelevant to my man at the machine.

I stood, and the doctor helped me into the wheelchair again.

As he rolled me back toward the elevators, he laughed to himself.

I hunched forward in my seat. Still felt the heat in my back, but at
least it wasn't moving.

"Why don't you sit back?" the doctor asked. "Get comfortable."

"I'm better like this," I said.

"Thanks for being a good sport. We'll figure out what's going on, don't
worry."

"What was that for?" I asked, pointing to the room we'd just left.

The doctor laughed loudly now.

"It was just for my own curiosity."

I tapped my hand at my forehead, like I was doffing my hat.

"Glad to be of service," I said.

He tapped my shoulder.

"No, no. I didn't mean it like that. We had to check, of course. It's just that looking at all your tests, and based on your symptoms . . ."

"Yeah?"

"It's silly," he said.

"Tell me anyway."

He laughed.

"Well, if it weren't *impossible*, I'd shake your hand and say congratulations, Mr. Royce. You're pregnant."

5

The Resistance

55

PREGNANT.

Fucking pregnant!

After hearing the word come out Dr. France's mouth, I fell into a quiet paralysis. He spoke to me on the elevator down, but I didn't listen. I couldn't. My mind searched for explanations, theories, to help me understand his diagnosis. And, more than that, to understand why his diagnosis felt oddly, impossibly, possible.

Reading newspapers every day wasn't a common occurrence for me before reaching the Washburn Library, but nine months of study had exposed me to important truths and worthless data in equal measure. Now one piece I'd read only a month before came back to me.

An article about a parasitic wasp called an ichneumon. The ichneumon flies around hunting for orb-weaving spiders. When it finds a target, it attacks and paralyzes the spider, then lays its egg on the tip of the spider's abdomen. Soon the spider recovers and returns to its life, weaving webs and catching insects, but now the wasp's egg is growing on the spider's abdomen, sucking out the spider's fluids all the while.

Just before the wasp larva finally kills the orb-weaver, it actually takes over the spider's mind. It forces the spider to weave a sturdy web, one that will protect the wasp larva after the orb-weaver has died. This zombified spider works against its nature so it can weave what its parasite needs most. A home.

All this time I'd been trying to understand what had happened to me in that sewer.

What if I hadn't been poisoned? What if I'd been made a carrier instead?

What if the Devils of the Marsh left something *growing* in me?

As this thought occurred to me, my legs shook, my feet slipped off the wheelchair's stirrups. My shoes dragged on the hospital floor as if I was trying to stop us from moving forward, into a future where the parasite inside me was real.

My next thought was simple: I have to get it the hell out.

Dr. France returned me to the exam room, and as soon as he left, I snatched the corner cupboards open, looking for something strong to ingest. Only two problems with my plan: I had no idea what to look for, and the room had nothing useful. Not unless I wanted to stuff cotton balls down my throat until I choked.

Dr. France had promised more tests, but I didn't need them. As soon as he'd said the word *pregnant*, I knew that I was. Didn't matter what that technician saw on the sonogram. I accepted what I'd been feeling. Wiped out. Nauseous. Even the raw nipples. I still had that checklist in my mind because of Gayle, the woman I got pregnant ten years ago.

Gayle knew she was pregnant even before the symptoms kicked in. Long before we took a test. I'd asked her how she could be so sure, and she'd said, "The body knows." At the time, I thought she was doing some of that mystical bullshit women get on. Where they act as if their menstrual periods control the tides. But now I realized what she'd meant. I'd *felt* different but didn't know how to name it. Couldn't imagine it until the doctor said the word.

It wasn't in my stomach, the ultrasound proved that, but even the heat between my shoulder blades had cooled. The Devil down in the sewer had stabbed me in my forearm. It must've injected the embryo there. But the little thing hadn't stayed still. Maybe it moved through my bloodstream. From forearm to shoulder, shoulder to neck. Where would it end up?

Better question: where would it come out?

In my examination stall I took the chance to roll flat, looking up at the ceiling. No pain between the blades. I squeezed my arms, my legs, my chest, but felt nothing strange. Wiggled around on my back. I snatched a tongue depressor from the jar on a shelf and pressed it against the roof of my mouth. No sign.

Then I remembered that I did have a particularly strong medicine with me already. Stuff I'd brought with me from Vermont. Six baggies of heroin, right there in my coat pocket. That much dope could kill some adults. What about a little parasite? So now instead of medicine I searched for a syringe. I could cook up all six bags, find the egg, and fire a hotshot into its heart. Heroin could save my life.

BIG MACHINE   229

I found calipers and colored medical shears on the shelves. Cotton tipped applicators and even extra rolls of exam table paper. But no needles. Not anywhere. The hunt left me winded, so I lay back on the table again. I had even started to sweat.

There was a rumble outside the examination room doors. Not an explosion, but an argument. Real yelling in the waiting room. Two women. Soon a nurse came to me, huffing, like she'd been in a race.

She said, "It's a lady out there says she needs to come talk to you. Says she's your wife."

"She said that?" I laughed.

"You got a wife?"

"Sure," I said.

The nurse frowned, unhappy to get the confirmation. She'd probably wanted to send Ms. Henry out on her ass. I didn't feel the same way. I know it was a lie of convenience, that's how Ms. Henry would explain it. "Family only" allowed in the examination rooms. But I felt glad anyway. She could've said she was my sister. I wouldn't have wanted to hear that.

"What did the doctor say?" she asked, once she got in back.

Ms. Henry pulled the curtain closed. She brought a chair to the exam table. Her dry lips were cracked, so she licked them.

"They're still running tests. How you doing out there?"

The Gray Lady said, "I'm getting itchy to move."

I swished my feet around on the exam table, and the butcher's paper underneath me crackled. Even though I kept up a conversation, I can't say I was entirely involved.

She said, "Now, here's the thing. It's past three A.M., and every minute I'm not after Solomon is a minute he might hurt more people. Who knows how many more bums with bombs he's got."

"Well, what do you want to do?"

She put her hand on the green plastic padding of the bed, her fingertips not even an inch away from my left hip. Half an inch. I didn't move any closer, but I watched her hand there. Instead of speaking she looked down at it too. It was like the sea rolling up to the shore. Below the surface they're already touching.

"I need to go," she said quietly. "But you stay here. Let the doctors do what they can."

Now I cleared my mind and looked at her. I sat up, though that took effort, even with the painkillers they'd finally administered.

"Just a little banged up, Ms. Henry. But I can go."

She looked around like she might ask one of the nurses, but it was a new shift and none of them knew me as the medical oddity. Even Dr. France had left to eat something and wouldn't be back for a while. My charts explained the curious situation, but information isn't useful until it's been unearthed. For now I was just a middle-aged man with no visible injuries. A little worn-out, maybe, but who's going to focus on that guy when there's a teenager with a bullet wound?

"The Devils of the Marsh," I began. "What kind of things do they do for the Voice?"

She squeezed her nose to wipe off some sweat. "Anything it wants, I guess."

I had trouble asking the next question. I leaned toward her. "Even reproduction?"

Now she snapped back fast. "You won't stop being a damn fool for one minute? I'd call you a child, but that would be an insult to boys!"

I scooted back too, and crossed my arms.

"You make it real hard to like you sometimes," I said.

Ms. Henry turned to me then, looked directly at me, and it felt as if I'd never known her before. The corners of her eyebrows sagged, and the lids turned so heavy they nearly shut. Her black pupils became passageways directly inside, and I saw a sadness dwelling there.

She nodded. "That is what people say."

Who knew she could be hurt?

I swung my legs over the side of the exam table.

"Go outside, Adele. And I'll get dressed."

I'D BEEN STRIPPED DOWN to socks and a gown, so I had a lot of clothes to put on. I couldn't do it fast. My tweed slacks, my chukka boots. I buttoned up my shirt and donned the Norfolk jacket. It took a good few minutes to do all this, and as I moved, I wondered where *it* moved. Where it grew inside me.

As I finished dressing, I thought of what had pulled me out to Cedar Rapids in 2002. What had gotten me onto that plane. Would I have gone to Cedar Rapids for anyone besides Wilfred? I doubt it. I doubt it. But by then he and I were the last of the Washerwomen's children still alive. He lured me out to Iowa with the promise of easy money, but he had to do that. He couldn't just tell me I was flying out there to die.

I put my hands in my pockets and felt something in the left. Found the battery-powered candle I'd bought at Laguna Lake that afternoon. It was still on, casting its electric light weakly, as ineffective as that congregation's prayers. Neither had protected the victims at Laguna Lake from Solomon Clay. I dropped the light into the trash. Its glimmer filled the bag. I shut the top.

Which is how I got the idea. One last place where I could try to find a needle. The orange medical waste receptacle sat in the other corner. A little reddish-orange bucket. I watched the curtain of my exam room, but heard no footsteps coming. I couldn't shoot up there, in the exam room, but if I found a needle, I could sneak it out with me. Inject that hotshot when I was alone.

I got on my knees and lifted the lid.

56

MS. HENRY STOOD at the hospital exit. And, boy, did she look tired. I'm not talking about a few days of work. How long had she been running around for the Library? She leaned against a column and smiled when she looked over, but it was a pinched grin. Maybe she was just as concerned about me. My strain must've been showing. But she didn't second-guess or send me back to bed. She just turned toward the sliding doors. As I hobbled along, following her, the television in the waiting room played some anonymous courtroom show. Then the television blared a little trumpet tune, and a graphic appeared that read, BREAKING NEWS.

Ms. Henry was practically outside. I'd almost reached the lobby doors.

A voice, scratchy and distant, spoke to the room.

"Solomon Clay is a lion in the wilderness. Solomon Clay is our universal friend."

Ms. Henry rushed back inside so fast that she spun me around in her wake. I had to balance myself against a column so I wouldn't tip over.

The rest of the waiting room wasn't as shocked as us. Talk about underwhelmed. The horn tones of the emergency broadcast threw most of them into a trance. It was like a signal to *stop* listening. A few shut their eyes for a quick nap. Only one guy actually got angry. He slapped his thigh and said, "They interrupted my Judge Maybelline!"

A grainy image blipped across the television screen. Figures shifting in the dark. People broadcasting from inside a cave. Another terrorist video from Iraq? Or was it Afghanistan? Or Belarus? There'd been so many, I doubt the general public really differentiated them anymore. I couldn't be the only one. Now the video paused midmovement and a news anchor's dry voice spoke over this picture.

"These are the images delivered to our offices less than an hour ago. A VHS cassette literally dropped at our doorstep. This from a group claiming responsibility for the recent incidents here in Garland. While their claims have not been verified, authorities *are* taking this video seriously. Please be warned that some of the language is of an adult nature."

The on-screen image moved again. One man in a cave. Two? No. Three. Sitting in a row. Hands in their laps. Faces hard to make out. Were they black or white or yellow or brown? Couldn't say. They were shadows.

The figure in the middle spoke in that same hoarse voice.

"We are the Church of Clay."

The two shadows on either side of him clapped their hands and shouted.

"Isn't it wonderful!"

"Isn't it good!"

I looked at Ms. Henry. She'd reached into her purse automatically, her hand sitting limp inside it as she watched. I placed my hand against my jacket pocket and felt the outline of the syringe I'd dug out of the orange trash bin.

"Do you recognize us?" the figure in the middle asked. "Even if I told you my name, showed you my face, it wouldn't matter worth a damn. You still wouldn't see me."

"Isn't it wonderful!"

"Isn't it good!"

Others in the waiting room sat up. Those who were napping opened their eyes.

"We are the sons of sorrow. The children you despise. And most of my life I thought that was all I'd ever be."

Nurses walked out from the examination room doors. One of them went to the intake station and found a flat, gray remote in a drawer. She pressed a button, and the voice on the television got louder.

"But then a man showed me that I'd been blind. Solomon Clay spat in the dirt, rubbed the mud over my eyes, and when I washed the mud away, I could truly see."

"Isn't it wonderful!"

"Isn't it good!"

The crowd in the waiting room looked left and right. Trying to understand exactly who these three shadows were addressing. I know he doesn't mean me. Must be you.

"You got the game fixed! Your slot machines won't hit the jackpot for people like me."

The other two shadows spoke quietly now.

"Is that wonderful?"

"Is that good?"

The television couldn't get any louder, but the nurse with the remote sure tried. She held the button down, and the little green bars lit up at the bottom of the big screen. They were so bright you thought they might illuminate the hidden faces. Even the children in the room had grown quiet. We all heard.

"But now it's our turn. It's time for our reward. You've had your round. The Church of Clay is going to wipe the board clean. The whole world will know our name. *Fuck* the meek. The despised will inherit the earth!"

The other two shadows clapped harder now than they had before.

People in the waiting room sat back. Some stood. They glared at the screen. One woman even spat with indignation.

"What the hell did I ever do to them?" an old man asked. "I'm just trying to get mine."

A younger woman, a teenager really, said, "They don't mean us. They mean the politicians. Or white folks. That's who they angry at."

A dozen people nodded. Not any of us. Not regular folks. We were exempt. This made sense to people. This comforted them.

"I don't care who you are!" the shadow on the screen yelled, as if he had actually heard us. "Not one of you is innocent, no matter what fairy tale you tell yourselves. Oppression doesn't make you noble. Or exempt. Did you sleep in the gutter last night? Are you chased out of bed by the rain? No! This is a new era. It's time to choose new teams. Not even your babies will be spared. The milk they drink will be pestilence."

Now the teenage girl jumped up.

"But that's not fair!" she yelled.

The shadows on the screen clapped and shouted.

"Isn't it wonderful!"

"Isn't it good!"

There could've been more, the shadows sure seemed amped enough to continue, but they were interrupted. Suddenly sunlight flared from the right side of the video. In a moment those three shadows changed from phantoms into old men. In this light you could see the one in the middle sitting in a wheelchair. They weren't in a cave, just a dirty hallway. The video stopped there, like it had been chopped. The moment took on the significance of a vision. Three old men, all in profile, jeering at the sun.

"They're black!" the teenage girl shouted.

Some black folks in the waiting room covered their faces from shame.

I reached out to grab Adele, but thought better of it. So instead I blew at the back of her head to get her attention. She touched her scalp and looked at the ceiling. Then back at me.

"What the hell are you doing?" she whispered.

I motioned with my head and we walked out the lobby doors. A news anchor came back on the screen and blabbered in an excited tone.

"That's By the Bay," I said. "That light was me walking in on them."

57

THERE WERE BENCHES ALONG the curved driveway outside Highground Hospital. They were filled with men of various ages, but similar style: drained, tired, though not from work alone. Just worn-out with living. They stared at Ms. Henry openly as we passed. The Church of Clay. How many members did it have?

"We're going to have to walk. I've fired Claude."

I laughed when she said that, because the oxycodone I was on could only manage so many miracles. The fact that I wasn't sweating much, wasn't collapsing, that was really an achievement. It seemed ungrateful to demand more of this drug. Like walking farther than the car.

I need to break in and admit that oxycodone is not the kind of stuff a former heroin addict should be taking. But a doctor doesn't know what a doctor isn't told, and when Dr. France asked me if there was any reason I couldn't take it, I suffered this odd, instant memory loss. Then suddenly, oh my, what's this yellow pill in my hand? Well, okay, I'll take it if you really think it'll help. Swallowing it was like getting a postcard from a dear old friend: Missing You! XOXO.

Ms. Henry went up a set of steps, and I followed her using the handrail so I wouldn't lose my balance. We'd walked about halfway down the block when I saw Claude's car parked on the corner, across the street. The lights were off, but he sat in front.

"You don't think we could ask Claude for one more ride?" I pointed across the way.

"He's done with us," the Gray Lady said. "And I'm done with him."

But the daunting look of 14th Avenue, empty and looooong, made me insist.

"Maybe he'd at least give us some of my money back, so we could call a taxi."

She shook her purse. "I've got the money here. And we need to conserve it."

"I bet Claude wasn't too happy about giving back that cash!"

"With a man like him, you can't just ask."

"So how'd you convince him?"

"There's a pistol in my handbag."

I laughed. "The fear of violence always works."

She said, "I shot him three times. He died."

I looked at his car again. Saw the figure at rest in the front seat, a body in the dark. His black Town Car looked like a casket now.

Claude.

"I thought you'd be happy," she said.

I would've thought so too, but I only felt overwhelmed. I touched my jacket pocket. Left my hand there a moment.

I'd wrapped the syringe I found inside layers of paper towels. It had been used before, drops of dried blood visible inside the barrel, but I didn't I care. I meant to use it, to kill that parasite. I tried to concentrate on that plan rather than Claude's death. The only thing over which I had any control. I just needed privacy.

"We have to get somewhere safe," I said.

The Gray Lady reached under her gold tam, scratched her scalp.

"I doubt those men have stayed at By the Bay. If they dropped off a tape, they must have a bigger plan. We have to get help," she said. "The estate's the only place."

We walked.

I tried to act unimpressed. The exhaustion helped, but I was already imagining my finger on a copper doorbell. Maybe the Washburns had a brass door knocker. Or, even better, a braided cable attached to a gong. The idea of the Washburn family still held some clout with me.

No buses rolled by.

No taxis on the streets.

With the quiet came a memory. Being dragged into Claude's Town Car. Kicking at his face. And then I wondered how much of that Town Car's leather was saturated with his blood. Had he even known what was happening? Had Daphne understood when Rose shot her?

The Gray Lady said, "Steady, Ricky. Steady on."

I moved beside her, but wouldn't look her way.

"We're going to use the rest of the bullets in my gun on Solomon Clay," she said. "Are you prepared for that?"

"Prepared? Maybe. But you're *eager*."

"We finish him, and that's that. We return to the Washburn Library."

"Happily ever after, right?"

The Gray Lady watched me. I saw her do this even though I pretended to watch the stars.

"The Dean's going to be pleased with you," she said. "You're tough."

"The Dean will like me? Hot damn, my life is complete!"

"Okay, Ricky."

"How about you tell me why you're so loyal to that man," I said.

She sighed. "It's not *that* man who earned my loyalty."

"Well, which man was it, then?"

Her mind flittered off to a memory or a feeling. I watched it happen. I couldn't follow and didn't want to. I counted my steps instead, which became monotonous, but it was still better than focusing on how cold and empty my right calf felt. Or my numb right foot.

It got hard to see because my vision blurred occasionally.

I'm breaking down. That's what I admitted to myself.

And just then I felt a hot jolt in my back. A knot in the middle. A mass, a form. A life. I thought of that parasitic wasp, the ichneumon, turning from egg to larva, sucking the fluid right out of its host. Would it kill me before I had a chance to stop it? This anxiety made me snap.

"There's not one person alive who's on your side, Adele."

Ms. Henry crossed her arms as she walked. "And you're surrounded by friends?"

"The closest you ever came to having company in Vermont was when the guards took your garbage on Tuesdays."

"I didn't want visitors."

I said, "No one trusts you, Ms. Henry. Can't you see that?"

She patted her chest with one hand. "It has occurred to me."

"The despised become despicable," I said.

She spat on the sidewalk. "Solomon told you that."

"How do you know?"

"I heard him say it once before."

"Look, Adele, *I* don't trust you. But I'm here. And I'll march with you all the way to the Washburn estate. I'll face down Solomon Clay. *If* you'll be honest with me now."

"And what if I don't?"

"Then your only friend is the Dean."

Adele dropped her arms, grabbed the fronts of her slacks.

"Two years ago," she began, but stopped.

Adele squeezed her eyelids shut and blew out a deep breath.

She said, "Two years ago I destroyed the Washburn Library."

This is the story she told me.

58

The Resistance

(An Adele Henry Adventure)

EVERY WINTER MORNING in the Northeast Kingdom is like the dawn of mankind. The world turns so frigid at night that all the living *must've* died. So when the sun rises, it bears witness to ten thousand resurrections. People wake, and the first thing they do is compare thermometers with their neighbors. "My house was down to thirty below last night, how about you?" And the one who had it worst gets to be the proudest. You're bound to learn something true about yourself in that environment; the wind blows off all your covers.

Adele Henry figured out two things after a few months in Vermont: she liked research and she loved drinking. (She may already have been aware of the latter.)

Each morning she'd start the day by spreading her paperwork across the dining table, then preparing a pitcher of manhattans. She'd spend the afternoon draining it. But never to the detriment of her work at the Washburn Library. Really. She loved the job too much to do it poorly. She would've been the last to guess how much joy research could bring her.

The only thing she wouldn't do was walk over to the Library every day. Enter those glass cages they called offices? Please. So while the other Unlikely Scholars left their homes each morning and marched into the building, she got down to business in her dining room.

She worked alone. If she needed anything, she just had the staff deliver it. Sometimes, if she was feeling too tipsy, she wouldn't even open up for them, just shout to "leave it on stairs." And yet the Dean didn't fire her, not in the first month or the third or the sixth. And that's because her dedication was clear. If she lost an hour because she'd napped in the afternoon, she made up for it with two more hours' work during the night. And she didn't just snip articles like those other chumps. She sent page-long explanations too, detailing her reasons for picking each one. Sometimes she heard the other Unlikely Scholars throwing dinner parties in their cabins, but when she felt a stab of loneliness, she just endured it, set her head down, and returned to the files.

That particular morning, in November of 2003, Adele had already sipped half a pitcher of bourbon and sweet vermouth (and a dash of bitters), so it seemed like nap time would arrive soon. When Lake came for her, knocking lightly on the cabin door, she didn't even register the sound. Not until it was over. She listened to the heavy scrunch of Lake's boots in the snow.

Adele finally got up and went to the door, but she had a funny way of walking. Kind of slow and wobbly. It's possible she had to hold on to the furniture as she moved. But she wouldn't say she was drunk. *She* wouldn't.

When Adele finally opened the front door, she saw Lake was already far away. Even from twenty feet off the man was large. Bigger than a breadbasket. Bigger than the truck that delivered breadbaskets.

"Hey!" she shouted. "Calling me?"

Had she slurred her words?

Lake turned around. "Thought you weren't there."

"Just sunbathing," she told him. Her hands and face already felt frosty in the open air.

"Better get your coat," he said.

"I'm fired," she said.

Lake laughed, and the sound rumbled like an avalanche.

"You've been called up," he explained.

"To meet the Dean?" she yelled, even as Lake walked closer.

"Yup."

In response to this momentous news Adele Henry went into the bathroom and threw up.

AFTER SHE'D BRUSHED HER TEETH, dressed, wrapped, bundled, and put on a scarf, she was prepared for the short march from her cabin to the side door of the Washburn Library. Hard to believe the other Scholars did this every morning when they could've been like her, stayed in and enjoyed a glass of port with their eggs and toast. How did she get all this liquor? That's easy, she drove to Burlington and bought it. It's not like the Library asked to see her receipts.

"You're as calm as anyone I've ever seen," Lake said as they walked.

"I've got a lot of courage."

He smiled. "About five pints of it. That's my guess."

Adele looked down and wondered if she'd been weaving as they walked. Did she smell? How had he known she was so tipsy?

Lake looked at her and said, "You're talking a little loud."

She nodded. "Is this better?"

"Yes," he said.

"Thank you, Lake."

They were almost to the Library door. The roof of the enormous building cast a shadow across them that took the shape of a great hand.

"Does the Dean just say hello and send me back to my cabin?" she asked, speaking but listening to herself as well. Monitoring the volume and clarity of each word.

Lake shrugged. "Heard they just bought a pair of tickets. You're off on a trip. You're going to meet the boss man, that's the rumor."

"What rumor? You're taking me to him right now."

Lake held the door open for her and hitched his slacks with the free hand.

"Not the Dean," he said. "Mr. Washburn."

ADELE TOOK THE WOODEN STAIRS that led to the Dean's office two at a time, treating this like a school yard race rather than a holy climb. She skipped so quick that she tripped when she reached the top. Fell flat on her chest. An echo they must've heard in Massachusetts.

No one came to help her up. Lake stayed hidden around the corner, at the bottom of the stairs, or maybe he'd even walked off by then. But someone was there. She heard giggling as she pushed herself up, and realized it was the other Unlikely Scholars, laughing in the lobby. They must've known she'd been called up even before she did. Maybe one of them had seen Lake making the trip toward her cabin.

So she heard them down there, cackling about her fall, and while she did feel some humiliation, there wasn't any pain. That's one benefit of a few strong drinks, you're invulnerable. So Adele picked herself up, steadied herself, walked to the Dean's oak door, and pushed it. When it didn't open, she rattled the handle. Then she kicked.

"Just wait for the buzzer!" the Dean shouted from inside.

"Well, hurry up and buzz it, then!"

Finally she stepped into the darkened room, didn't even hesitate, swung the door closed behind her.

"Do you hear my voice?" the Dean said solemnly.

"Course I do," she said.

"Follow it."

She moved much faster than she should have, and in no time she smashed right into a table. Its edge clocked her clear in the belly. But did that stop her? No. In fact, she climbed right on top of the table and walked the length of it. The wood wobbled beneath her. The legs creaked, but she didn't care. Being drunk made her just fearless enough, and when she reached the edge, her step hardly faltered. She hopped down and landed clean. She smiled in the dark.

The Dean turned on the small lamp sitting on his desk.

"You got footprints on my table," was all he said.

The Dean looked at his shirt and brushed away dust that wasn't even there. It had been six months since the welcoming banquet, the last time she'd been this close to him. He still seemed rigid in the way small men can be. Anticipating disrespect from all directions.

Maybe Adele was being too hard on the man, but she didn't think so. The Dean gave her this feeling because of his crisp clothes. They were so freshly pressed. Not ironed each morning, but hourly. The Dean probably thought wrinkled pants were a sign of bad breeding. Nonsense. And yet, Adele ran hands over her own dress. Smoothing out the fabric before she realized what she was doing.

"Now sit down," he said. "And let me tell you about Judah Washburn."

She sat, but it took all her concentration just to listen, no murmurs and no questions. When he was done, she had no reaction.

Now he tapped his computer and, nearby, a group of printers started. She heard them chugging and turned to stare while the little man spoke, at length, about what they were printing. That the field notes were like Scripture. An American gospel. When she turned back, the Dean watched her, his head cocked to the left.

"You don't seem all that . . . enthusiastic."

Adele said, "I'm glad to know all these things, sure."

"But?"

Adele remembered what her mother used to say when grandma called and asked if the pair attended church in the proper way. Adele's mother would throttle the phone and say, "God and the Devil have decided they're unreachable. So I've stopped trying to reach them." This best described Adele's faith, even now. Thus, the Dean's zeal didn't convert her. She tried to think of how best to explain her belief system to the man.

She said, "I'm a working person. That's it. So why don't you tell me what you need and let me go do it. The quicker I'm back in my cabin, the happier I'm going to be."

The Dean leaned forward, chin over his desk. Her disinterest seemed to make *him* work harder to woo her. Even he seemed surprised when he related his own story.

"I was a crew member on the SS *Antonio Maceo* before I came to the Library. A steamer in Marcus Garvey's Black Star Line corporation. I loved Mr. Garvey, very much, and looked up to him like a god. I got his attention by contributing quite a few big checks to the UNIA. Unfortunately, I must admit, those checks were forgeries. All of them bounced. And yet, when he found out, Mr. Garvey didn't throw me in jail. He was forgiving. He said I could make it up to him by serving on the crew of the *Antonio Maceo*. I didn't hesitate. I was joining a great Negro empire! But you know how it is. The reality didn't live up to the dream. Our ship had more troubles than the African continent.

"On our maiden voyage, from New York to Cuba, me and a brother named Hastings were working the boilers. They'd been giving us trouble from the moment Mr. Garvey bought the ship. Hastings and I were posted at those boilers to guard against any . . . embarrassments. The work was dull and stressful at the same time, like waiting for your sick child's fever to break or become an emergency. Then I heard a splash off the larboard. A woman calling out for help. I ran to her, confused. We didn't have women in the crew. Hastings stayed behind.

"When I reached the water, all I saw was a school of bluefish. I'm staring down at them, but I still hear the woman's voice. I'm thinking she's *under* them somehow, but that doesn't make a damn bit of sense. Those fish would've scattered before she even touched the water. And now the sound changes; she stops calling for help and starts speaking. To me. I hear my name. And I find myself leaning over the side of the boat, stretching and stretching, straining to understand her. And then, splash, I fell right into the water. The bluefish shot right off."

The Dean patted his forehead with a handkerchief. He'd started to sweat.

"Before I even called for help, the boiler exploded. Just like that. Hastings died right away. I was in the water two nights before rescue found me. It wasn't so long before the Library's invitation arrived."

The Dean lay his hands flat on his desk and breathed deeply. He said, "How would you describe what happened to *you* in Paterson, New Jersey. In 1997?"

"I wouldn't," she said, suddenly more sober than she'd been since sunrise.

She understood the Dean knew something, had a general idea about her ordeal in a New Jersey motel room, maybe, but no one was getting the particulars. If she hadn't told her own mother, why would she tell him?

The Dean drummed his fingers on the desk.

"Do you understand this is a rare opportunity? To be invited here. To speak with me?"

"Yes, I do," she said.

"And would you like to stay?"

"I know I don't want to leave."

He dropped his elbows onto his desk so he could lean even farther across it. He seemed exasperated, but maybe a little intrigued too. Most of the Scholars would've swallowed sawdust to be in Adele's chair.

"Each Scholar's moment of clarity is never completely clear, Ms. Henry. Interpreting the field notes is like listening to a conversation through a closed door. I can't pick up every single thing, but I get the idea. Will you at least tell me the promise you made in Paterson? "

The Dean leaned back, crossed his hands on his flat stomach, then undid one button of his vest.

Adele hadn't been the kind of girl who'd always wanted to be pretty. She'd just wanted to look cool. As juvenile as it sounds, at thirty-eight, that was still all she wanted. But when she leaned forward in her seat, the chair pinched the sides of her thick thighs. And when she leaned back to try to cross one leg, the top leg slipped off. Too much meat below the waist. She felt she wasn't built for swank. In this chair Adele had to sit straight, which made her feel like a child.

Adele remembered that motel in New Jersey. Being held down in the tub, nothing to stare at but the water-stained ceiling tiles.

"I promised to get them before they get me," she said.

The Dean nodded. "Well, then, maybe you can do what I need."

The Dean stood up, walked to the four printers. They hummed in the darkness. He returned to his desk with a sheaf of printed pages in his hands.

"I'll make it plain. The Library is under threat, Ms. Henry."

"And what do I have to do to protect it?"

"Whatever is required to keep it secret, to keep it safe."

"Why does secrecy matter?"

He said, "You want the cosmic answer or the pragmatic one?"

She didn't even speak, just curled her lips and tilted her head.

"We pay our staff in cash, and the Unlikely Scholars don't file. That's one hundred fifty years of back taxes. If the IRS came looking to be re-paid, we'd go bankrupt for sure."

This answer actually pleased her. Simple, practical, commonsense. The Washburn Library was dodging its bills.

The printers rattled, and the small video panels on their sides turned bright.

"So if we lose this fight, I'll have to pack up this office," he said. "And you'll get booted out of that little cabin you love. Right out on your ass. And then where will you go?"

"I could find something," she said, defensively.

"Go back to selling that ass?" the Dean muttered.

She stood, shot right up. "You speak like that one more time. Go ahead and test me."

The Dean smiled. "No, Ms. Henry, I wouldn't want to do that."

"So *what's* the threat?"

"Mr. Washburn. He's the threat. He means to shut us down."

She flopped down into her chair again. "Why?"

"He isn't as devout as we are. Do you know Solomon Clay?"

"I've read his files . . ."

"I'm sending you west. With him."

"With . . . ?" She squeezed the arm rests of her chair. "He's here?"

The Dean opened the middle drawer of his desk and set a thin gray manuscript onto the tabletop. "You can have the life you want, Ms. Henry. The one you deserve. I promise you."

She looked at the book.

"And what's it going to cost me?"

"You just have to remember who gave it to you," he said, opening the cover.

The Dean flipped through a series of yellowed, aging pages. Adele saw lines of writing in black ink, red ink, even scrawls made with something like ash. Different penmanship, maybe different eras. She couldn't read the words with the ledger upside down.

"I'm sending you with Mr. Clay. He's going to try and convince Mr. Washburn to change his mind, but you're my fail-safe. Solomon thinks of himself as the Scholar of all Scholars. More a prophet than a worker. He won't get blood on his hands, if it comes to that. But you will."

"So you don't really trust him?" she asked.

"No. But I don't really trust anyone."

"So why send me?"

The Dean smiled. "I trust your greed."

And Adele felt slightly pitiful. This came on suddenly, overwhelmingly. It was because she knew instantly that she would do it. "It" being *whatever* was required to keep what she'd been given. Earned. *Deserved.* A cabin. Nice clothes. Groceries. Even the research. The shame wasn't in discovering that she had a price; everyone had one of those. Maybe it was just in learning, so concretely, that this was what she cost.

AND YET, no matter how earthshaking a moment is, there's that minute right afterward when you return to the unconcerned world. Which is exactly what Adele experienced after she'd heard all the Dean had to say. She signed on for the work because there were no competing bids, then stepped out of Armageddon and onto a wooden staircase. Found that reality hadn't shifted noticeably. Her bra still cut into her shoulders. She still stood five-foot-one.

Adele took the stairs one at a time. When she reached the bottom, she meant to sprint toward her cabin and finish off the pitcher of manhattans, one big gulp before the epic trip, but she couldn't get around the man waiting for her down there. A myth stood in her way.

He overshadowed her. Not Lake. Too skinny. "Don't moisten your panties," he said.

"Excuse me?"

"That's been known to happen the first time a lady meets me."

"Meets who?" she asked.

"I'm Solomon Clay."

She felt a wave of awe powerful enough to knock her down. But the guy seemed so pleased with himself that she refused to show it. Adele struggled to keep her balance and pressed one hand against the wall. Which made Solomon Clay laugh.

"Yeah," he said. "You know me."

Solomon Clay extended his right hand as if it were the tip of a scepter. It was narrow, rough, gnarled; glorious and unnatural; as stirring as a rusted red bridge abandoned in the countryside; you see one and think, That thing will never fall.

He left the hand out there so long she wasn't sure if he wanted her to kiss it or to bow. Finally, she forced herself to shake his hand, the least objectionable option.

Adele shivered with revulsion at the touch.

"Did I just give you a climax?" he asked with a smirk.

What kind of prophet was this?

As soon as he let go, she put her hand in her coat pocket. The fingers all but quivered, and she hated to think Solomon Clay read this as excitement. She felt tempted to explain everything about her ordeal in Paterson, New Jersey, just so he'd understand her reaction clearly. She'd give him answers that she'd denied her own mother if it would remove that gloating grin.

But before she could decide, Adele heard another sound in the long hall. A familiar voice. One she'd last heard in 1997. It wriggled across the stone floor. It curled up the length of her right thigh. It settled in the pocket between her upper thighs. She actually felt a weight press against her pelvis. It reminded her of that gruesome weekend, the last time she'd been held tight.

You're my special flower.

But that whisper wasn't real. It wasn't. Was not. Only a memory activated by touch. Now her own hand, still in her coat pocket, felt as hot as an ember thrown from the flame.

"So you're my shield bearer," Solomon said.

"I'm what?" she asked. She hadn't quite heard what he said because she was looking past Mr. Clay, peeking into the far corners, just in case. Just in case.

"You know the tradition? The shield bearer accompanies the veteran soldier into battle."

"I thought we were Scholars."

"Not in the field. Out there, think of yourself as my valet."

Adele watched Solomon's face. Did he know, even suspect, what the Dean had told her? He might be the legend, but she was the fail-safe. Solomon Clay seemed too confident to consider such a thing.

They walked along the hallway now. Past the guard's desk and out the side door of the Washburn Library. Eventually it would be summer, the better of the three seasons there in the woods (rainy season being the third). In summer the wind would romp with the fallen leaves. Right now the snow simply pinned the whole world down.

"Where are you from?" she asked.

"I came up in Chicago," he said quickly.

"Then where'd you pick up all this shield bearer mess? Ancient Greece?"

"What's wrong, woman? Are my big words confusing you?"

He sneered and looked down at her. He was a light-skinned black man. Her friends used to call them yellow-boys. Girls dated them and girls hated them, usually at the same time. Boys who'd been told they were beautiful only because of their complexion. They might have a face like a bullfrog's balls, but with that golden skin they couldn't fail. She loathed that deeply bred confidence. And, of course, she also envied it.

He walked her all the way to her cabin, and when they got there, she felt surprised they'd gone so far so quickly. She wasn't tipsy anymore. Being insulted by this prick had sobered her right up. Big words, my ass.

And yet, she had to admit a certain admiration for the man. If nothing else he looked astoundingly young. Solomon Clay had to be seventy, but he looked forty-five, at most. As they moved, he smoothed his wavy hair and tapped down the fine wisps above his ears. He even smoothed his eyebrows. Half-pathetic for a man his age, maybe, but he was strangely beautiful for a man so old. Men grow handsomer over time; women just mature. Everyone seemed to agree.

Oh, she knew it was silly to care so much about aging. To think like those ladies whose comfortable lives let them be conceited full-time. But rich women weren't the only ones yearning to save their sweet faces. What girl doesn't watch her loosening skin with regret? Maybe even lady alligators sigh at their reflections in the river.

"Lake is inside packing your things," Solomon said. "Then he'll drive us to town. You handle our tickets."

He pulled an envelope from a pocket inside his jacket. She snatched it from his hand, in a hurry to get away from him.

"That's bad manners, Adele. You better work on that."

"Or else what?"

She cocked her arm slightly and squeezed her hand around the envelope as if it were a weapon she could use to crack Solomon's skull.

"You know I stopped calling you new folks Unlikely Scholars years ago."

"What do you use instead?" She crossed her arms to defend against the inevitable insult.

"You all come here and start dressing like businesspeople, so I just call you pros."

He looked her up and down.

"But I'm guessing you've been called a pro plenty of times before."

He walked off, and she watched him go. He swaggered like a child.

The Dean had told her to crush anyone who threatened the Library. They might be going out into the field to negotiate with Mr. Washburn, but she hoped Solomon Clay would give her an excuse to inflict a little violence on him while they were there. Hurting a man like that would be very satisfying.

INSIDE THE CABIN Lake had finished putting her things into suitcases, even her underwear. When she walked in, Lake stood by the kitchen table. He unplugged the old toaster on the kitchen counter, and in his enormous hand the black cord looked like a line of thread.

"I'll take your bags down to the truck," he said. "You can meet us there in fifteen minutes. Will that be enough time?"

"I'm sure."

He went to prop the door open, but she stood there already and held it for him. So he went back to the kitchen table and lifted both bags. As he came closer, she couldn't help it, she stepped backward as far as she could without letting the door swing shut.

Lake stopped there and said, "Mr. Clay was giving you hell."

"You heard?"

"Through the door."

"He's the legend, I guess."

Lake shrugged. The suitcases seemed weightless when he held them, but she hated to think how much heavier they'd be when she was on her own.

"He's not actually from Chicago, you know. He's from a town called Elgin."

"Oh," she said.

Adele knew what Lake was doing, trying to pop a few holes in that asshole's balloon, but geography wouldn't reduce him. She still felt small in comparison, intimidated by Mr. Clay. She appreciated Lake's attempt, though, and smiled politely.

"Also, Solomon Clay is not that man's given name. He took it on when he got here."

Lake stooped and looked into her eyes.

"What's his real name, then?" she whispered.

"Maurice Storch."

Maybe Lake caught the first chuckles bubbling behind Adele's eyes, but he didn't wait around to watch.

Adele spent the next five minutes in the bedroom lying on her star of Bethlehem quilt, laughing herself into a stomachache. She imagined introducing herself to old Mr. Washburn. Hello, I'm *Maurice's* shield bearer!

After that was through, she spent another five minutes talking to herself about this new position with the Library. Convincing herself to embrace it. To be brave. The sight of the Vermont woods through her cabin window helped give her courage. You made it here, she thought. And who would've believed you could? Not even you.

Adele went to the vanity table near her bed and pulled her hair down from its ponytail. The straight brown locks barely reached the tops of her shoulders, but she still felt good about the look. It had taken her six years to grow this much back. She brushed it a little, but not too hard because her scalp had always been tender. Then she pulled the brown hair together again, twisted it, and tied it off with a little maroon hair band. Adele turned her head and looked at the ponytail in profile. Like this she appeared business-minded, professional. One serious brunette. Adele Henry.

Keep going, she said to herself in the mirror. Keep going.

After that she put a few last supplies into her old purse, the big green one she'd brought with her from her previous life. The only item that re-

mained from those decades. Only as she left the cabin did she open the
envelope and look at the pair of tickets she'd been given. Final destination: Garland, California. But the trip out there would take days, not
hours.

Adele Henry and Maurice Storch were going Greyhound.

SEEING AMERICA BY BUS is like touring the Louvre in a Porta Potti.
And that's all that will ever need to be said about that.

THE LOUNGE of the Garland bus station collected dust better than most
vacuums. It wasn't a dirty place, exactly, no trash on the waiting room
floor, but Adele nearly had a coughing fit the moment she opened its
doors. Solomon Clay didn't make things any easier when he refused to
carry his own bags inside. She had to make three trips from the bus to
the waiting room, first carrying his things over, then hers. By the third
trip she was heaving, inhaling great quantities of the gritty station air.

Meanwhile Solomon Clay sauntered over to the public telephones as
if he were about to ring up another assistant to take her place. She got
to rest, really gather herself, only after hauling in all five of their suitcases, and at one point Adele felt nostalgia for her carefree days at the
Scarborough Women's Correctional Facility.

Water, that's what she needed, so she got in line at the concession
counter but didn't realize she had no money until the woman demanded
a dollar. Mr. Clay had been buying all her meals at different spots on the
road. She hadn't received even a nickel before leaving the Library. Embarrassed, she slinked away.

Adele didn't run right over to Solomon now, because then she'd feel
too much like a kid looking for her allowance, and this guy didn't need
any more help treating her like a pup. So she crept toward him instead.
He kept his back to the waiting room, phone receiver against his ear.
Adele came close enough to pick Solomon's pocket (which she considered), but then she heard him say, "We're at the Greyhound station, Mr.
Washburn."

Hearing that name gave her the wobbles, and she couldn't move any
closer. Instead she stumbled over to some vending machines in an alcove to the right of the phones. Adele flopped against the plastic face of
one machine so hard the candy bars shook in their silver coils.

Washburn.

Even though Lake had told her the rumor, she hadn't truly believed it.
Even when the Dean confirmed it, she'd remained suspect. But now, in

this city, hearing Solomon say the name, Adele was surprised to find just how much power it held. All those months of working at Mr. Washburn's Library had deeply affected her.

Old Mr. Washburn. What would he be like? She imagined Moses and Frederick Douglass rolled together. A stooped but powerful old man with a curly gray beard and a walking stick. Lightning bolts shooting from his mouth when he spoke. She realized she was thinking of Judah this whole time. She'd come across some wild ideas at the Library, but a two-hundred-fifty-year-old man was the wildest yet. It wasn't possible. Was it?

Solomon hung up, and Adele stepped away from the vending machine, saw herself in the plastic's reflection. Did she look right? She snapped the collar of her powder-blue box coat. She rubbed the shine off her forehead.

Washburn!

Despite the noise she'd made when she'd smacked against the candy machine, Solomon didn't realize she stood so near. He couldn't see around corners, after all. So after hanging up with Mr. Washburn, he made a second call. Spoke as loudly, as calmly, as he had during the first.

"Hello, sir," he said. "I'm in Garland. Just now. No, she made it too."

Adele heard him turn, the creaky sound of a metal phone cord stretching. Was he speaking to the Dean? Must be. Only the Dean or Mr. Washburn could coax respect out of Solomon Clay.

"She *was* bringing in the luggage. Now? Eating a snack, probably." He laughed.

Adele stepped back and looked at herself reflected in plastic again. She patted her waist with both hands sympathetically. Then she squeezed the flesh so hard it hurt.

"I've just spoken to him. We're getting picked up. Yes. Why do you need to know? Don't you trust me? Okay. Okay! I'm taking Mr. Washburn to the Devil's Well. That's right. I believe I do know where it is. I didn't tell you because you would've wanted to come too. It's bad enough I've got this bitch with me."

Solomon Clay cleared his throat. His voice quieted, but she could still hear.

"I'll take him to the Devil's Well. That's where I'll plead our case. Judah heard the Voice there. Maybe we will too."

Adele didn't have time to search for a pen, so she committed the words to memory: the Devil's Well. She'd investigate. TheDevil'sWell. But where to start? TheDevilsWell.

Why this instant desire to remember these words? Sniff out their meaning? Why not just wait until Solomon Clay led them there? Or ask

Mr. Washburn when he arrived? Adele remembered what the Dean had told her in his office. He didn't trust Solomon. He didn't trust Adele. Didn't trust anyone. Considering the company, that seemed like the smart move. Who should Adele trust? Only herself. She would find her own answers, thank you.

"Window-shopping?" Mr. Clay asked. He stood behind her now. She watched him in the reflection. How long had he been there? Had she been repeating those words in her head or out loud? She'd been staring at the ground, trying to concentrate, but now she acted as though nothing could be more fascinating than the 3 Musketeers bar on bright display.

"You want something?" he asked as if she were a dog that wanted its bowl refilled.

She nodded. The Devil's Well.

She repeated this to herself. It seemed like such an easy term to remember, but she didn't entirely trust herself. Her drugs of choice back in the day? Amphetamine, dexamphetamine, and, of course, methamphetamine. All of which can have a negative effect on a person's memory. Names and dates and places and faces.

Solomon went into one of his coat pockets and pulled out his wallet. Removed a dollar. But instead of giving it to her, he fed the bill to the machine and asked, "Which one?"

Adele imagined Mr. Washburn now as a man crippled by senility, a figure slouching in a tarnished wheelchair, his dirty gray beard just a matted mess. Who would protect this feeble codger? She tapped the glass lightly, mechanically.

Solomon Clay leaned forward. "CJ7."

He punched in the code, and a blocky Whatchamacallit bar plopped down. The plunk of coins echoed in the alcove. Solomon stuck one long finger into the proper slot and retrieved a dime and a nickel. He left Adele to stoop and fish out the candy.

Which she did because she was hungry as hell.

But forget asking about another dollar for that water now. She'd drink out of a bus toilet before begging Solomon Clay for anything. While they waited for their ride, Adele went upstairs to the ladies' room and drank handfuls of water out of the tap at the sink. Then she took a length of brown paper towel and wrote the term she'd heard with her lilac liner pencil.

The Devil's Well.

Could Judah's story be real? Why did this idea scare her more than anything else ever had?

When Adele returned to the lobby, some big guy was swiping her suitcases.

She came down the stairs and found him running off with her things. Solomon Clay was nowhere near. He'd just left their bags unguarded! Now some dude, dressed like a dockworker, was robbing her. His silhouette was as massive as the Grand Teton, but Ms. Henry didn't hesitate. Hell, no. She jumped his ass. Practically landed on his back.

"I will beat your *ass*, motherfucker!"

This is what the lady yelled.

And that is how she introduced herself to Mr. Washburn.

AFTER AN EXPLANATION, disentanglement, and mutual apologies, Adele and Mr. Washburn caught up to Solomon Clay. He waited for them out on San Pablo Avenue. A street that offered any of a dozen places for the poorest to flop: the Carson Arms, Sunshine Manor, By the Bay. Right now Adele Henry would've preferred to stay in any one of them rather than spend another millisecond in Mr. Washburn's presence.

She was so embarrassed. Bum-rushing the boss. And using foul language too! All this because he'd been trying to carry her bags out to his car. After they'd cleared up the confusion, she wouldn't let him touch her suitcases again, insisted on lifting them herself.

And now she stared at the ground, muttering, beating herself up even more. Putting down her own professionalism, her intelligence, her bad temper, even the way she wore her clothes.

How could you do that to Mr. Washburn? He's going to send you back, and it's all your fault. But you don't deserve to be here anyway. You aren't brave enough. And you're just so *stupid*. Too violent. Too short. You're no damn good at all. This is what she said to herself as they walked out to the car.

But Mr. Washburn didn't seem to notice her turmoil. While Solomon Clay clearly didn't care. Both men were too busy trying to fit three people and five suitcases inside a 1977 Mercedes-Benz 450 SLC Coupe. This wasn't the slick roadster, that two-seater with lots of spirit, but its chunky cousin. A cheaper model, if we're being blunt. Slightly roomier backseat, a little more headroom, but very little else to recommend it. A bit of a beanbag, as far as coupes go. Mr. Washburn opened the trunk and worked much more luggage in than physics should have allowed. Until finally only one suitcase remained, one of Adele's.

"I can hold that on my lap," she told him.

Mr. Washburn looked like a bear, but spoke softer than a child. His chubby face betrayed his age; he couldn't have been more than twenty-five. Not the real Mr. Washburn. More like Mr. Washburn's great-great-great grandson. There's a tendency to think people who smile too much are dumb, but this boy wasn't. His grin worked to balance out his small, intense eyes. They were as black as polished onyx, and just as brilliant.

He smiled at her. "This is a pleasant surprise."

"Me?" she asked. Confused by what he'd said, but also by the fact that she felt flattered.

Mr. Washburn winced, but recovered. "Well, yes, *both* of you."

Solomon cut in. "We didn't have time to let you know we were coming."

"No," Mr. Washburn said. "I guess you didn't."

Adele climbed in back, her last suitcase heavy in her lap. Solomon Clay moved into the passenger side of the car and pushed the seat as far back as it would go, then turned to the uncomfortable Adele Henry and said, "He doesn't know we're here to change his mind."

"You don't think he's guessed?" she whispered.

"Why? He hasn't told *anyone* he's closing the Library yet."

"Well, then, how'd the Dean find out?"

"Didn't he tell you?"

"You mean that oracle bullshit?"

Solomon sneered. "Still think it's bullshit?"

Mr. Washburn walked around the car, checking Solomon's door, then the trunk, before getting inside. They needed to roll down the windows just so Mr. Washburn and Solomon Clay had room for their outer elbows. That car was packed tighter than a slave ship.

As they pulled onto San Pablo, Adele felt the close quarters of the car as a clutch around her body. She felt a breeze slinking up the space between her skin and her clothes. When it reached her collar, it came out as a fetid breath. A voice, whispering into the crook of her neck.

You're my special flower, aren't you?

How much does that flower cost?

The memory of that voice, its flirtatious venom, agitated Adele. She must've looked tense to Mr. Washburn as he watched her in the rearview mirror. His small eyes showed concern.

"I know you must be tired, Adele. That bus trip is long."

"Yes," she said, absently.

"I'll drive as quick as I can. There's a nice bed waiting for you."

Adele looked back at him in the rearview mirror now.

"Thank you," she said.

THEY DROVE to the Washburn estate, but before Adele could register the grandeur of it, she'd been dropped off at her own cabin and told to rest until morning. It wasn't her cabin for the night or the week, or even a month; it was *hers*. Mr. Washburn parked in her driveway, walked her bags inside, and showed her the paperwork sitting on the dining table: Adele Henry's rent was one dollar a month, with a lease good for ninety-nine years. Best land deal in Northern California.

"Why are you giving this to me?" she asked.

"We appreciate your work for us, and we believe in repaying those kinds of debts."

She smiled. "Don't you think you should ask your father about this first?" Adele waved the lease, but didn't let it go.

"My pop died when I was eleven. After he was gone, Mr. Clay was there for me, like an uncle, but I'm the head of this family."

Adele set the paper down and clasped her hands.

"I didn't meant to insult you, Mr. Washburn. I guess I'm not too good with people."

He said, "My first name is Snooky. And you're doing just fine with me."

They stood quietly in the warmth of the living room, close to each other.

"Snooky Washburn," she said.

"Snooky Washburn the third, actually."

"Is there a fourth?"

"No. Not yet."

He really did have a lovely smile, Adele felt. She offered one of her own.

"But my wife and I are trying," he added quickly.

Adele experienced a coughing fit just then, call it the soundtrack of her embarrassment.

"Well, shit!" she shouted once the coughing stopped.

He sensed the awkwardness between them and stooped lower. He'd learned that trick that big men do, of folding themselves in half so others might reach them.

Adele couldn't even look at him. She touched her face. "I always say the wrong thing."

Snooky Washburn laughed, and it was so loud she felt it echo in her chest.

"You haven't said the first thing wrong, Ms. Henry. Some of the things you say can be *surprising*, but the best thing about life is the surprises. Like I didn't expect to meet someone as nice as you today."

Adele grinned again, but he didn't see this because she wasn't looking at him.

"Okay," she said. "But if I call you Snooky, then you have to start calling me Adele."

He agreed and left through the kitchen door. She watched and waved as Snooky got into the car and backed out of the driveway. She didn't laugh at herself, at her big old putty heart, until she was alone.

NO REST ALLOWED, however. After one thing's done, there's another waiting. If she didn't get to it, who would? Where was the Devil's Well? And what was it, really?

Adele's cabin was big, three bedrooms big, generous beyond all reason, so much so that Adele wondered if she'd be getting roommates soon. She knew she wasn't, but still feared she could. One closet even had a pair of men's suits hanging in it. The last tenant's, maybe. This suspicion forced her to get up and check the driveway every few minutes. Even in the middle of taking off her makeup. With cold cream daubed across her face she crept into the kitchen, expecting to see a van full of Unlikely Scholars arriving to invade a space she already considered her home. Hers alone.

One canopy bed stood assembled in a room now officially "the bedroom," though it didn't have a vanity as she'd have liked. She had to remove her foundation at the bathroom mirror. Without makeup she looked at her wide face, cheeks as round as tennis balls. Hair so brown it almost looked black. It was her mother's face.

On sick days, when Adele had stayed home from school, Maxine Henry had cooked up Spanish omelets as a special breakfast treat for her girl. Two eggs beaten and poured into a pan; minutes later a puffy yellow disc slid onto a plate. While the eggs cooked, Adele's mother chopped onions and tomatoes, green peppers and mushrooms, then dropped them all into a second pan of crackling corn oil. Maxine would fry those vegetables until they'd browned and the onions took on a sugary taste. And finally, the magic ingredient, add teaspoons of ketchup to the nearly finished pan. The ketchup turned the corn oil into thick gravy. Pour that pan onto the cooled eggs and fold the omelet in half. As the thick oil soaked through the eggs and across the plate, Adele would dip a finger to taste. Perfection.

Then, while Adele ate, Maxine Henry would run around the house yelling, "Where are my keys? Where are my keys?" because preparing this breakfast always made Maxine late for work. The sight of her frantic mother made young Adele giggle, so her mom would shout even louder just to make her baby howl. Adele might try to mimic her mom, but the words all rushed together until they became another language. Wherearemykeys! 'Rarmykeys!

Eventually Maxine would find them and go to work. Adele was a little young to be left home alone, but there weren't any other options.

Adele had memorized the number for her mother's job and knew how to dial 911. Beyond that, Maxine simply had to have faith her daughter would be okay.

As Adele looked into the mirror now, at her naked face, her mother felt incredibly near.

Guess what? Do you know where I am? *California*. Can you beat that?

Maxine Henry. Only a few thousand miles away. As close as a phone call. Except Adele had been refused the new number. Accessible by mail if only Adele's mother had been willing to give her the new address.

AFTER A BATH Adele brought the suitcases into the bedroom and laid them flat in a corner, opened both, and hung all the clothes. She changed out of the box coat and skirt and put on a cotton crêpe kimono. Now she checked the kitchen, searching the cabinets. Yes! They'd stocked her cabin with the important provision. Liquor. Maybe the Washburns didn't teetotal quite as vehemently as the Dean. She made a gin rickey, full of ice, and drank it reclining in the lounge.

Then she poured one more.

Adele walked through the house, her house, and touched all her walls and every window. By the time she'd made the circuit, she was ready for one more glass.

Eventually she took off her kimono, put on a khaki two-piece riding suit, and her most comfortable shoes, four-buckled gaiters. She stood on the edge of the tub in the bathroom so she could see the outfit in the mirror. She looked courageous. Strong. If you asked her to go into the bush and kill a rhino, she could do it. With her hands.

Time to work.

She found a bike in the garage behind her cabin. Leaning against one wall. This big silver monstrosity. Fifty soup cans molded to resemble a Pashley Roadster, but warped. The bike looked like it had just survived a collision with the fourth dimension. She pulled it out and checked the mildly rusted chain, bounced up and down in the lopsided seat, even dropped it on its side; she was flawed, but she was sturdy. Adele took the bike along the small path, back around to the front of the house, popped the kickstand, and went inside for a hat.

While she'd been rummaging in the garage someone had come along and flipped an envelope under her front door. Periwinkle paper with writing on the face. It read: "Per Diem—$50." She opened it and found four hundred dollars inside.

She washed the glass she'd used (sipping at the last drops of gin rickey first), then grabbed her green purse and a newsboy cap. She walked around the cabin to be sure the windows were shut. Looked to see if she'd left any lights on by mistake. She'd really developed the home owner's mind-set right away.

Adele Henry, quick study.

Adele Henry, pedaling fast.

ADELE HENRY COASTED DOWN MacArthur Boulevard in that two-piece riding suit, on that battered bike, but had no idea where to go. She had one phrase, but no sense of its value. She'd decided the Devil's Well was a place, maybe a famous landmark. A location she could find. So she stopped her bike in front of a coffee shop, went inside, and asked to see a phone book.

The coffee shop felt like a grotto. Cozy and warm, the deep brown walls hugging close, and even the tabletops were made of stone. Since the smaller tables were already occupied, Adele sat at the one great table nearby, big enough for a dozen chairs. Six were already in use. She took a vacant corner and opened the phone book, leafed through the pages, and listened to them flap. She was waiting for the coffee she'd ordered. When they called her name, she took everything up there with her, her purse and coat, even the bulky phone book. She trusted no one.

In the seconds it took to walk up to the counter, a man had settled into the chair next to hers. Just appeared out of nowhere. Adele scanned the shop for another table, but no luck. She put her drink down, took off her coat, sat, set her purse between her feet, and started her research. She scooched her chair another inch away from the stranger.

"Yeah," the guy muttered.

Adele didn't respond. She only went into her purse for the brown paper towel.

The man beside her had a newspaper, a good sign (he could distract himself), and while he opened a section, she searched . . . for what? Was there going to be a business called the Devil's Well? Maybe. So she checked, but that was a bust. Was it a park, a gully, a mountain? Nope.

"Personally, I think you're right to wear those gaiters out. I'm pretty sure it'll rain today."

Adele ignored the man, even if he was complimenting her boots. She set the coffee cup on one end of the paper towel so it wouldn't blow away as people opened the front door.

"When I get out to hunt, I like to wear something similar. I wear those rubbers, you know, the slip-ons? Sometimes you're standing in six inches of mud. You don't realize it, but that environment can really abbreviate the lifetime of your footwear."

Well, what about a community group? A theater? The Devil's Well. Adele's ideas were crusty. A gang? Why the hell would a *gang* be listed in the phone book? Well I don't know, she snapped at herself, but let's just check anyway!

"Mushing around for an hour or two seems worth it if you get a few good hits on your detector, though. Most days I find nails and bottle tops, but I dug up a watch two weeks ago."

Other people at the table huffed to try to shush the man's patter, but he wouldn't be deterred. He didn't require responses. Probably held conversations with the shampoo bottle in the shower.

Adele slumped in her chair, but didn't sit back. There had to be something she could do.

"Say. Are you a teacher or something?"

Adele sipped her coffee.

"A reporter?"

She picked at lint that had gathered on her pants.

"An archeologist?" he asked, but without hope of a reply. Now he sighed and snapped his newspaper, lifted it to his face.

Adele decided she'd at least finish the coffee before crawling back to her cabin.

He muttered. "Why else you bothering with the Devil's Well?"

She turned to him quickly. "What did you just say?"

He lowered his newspaper.

"Well, hello! So nice of you to notice me."

She pointed at the phone book. "I was so busy."

"Oh, of course you were," he agreed.

He gloated, but didn't seem angry. His gray hair exploded from his head in all directions, wild and windswept even indoors. He looked like a dandelion. His body as thin as the stem.

"I thought you were ignoring me because I'm white," he said as he folded his paper neatly. "Crazy old white man in the coffee shop!"

Adele looked at her hands. "That's not true," she said. "I would've ignored you no matter what color man you were."

He nodded faintly. "I guess I can live with that."

She put her hand on the paper towel. With the letters written in her hurried script the thing looked like a scroll.

"So these words, you recognize them?"

"The Devil's Well? I sure do."

"Will you tell me?" she asked.

He leaned forward and widened his eyes. "Do you work for a museum?"

"I'm really not sure what I'm doing," she said. "But if you could just tell me . . ."

He smiled. "I can't really explain that much. My powers are limited. But I know where you could go. Someone you could talk to. She can answer anything."

Adele lifted the green purse from between her feet. This time she had a proper pen instead of a liner pencil. "I'm ready," she said.

"You know what I'd love?" the man asked, leaning back. "One of those prosciutto bruschetta sandwiches."

He grinned.

She looked at the register.

He winked playfully.

Adele put the pen down and took out her coin purse, turned away from him and swiffed a twenty-dollar bill from the roll. "You want anything to drink with that?"

He lifted his mug. "I've already got the coffee, thanks."

Adele Henry, diplomat, traded food for information.

THE GARLAND FOLKLORE SOCIETY KEPT ITS OFFICES in the last Victorian home on the shore of Laguna Lake. Even without the directions Adele would've noticed it. The rest of Laguna Lake's architecture spoke of late twentieth-century prosperity, high-rise luxury condos and high-rent apartment buildings. It was like the skyline on Garland's postcards. And tucked down amid those titans stood one cream-colored two-story home.

She walked her big bike up the little driveway that led to a porch and, having no lock, hefted the silver monster up the steps. As she did, she heard someone inside, coming to answer the knocks and rattles her bike made.

"Can I rest this inside?" Adele asked when the door opened.

The woman at the door sighed. "I don't care."

She stepped backward to let Adele and her steed in.

They entered a long hallway, and Adele propped the bike against a table covered with local history brochures. Then the woman went to the right, into a parlor that had been restored to its original beauty. A warm room, though a little crowded. Three settees, one against each wall, and a dozen parlor chairs, six of them huddled around the fireplace. Five walnut marble-top parlor tables were scattered around. It was as if they'd tried to fit three parlors into one.

"Welcome to the Garland Historical Society," the woman began. Her tone was flatter than Formica tile. "While you are standing in the last Victorian home along Laguna Lake, it wasn't always alone. The lake was once surrounded by houses just like this one."

"I'm not here for the tour," Adele said, realizing this woman had a lot more lecture left.

"Oh, thank God," the woman said, and rubbed her tired eyes, but then she hopped back like Adele had pulled a gun. "Are you a process server?"

"I promise," Adele said. "I'm not from the courts. A friend of yours sent me over. I have questions and he said you could answer them."

The tour guide's long black hair hung across her face and over her shoulders. Her eyes were entirely hidden. Adele just saw a full nose and the thin lips beneath it. The woman pulled her hair back to expose her whole face and laughed quietly.

"No friend of mine would send *more* work my way."

"White guy. Older. Loved talking about his metal detector."

"Barry Sometimes!" she yelped.

Adele looked over her shoulder as if the man had suddenly appeared.

"I call him Barry Sometimes because he makes appointments for my tour, but then he only shows up for half of them. I never know which ones. Sometimes he shows, sometimes he doesn't. He feels so guilty that he sends people over to me. He thinks I *want* to help people."

She had a deep voice, husky, even sensual. She didn't sound like a smoker, more like a smoky room.

"But you don't want to help people?" Adele asked.

"God, no," she said. "I'm an academic."

Adele nodded and tried to smile. That was meant to be a joke, but she couldn't understand what part of it was funny.

"Listen to me," the woman said. "Pissing and moaning. Sorry. I'm Joyce Chin. The least professional historian in America."

"I'm Adele Henry, the world's most clueless detective."

Joyce clapped. "That's the spirit."

"I thought this was the Folklore Society. That's what Barry said."

Joyce pointed to the ceiling.

"We just took over from the Garland Historical Society last year. We got the top half of the building, but the first floor is still theirs. We're shuffling things around, as you can see. A lot of this furniture used to be upstairs, but now the Folklore Society is on the second floor."

The two of them shrugged and seemed awkward. A third party, some kind of translator, might've helped.

"Listen," Joyce finally said. "My office is up there too. It's the only place in Northern California where I can smoke without being called a murderer. Do you mind if we go up?"

Adele nodded and stepped aside.

"Your outfit belongs down here," Joyce joked as they walked down the main hallway. At least Adele *thought* it was a joke, but the lack of affect in this woman made it hard to tell.

Finally, they reached the stairs and ascended from history into folklore.

ONE OF JOYCE CHIN'S OFFICE WALLS was covered with crude drawings, and a second with college degrees. While Joyce smoked, Adele looked at all these decorations. Seeing the bachelor's and master's degrees, the Ph.D. certificate, turned Adele into a calculator. She saw the dates when each had been issued and tried to think of what she'd been doing while Joyce studied at school. The doctorate read 1997. Where had she been then?

That's all you charge for your little flower?

You make me want to go and start a garden.

"It's a myth," Joyce said. "The Devil's Well. Just a story. Are you Native American?"

"No."

"How'd you hear about it?"

Adele's paranoid streak ran through all two hundred six of her bones, so she avoided specificity.

"I overheard a man I work with talking about it."

"And what did he say?"

She paused. "I guess he said he knew where it was."

Joyce sipped at the filter of her second cigarette and leaned back in her seat.

"Well, so what?" she said. "People claim they know where Atlantis is. It's just talk."

"My coworker isn't a man I trust," Adele admitted. "He's planning an expedition."

"To where? Jupiter?"

"Underground," Adele whispered, tapping at the arm rest of her chair.

"You think he might be putting others in danger?"

See that. Adele *knew* she'd make a mistake. Now Joyce Chin would ask names, maybe call for police, who would detain Adele, and soon enough she'd have to face a very disappointed Snooky Washburn. She didn't want to be known as a blabbermouth.

"We work for a library, Ms. Chin. The greatest danger we face is paper cuts."

Joyce puffed and laughed. She blew the smoke out from the right side of her mouth.

"Then, what do you think may happen, Ms. Henry?"

Adele feared she couldn't outthink Joyce Chin, so she told the truth elusively.

"I'm just afraid of what may happen if my coworker doesn't get his way."

"A man reacting badly because he's been denied? I've never heard of such a thing."

Joyce and Adele laughed harder at this than anything yet.

Finally, Adele said, "The head of our library seems like a good man."

Joyce completed her thought. "And you'd like to protect him."

Watching Joyce with that cigarette only made Adele want to drink. She thought more clearly with a tumbler in one hand.

This large room was crowded with books. Some in stacks on the floor, many more on the metal shelves. From her seat Adele could see some of the books were upside-down, others with spines turned in. Well-used and dog-eared. These weren't display items.

"Take a look at this," Joyce said, rising from her seat. She dropped her lit cigarette into an empty metal garbage bin, then pulled an oversize book from one shelf. Its covers were stiff, forest-green, somewhat new, but the pages inside were so old they'd gone yellow and brittle. Joyce set it down on her desk and opened it. Adele leaned forward in her seat.

"Garland, the city as it is now, began when a Spanish general named Gabriel Pereyra was given 44,800 acres of land in recognition for his lifetime of service to the Spanish king."

Adele brought her fingers to the page and touched it very lightly. It showed a map of these 44,800 acres. The date in an upper corner read 1774. The illustrated land looked unpleasant, uninhabitable, excessively natural to her urban eyes.

Joyce walked over to another bookshelf, leaving Adele by the map.

"One of Pereyra's cooks, a drunk, kept a journal. Mostly just a listing of the kitchen's diminishing resources. But he does have one entry, just one, where he claims he stumbled onto a path that led underground. Not far from here. Back when Laguna Lake used to be nothing but marshes. Hundreds of tunnels. That's what he describes. Filled with water. Like canals."

Joyce Chin returned to the desk, carrying another large old book.

"The Devil's Well," Adele said.

Joyce Chin grunted. "A myth. A myth begun by these guys, the Heurequeque Indians."

Joyce tapped the page of the open second ledger. Adele expected to look down and see photographs. Like a few hundred years ago these Indians might've taken a few snapshots to preserve their special moments. Instead she saw a series of sketches, a couple on each large page, sketches so rough that few people today would call them maps. More like tracings, only vaguely recognizable as Garland's boundaries.

"They were nomadic people who'd been going up and down the California coast for at least a thousand years before the Spanish arrived. And this sunken bowl of marshland? Here. The one that used to stretch for miles, from Grand Avenue all the way to the San Francisco Bay? *That's* what they called the Devil's Well. So it's like the Bermuda Triangle, in a way. Your coworker might know *where* it is, but that doesn't mean the magic is real."

Adele nodded. "But why did the Indians give it that name?"

"Because the Devil lives there."

Adele looked up at Joyce, who couldn't stop smiling. She'd been indulging cigarettes, but truly enjoyed this.

Joyce Chin corrected herself. "Devils. Plural."

She turned three brittle pages in the second book and swept her thin hand over one huge drawing, all curving lines and dots. This was a map too, but on a grander scale, not a sliver of land but a constellation of stars.

Joyce said, "The thing about cities, about what we call civilizations, is that they blind you. We evolve for the better in some ways, but lose sight of other things. Ms. Henry, I want you to imagine this land long before there were any streetlamps or headlights. Nothing brighter than a small fire where people gathered round."

Adele stood and walked with Joyce to one of the windows of the office. They looked down on placid Laguna Lake.

"When you looked up, you could see the sky clearly. You could see stars by the hundreds. Thousands. The Heurequeque used to sit together and witness the night. They mapped whole star charts. Observed galaxies."

Now Adele leaned forward until the tip of her nose brushed the cool glass.

"The sky was so clear that the Heurequeque's ancestors were able to see directly into the eyes of their Creator. That's the story. And their Creator basked in its children's attention. In return it would sing to them. But so quietly that they could only hear it in the breezes or the rustle of marsh grass. So they called their Creator the Whisper."

It wasn't hard for Adele to imagine that the Heurequeque's Whisper was also Judah Washburn's Voice.

Adele looked up at the ceiling now, as if she would see through it if she concentrated.

"The Whisper created suns and planets, insects and beasts, right before the Heurequeque's eyes. A single breath from the Whisper's lips, and deer appeared in the world. Venus was created with a hum."

"It's the brightest planet," Adele said, which she'd learned from a children's science supplement in the *Pittsburgh Post-Gazette*.

"But all this work takes its toll, even on a god. The Whisper was busy. It needed help."

"It needed scouts," Adele said.

"So the Whisper pursed its lips, blew out, and just like that, poof, twelve attendants appeared. They set the clouds in the sky. Churned rivers. They did the Whisper's bidding in the world."

Adele opened her purse now, reached inside, and grabbed the brown paper towel. She didn't take it out, but felt the need to touch it.

Joyce said, "And after all the rest was done, the world in order, the Whisper cast them to earth, to this land we now call the East Bay. And gave them one last task."

"What was that?" Adele asked quietly.

"To teach the Heurequeque!" Joyce shouted. This story animated her like nothing else so far.

"How to live right," Joyce said. "How to earn the divine rewards."

Adele tapped the window with a knuckle. "But they didn't live right?"

"No. The Heurequeque saw the Swamp Angels and were disgusted. They looked vile to human eyes, so the Heurequeque ran in terror. They despised the Swamp Angels, turned their backs on the Whisper's emissaries. Called them 'the Devils of the Marsh.' Hunted and killed as many as they could. The Heurequeque fell from grace. Myths and folklore try to remind us of truths like this. That's their purpose."

"Truths like what?" Adele asked.

"That the face of goodness may surprise you."

Adele Henry and Joyce Chin stood over the desk again. Joyce lit her next cigarette. The pair looked down at the two open books. Joyce touched the pages and smiled at the maps.

The face of goodness may surprise you, Adele repeated to herself.

"This is really what you do?" Adele asked. "Digging through these freaky things?"

Adele waved at the bookshelves. They reminded her of the shelves in her own cabin, even though Joyce had a lot more. It felt like seeing your favorite dress on another woman and wondering if you looked that good.

"I mean, you don't ever second-guess this kind of life?" Adele added. "Like what kind of difference it really makes?"

Joyce Chin crossed her arms; the lit cigarette fumed in her left hand.

"I know," she said. "Believe me, I know. Who cares about all this nonsense, right? Folklore. It sure won't make you rich! It's quilts and handicrafts and ridiculous stories. Even the people I study don't care about it much. But I *do*."

Wait! There'd been a mistake, an error in the translation. Adele hadn't meant to insult Joyce, but to admire her commitment, her expertise. Her rigor. She'd meant to say, Thank you for knowing all this. Thank you for sharing it with me. Thank you for being an example. Oh, what was the point? Adele would never be able to explain. She'd only say the wrong thing.

"I just never met a woman like you before, Ms. Chin."

"Sure you have," Joyce said. "I'm a woman like you."

ADELE RODE TO TOWN in a bus that morning, and that evening she steered home on a bike. Adele preferred the second, even though it was more work. In fact, the work was the best part. Your body's made to act, and once you finally let it, when your lungs turn to bellows that rouse the spark of life in your throat, that's when you'll breathe fire. Just as Adele did now. Sure, she'd survived some hard times before, but surviving is far from thriving. Thriving is like this, the simple trick of pedaling up a hill. It got her mind working.

She'd expected trouble at the front gate of the Washburn property, but the guards already knew her and waved her by. Also, they didn't seem to care much who went in and out. They were only paid enough for attendance, not effort.

Instead of riding down the main road and making a loop around to the back entrance of her cabin, a trip across flat land, she snapped the silver bike into first gear and attacked the steep slope veering off to the right. She felt that good. Adele made it about three feet up before she thought, Fuck this. She got off, walked the bike. There's passion, and there's pulling a muscle.

At the top of the hill she saw the San Francisco Bay and a bridge, though it wasn't the famous Golden Gate. Something smaller that connected Garland, Oakland, Berkeley, the East Bay to the legendary Pacific city.

Seeing all that structure, the obvious permanence of it, Adele realized why she'd had such a hard time with what Joyce Chin told her. As a human being you tend to think your present moment is the pinnacle, the summit, of life's achievements. Or at least she thought that way. And yet she couldn't help feeling envious when she imagined those Heurequeque under the stars. Not because their lives were simple and rustic, none of that nonsense. She doubted that a life like theirs was much more than toil and sleep. But the idea that they might've seen their Creator simply by peeking at the night. What a gift. Maybe this was why the idea of Judah's story being true bothered her, too. No one wants to envy a folk tale. But the wish to see *something*, maybe even for her, was no myth.

WHILE MOST OF THE GROUNDS of the Washburn estate had a sculpted look—even the creeping vines on the sides of the guardhouse clung in a decorative *W*—the woods around Adele's cabin were berserk. She knew she'd almost reached her place when the trees rose up in clusters, crowding one another for space, and the underbrush spread with violence.

The driveway wasn't even visible; you had to know where it was. She found it after a moment's confusion, and rode its curve to her Spanish-style cabin. A nubby white chimney rose from the orange tiled roof, and all the blue window frames looked even brighter because of the white walls surrounding them. Talk about a stick of butter! She couldn't help feeling full. The feast of her new life tasted richer when you threw this cabin in.

She wanted another hot bath. She undressed and put on her kimono, a pair of fleece scuffs to keep her feet warm, and while going through this, Adele reviewed what she'd learned.

When the Dean told the story of Judah Washburn, there was a figure Judah had followed while underground. *Too tall to be a man.* That's what the Dean had said. What about a Swamp Angel, doing the Voice's will? Leading Judah to his fate.

And what was hers? In her experience, the only fate you had was the fate you made.

I'm not a cop.

I promise you.

How can I put your mind at ease?

I won't enjoy myself if you're nervous.

But forget that awful weekend, Adele. Forget it, forget it, cut it out. Take a bath.

Adele went into her suitcases to find that Lake had packed her scented candles. She got a pair of saucers from a kitchen cabinet by the fridge, lit both candles at the oven, placed them on the saucers, and walked them into the bathroom slowly. Set them on the bathroom sink. She shut the door, turned out the light, took off her kimono and slippers. The fat candles offered just enough light to see.

Just open the car door and get inside.

Come on, now.

Be good.

"Shut up," she told her mind. "Shut up."

The water bordered on boiling when she ran it, but soon it settled down to just pretty damn warm. A temperature that suited Adele Henry well. She got in and felt her legs go jelly. Once her lower back sank under the waterline, the heat untied a knot she hadn't even realized hid there. The candles burned long enough to release their lilac scent, and because of the closed door and window Adele felt not just surrounded, but overpowered by the smell. She wanted that. It helped her to stop thinking and worrying and remembering and reliving, so she could find her way back to happiness. She hummed to herself because the house lacked a radio.

She whispered, "Met him on a Thursday, sunny afternoon. Cumulus clouds, eighty-four degrees."

You fall asleep when treated this nicely. Adele lay in the water until it cooled and her eyes fluttered shut and the trees outside the bathroom window brushed themselves against the cabin walls. Eventually she woke up and climbed out of the bathtub, blew out the candles, dried herself off, put on the kimono and scuffs again, made her way to the bedroom in the dark. Moonlight filtered in through the curtains.

Adele sat off the corner of the bed, opened her kimono, and spread her legs. Pressed her left hand against her belly. She leaned forward so the firm mattress edge rose up against the bottom of her pelvis, and she slowly ran her right hand down into the pubic hair. The way she'd been masturbating since she was a girl.

To be fair, the man she imagined walking into her room just now wasn't actually Snooky Washburn. He only shared the man's size and complexion. And face. You and I, she said to him. He said her name and then stood before her. He wore a navy-blue suit. She stood and took off his jacket, but one of the buttons on his shirt had fallen off. Adele pressed her finger to the empty buttonhole, and he watched her do this but didn't move. Then she slipped her hand inside his shirt and touched his beefy chest. Her pointer finger found his small, hard nipple. Whose skin felt warmer, hers or his? You need my help, she said again, but he put his big hand over her mouth. She went silent. His hand moved behind her now. His heart beat out strongly. He didn't slide her kimono off, he tore it away.

Adele Henry leaned nearly off the edge of the bed now, her middle and ring fingers going frantically while her left hand grasped the side of the mattress for balance. She hissed as she ground down against the corner of the bed, eyes squeezed shut, back gone all straight, and kept going until her thighs began to shake. Hot shiver in her belly.

And soon she fell into a lovely sleep.

LOUD KNOCKS WOKE HER, and she stumbled to the cabin door confused, not even sure who she'd meet on the other side. And when it was

Snooky, she felt embarrassed for oversleeping, for answering the door in such a state, and for the fantasy that had sent her to bed the night before.

"So, good morning! How do? I made some breakfast for you."

Snooky wore black jeans, workman's boots, a green sweater, and a warm coat, much like what he'd worn the day before. He probably hadn't ever gone in for those bowler hats and handmade vests like the Unlikely Scholars wore. Costumes of importance. But why would he? His authority lay in his name.

Adele still felt too shocked to answer, so she stepped aside, but Snooky didn't come into her cabin. He carried a plate covered with aluminum foil, and only a third of that plate crossed the threshold. She took the plate by its edge and tipped it backward so it left his palm and rested on one of hers. Even through the foil she smelled the biscuits.

The same green Mercedes 450 SLC sat at the top of the driveway, with Solomon Clay in the passenger seat. Seeing him dressed in a beige tweed jacket was her first reminder that she'd answered the door in her kimono.

"I can meet you at the car in fifteen minutes," she said. It was sillier to stand there speechless.

He laughed quietly. "Eat one of my biscuits, and you'll need to lie down for half an hour. I've got some orange juice for you too. I think I made it the way you like."

She took the carafe of orange juice by the fluted tip. She swished the orange juice quietly.

"Why do you Washburns do all this for us?" she asked.

"Maybe it's what you deserve. Is that good enough?"

She laughed just once. "Folks like me aren't usually on the list for prizes."

"You're on mine," he said, and walked back up the driveway.

HE WASN'T LYING about those biscuits. Adele knew there were people in the world who were entirely too healthy for a meal like this. Had to be four eggs in that omelet, four at least. Half a block of cheese. It wasn't Maxine Henry's Spanish omelet, but nothing could be. The orange juice was prepared perfectly, though. With champagne.

Adele took a half hour to eat, finish the mimosas, wash the dishes, wash herself, and choose a uniform. She felt self-conscious about taking so long, but believed Snooky would forgive her.

She decided on a gray plaid riding outfit with jodhpurs that fastened along the outside of both calves, and a long, belted three-button jacket.

She went into the bathroom and applied a full face of makeup. Adele brushed her hair quietly and wished to wear it in braids again, the way her mother used to do it. Adele remembered the comfort of her mother picking through her hair. How safe she felt when she draped each arm over her mother's strong thighs.

Maxine.

Adele's outfit felt a bit snug. She worried about the way it squeezed her belly and thighs. That it made her look grotesque. No one else will notice if the clothes are a little tight, she reminded herself. You're the only one who cares. So stop being silly and get out there!

Adele walked up the driveway and reached the car. Both men had stepped out to stretch. Solomon Clay posed in his loose tweeds. He looked as elegant as a solid Brigg umbrella. He pointed at her riding suit and said, "Your suitcase is overpacked."

As Adele climbed into the car, she stepped on his Chetwynd shoes, scuffing one toe murderously.

As Snooky drove them off the estate, he said, "Was I right about those biscuits, Adele?"

"You were. And how did you get the omelet so fluffy, *Snooky*?"

Solomon Clay cackled. "Snooky's *wife* cooked your eggs."

IF A PERSON HAD TO GUESS the least likely destination for Snooky Washburn, Solomon Clay, and Adele Henry, it's still doubtful anyone would have come up with the Albertsons supermarket on Lakeshore Avenue. Nevertheless, that's where Snooky parked.

Adele climbed out of the car while Solomon Clay walked ahead, his long legs covering yards with a stride. As he moved toward the front of Albertsons, Adele hissed for attention.

"Snooky," she whispered, "do you know where we're going?"

Snooky stopped by the trunk of his car. "Sure I do. I've been told about Judah and the well since I was in my crib."

"Then you believe it."

"I believe the story is important to people," Snooky said.

She wanted to grab his wrist, pull him back into the car. "If it's just a story, why go?"

"You have to do it. It's like walking on Mount Sinai."

In the distance Solomon Clay realized he was alone and came jogging back.

Adele spoke quickly. "We're not here just to give you a walking tour."

"Oh, no?" Snooky said. He was playful, but to her he looked childish and naïve.

"We know you're going to shut the Library down."

The smile left Snooky's face, and he leaned against the car. The metal frame creaked with the weight. "What did you say?"

"We *know*, Snooky."

"I haven't even told Cherise yet."

Cherise. Adele almost said the name out loud, but caught herself.

Solomon Clay arrived. He watched Snooky's stunned face closely, then turned to Adele.

"You told him."

She said, "He had a right to know."

Snooky, still leaning against the car, spoke softly. "How?" he asked. "*How?*"

Solomon smiled. "We're onto something at the Library, Snooky. Let me show you."

The two men moved. Mr. Clay led Snooky by the shoulder, and this made Snooky look so young. Solomon pointed back at her. "You stay with the car."

Adele said, "I bet I won't."

He glared. "What did I tell you about that tone?"

Snooky found himself again. Shook Solomon's hand from his arm. He said, "She's a grown woman and she can come if she wants."

Solomon pouted like Snooky had snuck a sandwich into his dinner party. He sped to the front of Albertsons in a rage. Before following, Snooky took out his car keys, opened the trunk, and found a small black case. He opened it, and Adele saw a pistol. Snooky slid the pistol into the front pocket of his jeans.

"Solomon was there for me," Snooky said. "I know he can be hard to take, but I respect him. And I trust him." He patted his gun through the denim. "But I'm no fool either. Don't worry, Adele. I'm still in control."

Adele wanted to believe Snooky, very much, but he wasn't like the Dean or Solomon Clay. Ruthless. Hustlers. Street veterans. Pros.

Was it progress that now black boys *and* white boys, yellow girls and brown ones, could be born so privileged that they never doubted themselves? So coddled they considered themselves infallible? Pity them. They dive into chaos where others have the common sense to run away.

As Adele walked behind Snooky, she realized her mission had changed. Before, she'd wondered if she'd have to kill to protect the Washburn Library. But now she wondered if she'd have to kill to protect Snooky Washburn.

THE NEWSPAPER of record for Garland's homeless population is the *Avenue Edge*, a collection of articles, essays, poems, harangues, and doodles sold by the homeless themselves on corners and in front of candy stores, coffee shops, and in parking lots. The salesmen with charm earn bills, and the ones without get bubkes. It's a dreadful feeling to end your day with just as many copies as when you started, so imagine the good fortune of our man in front of Albertsons that particular morning. A disagreeable guy. Glowering. Utterly without hope of generating even a quarter that day, and he lucks into Solomon Clay.

He said something to Solomon, the same grumble he'd inflicted on the Albertsons employees who'd opened the store, and on every customer that morning, but this time his grumble worked. The man passed him a twenty-dollar bill and slipped a copy of *Avenue Edge* from between those gangly fingers.

Adele and Snooky passed the homeless peddler, but he didn't try getting money from them. He was too busy staring at the bill in his palm.

Adele went inside the supermarket and followed the others down the shampoo aisle. Solomon Clay at the front, Adele Henry in the back, and between them one member of Garland's aristocracy.

At the end of the aisle they passed a refrigerated egg display, and Solomon Clay went through a pair of brown industrial double doors. They reached a medium-size package room, dirty concrete walls and flooring, racks of packaged bread ready to be shelved, boxes of vegetables ready for their bins.

There was a large elevator door there. Solomon Clay pressed the button, and they got in. When the doors opened again, they were in a sub-basement. Lightbulbs hung on wires from the ceiling, and the wires were frayed.

The three of them walked in the same order and did it quietly. The smell of mildew brushed their noses. Adele swatted in front of her face because there were flies. Finally they reached two locked gray metal doors.

The Devils' Well, she thought.

Solomon Clay opened the doors. She expected them to creak, but they moved silently, like they'd been freshly oiled. There was a smaller room inside. An incandescent vapor-proof aluminum light hung on a wall, but it only lit the manhole cover in the middle of the floor. Solomon Clay touched one of the darkened walls, found a shelf and two metal keys that looked like large red soda pop tabs. He inserted the keys into the manhole cover and pulled the lid up.

There was one black equipment kit tucked into a corner of the chamber. Solomon Clay grabbed it and climbed in.

"You don't have boots or anything?" she said to Solomon. "Something I could wear over my outfit, to protect it. Even a plastic bag for my hair?"

Solomon spat down into the darkness. "Maybe you'd like Snooky to carry you around?"

As Solomon descended, he muttered, "You could sit on his face."

THESE WEREN'T SEWERS. Adele figured that out pretty quickly. Just as soon as she noticed the complete lack of human waste. They were in a wide tunnel, filled with muddy but fresh water that came up to her knees. Like canals. She thought of Joyce Chin, who might've appreciated knowing the old Spanish cook hadn't lied. These catacombs were quiet and dim, but only two people shrank. Down here, Solomon Clay bloomed.

"The first time I found my way down, I never wanted to leave," he said. "I wonder if each of us gets made for a certain kind of environment. Like it's not even up to you. This is just where you're supposed to be." He carried a flashlight. Each of them did now. Solomon waved his to and fro.

"These tunnels feel homey to you?" Adele asked.

"I don't mean standing in water. I mean down below instead of up there."

Solomon touched the ceiling, and his light stabbed at the surface like a lance. His case had been full of trusty little items like this: flashlights, batteries, bandages, even face masks.

But Adele didn't feel like entertaining the philosophical jabbering of Solomon Clay. Instead of responding to him, she said, "So it's really true, Snooky?"

He looked back at her and nodded somberly.

"Yes, Adele. I guess it is."

She hadn't wanted to hear him say it. The Dean could, Mr. Clay could, but it wasn't true until Snooky did.

"Are you running out of money?" She didn't care if the question sounded coarse.

"That," Snooky said. "And patience."

Adele's light played across the tunnel walls. They were only dirt, not concrete, but the earth had been sculpted, smoothed, hardened. Glazed by a process too mysterious for Adele's best guess. Solomon, Snooky, and Adele sloshed through the heavy water and gave up trying to keep their clothes dry. Soon enough their wet clothes gummed up against their bodies, outlining every paunch and jiggle. Adele kept tugging her shirt off her belly. The water rolled away from them as they moved along, slapping against the tunnel walls on either side, then returning with a slurp.

"Did the Voice tell you to shut it down or something?" she asked.

"My accountant told me to."

Snooky Washburn was doing the worst of all down in the tunnel. Kept bumping his head on the ceiling and then stooping down too low and getting water in his mouth when it splashed up against his legs. Then coughing violently enough to bring tears to his face.

And yet her sympathy only came in waves. When it ebbed, it was because she thought of his plans for the Library. He could just shut it down like that? she thought. Shut *me* down?

She realized she'd already told herself a whole story about Snooky Washburn and Adele Henry. Teammates. Partners. Maybe in love someday. All this in the span of a day. Despite Cherise. Despite the difference in their ages. And why? Because this is what she wanted. A man like that beside her. Not in front or behind. It took only hours for her to plan out their years, and yet look at Snooky over there, oblivious. Just a man who'd decided to throw her good new life away.

THEY CAUGHT UP to Solomon in a larger chamber just a few yards ahead. Adele thought it was their destination, but three more paths led out from there. If these tunnels were roads, they'd reached an intersection. She looked up, half-expecting to find a traffic light.

Solomon Clay clapped once, but the echo in the catacombs made the sound tremendous, as if a set of great doors had slammed shut behind them.

"Judah waded in these waters, Snooky. Your ancestor touched these walls."

Snooky looked at the ceiling. How many times had Solomon practiced these words just to make them seem effortless and improvised now?

"He had every reason to give up, to just drop in the dirt and die."

"But he didn't," Snooky finished.

"That's right. He maintained. He persevered."

"I know where this is going," Snooky whispered. "But I'm not changing my mind about the Library."

Mr. Clay said, "That's all right. I didn't bring you down here to talk about that place."

Solomon walked ahead again. Snooky Washburn followed him, drawn perhaps by curiosity. And what about Adele? Why should she continue?

Adele thought of all the troubles she'd faced in the past. Too many. Would that change if she ran away? Trouble comes, that's unavoidable. Might as well have it out now.

Adele thought of Maxine Henry again. Her estranged and disappointed mother. A woman practically driven into hiding by her daughter's criminal life. A relationship that wouldn't be saved in a thousand years. And despite their history Adele called to that woman now as she trudged toward the Devils' Well. This wasn't the first time she'd prayed to her mother for protection. She'd done it in Paterson, New Jersey, too.

Keep me alive, Maxine. Please be with me.

Adele continued on, behind the others, into the deeper gloom.

WELL, LOOK AT YOU *just standing around in the cold. You remember me?*

You're my special flower. That's right.

I'm lucky to find anything so precious growing in Paterson.

I told you I wasn't a cop. Will you trust me this time? Don't run off like before.

Climb inside. It's fine. That's fine.

I want you to talk to me the whole time, okay? Call me Honeyspot. Okay?

Yes, that's what I said. It's funny, right?

I'm like a bear, I guess.

I find a woman's honey and I steal it.

EVENTUALLY THE CLEAR TUNNELS DETERIORATED, and rubble turned the ground beneath the water into an uneven pathway. The catacombs became wilder. The air so hot that sweat bubbled out of every pore in Adele's face. Eventually she stopped wiping it away. Tree roots cracked through the ceiling and grasped at the tops of their heads. It was as if they were marching backward in time. From the modern day, as far back as the dawn.

They walked single file and kept a quiet line. Thicker tree roots dangled down, and cordgrass grew out of the water; the tops of it brushed as high as her knees.

I SAW A MOTEL *on my way over here. Would you mind going there?*

Don't worry about the money. I want you for hours.

Okay. You can have half of it now and the rest as soon as we're done. That sound fair?

You know what you seem like?

You seem like a good girl to me.

ALL ROADS END. Aboveground or below. This tunnel stopped at a closed door.

The door was a disc, easily six feet across, and made of gray stone. An aspirin tablet for one very big headache. There was a hole as wide as the tip of a baseball bat right in the center of the disc. Solomon Clay leaned forward, put his hand into the hole, and pushed the door to the left. It rolled open with a rumble.

Snooky spoke in a hush. "Is this . . . really?"

"That's right, little prince."

The inside of the chamber looked even darker than the tunnel where they stood. An impossible kind of night, the last night. The way it'll look when every star goes extinct.

Mr. Clay walked calmly into the open doorway, but Snooky hung back, stiff. Adele reached his side, and the man couldn't even blink. His mouth hung open.

"Snooky," she whispered. "Snooky, it's all right."

"I can't go in there," he said.

"You want to run?" she asked.

"I never believed it," he admitted.

"Let's run," Adele said.

Now he blinked. And breathed. He looked at her. "I'll bet you've been through a lot worse than this, Adele. You don't seem scared, but I can't even move my legs. I thought this was just a story my father told me at night to scare me. I can't do this . . ."

"You can do whatever you want to, Snooky. And you'd be surprised what you can survive."

He smiled weakly. "Can I give you this?"

Snooky pulled the gun from his pocket and handed it to her, handle first.

"The way I feel right now, I'd probably just end up shooting myself."

Adele took it. "Think of me as your bodyguard," she said, trying to sound cool.

But this bodyguard had to face the fact that she'd never fired a gun. The thing was as heavy as a heart attack. She must've been looking at it strangely.

"If you have to use it," Snooky said, "don't pull the trigger, just squeeze it."

They went in together, side by side.

THERE YOU GO. *Good girl.*

How do you like this room?

Come, now. No crying.

Oh, I see. Those aren't tears. That's blood. Your scalp's not holding up well.

But it doesn't even hurt after a while, isn't that right?

My special flower.

If they do let you into heaven when this is over, tell God how I plucked you tonight.

THE CEILING OF THE EARTHEN AMPHITHEATER ROSE to thirty feet. After being stuck in those cramped tunnels, it felt as disorienting as deepest space in there. Adele felt nearly weightless, and she went cockeyed trying to adjust to the dimensions of the new room. She'd become used to reaching out and touching the tunnel walls or ceilings, and without this she drifted. If there hadn't still been water around her thighs, cordgrass bunching around her shins, she really would have believed she was floating. Adele stood a mile below Laguna Lake, but it felt like she'd left this old world.

Snooky Washburn rose to his full height for the first time in an hour, and even Adele's back felt better when she saw him stretch that way. The room was darker than the tunnels, but her eyes adjusted. The beams from her flashlight seemed to float in the air, pockets of illumination that helped her see.

The cordgrass below the water had been growing and dying for centuries. All manner of tiny organic life had come to be and come to pass in this chamber too. Their fats and cellulose and proteins broken down by bacteria in the mud and sediment of the marshy floor. This process produced swamp gas. Methane, mostly. Colorless and odorless, but not exactly harmless. The Devils' Well appeared empty, but it was actually quite full.

Snooky walked ahead, into the middle of the chamber, where Solomon stood too. The water rose as high as each tall man's waist in that spot. Adele hung back a bit, staying closer to the only door, and took the gun out of her pocket. She pointed it down, toward the water.

Really she was aiming at her own foot, and when she realized this, she lifted the gun, pointed straight out, and moved her arm until she had the gun aimed at Solomon Clay. But she couldn't maintain the pose for long because the weight of the gun exhausted her shoulder.

Solomon Clay said, "I'm disappointed in you, Snooky. And the Voice is too."

WHEN YOU SCREAM, *it forces me to put things in your mouth.*

SOLOMON CLAY PURSED HIS LIPS. He made a long slow hummed note. He hummed all the way through Snooky Washburn's protests. And when Snooky raised his voice, Solomon only hummed louder. Finally Snooky stopped trying.

"I didn't bring you down here to talk about your money, Snooky. I didn't bring you here to have a debate about your *wealth.* You could say I'm concerned about your soul."

Snooky groaned. "Not one of these talks—"

Solomon interrupted. "I first met you when you were eleven years old. At your father's funeral. I walked down the line of family, and most of them didn't even want to shake my hand. Maybe they blamed the Library for your daddy's death. Maybe they thought of us as a god damn cult, I don't know. But then I got to you and I introduced myself, and do you remember what you did?"

Snooky looked away from Solomon, into the empty dark all around him.

"I offered you my seat."

Solomon nodded. "And you wouldn't let me say no. You had me sit with all the Washburns, like I was just as much your father's family as any of them, and I knew you had an honorable heart."

"That was years ago," Snooky said.

"Not so long, Snooky. And I still see that upright young man today."

"I appreciate that," Snooky said. "I really do."

The chamber returned to silence. Adele and Snooky had entered shoulder to shoulder, but just now she couldn't help feeling a little like the odd one out.

I'M GOING TO PUT YOU *in the bathtub now.*
Can't have you bleeding through the mattress.

ADELE COULDN'T SEE QUITE RIGHT. Solomon had turned his flashlight in her direction. She squinted in the glimmering cave.

Snooky shouted, "But how long am I supposed to keep bankrolling you? For real. *How long?* Fifty more years? A thousand?"

Now Adele sloshed forward in the water, only two steps, raising her free hand as if she had the proper answer.

Solomon pointed his light back at Snooky. "I told you, I'm not talking

about your *got damn* money! Keep it all, I don't care. I want you, Snooky
Washburn the third, to come with me and meet the despised children."

Snooky spoke wearily. "I meet them every time the Dean sends them
from Vermont."

Though she knew Snooky meant every Unlikely Scholar who'd arrived by bus, plane, or car, she couldn't help thinking of when they'd
met, tussling on the Greyhound station floor.

"You think I'm talking about a bunch of puffed-up washouts? They
think a brand-new outfit means now their shit don't stink. Well, the
Voice isn't just a path to prosperity."

"I have a family!" Snooky shouted, as if his family were a weapon hidden in his sleeve. "And an inheritance that's running out. I have to worry
about my own."

Adele tried to see Snooky's face. Was he looking her way right then,
begging her to squeeze that trigger and protect him? The swamp gas was
making her faint, woozy; she swung her flashlight wildly, trying to find
him. The light seemed to hover in the swamp gas until a sickly yellow
fog filled the chamber, covering the waters like a shroud, obscuring the
two men even more.

There were great splashes, and the water sloshed around Adele's
knees, and in her confusion the water seemed to bubble and churn as if
she were being boiled alive.

"*That's* Judah's real legacy," Solomon said. "He was selfish down to his
soul too."

Adele jiggled the gun, which rested in her grip, but her shoulder
wouldn't work as expected. It wouldn't lift. Too tired. She ran forward,
into the cloud of swamp gas, and found the two men wrestling.

Solomon huffed. "But I'm going to beat that demon out of you."

Snooky was fifty pounds heavier and fifty years younger, but the old
man was filled with an unquenchable fire. He had Snooky stooped forward, head down toward the water, both arms pinned behind the back.
They looked like prehistoric beasts, like two dinosaurs battling. They
gasped and panted, and their breath seemed to mingle with the swamp
gas until Adele really felt she'd stumbled into a clash at the dawn of
time.

She shouted, "Let Snooky go!"

Solomon raised one arm and brought the elbow down on the back of
Snooky Washburn's head. The big man went down with a splash.

Mr. Clay turned to Adele. "Or what?"

Her right arm felt stronger now, thanks to a sudden rush of self-
preservation. Adele held the grip of the pistol loosely, and with a grimace
she raised the gun.

DON'T YOU WANT TO TALK? *The others always do.*
   Come on. Eyes open.
   I like to hear the begging.

SOLOMON CLAY PUT HIS ARMS UP, but his smile told her how little he feared.
   "I've survived a bullet or two, Ms. Henry."
   "How about six?" she asked.
   Adele didn't want to duel with this maniac. Didn't want to hear about the Voice or Judah Washburn. Real or not, none of it mattered. Not at all. This is why her religious grandmother had never made headway with Adele or Maxine. Her grandmother thought that if she just made a convincing argument for belief, her daughter and granddaughter would come to God. Just as Solomon seemed to believe he could convince Snooky to become magnanimous through the word or the fist. But she suspected Snooky, like herself and Maxine, just refused belief. It held no value for them. A concept that baffles believers. Adele wanted to leave this cave and return to the life she'd been enjoying. That's it. Whatever got her back to that comfort was the plan she endorsed.
   Snooky recovered and rose from the water. His soggy jeans and sweater clung to him, and he looked like a child who'd been dunked in a pool. He turned to Solomon Clay, whose hands were still up because of Adele and the gun.
   Snooky raised his fists. "You won't catch me sleeping twice, Solomon."
   Adele shouted a question, but it was for Snooky not Mr. Clay.
   "Why now?" she said to Snooky. "Why shut it down now?"
   Snooky heaved, caught his breath. "When would be better?"
   "After I'm gone," she said. She couldn't help it.
   Snooky nodded gravely. "It's not personal, Adele."
   That was the most hurtful thing he could've said.
   "It is for me."
   Adele stepped forward and felt the ground beneath the water dip just a little, but she kept her balance. The tide rose to her pelvis. Her tired arm shivered, then lowered involuntarily.
   Solomon dropped his hands. "You'll be back to selling your rotten twat within a week when he closes the Library. At least I can take some comfort in that."
   With great sadness, and exhaustion, Adele Henry raised the pistol one last time.
   And then the Devils descended.

WAKE UP NOW.
Wake up.
We're not done.

THEY CAME OUT of the swamp gas, gliding down from the dark. When they twisted in one direction, she saw them clearly, but when they turned again, they seemed to disappear. They were as thin as sheets, human forms but only two dimensions. They fluttered like the fumes above a fire. They had two arms each, a head, a torso, two legs, and the skin looked sea-green in the dark chamber. They looked like they belonged in the deep rather than on land.

And now she thought the queasy yellow glow in the chamber hadn't been her lights playing against particles in the swamp gas, but these . . . things. A yellow radiance seemed to emanate from their bellies. It seeped out through their slick skin.

Adele felt sympathy for the Heurequeque in an instant. Their repulsion must've felt just like hers now. Her mouth pinched as if she'd tasted something sour, and her throat closed until it felt like she was choking.

There were five of them. And when they landed, they surrounded Adele, and with her free hand she covered her eyes. But then she felt a touch, on her skin, and when she looked, she saw one of them had grabbed her hand. The hand that held the gun.

Adele tried to remember the lesson of Joyce Chin's story. The face of goodness may surprise you. But the *feel* of them against her. Cold and tough. She couldn't see their faces, couldn't see if they even had faces, and this made her shiver from her scalp to her toes. Somehow her throat closed even tighter and she thought she would black out. It was an instinctive reaction. *Terror* is the word.

She watched as all five now wrapped their slippery arms around her. They grabbed at her wrist, her elbow, her shoulder, her fingers. She thought they were attacking her, but in a moment she realized the weight of the gun had disappeared. They were helping her lift it. They were helping her aim. They pointed the pistol at Solomon Clay.

They want me to kill him.

He and Snooky moved much more slowly than she did now. She and the Devils of the Marsh worked in accelerated time. Snooky's mouth still hung open, his last sentence just finished.

It's not personal, Adele.

They pointed her hand, the gun, directly at Solomon Clay's head, guiding her.

The Voice wants me to kill him. That's my fate.

But Adele Henry pulled her arm away from their influence. She tore herself from their control. If she was going to be guided by anything, it would be her own will. The Dean really had known her, even better than she knew herself. She would protect the Library.

Her shoulder hurt again as she aimed the gun, all alone, at Snooky Washburn's chest.

She fired.

BIG AS HE WAS, burly as a bull, Snooky Washburn couldn't resist a bullet. The first one made him stumble; the second sent him flying. His body went into the water and floated off like a basket lost to the reeds. It drifted, and Adele saw it move.

I just killed a man, she thought.

I murdered him.

The Devils of the Marsh moved away from her then, like scattered birds. To fly they flapped their bodies, which were as flexible as wings. And when they did this, all together, a great wind blew through the room. Fresher air sucked in from the tunnels.

I defied the Voice, she thought.

I defied God.

She righted herself and waved the gun in Mr. Clay's direction because she thought he should be next. Snooky, then Solomon, then those Devils. Then herself. She thought she might cry. In fact, she might have been crying already.

Solomon Clay stood in the same place he'd been, and watched Snooky's lifeless body for a moment more. Then he turned to Adele. His eyes were wide and his forehead wrinkled; the lines around his open mouth were deep. He'd been stunned into looking his age.

He said, "You treacherous bitch."

Solomon Clay stepped through the swamp gas, approaching her.

He snarled. "Human beings are no damn good! You've finally taught me that, Adele. The despised become despicable. God damn! We're worse than animals! We're like monsters."

Adele didn't argue. She just pulled the trigger again.

But this time it caused one hell of an explosion.

When Adele Henry pulled the trigger, the muzzle flash lit the fuse of methane gas newly mixed with the oxygen that had been sucked in when the Devils of the Marsh took flight. The gas had become explosive.

The methane blast shot toward the only open doorway, and the fire passed over Adele even as she turned instinctively. She went facedown into the water and the fire singed the back of her clothes. She lifted herself out of the water when her breath ran out, and the air was still hot enough to prickle her face. The boom had left Adele temporarily deaf.

But why wasn't the heat burning her? It was hot enough to melt the gun in her pocket. And yet, it hadn't hurt her. These questions occurred to her slowly, casually, almost as if she'd left the tunnels far behind and had the time now to recollect with patience. She looked down and saw herself there, wading in the water. Down there and up here, both at once.

How am I alive? she thought.

Then her ear tingled, the way it does when someone stands right behind you and whispers sweetly. She felt the warmth of someone's breath. She heard a sound, but it remained a mumble.

Adele felt a sudden desire to turn. Not to shift her head down there, but up here in this dreamy state. To turn and see who stood behind her. Perched right there, whispering into her ear. Would she see Maxine Henry there? Or the face behind that face? She tried to turn, but the more she moved, the slower she went.

Why did you save me? she asked.

I'm not worth a damn thing.

And now Adele could finally make out the phrase being spoken into her ear. No longer a mumble, more like a command. Four words . . .

Four words.

Adele's head cleared, but a high ringing persisted, one long note running right above her noggin. She touched the tunnel walls, and the grit of loosened dirt felt soothing. She touched her scalp, and a few curls dropped into her hands.

They were all bone-white.

Splashing registered throughout the chamber. Her hearing had returned.

Then she saw one Devil of the Marsh, deep inside the chamber. It fluttered, snapping as violently as a flag, but it didn't scream or moan. It was on fire, but it couldn't wail. This only made it seem more anguished. Its body shook so quickly that it floated on the air. A levitating silhouette, all aflame. She saw that shadow die and drift back down to the water.

Did I kill them off too?

It was too much to bear, and this wasn't the place to formulate answers. Adele ran back, toward the circular doorway. Just get to the tunnels and follow the path out. You're the only survivor. No one has to know what happened. Get upstairs, get on a plane, get back to Vermont. Get in your cabin.

Run, Adele. Run your ass.

Behind her she heard a retching noise, coughing or choking, a person in great pain. She didn't look back until she'd passed through the doorway. Then she turned, put her hand on the great stone door, and rolled it back. She closed the cave. The gun in her pocket, a lump of fused metal, still served a purpose. She set it down, under the water, so it blocked the door. So nothing inside could get out.

She looked inside now and saw him, Solomon Clay, shambling out of the darkness. How could he have survived when Snooky's body had been burned to ashes?

Solomon's body shivered; his legs were stiff as he stumbled. And his face. His face.

It glowed.

He slammed against the doorway. He pressed his lips to the small hole. He sang, out of key, an old Christmas carol. "Do you hear what *I* hear?"

As Adele ran down the tunnel, she listened to Solomon slam against the door again and again. In time he might actually break it down. The hole in the stone amplified Mr. Clay's weak breathing, still going, still going. The panting lingered with Adele so long that eventually it seemed to be her own.

AFTER TWO DAYS of torturing Adele Henry in that motel in Paterson, New Jersey, the mass murderer James Cuvell, who later demanded that newspapers call him Honeyspot, left her there faceup in a tub. The drain was clogged by all the hair he'd pulled out of her. Her big green purse was hooked over the bathroom doorknob, close enough to grab on to and pull herself out, but he believed she was too far gone for any such thing. He underestimated her. And as she slowly rose from the tub, she made a promise, to always get them before they got her.

James Cuvell left her there because he knew she was dead, had to be dead. The other women had all died. Absolutely dead because a body only has so much resistance. A body couldn't possibly survive.

But a body did.

6

Electricity

59

OKAY, so Ms. Henry told me all this business, everything she went through two years before, everything she did, an ordeal that would've killed a dozen men, and yet I said only one thing when she finished.

"So you really *liked* that Snooky Washburn, didn't you?"

Ms. Henry nearly stumbled to the ground.

"That cannot be the only thing you heard," she said.

"Not the only thing, but it's a big one."

She stammered. "Well—that's—not—"

She threw out her arms. "Why are you acting like this?"

A different question occurred to me.

"Didn't you say you were *loyal* to Mr. Washburn?"

"Sure, I did. So?"

"You shot him in the chest!" I shouted. I regretted being so blunt just as quickly. "I'm sorry, Adele."

"Yeah," she muttered. Then she recovered. "But that's why I went back to Vermont. To the Library."

"Out of loyalty?" I said, totally deadpan.

She shook her head like I was the dunsky. "I couldn't just leave the Library to men like the Dean or Solomon Clay. Could I?"

"So you came back to honor Snooky's memory?"

"Right," she said, though she hardly sounded sure.

"But then you just locked yourself up in your cabin."

"Why you have to ask so many damn questions?" She bared her teeth. Only then did I realize what I'd been doing to her. A game of questions and answers just like the Washerwomen once taught me. But I wasn't feeling self-righteous or out to win any childish game. Listening to her fool herself had me thinking about, fearing, all the ways I might be doing the same. When this was over, if I survived, wasn't I expecting to return to the Library? Didn't I look forward to its comforts? What kind of backflips would *I* do to clear my conscience?

Adele, meanwhile, hadn't been privy to my thoughts. Her skin still stung from the way I'd pinched her.

"And what about you?" she growled. "You never did anything you regret?"

I pointed at the gates of the Washburn estate.

"We're back," I said.

It was five A.M. when we entered the estate's grounds. The sounds of early morning had begun: that first wave of snorting cars; the way night burns off as dawn approaches and the sky seems to hiss like paper thrown into a fire.

When we passed the guard booth, it was empty. Not closed, but abandoned. The little television on the desk hadn't even been turned off. It flashed a local weather report. The day promised to be bright and cool.

"Come on," Ms. Henry whispered. She looked down the main road that led to the mansion, but the only thing moving down there were the branches of the trees. They shivered in the wind.

We went down this road quietly, looking into each darkened utility building that we passed. There were no cars parked along the road, and I found myself wishing for the pickup I'd seen the day before, the one with the busted windshield. It would've been a landmark I recognized, one that would've helped make the grounds feel more familiar. But it was gone.

I had to stop and lean over and dry heave. Twice.

Morning sickness? I thought.

My God.

I just had to get to the cabin. Finding this thing, wherever it had hidden itself under my skin, wouldn't be so hard if I had some time alone. All those years of tapping veins had taught me how to probe my body.

Ms. Henry said, "Let's go see what the Washburns have to say."

"Who's left?" I said, and regretted it.

She recited in a monotone. "Snooky Washburn is survived by his wife, Cherise, and their two children."

"You really think that woman will want to help us?"

"Who else can we go to? Snooky's gone. The Dean's in Vermont. The cops would arrest us or throw us in a mental ward. We're running out of support."

We walked in the road because neither of us even had the energy to climb back onto the sidewalk. I was finally going to get inside that mansion, but I didn't feel awake enough to care. Just lead me to a guest bathroom. Give me a lighter, a spoon, and a few uninterrupted minutes.

As we got closer, I had a better sense of the mansion. Enormous, of course. Four stories tall, and it seemed a mile wide. There were dozens of sash windows in the façade. All their curtains were closed, so the mansion looked like some great sleeping beast.

Now there we were, hoping to wake it.

Up the circular driveway, across a little strip of lawn, to the front steps, onto the little porch, and finally, the front door.

I waited for Ms. Henry to use the bell or the brass knocker or the cable attached to a gong, but she just kicked at the damn door. Hard. When her foot got tired, she used her fists.

But no one came.

"They're avoiding us," she said.

"Maybe."

"Well, what else could it be, Mr. Rice?"

I pointed at the dawn. "They might just be asleep."

"Oh," she said. "Right."

Ms. Henry looked at her fist, the one that had just done all that pounding.

Then the door popped open. Not all the way, but enough for a little head to peer out. An older Filipina with a small bald spot in her hair.

"Uhh?" she said, sounding both tired and annoyed.

Ms. Henry smiled. "Tia Quina, I'm sorry to wake you up."

The woman reached into her nightgown and pulled out a pair of glasses in big plastic frames. One of the arms of the glasses was missing so she had to hold the frames with her hand even as they balanced on her small, round nose. The woman scrunched her face, puckered her lips, squinting at Ms. Henry.

"Ehh? Is that Adele? My Lord and my God. How are you?"

"Tired," she said.

"Yes, yes. I see. And I am tired too, from being wake up just now!" She laughed when she said this, but that didn't hide her irritation.

"I'm sorry," I said.

Tia Quina looked at me. She held the glasses a little farther down her nose.

"I don't know this man here. What's this, Adele? You get marry, hah!"

"This is Ricky Rice. He's one of the Scholars."

"Ah, then it is good to meet you, but my Lord and my God it is too early!"

"I'm sorry," I said again.

Tia Quina waved her other hand at me, as if I was being foolish for apologizing.

She said, "I will forgive. I can forgive."

Ms. Henry said, "Tia, we're looking for Ms. Washburn."

"Ah-ha. I see. She gone, though."

"When?"

"Yesterday. They pack up, pack up!"

"They?" I asked.

The sleepy woman became somber and dropped the hand that held the glasses.

"The Washburns," she said. "They go. Even the kiddies."

"So you're here all by yourself?" I asked. It seemed spooky to be alone in fifty rooms.

Tia Quina smiled. "Ah, no. No, no. I bring my family in already! My sisters all are staying in the third floor. My Lord and my God, they like it here!"

She laughed quietly, and I thought it was funny too, but Ms. Henry seemed grim.

Tia Quina cut her off before the Gray Lady could lodge any complaints.

"You going now, Miss Adele? Ah? Back to your house they give you?"

Ms. Henry didn't answer, so I said, "Yes, we are."

Tia Quina nodded at me. She shut the door and locked it, but I didn't hear her walk away. She waited to see what we'd do, just as I waited to see if Ms. Henry was going to kick a fuss.

Ms. Henry only gaped at the mansion's windows. I wondered if I'd made that same face in the stairway when the Washerwomen had pulled their guns. The dread you feel when your institutions fail you.

"It's just us," she whispered.

I tried to ignore the panic in her voice.

60

WHEN WE FINALLY REACHED THE CABIN, Ms. Henry walked into one of the back rooms, the bedroom, and returned to the living room with a pillow and heavy comforter. She dropped them on an orange love seat and gestured that this was for me.

I hadn't felt that throbbing, flapping, beating—whatever you want to call it—in my back for a little while. Not during the whole walk from the hospital. This made me anxious. I couldn't stop thinking of it like that wasp's egg. Had it snuggled off somewhere else, my thigh maybe, and transformed into a larva? How long until the last stage, the spider's death? I got so antsy that I reached under my shirt, patting my skin up and down, right there in the living room.

"Don't take your shirt off in here," Ms. Henry gasped as she came back from the kitchen with two snifters in her hands.

"Oh, calm your ass," I said.

She slammed my drink down onto the close edge of her dining table, then went to the far end and sat, keeping as much birch veneer between us as possible.

Ms. Henry and I drank our glasses of Old Grand-Dad quickly, just two gulps, and she went to pour two more. I guess she wanted the drinks to help us calm down. I wanted her to have enough that she'd just black out. Leaving me alone long enough to take care of things.

There was an old radio above the fireplace. I clicked it on and dialed through channels slowly. A millimeter to the left or right meant the difference between pop music or R & B or oldies rock, and I didn't want any of them just then. Didn't feel like hearing anybody crooning. If someone had started singing about love, I'd have strangled the speaker.

When I found a local news station, the drone of the reporter— sounding neither male nor female, age and regional accent disguised— filled the cabin with its comforting, bland tones. The kind of voice that will discuss a cataclysm or clam chowder in the same mellow key. Yes, please, listener-supported radio, tell me about the weather in Alameda, please speak of nothing else.

"The Bay area awakes in fear this morning. The recent spate of explosions in Garland has caused a sense of panic throughout Northern California. While an official state of emergency has not been called, National Guard troops from as far off as Portland have been called in to provide assistance."

I felt betrayed by the newscaster. He or she (it was hard to tell which) was supposed to shield me from crises with inane reports about bluegrass festivals or the history of double Dutch.

"Security checkpoints are being set up across the Bay area. Access to the city of San Francisco is being controlled, as it remains the likely target of any serious terrorist threat. The outlying cities of Berkeley and Oakland are receiving greater security attention as well."

I played with the volume knob, was tempted to turn it all the way to the left, until the radio clicked off. But I didn't do it. I wanted to know what was being done for Garland.

"Mayor Brandy has reported that he's spoken with Governor Lilyfield, and the governor promises Garland is not being overlooked. The president has also guaranteed federal support, saying the American government would never abandon a U.S. city in crisis."

The newscaster paused there, and I heard a snort of breath, derision, the sound of his professionalism being punctured by his disbelief. It seemed Garland was facing a revelation like Adele's only minutes before, looking up at the mansion to find there was no one inside who would help.

I stopped listening because Ms. Henry came back from the kitchen with our cups of 100 proof whiskey. I took mine and held it tight.

"You just had to turn that on," she said. She sat again and held her drink to her breasts.

Now a different reporter coughed once into the microphone, a live feed. I heard the sounds of traffic behind him.

"I'm standing below I-580 in Garland, and even though it's only five-thirty, you can already hear the sounds of gridlock. The National Guard have set their checkpoint on the western end of Stitch Bridge. Any car or truck entering San Francisco is to be thoroughly searched for any potential threat. While this is an important security measure, it's causing a backup that threatens to cripple an already nervous East Bay. The highways are turning into parking lots. Mayor Brandy has asked employers to give people the day off, but he can't demand it. So far most employers have stated that in this economy they simply can't afford to close for an entire day. "

Ms. Henry held the glass of whiskey to her chin and shut her eyes, as if the Old Grand-Dad fumes were helping her think.

She said, "Solomon doesn't care about secrecy like the Dean. Can we agree on that? He doesn't want to hide with his people in Vermont."

"That video was a threat to Garland *and* a commercial for the Church of Clay," I said.

"Okay. And why would they want to advertise?"

I said, "It gets a certain kind of person interested in Solomon Clay."

Adele finally sipped her drink. "He won't need to send out handwritten invitations. The despised will come find him. He got the news to broadcast a recruitment tape."

"I'm afraid two bombs and a video still won't be enough, though," I said.

Adele brought her cup to her lips a second time, but she didn't drink. "He'll need to do something even bigger."

"A real display of his power," she said.

On the radio the reporter started interviewing people stuck in their cars. It sounded like he was just moseying from one driver to the next. They weren't going anywhere.

"All those people," Adele said. "Just sitting out there."

Both Ms. Henry and I finished our drinks in a swallow. I waited to see her eyes shut, but instead both Ms. Henry and I fell asleep. Not even that. We blacked out.

Right in our chairs.

Facing each other across the dining table.

Unconscious for an hour and a half.

I WOKE UP and Ms. Henry had left the table. I listened for the shower running, but the only sound was of the radio rattling on with breaking news reports.

The doors to her office and her bedroom were open. I stepped into the office. Empty. Peeked into the bedroom, one hand over my eyes. Nothing. I heard a flush in the bathroom. Then another. And a third. I would've laughed if I hadn't needed to get in there myself.

The bathroom door opened, and Ms. Henry looked up at me grimly. She lifted her right hand: six empty baggies.

61

"YOU DON'T KNOW what you've done," I said.

I couldn't even look at her face, too mesmerized by those transparent glassine bags.

"I saved your life," she said. " 'Cause if you shot up, I would've killed you."

"Like Snooky Washburn?"

Yeah, I meant to hurt her. But she was invulnerable because of her indignation.

"I figured the whiskey would pacify you. Then I could see what you were holding."

"Is *that* why you kept pouring?"

"Of course," she said. "Why else?"

" 'Cause you're an alcoholic?"

I stepped backward, and she did too, me toward the office and she into the bathroom.

"How'd you even know I had anything?"

"You've been staring at your coat pocket since we left the hospital."

"Really?"

"Don't become a poker player, that's my advice to you."

Now what? A fine question. I slumped against the doorway to her office.

"And where did you find that needle?" she asked. "In a corpse?"

I waved her away. "Why don't you let me take a shower."

She grabbed the doorknob with the same hand that held the baggies. I listened to them crinkle, like a bear hearing the last gasp of its cub.

"I didn't throw them out to hurt you, Ricky."

"And yet . . ."

Ms. Henry walked into the living room. She took our glasses to the kitchen.

IN THE BATHROOM I shut the door, washed my face, dried off with a towel, then looked in the mirror. I tried to see if I looked any different. Were my cheeks puffier? Did I already see jowls at the bottom of my face? How could I feel so different, but appear unchanged?

I remembered when Gayle used to do the same thing. Standing in the bathroom, pulling at her face. Gayle said she knew she was pregnant long before we took the test, but I only believed her in retrospect. Years later I would think back and remember the way we'd lie down for bed at night, and at some point she'd just rest her right hand on her belly. Not directly on top, but slightly to the right of her belly button. She wouldn't squeeze, just lay her palm flat against the skin, like she was checking a special temperature.

I took off my dress shirt, hung it on the doorknob. Looked at my bare chest in the mirror.

Where are you? I thought.

What are you?

Ms. Henry knocked lightly. I heard her lean against the door handle for balance. She didn't say anything, just stood there.

"How come you never told the Dean what the Voice said to you?" I asked.

"I went back to Vermont and chose to forget it."

"I guess the Dean can't see everything in those field notes."

She spoke again, as if I hadn't said anything. "The words didn't even make sense."

I touched my collarbone, my chest, my side. "But you didn't forget them."

"Of course not," she said.

I might've pushed, asked what those four words had been, but I had my own troubles. Let them remain her burden. I had my own hiding under the skin.

"I thought I'd take that story about Snooky to my death," she said.

"I can see why. You don't come out looking too good."

She hit the door once, hard, and stomped off. I ran myself a shower. Once under the water my legs shook so badly that I had to lie down in the tub. Lay flat and let the shower pulverize me. It felt better than a bath because my muscles needed the spray to force out my poisonous fatigue. I turned around and stayed on my hands and knees so the water would do the same for my back. When I did this, I felt a quivering under my skin, right in the middle of my spine.

I'd been attacked only days before, but now I realized I'd really started down this path three years earlier.

62

I FLEW OUT from LaGuardia Airport to Cedar Rapids, Iowa, with twenty-four thousand dollars strapped around my knees. It's harder to move cash than people might think. You can't just wire that much money through Western Union. Using a courier is the surest way. It was my first time on an aircraft. I mean ever. This happened in 2002.

But I wasn't nervous about getting caught at the airport, because the attacks on the World Trade Center and the Pentagon had changed my threat status. Before September 11, the skinny, jittery black guy made security think one thing: drug mule. But after the attacks, security only cared about bombs. So it was the Arab guys, the Puerto Ricans and Indians, even white men, that got searched. I was too dark to make people worry on a plane. Still caused fear in elevators.

The flight went fine because I'd brought a couple hundred milligrams of Thorazine too. I shut my eyes in New York and opened them again in Iowa. I took a cab directly to the address I'd been given.

My host opened the door of his HUD home, a building that would've been condemned if the government hadn't zoned it for the poor. He looked me over and smiled.

"You old crackhead," he said.

"You fat fucker," I answered back.

I stood face-to-face for the first time in a decade with my former rival for Annabelle Cuddy's affections. The only other of the Washerwomen's children still alive. Big Wilfred Tanner. He's the one who'd invited me out.

We hugged each other like men do, without touching below the waist, just that stooped clutch like grappling bears. I smacked his back with an open palm, and he squeezed my neck with one soft hand.

He led me inside and showed me to the back. He silently directed me into the bathroom, and when we were both inside, he stood blocking the door. There was a big hole in the ceiling where snow and rain could come through. He'd laid a plank of wood on the roof to cover the gap, weighted bricks on top so it wouldn't blow away. We stood there a little longer, quietly. He wouldn't step out of the way.

Finally I said, "You going to show me the rest of the place?"

He sniffed. "Take off your pants."

I said, "I can't get a sandwich or something before we do business?"

Wilfred gripped the doorknob so tightly it yelped.

I took off my pants.

He pulled the money from my legs so fast that the tape left burn marks.

WHILE HE WAS GONE, I took a nap because that Thorazine was still in my veins. Even with a bit of a rest it kept me cloudy. When I moved, it felt like I was dragging a couch by my ears. I settled into the sofa in Wilfred's den.

Den. That's me being polite. I think a family of rats would've decorated his place with more class. Where some people hang artwork on the walls, Wilfred just had promotional posters from bars. Killian's, Heineken, King Cobra malt liquor. (I think he had the last one up just so he could masturbate to the woman in the ad.) Seeing the state of Wilfred's place made me feel better about myself. At least he hadn't cleaned himself up either. I might've been a junky, but this man was a boozehound.

When he came back, he brought a couple of pulled pork sandwiches and a twelve-pack of Leinenkugel's Honey Weiss. This was the celebration for a job all done. We didn't talk about the money. He'd tracked me down in New York, said I was the only person he'd trust to take some loot across the country. I figured it was just that his drunk ass didn't have ties to anyone else in the East. We'd been in contact now and then, so he knew I was all about the heroin. Why trust a junky unless you had no choice?

We sat on his lopsided couch, and he finished three beers before I'd opened one.

"You still on that stuff?" he asked me, his mouth full of pulled pork.

"I'm on a lot of stuff," I said.

He sneered, which made him look like a sow. When he snorted, I wanted to check for a curly tail. "You ain't doing no drugs in my fucking house, you feel me?"

"But I brought enough for both of us!"

The pork rested in the space between his lower lip and gums like a wad of chew.

"You always had jokes," he said.

We went like this for a little while. He and I were the last two child survivors of a long-forgotten cult. We'd suffered through mass murder in a stairway. Had both been fed into the foster care system at age ten and had spent the next eight years in the same group home, one that was affiliated with the Creedmoor Psychiatric Center.

It was funny to me that Wilfred could be intolerant about heroin, but turn a blind eye to his own abuses. That reminded me of my old friend Bottlecap, the one who used to hear from the Lord. He was such an infamous drinker that even the beer distributors around Troy knew his name. His favorite bar, the Alleycat, used to send him birthday cards by certified mail if he stayed away too long. If he signed for it, that meant he was still alive. And yet that drunk looked down on me for being a junky. Bottlecap, like Wilfred, believed that if your drug wasn't fermented, you were out of order.

After a half hour of sniping I'd had three beers and he'd finished eight.

"You want to get some pussy?" Wilfred asked.

"Always," I said.

He suggested we visit Czech Village. A tourist zone that celebrated the ethnic origins of the city by selling glass figurines, garnet jewelry, baked goods, and meat. He knew two bowlegged women who worked down there. They might let us buy them drinks. Wilfred drove us in an old cargo van, the kind you could live in but shouldn't.

Before we actually got moving, he gave me my money. Eighteen hundred dollars. All fifty-dollar bills. I counted and recounted them as he started the van. It took him a couple tries, so I counted twice. Right then I believed I really loved Wilfred.

Ten minutes into the trip he said we should stop at his friend's first. A guy who sold cloned cell phones and doctored driver's licenses. Those were the kind of crooks I enjoyed. I liked my criminal life lite. Wilfred said everybody called this guy Murder, but I shouldn't take that too seriously. They only called him that because he had some Belgian last name no one could pronounce correctly, so no one bothered. *Murder* was close enough.

He didn't have to convince me. I wasn't scared of anything just then.

Not anymore. I'd expected to land in Cedar Rapids, bring the money to my cousin, and be greeted by two ugly guys who would cut me into pieces. Then feed the parts to a dog. I was afraid Wilfred had started hanging around with heavy crooks like that, but in this life you couldn't always avoid such a risk. So why did I come to Cedar Rapids if that was my fear?

Eighteen hundred dollars!

And Wilfred suggested that it could lead to more. So when I didn't get killed, I coasted. We drove past Mount Mercy College, which watched Cedar Rapids from a hill, then alongside Tomahawk Park. Soon we reached Longwood Drive. I memorized the names of places and streets in case Wilfred abandoned me in a cornfield. As long as I kept track, I could find my way. I had no fears, but I wasn't dumb.

We parked, and I stepped onto the sidewalk. It was warm out. The air smelled like cereal, even this far from the Quaker Oats factory. That made the afternoon seem fun, even silly in a good way. Wilfred and I shared a smile.

I felt positively sanctified as I entered Murder's home.

63

A SUIT LAY FLAT on Ms. Henry's bed. I heard her in the kitchen and I smelled toast. Didn't even bother acting bashful as I walked from the bathroom to the bedroom with only the towel around my waist. See me shirtless if you dare, Ms. Henry!

She'd left me a fine outfit, two-button double-breasted brown worsted wool, serge weave and a green pinstripe. A white dress shirt lay underneath. No tie. I'd have to go without, back to a Byron collar for me.

I thought of Adele's story again, the two suits she'd found hanging in the closet of this cabin when she'd first arrived in 2003. Some Unlikely Scholar had left the outfits, never returned to reclaim them. He never reclaimed this cabin either. It was as much of a relic as his coats—both had held his body. Where was he now?

As I dressed, I remembered Gartrelle Meadows. The Unlikely Scholar whose files I'd been reading in Vermont the week before. The man who'd walked into the South Bronx parking garage and recorded the ghostly voice repeating itself. *Electricity. Electricity.* I'd felt warmth for my man as I'd leafed through his notes. Camaraderie. Even though I'd never met him, I knew him. But what about the people who'd been a part of his life before the Library? Would they have been as charitable about his memory as me? I doubt it, and I don't blame them. You can only abuse people's faith in you for so long.

How many years had I been doing it?

In the living room Ms. Henry had already set out the toast and butter, some jam and a small plate of sausages. Her order at one end of the table, and mine, six feet away.

I walked into the kitchen. She looked wrecked. It didn't help that I had showered and changed but she hadn't. Her riding suit had dots of Claude's blood along the right sleeve.

"You need help?" I asked.

"I'm all done. Go sit down."

She came out with two glasses of orange juice, put mine next to my plate of toast, and walked to her table setting.

"I wouldn't have thought you'd do all this," I said. "Making a meal for a man. Like you want his company."

She sipped her orange juice, then sighed.

"I need men, Ricky. Men are the ones who act like they don't need me."

"It's only an act," I said.

We ate quietly.

Finally, she said, "I'm used to knowing exactly what I need to do to get what I want."

"But you don't know what to do now?" I asked.

"I don't know what I want."

"You and me could go anywhere, Adele. You got our money back from Claude. We could buy two bus tickets. All the way to Seattle."

"You think we're going to blend in, in Seattle?" she asked.

"They've got black people in Seattle," I said. "Don't act like it's 1910."

She took a couple bites of her toast. "Is that what you want to do, Ricky?"

"Part of me does," I said. "But the rest would be ashamed if I did."

Adele looked to her right, out the window of her cabin, at the handful of trees growing a few yards down the hillside.

"I been on my own," she said. "Looking out for myself since forever. When I got the invitation from the Library, I couldn't get up there fast enough. And when they welcomed me, I just couldn't believe it. A person like me."

She tore at her napkin, dropping the bits right on top of her half-eaten breakfast.

"I'm just supposed to give that up?" she asked, more herself than me.

"But you're not alone now," I said.

Adele looked at me again. "You know the last time my mother was really proud of me? Seventh grade. I won a spelling bee. Beat everyone in my school."

"What was the winning word?"

"*Exalted,*" she said.

"Exalted? That's it?"

"It was a bad school." Adele laughed. "But Maxine kept my certificate on the fridge for a year."

"I bet she still has it," I said. "Folded up in a drawer somewhere."

Adele sucked her teeth. "You think so?"

"She's your mother, Adele. She hasn't given up on you."

Adele rose from the table.

Once she'd showered, she dressed in an olive middy blouse and walking skirt, a Crusher hat, and black gaiters. I whistled when I saw her. She looked well-qualified for the job. Adele turned, to show off the outfit, then caught herself and stopped.

Her old green handbag carried a compact umbrella, two road flares, and that pistol of hers, a little gray automatic. She gave that to me.

"You went back down to the Devils' Well to get this?"

"That was a revolver. This is an automatic."

Ms. Henry walked me out and along the side of the cabin. Adele's blue garage door swung upward with one good tug. It wasn't the cleanest place. Insects had done a lot of decorating. An immense spiderweb filled one small window. But forget that, how about the car: a green 1977 Mercedes-Benz 450 SLC Coupe. Snooky's chariot.

"His wife didn't mind you keeping this?"

"She didn't want it around. She was going to sell it, but I asked for it."

"And she just handed it over?"

"As far as she knew, Snooky died believing in the Library. Cherise loved him too much to cut us off entirely."

I walked to the passenger door of that old Mercedes-Benz. "Let's hit it, then," I said.

She stood by the taillight. "Wrong side, Ricky."

"What do you mean? I can't drive."

Ms. Henry pressed one finger against the rear window. "But it's an automatic."

I looked inside. "That's a stick shift, Ms. Henry. And I can't work either one."

She looked again while I leaned back, my butt against the side of the hood. Me and her, she and I, a pair of city kids. We'd never learned how to drive.

"How'd you even get it here?" I asked, pointing at the garage roof.

"It was towed."

"Well, I'm not walking," I said. "That's out. It's just not possible."

"You want to ride on the handlebars of my bike?" she snapped.

She pointed to that silver beast of hers, propped against the wall. It looked even more monstrous than I'd imagined. Half-mechanical, half-animal. The curved front fender looked like a lip drawn back into a snarl.

"This is great," I said. "Maybe I can steal some kid's skateboard."

Adele looked ready to yell, but she contained herself.

"We can find another bike," she said. "The Washburns couldn't have taken all of theirs."

They were going to be helping us out after all.

64

AS SOON AS WE'D WALKED into Murder's living room, I knew Wilfred had set me up.

It's frightening to step into a place and understand you're a victim. I'm not talking about a bad feeling or a vague sense. I mean knowing. A quick fire runs through your heart and limbs. You go stiff because you're aware something's about to happen, but you can't think clearly enough to escape. I shivered, involuntarily, and then hands swarmed over me. That's it. The front door shut and I was trapped. Murder didn't even get out of his love seat. He had plenty of friends in the room.

Those hands pushed me to the ground so quick that I didn't even scream. No thoughts of any kind. One minute I'm nodding at our fat Belgian host, and next there's carpet fibers scratching my neck.

The living room was small. This was one of those houses that look bigger on the outside. Lots of little rooms, instead of a few large ones. This house was probably built back when people were only waist-high. One hundred years old? Two hundred? The air stank of timelessness.

From my place on the ground Murder looked bizarre. I don't know how tall he was. Like I said, he never stood up, but the man had to be five feet wide. Not hard to guess how he got that way, because he had a supermarket bag full of butterscotch candies in his lap. Murder didn't suck on those sweets either. He'd pop one yellow disc in his mouth and chew it like a potato chip. If I hadn't seen that it was candy, I would've sworn he was eating glass.

"Your cousin does this to you," Murder said, between bites. "You understand?"

The man barely opened his mouth, so his accented English was forced through his pinched little lips. The Belgian didn't speak. He spat.

"Wilfred?" I shouted. "Wil?"

The Belgian nodded, but I hadn't been speaking to him. I was just calling out for the boy who'd held my hand in that stairwell twenty-seven years before.

But he wasn't there. Wilfred Tanner, the man he'd become, said, "We're not related."

Murder sucked another butterscotch into his mouth and chewed it to shards.

"But this is what you tell me. 'Cousin Ricky is bringing money.' Isn't it what you say?"

"Me and Ricky don't share blood, that's what I mean. We spent our lives together. That's why I said cousin."

Murder laughed. "But you don't say cousin now."

Lying facedown on the ground, I saw all these butterscotch shavings clotting the carpet. Whatever didn't make it down his throat fell to the ground. His bare feet were covered in the stuff. Had Murder ever moved?

"You must be careful who to trust," the Belgian said to me.

I spoke to him for the first time. I said, "I promise never to trust Wilfred again."

The men holding me down laughed at this. One of them was stepping on the small of my back, and I felt his laugh when he pressed harder into my spine. How many of them were there? Five or six probably. I couldn't say. I hadn't had time to count. They'd all been gathered right inside the doorway. That seemed like a lot of muscle just for skinny little me.

"Do you want to say something more with your cousin?" Murder asked.

Wilfred bent low. His fat shoulders and head filled my view. He smelled like ketchup and beer. "Doubt is the big machine. Don't you remember, Ricky? Ain't you learned that yet?"

I said, "For where your treasure is, there will your heart be also."

Wilfred snorted. "Shut up, crackhead."

Then he went into my pants and took back his eighteen hundred dollars.

"What is that money there?" Murder asked.

Wilfred stood again.

"That's what you paid me this morning. He wouldn't have come in here without it."

"That is a good idea," Murder said.

"Yeah," Wilfred said, almost casually.

I listened to him count the fifty-dollar bills, and in that time Murder watched him. The men on top of me shifted and sighed. I think they wanted to get to their work. Chopping me up and feeding the parts to dogs, no doubt.

Fucking Wilfred Tanner.

Murder said, "You are staying with us."

He made it sound like a bed and breakfast. Murder's B & B, butterscotch served at nine A.M. How I wish I could've said something like that, witty and cool. Instead I groaned.

"All right, then," Wilfred muttered. "I'm gonna go."

That bastard even sounded bored.

Murder said, "I was speaking of you too, Wilfred."

Talk about screaming! My cousin worked his lungs.

But of course the Belgian was in the right. Instead of taking twenty-four thousand dollars to the thug who was owed, Wilfred had brought it to Murder. Got paid eighteen hundred dollars for the service. With me dead Wilfred could just blame the loss on some unreliable junky. It all smacked of a loser's logic. The kind of plan hatched by an idiot at last call. But now Murder wanted to make sure there was no one alive to speak his name, because the Belgian wasn't a fool. Wilfred should've just sent me in there alone and sped away. But he knew I'd never have stepped inside by myself.

When Wilfred went to the floor, it trembled. The wood planks beneath the carpet rolled like a wave. Even Murder lifted an inch out of his seat. But he didn't drop that bag of candies.

After the screaming stopped, Wilfred promised that he wouldn't speak a word of this. He'd erase it from his own memory. He'd move out of state. Today.

The Belgian reached into his plastic bag and swept his fingers through the butterscotch candies. They clacked like gnashing teeth.

Murder said, "I doubt this."

65

THAT MORNING HAD TO BE the worst traffic day in Garland's history. Intersections lose their definition when you can't turn left, right, or around. And the problem wasn't just down there on MacArthur Boulevard or along Lakeshore, but above our heads too, on the elevated lanes of I-580 west, headed into San Francisco. Full-on frozen. Packed streets and highways. Ms. Henry and I rode our bikes on the uneven sidewalks, and we were the fastest things moving.

People in their cars craned their necks trying to see something, *anything*, as if a solution was just up the road. I felt surprised so many people had come out of their homes at all, considering the threats and the bombs. But if employers hadn't closed their businesses, then most employees couldn't afford to skip work. Paychecks pulled them out of hiding.

Garland's manners were breaking down around us: car horns played by the dozen, drivers yelled at other drivers through rolled-up windows. Some wore a look of rageful contemplation, thinking about pressing the gas and plowing through. Others only cradled their heads.

As we crossed Lakeshore Avenue, we had to get off our bikes and walk them between car bumpers. We stopped in front of a burger joint. They were open, but weren't busy. It wasn't a sit-down place. You walked up to the glass and made your order, watched them prepare it. Then they slid it through a door in the bulletproof shielding. Inside, a man and woman in clean white T-shirts leaned against the counter, watching the congestion. They stared at the gridlock the way one might stare into the Gobi Desert, with a mix of awe and depression.

Ms. Henry pointed to a walking bridge above the highway.

"Let's go up and see what we can see."

We had to walk our bikes uphill along the southern side of the highway. At the top of the hill I-580 was almost hidden, tucked down between trees and bushes. The westbound lanes were so congested that people had stepped out of their cars. Some climbed onto their trunks, trying to see how far this mess went, but even from my place on the walkway—twenty-five feet above them—I couldn't see the end of it. It ran right up to Stitch Bridge, and across it. Many people mingled in the breakdown lane.

The parking lot of the burger joint lay just below us, had a couple of cars parked there. I saw a figure crouched down behind a hatchback, couldn't tell if it was a woman or a man. Trying to take a quick piss, I thought, and this made me nostalgic for New York. So I actually stared on, waiting for that special gesture of relief, the shoulders relaxing as the bladder empties. And because of this I was the first to see the figure rise to full height. Not pissing but vomiting, not a woman but a man. A bum. He stepped out from behind the car.

He slumped forward as he walked. The guy looked downright malarial. His motto was malnutrition. He teetered toward the crowded street carrying a small green sack.

"Ms. Henry," I said, and pointed down to where we'd just been.

The guy threw out his arms and screamed, "Solomon Clay is a lion in the wilderness!"

Every face turned to him.

Ms. Henry was on her bike seat in less than two heartbeats, and I managed almost as good a time. But we were slowpokes by comparison. Down below, a red Volkswagen lurched from the street onto the sidewalk. It clipped that homeless dude right in the leg, sent the wasted man backward, five feet into the parking lot. He lay still for a moment, but then stood again.

The driver popped her door and shouted to a passenger. Meanwhile the man and woman inside the burger joint ran out from the safety of their bulletproof glass. The guy carried a spatula and the lady held a long knife.

The homeless guy didn't run. He lifted his arms again and smiled.

They kicked and punched. The guy with the spatula brought its handle down on the homeless guy's head like he was driving in a spike. The woman waved the knife, but used her foot instead. Three other people got out of their cars and ran toward the fracas. They surrounded the homeless guy. They beat him.

They beat him pretty bad.

When they were done, the woman from the red Volkswagen pulled up on the guy's ratty coat, and his head fell back, limp.

"Why didn't he just blow them up?" Adele asked.

"Maybe he didn't have time to light the fuse."

"He stood there and taunted them. Why?"

Ms. Henry looked back to the highway, the eastbound route, at the crowds gathered in the breakdown lane. And then off to her left, to Grand Avenue below.

"Look there," she said.

I leaned against the warm metal and felt heat through my sleeves. I watched the street, but only saw more gridlock. Some pedestrians crowded bus stops while others walked to work. And a little ways behind that scene lay Laguna Lake, cordoned off by police tape.

"Forget everything else," Ms. Henry said. "Look at those men."

She wiggled one finger to lead my eye.

Fourteen men marching in single file.

But nobody on the street paid attention to them because their clothes weren't tattered. They'd dressed better than they'd probably done in a decade. Either sweatpants or khaki slacks. Button down shirts and cheap sports coats. Camouflage.

But Ms. Henry recognized them. And I did too. Those men slinking down Grand Avenue had a familiar posture, stooped from a lifetime of defeats and dirty dealing. A bum by any other name is still as shabby. Each carried a gym bag or a briefcase or a book bag.

Ms. Henry said, "That other guy was just a decoy."

66

WE WERE CARRIED DOWN CONCRETE STEPS and left in Murder's base-ment. Wilfred made faint panting sounds as soon as we were alone. He seemed to be hyperventilating, but I wished he was choking to death. And told him so. I whispered threats first, then questions. How could you do me dirty like this? Did that for a long while, but stopped asking eventually. He wasn't going to answer. He cried and he muttered, that's all he could do. The tears ran down his round cheeks and into his gap-ing mouth. It actually calmed me to see Wilfred's panic. It was like watching distant lightning in the dark. The storm over there means it hasn't reached me yet.

At least the basement floor was padded. That's what I noticed when I looked away from Wilfred. There were old mattresses on the ground and piles of torn clothes, discolored sheets stacked on top of them. It looked like someone had robbed a Salvation Army bin and then left the spoils there to rot. We were having a sleepover party at the dump.

It was an unfinished basement. Dirt floors peeking up from areas the mattresses didn't cover. And there wasn't any heat. Exposed pipes and wiring ran just above our heads. There were holes in the foundation, but it didn't matter. I wouldn't be crawling off, because my hands were tied behind my back and my ankles wrapped in rope. In the face of Wilfred's silence, I lay there for an hour, lost in my own quiet fog.

"How's your parents?"

I was so used to Wilfred's heaving breathing that I didn't even realize he'd spoken. I looked around in confusion, as if a lump of clothes had asked the question.

"Your mom and dad," he said.

Then I realized it was him. I guess he'd finally swallowed his fear. But I didn't respond.

"My mom got saved a couple years ago," he whispered. "She's living in Wichita."

We left it at that until nighttime. I could see the light change through the holes in the walls. And when it got dark, a horde of feral cats crawled in through them. About a dozen.

They casually rambled through the holes and broken basement windows until they noticed us and stopped, midmovement. Two dashed back out immediately, but the others stayed and sniffed the air. They padded around our bodies, keeping far enough away, and watched.

They looked at one another.

Which of them would be brave?

Eventually this one bobtail crept closer. A long-haired cat, its fur a mix of silver, black, and just a little gold. Tufts of white hair stuck out of both ears. Its short tail lay flat against its ass. The bobtail inched closer to see if we'd lash out, but we couldn't use our hands or feet. That wouldn't have mattered anyway, because Wilfred was half-passed-out and the lack of dope in my system was already making me a little weak. Soon enough the cats knew we were harmless. When you considered diseases and fleas, their claws and teeth, we had more to fear from them.

They settled into the pillows and curtains all around us. That bobtail, the brave one, plopped down closer than the rest.

They formed a semicircle around our bodies and stared. A jury of feral cats.

Then I heard Wilfred repeating his name.

"Wilfred Tanner," he whispered. "Wilfred Tanner." As if introducing himself.

And upstairs?

Murder's house mumbled throughout the night. Pots being dropped onto the oven range, loud as shouts. The murmur of boiling water. They might've been making pasta or cooking crack, I couldn't say, because my nose was already blocking up and I couldn't smell anything. That's when I understood I was going into withdrawal.

But my ears hadn't stopped up yet, something that usually happened to me whenever I tried to quit. So I could hear. And always, always, the creaking floorboards. I imagined Murder moving above me, dragging his weight from one room to the next. That big Belgian finally on his feet, dancing on my grave.

THE NEXT DAY, in the afternoon, I had such awful diarrhea that I expected Murder to send someone down to spray me with a hose. But no one came, and by evening the backs of my pants had dried and stuck to my skin. I felt lucky for the stuffy nose then. All the feral cats had run off except for the bobtail. It was still there and, if anything, even closer. It wasn't more than a foot from Wilfred's gigantic skull, which only made the cat seem smaller, like it was resting in the shade of an enormous hill.

And you know what? I got jealous. I was lying on my hands in some Belgian's basement in Iowa, couldn't even feel my fingers anymore, a powerful thirst was scratching at my throat even as my withdrawal chills were getting worse, and yet all I wanted was for some dumb cat to come play with me. The bobtail had chosen Wilfred, and this seemed like the last insult. The final injustice. Talk about pathetic. I watched it huddle near Wilfred and felt the deepest outrage.

"Hey, cat," I whispered. "Get your ass over here!"

Surprisingly, that didn't work. The bobtail only blinked at me and snuggled closer to him. Wilfred Tanner opened his eyes then and gave me a very dizzy smile.

"It's just like Annabelle," he whispered. "Ladies love Wilfred."

He giggled, the sound coming through his runny nose.

"Annabelle Cuddy killed herself," I said. "She jumped in front of a train in 1993."

I knew it would hurt Wilfred to hear that, so I told him more hurtful things. I couldn't yell at this point. Anything more than a whisper tore through my dry throat. We'd been down there for nearly two days by then.

I said I'd probably shot up with his now-saved mother in some tenement years before. That I'd watched his father turn her out just to buy more crack. My God, the things I told him. And he didn't argue, not even about his mother's honor, which surprised me, because that boy loved his junky mom more than Navajos love fry bread.

As the second night wore on, I thought of more taunts, but I'm too ashamed to share them. While I spoke, Wilfred inched himself up. He had the silhouette of a manatee that's made the mistake of washing ashore, but really he was just a scared man looking for something, anything, that would provide a little warmth. The bobtail was a better bet than me. It touched him. It didn't run away.

"Annabelle," he said throughout that second night and into the dawn. "Annabelle."

He wasn't listening to me, I felt pretty sure.

It wasn't until the next morning, after the bobtail woke and skipped off, that I could see.

Wilfred Tanner was dead.

He didn't *seem* dead, though. His eyes had rolled up slightly, but it only looked like he was thinking about the answer to a vexing question. That deep, rich skin of his hadn't lost its glow, and I'll bet that if I could've touched his face, the skin would still have been warm.

I only knew Wilfred was gone because of his tongue. It hung down between his teeth, oily and pink, and it brushed against the old pillowcases under his chin. Loose, limp, a piece of stretched taffy. That one thing, that's all it took to convert him into a corpse.

But I didn't see how he could've died so quickly. He hadn't been shot or stabbed, hadn't been beat. So what had done it? Maybe none of us had actually lived through that night in the stairway so many years before. It just took some of us longer to realize we were dead.

67

WE GOT DOWN from the overpass and pedaled to Grand Avenue, but soon enough our bikes had to be abandoned. The streets were crowded, but now the sidewalks were too. Grand Avenue feeds right into Garland's business district, and many workers were hoofing it that morning. We asked people to move aside, but that didn't work for even a minute. If we'd tried to plow through on our bikes, folks would've become violent.

I saw the men moving ahead of us, but Ms. Henry and I couldn't catch up. Worse than my numb leg was the thump of heat along my spine. It seemed to beat in time with my own heart. I kept slowing down as I listened to it.

There were four bus stops on three of the corners at West Grand Avenue and Adeline Street. Each bus stop had generated a crowd. These poor folks looking to the horizon, when it was clear no bus would arrive. There were too many stalled cars blocking the way. Maybe four hundred people, including the ones in their cars, utterly unaware. The Church of Clay snaked right through them undetected. We even lost sight of those men for a time.

When we finally caught them again, their flock had thinned down to just one guy standing by a telephone pole. Where were the others? No time to check. This one had a blue duffel bag at his feet, the top already unzipped. He shuffled his weight from the right foot to the left, a pan-handler's dance. The guy went into his pants and took out a book of matches.

He struck one match, then lit the whole book.

The homeless dude held the book up as it sizzled.

This one wasn't a decoy.

It's amazing what folks don't notice. Even two men on the other side of the telephone pole hadn't realized what was happening. They stood with their backs to the bomber.

We were only yards away, close enough to be turned to ash, but unlike Martin at the lake, this guy wasn't sticking around. That boy might've been willing to sacrifice his life, but this older man hesitated. And that's what saved us all. His will to survive.

He dropped the burning matches onto the bag, but turned to run at the same time, and he kicked the duffel bag over. A little of the liquid inside splashed onto his cuffs, but most of it soaked the concrete. The hot matches landed on top of the upside-down bag. Nothing would ignite until they melted through.

The only people moving were the homeless guy and us. The rest of the crowd was too confused to blink or breathe. We reached the bag, and Ms. Henry scooped the matches up in her left hand even as she continued to move. The fire sat in her palm and she grunted with pain. Then she snapped her hand shut and strangled the fire until it died.

With that danger passed, the Gray Lady changed direction. Back after the homeless man. He shot off, running south down Adeline. She didn't glide, I wouldn't call it that. More of a forward-moving stumble. Ms. Henry went like an off-balance bat out of hell. And I was right beside her, a spasming snail. Quite a pair of heroes.

68

MY EYES CLOSED, I didn't close them. And hours passed, though it only seemed like minutes. When I opened them, the sun had set. Could it really be the third night in Murder's basement already? The pains of withdrawal were nothing compared to the start of dehydration. My heart burned so badly I thought it would rip the muscles of my chest apart. My gut rattled hard enough to hurt my hips.

These pains distracted me for hours, so it took me a long while to notice that Wilfred's body had been taken away. Upstairs I heard the pots banging on Murder's stove again, and then the weak creak of an oven door opening and slamming shut.

What were they cooking now?

My shoulders had swollen up because my hands had been tied behind them for seventy-two hours now. Those shoulders felt as big as grapefruits tucked under my clothes. And my hands, where were my hands? I couldn't feel them at all.

I tried to sit up, but the most I could manage was rocking side to side. My arms didn't like that, and neither did my breastbone, but I wanted to get onto my belly, needed to be in any other position. My sanity relied on a little movement just then. I didn't turn over, but I did get my left arm out from under me, and as it snapped to my side, the pain was a series of blasts, bright flashes behind my eyes. I wanted to move my right arm too, take advantage of the fact that the rope had come free, but that was too much to do all at once, so I rested.

In a little while the feral cats returned. The bobtail was last to come inside, but remained the boldest. It didn't even creep toward me cautiously. It practically hopped into my arms.

Now, even more alone, I concentrated on the closest living thing: that cat. It looked older somehow. Little white dots freckled its gray nose, and the gray hair didn't just poke out of its ears now, it seemed to spool down as far as its legs, which made the thing appear ancient.

But instead of feeling happy for the company, I entertained a different line of thought. I wondered why that bobtail had been so quick to settle right next to my cousin. Maybe it was more than body warmth, more than playing favorites. The other feral cats had frolicked and fought nearby, but none had been bold enough to make a bed by Wilfred's ear. Except this one.

I'd always heard that dogs could smell fear. Maybe cats could smell death? Smell death and even feel attracted to the scent. I can be a superstitious guy. Suddenly I didn't want the bobtail's company quite so much.

But it wanted mine.

I tried to scare it away, hoped to push it back with my newly freed hand, but that arm must have thought I was crazy. It couldn't do more than throb. So I tried to scare the cat away by making gruesome faces and spitting and whispering curses, but that old thing only hissed at me until I went silent again. Then it crept in close. I felt its wet fur as it tucked against my neck. It huffed hot breaths, and I held mine. I passed out while it slept.

ABOVE ME I heard dishes being washed in Murder's kitchen. That's what brought me back to consciousness. I didn't have much of a voice at that point—very late on the third night. I doubt even the bobtail would've heard me. And it was still right there, perched against me. I felt it but refused to open my eyes and confirm. Who would I have called to anyway?

I heard a broom brushing Murder's floors. That *chuff-chuff* noise as the bristles reached a corner, the hard clack of the shaft knocking the walls. It seemed worse to hear domestic acts up there, better if they were torturing animals or firing cannons. At least then it would've been hell above and hell below.

The bobtail gave a deep sigh.

I peeked now, impossible to deny the damned thing any longer. I watched it cross its paws, rest its chin on top of them, and shut its eyes again. What could I do? It was like sleeping in the same cell as your executioner. I shut my eyes too.

AT DAWN the bobtail remained there at my neck and let out creaky, squeaking breaths while it slept. As the faintest sunlight began to enter the darkened basement, I could see the old cat better. This little peanut was as fragile as me.

You want to share feelings, you want to empathize with living beings, humans do. That's what I believe. Some sense of communion with life, *particularly* as death approaches. Even a death-smelling feral cat will suffice, if that's your only choice! My left arm had healed enough to move, to touch and feel, so I tried to overcome my crazy fears and super-stitions.

An old cat would just need body heat where it could find it, I told my-self.

First with Wilfred and now with you.

It didn't kill Wilfred. It's not here to kill you.

It's not to blame.

It's not to blame.

Then I bent my left arm, and the tips of my fingers brushed the bot-tom of the bobtail, but the cat didn't flutter, so I left my fingers there. Touching. It felt wonderful.

I wanted to laugh because I'd thought it was going to wake up, claw me in the face, and run. Instead we reached a weary peace. In my blunted euphoria I looked around the rest of the basement, and then saw there, down near my waist, on my *right* side, a second bobtail curled up and sleeping too.

But it wasn't a similar cat. No. It was the same cat. Had those white freckles on its snout, threads of gray hair coming from its ears, chin propped on top of its paws, and even the sickly wheeze that had made me feel tender minutes before. The only problem was that the first bob-tail hadn't moved. It lay there against my neck.

But it also slept down there beside my waist.

Okay, I told myself, it's no surprise. You've just gone crazy. No one could blame you for a few hallucinations. It's been almost four days without water or food. And you weren't in great shape to start. The one on your right is just a pillowcase. It's still a little too dark in here and you can't see straight. That's all.

But you know how it is when you try to convince yourself of some-thing rational: the more you tell yourself the sane explanation, the more you believe the insane one. That's how it was. I'd rested myself awhile, and though it hurt even worse than the first time, I twisted my right arm out from under me. As it popped back into proper alignment, it made the same horrible snapping sounds the left had, but my mad curiosity overcame my pain.

And through all that, neither bobtail moved. They were waiting to see what I would do.

See that? I thought. Look how you're thinking. The cat hasn't moved, and that pillowcase down there *can't* move.

Eventually my right arm recovered enough to twitch, and once it twitched, it wasn't long until the spasms, and after the spasms I regained bodily control. That lump down there is just a blanket, I said to myself. It's a couch cushion. Now prove it to yourself.

I put my right hand out.

I touched it.

69

MS. HENRY AND I WATCHED in shock as Garland swarmed over the fugitive. They came out of their cars and off the sidewalks to catch him. He ran down the middle of Adeline. Trying to catch up with the others, I guess. When cars doors opened to block him, he switched and ran across trunks, over roofs, down onto hoods. But the crowd stopped him, they snapped him up. One moment he's on the hood of a Subaru, the next he's yanked to the ground. And after that? I couldn't see. I shouldn't say. The crowd worked as one mind and didn't even notice us. Ms. Henry and I didn't wait to see if they would.

We ran, but not for long. We got winded after three blocks. As we speed-walked, I looked at this woman beside me. She'd developed a limp, but wouldn't complain. When she stepped down on her left foot, she winced slightly and lifted her meaty shoulders the tiniest bit.

The Gray Lady.

Ms. Henry.

Adele.

"How's your hand?"

She opened and closed it. "Burnt."

She'd admitted a lot to me by now. A bit too much about Snooky Washburn. But a person like her doesn't do that easily. It felt unfair to play dumb anymore. I didn't want to keep secrets either. Now's the time, I thought. To tell her what happened, what was inside me.

"Adele," I began. "When we went down to the sewer . . ."

"Ricky."

"I'm not asking more questions. I'm trying to tell you something."

"Ricky," she said, "turn around."

Two Devils were falling out of the sky.

Their arms opened wide.

It's exhaustion that makes you brave. I went for the pistol in my coat pocket quickly, and yet I hardly realized I was doing it. But even before I gripped the gun, the Devils were on the ground. They reached us in a blink.

The Devil beside me landed on its feet and quickly pulled my left hand out of my coat. It stooped over me, leaned close, so I couldn't see it clearly. I only registered the touch. Its skin felt rough on my wrist. Imagine being squeezed by a squid. I tugged hard, hoping to free myself like Adele had done in the Devils' Well, but it must've learned from that encounter. It held me tighter.

The other one grabbed Adele in much the same way, pulling her right hand out of her purse, away from her flares.

Still holding us, they rose to their full size and cast shade across our bodies. Both were very tall, maybe eight feet, but their bodies were nearly as flat as flags. With sage skin everywhere, but their bellies were lighter, almost yellow.

They had faces, in a way. Two tiny milky eyes that looked like pearl onions. And below those eyes two small nose holes, each no wider than the head of a tack. And just below that a wide flat mouth, really just a slit in the skin that curled down at either end so they seemed to be frowning.

This close up I could even see they had tails that hung down and whipped side to side. I heard something scraping the asphalt, and looked down to see sharp nails at the tips of their tails, the nails as gray as old bones. That must've been how one of them had stabbed me, how it impregnated me.

These were Angels? In whose creation?

The one grabbing my hand shook me hard again. I stopped fighting. Let go of the gun, and it fell into my coat pocket heavily. I tipped my head back and beheld the Devil's face again.

Are you the one from the sewer? I thought.

Is one of you growing inside me?

But it didn't respond, not one word. What do you do with all that silence?

Then it let go, flapped its body once, and flew into the air. It landed again, half a block away. The second one let go of Adele and did the same. We'd come pretty far along Adeline Street, but there were still a few cars on the street, still some adults waiting at another bus stop. But none of them screamed, none ran in terror. Maybe no one else could see the Devils of the Marsh.

"Yo!"

Adele and I turned around to see a big yellow school bus with young kids sitting inside. Third or fourth graders maybe. Girls and boys had their faces pressed to all the windows on the left side, facing us and the Devils. The bus driver only looked ahead, at the traffic.

The bus chugged as it moved forward. The driver snaked that bus through gaps that seemed dangerously narrow. The kids all opened the windows on the side near us. Some stuck their heads out and gaped. Others crowded the glass door at the back. One boy had an arm out, as well as his head. He pointed at the Devils of the Marsh frantically, trying to direct the eye of any adult nearby. He shouted again. It sounded even louder with his window down.

"Yo!" But that boy wasn't horrified at the sight. He was smiling.

Swamp Angels. That's what *he* saw.

The kids kept diligent watch until their bus reached a corner. When it turned, the young faces moved to the right side of the bus. They remained there, rapt, until the bus disappeared.

Is this how Jacob felt when he met the angel? Or Mohammed as he witnessed Gabriel?

I turned back around and found the Swamp Angels still waiting on the asphalt. Two greenish silhouettes rippling in the road.

They turned and moved farther down Adeline Streeet.

"Part of me just wants to kill them," Ms. Henry said, gesturing ahead with her chin.

But I didn't answer her, I couldn't. Suddenly my face burned and my shoulders tensed. To my surprise I'd taken what she'd just said personally. It felt like she'd threatened a member of my family.

70

IT WAS THE FOURTH DAY.

I never took so long to move so little, but when you want to avoid the truth, a walk across the room can take a thousand years. As I inched my right hand toward the gray lump in Murder's basement, the bobtail by my neck never moved. It stayed so still I thought it wasn't breathing anymore. Murder's basement took on the damp smell of a coming storm, and I wondered if the room would flood during a heavy rain. Imagine, after all this, if I drowned instead of starved. At least I'd finally get some water.

Then it really did begin to shower out there. I didn't hear any thunder, only the first few spats of rain against the outside walls. The sound grew into a dull roar, which filled my head and only added to my confusion.

Listening to the rain distracted me so much that I didn't even realize I'd touched the little gray bundle on my right, until it purred. And a moment after that one began, the other bobtail, the same bobtail, purred into my left ear. The hum of the cats mingled with the drumming rain until the storm seemed to enter the basement and those old cats became as elemental as the weather.

I didn't have the power to pull away. I couldn't move, couldn't stand, and while my weary hand rested against the second cat, the first cat finally moved, uncurling itself from against my neck and shaking when it stretched. It looked past me to its double, still lying under my fingers.

That one woke too.

It stretched and shook and looked across my body.

And I lay there listening to both cats purr, to the steady rattle of the rain, focusing on these sounds rather than the four yellow bobtail eyes.

My neck tickled as the first cat paced along the left side of my body, bumping against my shoulder, my wrist, my knee. It reached the bottom of my left foot and stopped, bumped me there one more time and perched. Then looked at the other.

The second followed, bumping my right thigh, knee, and shin until it sat beside the first. They posted together, dispelling any doubt they were the same. Even their movements were synchronized. How could this be real? I hoped I was insane. That would only mean my mind had broken, not that the world was uncanny, unfathomable.

Squeezing their eyes in unison, breathing the same heavy sigh, the cats denied me the comfort of delirium. They were there.

Together they sniffed the bottom of my left foot, and even though I wore sneakers, I felt their wet noses against my skin. But when they pulled back, I felt my cold sock again, pointed my toes and heard the canvas of my sneaker stretch. It was like they'd passed through my clothing.

They pressed their noses to my right foot now, and instantly I felt their breath again. Even worse, when they licked their lips, the tongues tickled my skin. I even felt a charge in my bones.

The bobtails favored my right foot, put their noses up against it again, and stayed there, prodding. It was like having someone pressing a knuckle against your arch, sharp that way. I felt them against my foot, and soon the pain increased. It became so bad I swore they broke the skin. And still they pressed harder.

My body moved for me, sort of flopping backward, away from them. Was it shock? Do people bounce around in shock? Either way, my body knew the command: flee! But there wasn't far to go. My head bumped against the basement wall. The bobtails didn't seem bothered by this. They just crept forward and closed the distance.

They continued devouring me.

Right down to the bones. When their mouths snapped, I felt the stabs in my skeleton. It felt like they'd reached inside me. They ground my shinbone between their teeth and I *heard* the rod cracking. It sounded like the limb of a tree being torn off in a storm. Wild sensations sparked across my body, a flickering light behind my right eye, an ache in the wrist I'd broken as a boy, a cool warm explosion above my left ear.

And then they chewed through the bone, down to the sticky middle. They reached the interior. My body trembled and my lungs tickled. I felt them bumping heads down there—*in* there I should say. In me. Smacking their skulls against each other in the tight glove of my skin.

My right foot looked so swollen the shoe could barely stay on. Below my foot I only saw the bottom halves of their bodies. Their tails rose and slapped against the ground firmly. Rose again and waved in a semicircle, then whipped back against the dirt again. They'd gone through my shoe, squeezed into my flesh, popped past the bone, and got down to the marrow. I figured that was as deep as they could get.

How forgetful of me.

Many bodies will be buried, but not so many do their dying in the dirt. By ending up with these cats in Murder's basement it was like I'd cut a few steps out of the process already. So why not simply shut my eyes and let the bobtails finish their business? By now my foot burned because they'd dug so far in there. It felt like my bones, my skin, had already turned to smoke and cinders, and the beasts would keep going up and up until my whole body returned to dust.

So just let it, I thought.

I was tired after all, almost ninety-six hours of starvation and thirst will drain you. My body would've run out of power even if the cats hadn't come along.

Let it go, Ricky. Let it go.

But it turned out I was wrong about the cats. They weren't gobbling their way through my entire body, because it wasn't my body that interested them. Instead they reached a certain point, just below my right knee, and then they hunkered down, raising their rears while tucking their back legs. And then they started to pull.

I lay there in the darkness listening to the rain and talking myself into oblivion. The best way to avoid massive pain was to just go limp. But when I felt them tugging, it seemed like they were pulling my skeleton out of me. I opened my eyes and saw the basement wall above me get farther away as I was pulled toward the center of the room. Were they going to thrash and tear me into smaller pieces and eat those pieces one at a time? How do you relax yourself through that?

But as the wall got farther away, an inch or so with each pull, I saw that my left arm had flipped up over me, reaching for the receding wall. And yet even as the wall moved farther from view, my hand stayed as close to the wall as it had been a moment before. And again, after another pull took me farther down, my arm remained in the same place. After a few more tugs I noticed the sides of my own face getting farther from me. What I mean is, my eye sockets seemed like two well holes and I was falling deeper into the earth. I was being pulled down inside my own body, and when they finished eating, there'd only be this husk left behind. That's what the cats were after. Not my flesh. My soul.

The surprise was that I even had a soul to eat.

I don't mean this in the self-congratulatory way that people with tough lives usually do, where we talk about all our terrible exploits and how we acted so badly, but underneath it you can hear us bragging.

What I mean is, even though I'd been raised as a Christian, I'd never actually believed in the idea of a soul. People hear that you grew up religious, and they can't imagine you'd have a complex relationship with faith. If you believe one part, you must believe it all. But who gets more chances to see the absurdities than the devout? An answer that's satisfying on Sunday becomes contradictory by Wednesday night. Belief is a wrestling match that lasts a lifetime. So I'd certainly been taught about the soul, cautioned to protect it, read relevant verses in various versions of Scripture, including the Washerwomen's own. And for all that, I must admit, it remained more an idea than a conviction.

But now, in Murder's basement, it wasn't my body and it wasn't my mind. So what else could these creatures consume?

I only found out I had a soul when I was losing it.

That's when I thought of my father.

71

THE SWAMP ANGELS USED THE WIND to move. They didn't fly, they glided. Sticking their chests out until their upper bodies took on the shape of a sail and trapped breezes against their backs. This lifted them so high they almost floated off, but before this happened, they'd anchor themselves to the ground by digging the tips of their thin feet into cracks in the concrete. They leapt forward from one groove to the next, moving five feet with each step.

When they reached the low fencing around a parking lot, they hopped up and wrapped their feet loosely around the horizontal poles, then curved their bodies forward, puffing their chests to let the wind push them. Sliding along the rail until they reached the end and hopped off, were sucked backward while in midair, and then floated toward the ground. Here they caught at more cracks in the sidewalk and did the same grip-toed tiptoe again. Their tails swayed from one side to the other, keeping their bodies balanced as they soared. It felt natural to be awed.

In the air their bodies fluttered slowly, their tails stiff behind them.

"They look like stingrays," I told Adele.

"Isn't that something to see?" she said.

72

I WAS THREE YEARS OLD when my mother, Carolyn, didn't return from her missionary assignment in the field as expected. She'd been in an accident on Route 2 in Michigan, but we didn't know it at the time. It wasn't unheard of for a parent to be a day or two late. It might be something as simple as road weariness that slowed a person down if she was driving back to Queens from Colorado.

But Sargent Rice felt eager to go on his assignment and wasn't willing to wait. For years afterward he justified leaving by saying the Washerwomen were strict about their missionary schedules. We called them commissions. But they'd have given him a little time if he'd asked.

My dad believed in the Washerwomen's teachings, I know he did, but he also just wanted his full hundred and fifty days away from us. He wasn't so different from lots of married people. For instance, our mother never lingered when her travel date arrived. Lots of good-bye kisses, all the hugs me and Daphne pleased, but her eyes stayed focused on the front door.

Our parents weren't getting vacations. They worked hard as they crossed the country, and endured levels of dismissal and anger that I can never imagine. But the other seats in their rented cars were vacant. The motel bed only had to accommodate one. No children demanding. Time alone is pornography for people with families.

So at this time I was three and Daphne eight, Mom still getting a splint put on her arm in Michigan, but Dad's discharge date arrived, and Sargent Rice had to serve. Other parents did the same thing occasionally, watching one another's tykes. They even had a buddy system to help one another out. My father left each of us with a family in the community and asked them not to tell the Washerwomen, who would've objected. This wasn't as impossible to hide as you'd think. People keep terrific secrets from one another even in a one-room shack. You think they couldn't hide a couple of kids for seventy-two hours? The Dhumals watched Daphne and Ms. Rush took me.

And off our father went.

But by the sixth day, my mother hadn't returned, and I became too much for Ms. Rush. Forty-eight hours she could handle, but not a week. She'd already been plenty generous to me. But never let me pretend that a religious cult attracts the stablest people. By week's end Ms. Rush left me and the Washerwomen altogether.

I didn't remember any of this, by the way. Daphne only told me about it years later. It came up right after I told my father about her hidden plastic yellow ring. An hour after my father made Daphne melt it on a frying pan, she was kind enough to explain this family history. Ah, siblings.

Ms. Rush left me in a Burger King on Main Street in Flushing, and the manager fed me fries until Social Services arrived. They weren't going to return me to three women who were rewriting the Bible in their own image, bet on that. Daphne escaped my fate because the Dhumals kept their doors shut. Sargent Rice, only six days into his assignment, had to come back from West Virginia.

The term *orphanage* sounds melodramatic, so let's say I was kept in the back of an office instead. Some space in midtown Manhattan, with a large sleeping area for the kids in back and a small room up front where a caseworker explained the circumstances to my dad.

Apparently, if you abandoned your kid in 1968, the Child Welfare Agency only gave you a verbal warning and asked you to sign two forms. That's it. Soon as he did this, my father was free to take me back. He received a date for a hearing in Queens County family court, but the caseworker told him it was pure formality. The city had respect for all religious communities. Just go to court and the record would be closed. The only way my dad could mess it up was if he didn't show. Then they'd leave the file open. And even if it took years, they'd find their way back to him and me and the Washerwomen again. Child endangerment. The city wouldn't forget.

Sargent signed and agreed but didn't listen. In his mind he was already back on U.S.-119.

Afterward, he didn't bring me straight home. Instead, my dad took me to lunch.

What happened at that meal? This is the question I always asked him, but his answer never helped. We ate. That's all he'd say as he sank deeper into the cheetah-print couch. But I wasn't asking for a menu, I wanted a diagram of his thoughts.

I could imagine him with a napkin tucked into his shirt collar, just the way I'd always known him to eat in public. How long did that hour feel? When did he make his choice? What did he say to himself as he returned to that midtown office and gave me back to the orphanage?

As the feral cats in Murder's basement chewed through me, I didn't think of struggle or escape anymore, only that lunch with Sargent Rice. And the question he never answered: how could my father leave me like that?

I asked myself this even as the cats ground their teeth deeper into my bones. The foundations of Murder's home soaked in the rainstorm, and a thick, moldy air entered my throat. I coughed and choked.

I got a lot of mileage from that story about my dad. Leverage against him, I mean. It was a pretty selfish act, after all. And, like children do, I punished my father with it whenever he asked too much of me. Whenever he annoyed me. By the age of ten I'd bring the story up if he just told me to wash the dishes. I even reminded him of it on that morning when the police surrounded our building. Rose had whispered in my ear, and he'd barged in, and I'd felt angry for the interruption. So when he asked me to leave with him, I said, You're going to leave me behind.

That shut him down every time.

But now, in Murder's basement, I'd reached the dying time, and that old game of manipulation seemed pointless. Self-pity was even worse. Sargent Rice died in 1998, and in 2002, at thirty-seven, I was following him. Did I really want to spend the last moments of my life throwing one more tantrum?

And there in Murder's basement I realized the real question. The one I should've asked my father when I had the chance: at a moment like that, when someone needs you, why does a man hide his heart?

WHEN I WAS TWENTY-NINE, I took my girlfriend Gayle to a women's clinic in Jackson Heights. We went in together. We'd argued a lot, but now we agreed. Then, soon after checking in with the front desk, Gayle begged me to take her out of there. We sat on a blue Arlington sofa. We were waiting for an older woman to call us in for Gayle's abortion.

Gayle worked in a cooking school at that time, helping affluent kids file their class schedules. Holding their hands through the paperwork process as if they were in grade school rather than college. They weren't nice to her at all. She was only an office temp to them. They sniped at her suggestions and mistrusted her kindness. At night I'd find her half-asleep in bed, still wearing her work clothes. I'd pull her pants and panties off, and while she lay on her stomach, I'd rub her butt.

She had such a sweet little butt. When I caressed her, our bedroom would get so quiet I'd think she'd fallen asleep, but then, very faintly, she'd groan. Not sexual. More like the contact reassured her, relieved her. At least one person cared. Everyone wants to believe that. Gayle was an office temp, and, at that time, I worked for a moving company. We scored dope on the daily. But at night Gayle was my woman and I was her man.

When Gayle and I sat in that women's clinic, she rested against my right shoulder and cried. She squeezed my arm tight, but pretty soon that charge wore out and she was left with nothing but those familiar groans. She did that as we sat right in the women's clinic. In front of three other couples going through their own private debates. Gayle called to me for relief, but this time I wouldn't give it.

Although she wanted that baby, I relied on one thing about Gayle: she was terrified to do it alone. Didn't feel she could manage the enormous work of a child, not with making a living and, of course, heroin. So I didn't have to threaten or force her to have the abortion. I only had to become intangible, invisible, hardly there. Hide my heart. Her own fears did the rest.

Gayle pressed her forehead against me, but I only studied my big dumb hands.

A woman stepped out from the back rooms, and she called Gayle's name.

73

WE CROSSED A LONG OVERPASS that led to the Port of Garland, and when we came down the other side, it was as if the whole city of Garland had been muted. We were too far away to hear anything but our footsteps. The two Swamp Angels were far ahead of us. It was just me and Adele and that pulse, still strong, along my spine.

There's a living thing inside me, I thought.

We moved down Middle Harbor Road, which showed signs of hurried escapes, cranes with shipping containers midway between the ships and the shore. Trucks abandoned in the road, their doors open. Some of the engines still chugged.

There were hundreds of shipping containers stacked a hundred feet high on either side of the road. Red, blue, silver, and orange shipping containers with corporation names painted on their sides. They surrounded us and rose above like valley walls.

"How could you kill the Swamp Angels if you know they're doing the Voice's will?"

"I don't know that. Joyce Chin suggested it, that's all."

"They tried to make you shoot Solomon Clay. If he'd died down there, the people at Laguna Lake would still be alive. The Church of Clay wouldn't exist."

She slapped her purse. "How the hell could I have known, Ricky? You can't put all that on me!"

I said, "I'm not trying to down you. I would've done the same thing."

"Please, Ricky," she said, looking at the street. "Don't lie to make me feel better."

"Half the world would've done what you did."

We hobbled along quietly for a few paces.

I said, "But now the Swamp Angels are leading us. They want us to do something."

"You don't know that. That's just what you want to believe. And stop all this 'Angels' mess."

"Why do you have such a hard time admitting what they are?" I asked.

"I'm a working person, Ricky. Nothing more than that."

"Stop hiding behind that bullshit," I said.

She flinched, faintly, but didn't argue.

"I don't know what the task might be, Adele, but I want us both prepared to do it. Maybe they want us to kill, maybe they want us to protect."

"Protect who exactly?" Adele asked.

San Francisco lay far across the water, but it seemed safe. Looked safe. Maybe because I knew there were National Guard units controlling its border. But much closer, just a few hundred yards to our right, I saw the majestic eastern span of Stitch Bridge. Its upper roadway looked like a reflecting pool as daylight glared against all the windshields, each car waiting to be ushered through the checkpoint. A process that didn't seem speedy at all. Those folks sat in their cars, aggravated but patient. Unaware. Unguarded. Men and women and kids.

Thousands and thousands of them.

74

MY RIGHT LEG FELT FRIGID, right up to the shin. A soul wasn't devoured in just one bite. My body shivered, but the hungry cats were as indifferent as erosion. My mind returned to Gayle.

The old woman led Gayle and me into the back of the clinic, where there were very few windows. The waiting room had been bright, but it turned gloomy here. The thick carpets were old, and they silenced our footsteps. The walls had been painted light green of all things, the color of nausea.

Gayle and I walked into a narrow exam room, and the old woman told Gayle to climb onto the table. She said this quietly, even nicely, but that didn't calm Gayle. There was a folding chair right next to the exam table, where I was meant to sit. The old woman left. There was hardly enough room in there for the two of us. The place seemed no bigger than a walk-in closet. And yet, in a moment, three more women fit themselves in. All young, in their twenties.

They helped Gayle onto the table, lifted her feet and rested each in a stirrup. The whole time they were talking, asking the same questions. Are you all right? Are you sure you want to do this? Are you all right? Are you sure you want this done?

Gayle couldn't be counted on for answers anymore. She cried quietly. I only knew she was crying because she sniffled. When I looked, her chin and cheeks were slick with tears.

"Are you all right?" the trio asked.

"Are *you* sure you want to do this?"

They wouldn't speak to me. They wouldn't look at me. And yet if I'd gotten out of that chair, if I'd tried to leave the room, those women would've bopped me in the head with hammers. If I wasn't willing to be a father, I better damn sure be a witness at least.

So I sat there quietly, looking at my feet now instead of my hands. The room only seemed to get darker as the three women moved around. There was only one window in this narrow room and too many bodies. Gayle lay to my left, only inches between us, squirming on the exam table, a woman holding each hand. The third rubbed the tops of her now bare feet.

"How are we doing?" the doctor said when he walked in. A guy in his fifties, kind of round and unthreatening. He smiled at her, and, when I looked up, he even smiled at me, but there wasn't anything calming in the expression. He looked like a man who'd stumbled across a grizzly bear. Make nice. Make nice.

"My name is Dr. Hamilton and I've been working with this clinic for seventeen years," he said. He spoke in a chipper tone, I don't know what else to call it. Like he was at an auto show, admiring a prototype car.

"It's always been my belief that a woman should have the right to make her own choices. That's why I'm here today."

Gayle squirmed less as he talked, though the three women didn't stop touching her. They surrounded her. The one holding her right wrist nearly boxed me out entirely. I stopped looking at my shoes and looked at Gayle, who only stared at the ceiling now. She hardly seemed conscious. She hardly blinked. Her lower lip jutted forward and drooped.

"All right," the doctor said. "Do you feel like going ahead?"

Gayle didn't speak, she only nodded.

He said, "This is called a speculum. You see? I need this so I can see your cervix."

I heard, but I couldn't watch. Only Gayle's head and neck were visible to me anymore. The woman next to me hid the rest.

"This is just a swab," the doctor said calmly.

And it went on like this, step by step, until finally the doctor nodded to the woman who stood right next to me, and she left the room. I didn't try to peek now. I looked at my feet. I looked at the door. Twice I looked at Gayle, but she wasn't studying me.

In that time the doctor might have said more, but I hardly noticed. When that woman let go of Gayle's wrist, it was as if Gayle had been untied. Her body squirmed. A new fear animated her. It was time. Could she really do this? Gayle looked to the other women.

"Are you *sure*?" one asked.

"You can still say no."

"Of course you can. *Of course.*" The doctor said this sweetly, but his arms were crossed.

I remained in my seat and listened for Gayle's decision. But we'd gone too far into the clinic, all the way to the last room, and she couldn't generate enough power to propel us—herself, the baby, and me—out again. Gayle wriggled and shivered, but that's all.

Then the third woman returned with a big machine.

It came in on wheels. A gray box with coiled tubing attached to the side. It looked like a jury-rigged robot in a 1950s movie. Nothing but a typewriter balanced on a wastebasket. The woman wheeled it over to the doctor, then she stepped between Gayle and me again.

The doctor turned it on.

In the pamphlets at these clinics they used one word all the time. *Gentle.* The speculum will gently stretch the cervix. The woman will feel a gentle tug. The machine will make a gentle noise. Obviously I can't say if the first two are true, but the last definitely isn't. Dr. Hamilton turned that machine on, and the sound of the vacuum was a terrible whir, as loud as a tree shredder.

The noise bounced off the narrow walls and only became louder. When I looked at Gayle, she'd stopped crying, but her head and shoulders were raised off the exam table now. Was she trying to see or to push? I couldn't say.

The buzzing got louder and louder until I expected the room's window to crack apart.

The machine worked too well. It was pulverizing my bones and my delusions. My teeth hurt, so I held my face.

And then it was done.

The machine turned off, and Gayle was led to a room for rest. I sat on the blue Arlington sofa again. New couples were in the waiting room. When Gayle was ready, I took her home.

We'd picked out two names for the baby, one for a girl and one for a boy. When I repeated those names to myself in Murder's basement, I felt like I was making introductions to that unborn child. Moving toward it. Near enough that it could hear me. That's when I finally cried.

I felt my whole body for the first time in days. Real awareness through every limb, all the accumulated pain. I had a chill deep inside me. The tears burned my dry eyes, and I blinked furiously, afraid my eyes would crack in their sockets.

Eight years earlier I'd had so many ideas why fatherhood was impossible: Gayle and I fought worse than Arabs and Jews. Worse than Arabs and Arabs. Even working full-time I had trouble covering rent. And of course there was the dope. How you going to bring a child into all that?

It's shortsighted. Selfish. A mistake. And while all those might be good reasons for caution, they weren't mine. Not really. Plenty of others had managed to raise a kid through the same, or much worse. The shame I felt wasn't because of *what* Gayle did, but *why* I got her to do it.

I was a coward.

I muttered apologies to Gayle, and to our child, for the first time in my life. Nothing specific, just that pathetic old refrain.

"I'm sorry," I whispered.

My father always used to say that to me when I asked about our lunch date in 1968.

"I'm so sorry," I said again.

The sight must've been high tragedy, that's what I thought. A fucking junky, dying on his ass, starving, face like a corpse, apologizing to a baby that hadn't even been born and a woman he no longer knew. Absolutely wretched. Imagine the portrait.

And there I caught myself.

I *was* imagining the picture, and it was absolutely romantic. Romantic like the boy who fantasizes dying on a field of war, killing a thousand enemies before being cut down. Romantic as the girl who envisions poisoning herself, leaving a corpse that'll indict the one who finds it, a plucked and corrupted rose. A man, coming to an end like mine, should perish in this pose: contrite, abject, mythic.

Is this really all I am? I wondered. A grown man acting no better than a *teenager?*

The image I'd always held of myself was so much more forgiving.

All this occurred to me as my soul was sucked farther down into my body by those feline mouths below. I watched as I slipped out from the comfortable space of my skull and down inside the tight, moist channel of my throat.

This is really happening, I thought. This is really happening!

When the bobtails finished chewing me up, there wasn't just death waiting at the end. More like a reckoning. The ancient Egyptians believed the god Anubis met each of us on the other side, and that he stood before a great scale on which our hearts were set. There each was weighed, tested, for its worth.

Every time I'd blasted my dad with the story of how he'd returned me to the orphanage, he'd gone into a real depression, and I'd thought, in a child's satisfied way, that he *should* feel pain. But in Murder's basement I realized I'd been wrong. Leaving me behind wasn't what had made my father feel guilty. Not just that anyway. He'd felt guilty because leaving me behind had been so *easy.*

When I sat on that blue Arlington sofa and stared at my hands, while Gayle groaned with genuine heartache, I only impersonated sorrow. I wasn't devastated when the old woman called us into the back. Not despondent when Gayle and I left quietly after, not touching.

I was relieved.

Was this the heart I wanted measured?

And right then, the cats stopped eating. Not when I thought about what my father had done to me, or even when I admitted what I'd done to Gayle, but when I asked myself if I was satisfied with the life I'd led. With the man I'd turned out to be. Then the cats paused. For a moment they weren't pulling me down.

And in that respite I willed my soul to climb. And though my arm, up there, out there, still wasn't moving, I scrambled back up my own throat. I returned my eyes to my face. My spirit moved with such gusto that my body sprang up at the waist and I sat upright on the unfinished basement floor. From this position I could see one of the exits the feral cats used, an empty window frame taped half-shut with cardboard. I hadn't been able to see it while on my back. Early evening outside, but still enough sunlight to see the foundation of the next home only yards away.

Can people change? I thought.

I wasn't addressing myself. Maybe the cats? Or whatever had created them.

I fell over on my left side and grabbed at the ground underneath the hard layers of cold clothes. With a grip in the earth I pulled myself toward the open window frame, finding handholds in the dirt the way a free climber scales a mountain. Carefully. Slowly.

I know I've been selfish. But there's still some good in me.

I can stop being a coward. I can be brave.

I promise.

When I looked backward, over my right shoulder, the cats rested on their haunches and watched me. They tilted their heads in unison, smacked their lips simultaneously. Blood on their whiskers and paws.

I was feeble, but determined, and sometimes that's all you need. My right leg, below the knee, remained cold, felt empty. I wouldn't even have known it was there if the weight hadn't dragged at my knee.

When I pulled myself out through the empty window frame, I lay on my back in the last warmth of the setting sun. I looked at Murder's home. There were figures moving behind the gold curtains on the first floor. They gestured wildly. I heard grunts and laughter.

They had a perfect system worked out. I understood it now. The bobtails devour the soul and then Murder eats the body. Once they were done, there'd be no evidence you ever existed, not on the physical or spiritual plane. This is how some folks go out. We don't die, we're erased.

I expected the veil to part, for Murder's red face to press against the pane, for him to catch me trying to get away. Instead of waiting to be yanked back in, I turned onto my stomach and dragged myself until I found a puddle of rainwater at the bottom of the next house's gutter spout. It was filled with fallen leaves and three dead gypsy moths. I drank until it was dry.

The cats came to the basement window, but stayed inside the frame. They watched me while I lay outside, lapping. Another puddle of rain-water lay a few feet closer to the street, and I crawled to that one, drank from it too. The cats stayed perched in the window frame, stomachs only partly full.

How much of my spirit did they get? I can't really say. Who can put exact figures on such a thing? But if I had to guess, I'd bet they gobbled up nearly half of me. That part remains there still, waiting in the belly of the underworld. Someday I would have to reckon with it, but for now I was alive. Left with, let's say, 60 percent of my essence. Not enough soul to be careless with but, if I changed, maybe enough to eventually tip that great scale.

75

"I CAN'T GO BACK to Vermont if we get through this," I said.

"Oh, Ricky, please."

This declaration, the decision, must've seemed to bubble up from nowhere, so I understood Adele's exasperation. But questioning her at the gates of the Washburn estate had left me contemplative. I'd been replaying moments of my life in my head as we marched. Like my escape from Murder's basement in 2002. And the promise I'd made in Cedar Rapids. *I can be brave.*

"I thought I joined the Library to finally prove myself. I thought I was being bold. But maybe it turned out to be just another place to hide."

The San Francisco Bay lay to our left, nothing between us and the sea but fifteen feet. The quiet gray water shined in the sunlight. I looked behind us, and the view was dominated by the sky, not the land. This didn't make our problems down below seem small, exactly, but simply ours. The Heavens were busy casting beauty.

"So you just quit and do what? Go back to the minimum wage?"

I smiled. "I'm not romanticizing that, believe me."

We'd gone about as far as we could on foot. The Port of Garland was the shipping hub of the city, so most of it was docks and shipping containers. All of which were protected by chain-link fence rising two stories high. Stitch Bridge loomed nearby, well over our heads, but I didn't see how we could reach it.

"Why'd they bring us this way?" I asked. "We can't get up to the bridge from here."

"Maybe they brought us out here to just kill us," Adele said.

"You really believe that?"

"No," she said. "I guess I don't. But what else? Tell me what good we're supposed to do from here."

"You act like I've got the answer," I said.

She looked up at me. "You sure you don't have any?"

I felt the life inside me as a steady, low vibration by this point. At times it seemed to buck, to move. To kick. For the first time I thought of it not just as a life but as a child.

My child.

Just ahead of us the two Swamp Angels changed direction, veering left, entering a small park that we reached a minute later.

Port View Park had a circular driveway that led to a small playground. There was a snack bar and bait shop on the same lot. And between them a long concrete pathway leading right out to the lip of the Bay.

"You see that?" I whispered.

At the end of the path, in that distance, three silhouettes. Three.

THE WATERS of the San Francisco Bay smashed against the stone shoreline. Breezes off the water so strong now that Adele and I got bopped around. As we got closer to the end, I saw an octagonal fishing pier. The thing looked so old, just a mess of warped wood. Room enough for fifteen fishermen to cast lines off the sides. A sign posted at the pier's entrance read: FIRE DANGER. NO OPEN FLAMES. NO BARBECUES. NO FIRES.

The three figures standing on it solidified as we approached. The Swamp Angels were perched on the top rung of the pier's railing, looking down. On the pier floor stood Solomon Clay. He raised his arms and waved toward Stitch Bridge. He didn't seem to notice the Swamp Angels. Maybe he couldn't see them. Maybe he never had.

"You've hurt a lot of people!" I shouted.

Solomon Clay dropped his hands, looked at Adele and me.

"I'll hurt a lot more before I'm through!" he answered back.

We had to yell to be heard over the noisy shoreline. I already had the gun out of my pocket, but I didn't know if I could hit him from that far. I had to get closer. If I'd been better rested, I would've run, but Adele and I were only being held together by the stitching in our clothes at this point. The best we could manage was a trot.

Solomon wore a sharp gabardine raincoat, buttoned up and tied off, which made it look like a monk's robe. The boards of the pier were dark with moisture. Soaked with that explosive formula.

"We've seen what that stuff can do," Adele shouted.

Solomon looked down at the pier.

Solomon climbed onto the first rung of the pier's railing, and his weight caused the wood to whimper. These planks were as brittle as tinder sticks. He said, "I'm only waiting to see if my flock is in position."

He had no fear of us. I was almost there. My boots beat on the concrete.

Solomon thumped the top rung of the pier with his fist. "That's their sign."

Adele and I followed his line of sight. From the overcrowded upper roadway of Stitch Bridge I saw a series of business jackets flitting through the air. Must've been thirty or forty of them, maybe even more. The Church of Clay had dressed for work today, just like anyone else. Their cheap coats floated from the bridge, the flags of a woeful country.

"Time for mine," he said.

I found the energy to run faster with the gun stiff-armed in front of me. But I still wasn't quite there. Twenty feet might as well be a hundred if you're not accurate. Solomon Clay undid his raincoat. The suit underneath looked baggy, sagging on his frame because it had been doused. Soaked. He removed a lighter from his pants pocket. Did I see his hands shaking? I wouldn't reach him with a bullet. I thought maybe I should try something else.

"I'm pregnant!" I shouted.

I would've expected him to laugh, most anyone else would have. Even in the midst of all this strangeness, what I said had to be the strangest of all. Adele's reaction was closer to expected. She fell. Tripped and rolled right into the fence running along one side of the concrete pathway. As if my words had come right out and swept her leg.

Mr. Clay? He didn't drop that lighter, but his thumb froze on the striker wheel. He looked away from the bridge, into my face.

"You're . . ."

And, that quick, he knew it was true. He *knew.* The lighter fell from his hand, clunked on the pier floor. I was close enough now. I raised the gun. I pressed the muzzle to his forehead.

Solomon said, "Not yet."

76

SOLOMON MOVED JUST HIS EYES, looking up at the barrel of the gun still pressed to his head.

"When would be better?" I asked sarcastically, as if we were planning a lunch. But really, I wanted to be talked out of shooting him. I didn't want to kill anyone.

"First let me understand."

I looked at my hand, the pistol, as if they weren't even mine. It took me a moment to remember I had control over them. Then I lowered my hand, but I kept the gun out. Behind me I heard the rattle of the chain-link fence as Adele grabbed on to it and pulled herself to her feet.

Solomon squinted at me now, and behind him the Swamp Angels remained perched on the top rung of the pier. Their bodies swayed with the breezes coming off the Bay. Had they brought Adele and me here to kill Mr. Clay or to hear him out?

"Are you kin to the Washburns?" he asked. "Long lost cousin or something?"

"No," I said. "Nothing like that."

Solomon patted his hands against his suit, and the fabric squished from the explosive liquid. He looked down at himself then and seemed almost surprised to find himself soaked with the stuff.

"I . . . ," he began, but he seemed confused.

Adele clomped closer to us, stopped right next to me. "That was good!" she shouted. "You sure surprised his ass. Mine too."

She pointed down at the gun, tapped the muzzle with her pointer finger.

"Pop him," she said.

I looked at her and said, "I wasn't trying to trick him, Adele. I am pregnant."

While Solomon was shocked into silence, Adele took the news a little less stoically. She went batshit insane.

Spit shot out of her mouth as she yelled at me, drops so big I swore she was losing teeth. If she'd had the gun, she would've shot me. Just out of distress, astonishment, and even fear. If she hadn't had the whole pathological aversion to touch, I'm sure she would've strangled me for a few hours. Why did she have to find out this way? she yelled. No damn warning? And in front of Solomon Clay! She'd revealed so much, but I'd held this secret. She had a right to be hostile.

Solomon stepped backward on the pier, and neither of us followed. Where could he go? He patted his face liked he'd patted his clothes, as if trying to wake himself from a nightmare. He looked at me. Eyed me up and down.

"I got passed over," he mumbled.

Solomon's quiet confusion, so out of character, actually snapped Adele's tantrum. She stopped fuming and looked at Mr. Clay. "What the hell are you talking about?"

"I got in the mud to dig out my men. To convince them they deserved better lives. I put in *work*."

I didn't challenge him. I couldn't. There are people who get neglected, whole generations of them, as if God just leapfrogged over their line.

"I got passed over," he said again, quietly.

He leaned back against the pier, right between the Swamp Angels, who looked down at him still. I thought I saw pity in their expressions, but that might just be what I felt for him. I put my free hand out to him, tilted my head and smiled faintly, the way you beckon a flustered child.

Solomon set his shoulders back. "Fuck you and fuck your pity."

He stepped forward, stooped to reach the lighter that had fallen to the pier floor.

He said, "The poor will always be with us."

He grabbed the lighter. His men on the bridge still awaited their sign.

"When you drive them out, they'll run to me."

He bashed his chest with a closed fist.

"And my name will be their war prayer."

We were so far from the bridge. That was my logic as I raised the gun. We couldn't see his people up there, that's why they'd needed to toss their jackets as a signal. And I doubted any of them had been outfitted with binoculars or spyglasses. So they probably couldn't see us either. A person doesn't become a martyr just because he's died. It's because those who know of his death speak of its righteousness. They tell the story. But only Adele and I were down there, and neither of us would spread his word. To prevent Solomon from becoming a martyr I'd have to turn him into a homicide. On a day like this, amidst the larger terror, would anyone really investigate some unidentified black male? To be sure we'd even have to strip his suit off afterward. He'd get chalked up as a drug murder of some kind and disappear into the mist of urban statistics.

Even as I formulated this plan, I couldn't help feeling ashamed of myself. I knew he had to die, but must I really serve him up to such humiliation? He'd only meant to defend the despised. Everyone else had overlooked them. But I knew where Solomon's kind of apocalyptic fury led: to a stairwell full of dead children. It wasn't religion, only wrath. Not faith, but nihilism. I was sick of seeing belief warped this way. And that feeling overcame my sympathy for Solomon.

I put my hand against Adele's purse and pushed her back. She stumbled on the concrete and fell, shouting, "Ricky, wait!"

I wasn't the only one moving. Now the Swamp Angels leapt down from the top rung of the pier. They dug their thin feet into the space between the boards. As I approached, they surrounded Solomon. Why had they waited until now to act? Two years earlier Adele had skipped her chance to stop Solomon. And now, if Solomon had been willing to call a truce, I would've let him go too. Maybe they'd waited until I finally understood that Mr. Clay wouldn't be appeased. To spare him was to condemn others.

Solomon still seemed unaware of the Swamp Angels, which seemed desperately unfair. All he'd really wanted was to brush against the divine. He'd ached for contact, and even now, inches away, they remained unknowable to him.

Then the Swamp Angels grabbed him. Each seizing an arm so he couldn't lift the lighter to his clothes. Couldn't set himself on fire. Couldn't transform from a man into a movement. And he looked down at his hands, mystified. No matter how he struggled, his hands wouldn't rise.

He looked left and right, searching for the cause. And he fell into these short, quick breaths. Gasping. Then I saw Solomon Clay smile. With his head cocked back he looked directly into the Swamp Angels' faces. And they looked down into his. He shivered with ecstasy.

"Oh," he said. "They're beautiful."

I pressed the gun to his right cheek.

Then I shot Solomon Clay.

77

WHICH IS HOW I BECAME a righty.

Thank God for shock, that's all I'm saying. My hand, the gun, his head, they all went to pieces, but because of shock I didn't feel much of anything. It looked worse than it hurt, at least initially. The bullet hit Solomon Clay, and half his face turned into a mist that floated out to sea.

The explosion came just a second later.

I hadn't intended that part, of course. Only meant to cap him, but the problem was muzzle flash, the release of superheated gases when the trigger is pulled. That's the same stuff that sparked Adele's methane explosion down in the Devils' Well. She understood that, which is why she'd been calling for me to wait. It's also why she crawled off as fast as she could when I didn't listen. I might as well have put a lighter to Solomon's clothes.

I flew backward, onto the concrete pathway. Collapsed. Wish I could've just fainted, but I didn't. Stayed awake, aware. My left hand, my forearm, they'd simply disappeared.

Adele was beside me in an instant, pulling the belt from around her coat and tying off my arm above the elbow. She made the tourniquet quickly and expertly, but it wasn't necessary. The blast had been so hot my flesh had seared. The wound got cauterized.

At least I wouldn't bleed to death.

I blinked my eyes furiously, I remember that. Made this low sound, growling or groaning, one of those *g* words. Grunting? Let's say all three. Growling, groaning, and grunting. My throat felt hoarse from the way I'd screamed when my bones turned to splinters. I'd howled louder than the gunshot.

I heard Adele behind me saying, "Aw, Ricky. Aww, no."

"I'm all right," I muttered. "I'm all right."

It wasn't true, but I felt I should say it. To convince her and to convince me.

She said, "You gave them the signal, Ricky. You sure did."

Too confused to understand, I looked straight ahead and saw the pier burning. To the Church of Clay, Solomon had just become divine. They were too far off to tell the difference between a victim and a volunteer. Maybe they wouldn't have cared. On the bridge I imagined the Church of Clay opening their briefcases and bags now, slathering their bodies.

I wonder what the people on Stitch Bridge saw. What they thought, I mean. It must have been so confusing. To see all those men stripping off their jackets and throwing them out to sea. Opening their bags and drenching themselves. By the time anyone might've understood what was happening, it was too late. The match flames came next.

Small explosions ran along the side of Stitch Bridge like holes in a belt.

And that side, the one facing us, simply collapsed.

So many girders had been incinerated that the upper roadway slumped violently—south side down. The cars that were jammed up there shook and shifted. Some flipped onto the backs of the cars in the next lane. And those in the fast lane, closest to the explosions, went over the side of the bridge. A dozen cars slipped between the newly broken spaces and splashed into the Bay. The people trapped inside wouldn't be saved.

I couldn't hear any screaming, but Stitch Bridge did enough groaning on its own. The sound only got louder when the girders on the other side bent and snapped too. They weren't designed to hold all that weight themselves. The upper deck slammed flat onto the lower. This turned out to be good news for the survivors on top—at least they wouldn't get pitched off the side—but terrible news for those one hundred or so cars below them in the eastbound lanes, crushing news in fact.

But Adele and I were too far away to experience the immediate horror. The flat-out terror. From Port View Park I saw the upper deck twist and squirm, and when it moved, it caught the sunlight along its metal frame. This caused a powerful glare, but I could still see the flat satin of the San Francisco Bay and the open, bright sky above. Caught between the two this gleaming bridge looked like a second sun, rising. I would've put my left hand up to protect my eyes, but my left hand was gone.

We were witnesses.

78

HALF AN HOUR PASSED after Stitch Bridge collapsed, and neither Adele or I could move. It took me that long to understand the damage done to my arm. It wasn't until I tried to stand up that it really registered. I set my left hand down to help me balance and found nothing there. I fell on my face.

Shock had helped me, certainly, but even that couldn't explain my relative good health. I should've been laid out or weak from loss of blood. At the very least I ought to have been screaming. But I wasn't. When Adele had been down in the Devils' Well, she'd been protected. That explosion should've killed her, but she stood here now.

And what preserved me? Maybe the child?

When I left Cedar Rapids, I really thought I knew how to make things better. How to balance the scales. Selfishness had been my problem for decades, but it had all culminated with Gayle. So I left Iowa expecting that all I had to do was go out and try again. Meet a woman, get her pregnant, have that child, be a good father. Repair your karma in four easy steps.

But when I tried, I failed. I impregnated a whole series of women after that, but not one of them ever gave me a kid. A few months into the process and every single woman had a miscarriage. It just wasn't working.

Now, though, in light of all that I'd seen and heard, maybe my mistake began when I crawled out of Murder's basement assuming I knew how to make things right. Maybe the solution wasn't inflicting my plans on another woman and child. The Voice was going to make me be brave in a way I would've never dreamed.

Because I was dazed, I only heard Garland's state of emergency. Fire trucks, police sirens, and ambulances making their way to the burned bridge. They were doing their best to shake the world with whistles, but it was open sky out there at the edge of the continent, and those bells sounded feeble trying to fill all that space. Soon the smell of hot tar filled the air, as if the city were being cooked.

And then we turned our eyes to the water where the pier had been.

The explosion had shattered the pier's supports, turned the railing into sawdust. Only about half the flooring remained intact, and it floated in the water. Solomon Clay's body lay flat on top. Flames traveled across the remaining wood, licking at his gabardine coat. And as the fire consumed him, his body shook and kicked.

The Swamp Angels remained there with him. Both of them. They held him down even as the fire that scorched Solomon did the same to them. Their bodies quivered, but it wasn't just the wind. They were in pain. Still they held him there. Sacrificing themselves to see the job through.

Then the Swamp Angels were engulfed in flames, and soon they let go of Solomon's body. They were dead. Their figures were lifted by the wind and were torn into small pieces in the air. Bits of burning paper, that's all they looked like now.

The pier tilted and Solomon Clay's body slid. The splashing waters of the Bay doused the flames around him. His clothes had practically burned into his skin. I saw his skull peeking through the shattered half of his face. Fire had burned so much flesh away.

Adele watched him. She gripped and opened her hands. She did this so forcefully that I heard her nails scrape each time they dug into her palms.

The pier had gone adrift. It bobbled in the water. A current dragged it toward the Bay. It twisted in the current, and the smoke coming off the pier surrounded it in a gray cloud. When the smoke cleared again, only yards offshore, I could see Solomon Clay's face even more clearly.

One eye remained, on the right side, but the other had burst or melted out of its socket. Half his face was covered in loose, bubbled flesh, and the other half was his exposed gray-white skull. They say a skull, without skin, looks like it's grinning. But this one glared.

It was impossible to look away, even with the horror of the bridge not far off. The pier dipped in the tide. It tilted at an angle and began to sink. Solomon's body remained limp.

But his eye shifted.

I swear I saw it move.

It looked back to Adele and me and it held a relentless fury. Bitterness and vengeance without end.

Then his body slid backward, off the pier, into the depths.

79

WE BACKTRACKED HALFWAY THROUGH the Port of Garland without speaking or even looking up from the street. My arm throbbed, but nothing worse yet. I didn't mention Solomon's eye. Had she seen it too? I didn't even want to ask.

We crossed over the footbridge, and Garland came alive again. Sounds and sights. A few cars idled at the corner of 3rd and Adeline. They weren't waiting for traffic lights, because the lights didn't work. No electricity. The drivers looked to one another, waved one another on, inched forward, and then stopped to see what the others were going to do. At the next block there were more crawling cars.

The population of this whole embattled city moved at a similar pace. In hopes of escaping downtown Garland, a great number of refugees had migrated here. This barren zone had to be safer than the city center. I didn't see the National Guard or the army. Those troops were all stuck on the other side of Stitch Bridge, protecting the stuff, the people, who'd been deemed important. We were on our own.

Attention Garland: chaos has been declared.

Prepare to see an American city tear itself apart.

But this was a funny kind of anarchy. A mood unlike earlier, when we'd biked through the panicked traffic. Different from the frenzy in the people who'd beaten that bum in front of the burger stand and the other one farther up Adeline Street. Now the drivers were more careful and the pedestrians held hands.

Cars on these roads filled fast. Groups of people climbed inside any passing vehicle with room, and they were welcomed in. On the next block two teenagers had a big red cooler open. They passed out bottles of water to anyone.

Couples, trios, and quartets of people walked together on the streets. Holding each other up. Some of them crying, others still shocked. But no one seemed abandoned. Someone grabbed you up if you were alone. They pulled you close.

We'd been left on our own, but Garland held itself together.

Adele and I made it another two blocks before she finally spoke.

"Where is it?" she asked.

I looked up and down the street. Unsure of what she meant.

"The . . . ," she said.

Then she cupped her small hands into a bowl.

"My back. Up by the shoulder blades."

She slowed and looked, checking for a baby bump. Her face drooped with disappointment when she saw that it wasn't there.

It was a cobalt blue morning, which looked as though it would turn into another warm afternoon.

We reached Market and 3rd Street. A triage center had been set up in the parking lot of a self-storage building. By triage I just mean that someone had come from a local pharmacy with bags of aspirin, ointment, and bandages. A small table carried bottled water and crackers. The folks on one side of the table looked as bewildered as the folks on the other.

"Can I touch it?" Adele asked.

We were across from that parking lot, in the shadow of a low brick building. She had her arms crossed and her eyes focused on the wall behind me. I didn't answer until she looked at me.

"Let's go around the corner."

"Do it here," she said.

"You see all those people right over there?"

She stepped between me and the curb, her back to them. "No, I don't," she said.

I pulled my shirt out from my waistband, and warm air snuck underneath.

I had to undo a few of the lower buttons if she was going to feel the spot, but that was difficult on my own, one-handed. I couldn't get the buttons open. She saw this and stepped closer to help, but she couldn't do it either. While I tried and failed at one, she tried and failed at another. We were both too busy shaking.

Finally we stopped and put our hands down to let them settle.

When I tried again, I had an easier time. I just sort of pinched them open, one by one.

She watched me.

The lowest button first. Then the next. Until I'd opened my shirt most of the way.

Adele looked at my exposed stomach. She lifted her right hand and spread the fingers wide to press her palm against my belly.

But she couldn't do it. Her body fought her mind. Or vice versa. I didn't interrupt.

Finally she rubbed the back of one finger, the pointer finger, against me. Not even the whole finger, just the knuckle. Right above my belly button. That's all she could do for a while.

When she turned her hand around and touched my side, I didn't even notice right away. Her caress sent me into a trance of my own. Her hand slid inside my shirt now, moving to the small of my back. Her arms weren't long enough to keep so far away. She had to step closer.

Adele's cheek rested against my chest.

She reached up my back, and the skin felt warm, both hers and mine.

"Is this the spot?"

"A little higher."

"Here?"

"There."

The fluttering began as something light, but then it grew stronger. It felt loud inside me. I thought, She might even *hear* it if she keeps this close.

I looked at the top of her head.

I said, "Adele. I'm going to put my arms around you now."

80

SO WHY TELL YOU ALL THIS? Any of this.

It's a fair question. Let's call this my testament, then. After all, it's been five months and you're nearly here. I can't say that as a fact—who knows exactly how long it takes a child like you to be born—but I feel it's true. You're coming out.

You've grown. I know that much, because I can barely walk anymore. I'm so stooped over that I've been looking at nothing but the tops of my shoes for three weeks. That's when Adele put me on bed rest.

And I'm worried, let me admit that. Suppose I don't survive the birth? I've been trying to keep healthy. No junk at all and I'm eating better food. I still have a few drinks now and then, which I hear American doctors don't like, but I doubt they'd have much good advice about you.

What will you know about your father if I don't tell it? That's why I've written all this business down. Maybe you'd only know what other people say. I'm not sure how many, besides your mother, would be kind.

You have five grandparents on my side of the family alone, that's how I think of it. Carolyn and Sargent Rice, naturally, but I'm including the Washerwomen too. Having that many grandmothers means you're a lucky baby.

But if you ever do get curious about my family, assuming you do grow up and that you can read, or even walk among human beings—wow, so many "ifs" to worry about . . . If you get curious, you'll find a handful of notices about the Washerwomen. And only two about the Rice family. One lists Daphne Rice, nothing more than a name and age, as a murder victim from that night in the stairway. She was buried in Nassau Knolls Cemetery out in Port Washington, the service paid for by an Episcopal church. The second lists the jail time both Carolyn and Sargent Rice were given (seven and twelve years respectively, though neither served half that).

And the last article about the Washerwomen will explain that all three sisters hung themselves on the same night, at the same time, in their cells. This despite the fact that they were incarcerated in three different prisons and never allowed to communicate.

BUT LET ME TELL YOU about when Adele and I reached the corners of MacArthur Boulevard and Fruitvale Avenue, a busy intersection where people stumbled around trying to figure out how they'd make it home. A hundred people, maybe more, waiting at the bus stop, watching the road, as if something as ugly as a city bus would reassure them.

Adele and I had stopped across the street from the crowd, in front of an empty bank. We acted as if we just needed to catch our breath, but maybe we wanted to see the bus roll up too.

The people across the street clapped and shouted now, and when I looked to my right, I saw a bus at the top of the hill. A bus covered in dust. This dirty, gray bank safe came crawling down the block, and folks nearly went to tears. There were passengers inside it already, too many, in fact. Even the bus driver sat at an angle, tilting to the left, her face pressed against the glass.

But the bus stopped. A few people got off, which meant there was room for a few more.

A debate started at the bus stop, who from the crowd would be allowed on board? There were mothers with tiny children, which was one good argument. A few very pregnant women who huffed and held their bellies from underneath. I felt a special sympathy for them. But finally everyone agreed: a quartet of senior citizens walked to the bus door. Each climbed inside slowly. Those left on the sidewalk glumly watched the bus go, then looked back to the horizon.

I pushed myself off the hot brick wall.

"Give me your phone," I said.

"Who are you calling?"

"The Dean."

She didn't like the idea, but I must've been grinning so hard she knew I wouldn't be deterred. I felt good. I felt righteous. She opened her purse and recited the number as I dialed.

"Ms. Henry!" the Dean answered.

"This is Ricky Rice."

"Mr. Rice! It's only been four days, but we miss you."

The way he said it, so casually, it nearly made me faint. Four days!

"I just thought I better call you."

"I'm glad you did. We've got to bring you home. What's all that noise?"

"That's the aftermath of your plans," I said.

"Oh, my. Was it bad?"

"Yes."

"Very bad?" he asked. The Dean's joy registered in sharp little breaths.

"Just turn on the news," I said.

"I certainly will do that. I certainly will."

"Ms. Henry drowned in the Bay," I said.

"And what about Solomon?"

"He's dead too. I'm pretty sure."

The Dean laughed into the phone. "How mysterious!"

"Thousands of people died!"

The Dean stayed silent on the line for a breath or two.

"That's unfortunate, Ricky. I'm sure it is. But the sooner you come back home, the sooner you'll forget them."

I couldn't believe this mug! If he'd said that claptrap in front of me, I would've dropped him into a mortar and used my left arm like a pestle.

"I'm not coming back," I said.

"Is that right?"

Adele mimed the "hang up" signal, but I turned my back.

"So what you going to do?" the Dean asked. "Get another sweeping job?"

"If I have to."

He growled into the phone, "How you going to raise a baby on that kind of money?"

The big phone trembled in my hand. "What?"

His voice changed, lost the playfulness and found the gristle.

"You listening to me now, junky? I'm like an oracle. I told you that. Did you think I was just jawing? I knew what was going to happen. That's why I sent *you*."

"You sent me because I did good work," I whispered.

"Are you stupid, or just dumb? Violet had you beat, straight up and down. But what if that thing kills you coming out? I'm going to risk my best Scholar on that chance? Hell, no."

"You're lying," I said.

"Want me to swear on a Bible?" He laughed. "Now you come back to Vermont *today*, or I'm sending Violet to tear it out."

"Violet won't do it," I said.

The Dean sucked his teeth. "Violet's *grateful* to the Library. She knows it saved her life. You really think she'd hesitate to show her appreciation? You sure didn't."

I didn't want to get into chest-bumping with this man. What were we really going to do to each other besides shout? Maybe I could make this conversation more useful to me.

"So you know what it is, then?" I tried to make it sound like I was testing him, but really I was just looking for some corroboration.

"It's an Angel, Ricky."

"But why put something like that in me?"

"Because their numbers are dwindling! And like any other species, they want to survive."

"How many are left?"

"Just two, Ricky. Now imagine if something happened to them."

Once again I saw their bodies burning down to ashes as they held Solomon on the pier.

"You'd be carrying the last Angel on earth," the Dean said.

"Why do you want it so bad?"

He hissed into the phone, "Imagine how powerful the Library would be with an Angel as our servant."

"That sounds like slavery to me."

Before I could say any more, the phone fell out of my hand. Adele had smashed me with her purse. The big plastic phone popped against the ground, but it was too sturdy to break.

"How long you want to chat with him," she shouted. "Maybe he's tracing the call!"

"He already knows we're in Garland!"

She slapped her purse against the concrete. "But now he knows we're not coming back," she moaned. "We could've used that extra time to run."

The big phone made a few noises then. Sounded like static, but I picked the phone up and heard the Dean hissing with laughter.

"Adele," he shouted, "is that you? Sounds like you survived after all."

She looked at me then, and her big cheeks sagged. Her eyelids drooped. I finally turned off the phone. I felt so angry that I cocked my arm to throw it into the street, let a passing bus crush it. But Adele grabbed the top of the retractable antenna and slipped the cell from my palm.

"You have the kind of money to be throwing phones away?" she asked.

She made a big show of looking into her purse. Into her purse and not at me. What were we supposed to do next? This wasn't much of an army. Adele and me. And you. Not compared to the Washburn Library or the Church of Clay. What the hell were we supposed to do now?

"Tell me what the Voice said to you, Adele."

She didn't have the energy to withhold anymore, so she just said it. Four words. And when she was done, I laughed bitterly.

"What the hell does that even mean?" I asked.

"You see what I'm saying?" She shook her head.

Adele was right. The command made no damn sense at all.

81

THAT'S WHEN OUR NEW LIFE BEGAN. I write this in the bed of a rented room off Route 2, a two-lane road that runs along the brim of the United States. My right-handed penmanship might even be called legible these days. It's late and I'm tired, but I always feel that way now. We might be in Montana—but, no, that's wrong. We spent time in Montana a month ago. After a few days we have to move.

We settled in Oregon for a hot minute, figured it was a good place for disappearing, but one morning we woke to find footprints in the gravel around our rented cabin. Was it the Washburn Library or the Church of Clay? I don't know, but I'm afraid both are after us. Maybe the Dean has read the right field notes by now and figured out the last two Swamp Angels died. That'll only make you more valuable to him. And the Church of Clay? We murdered their prophet. That alone is a good enough reason to hate us. We never did find those other thirteen men we saw from the highway overpass. That's enough apostles to found a faith.

In North Dakota, a town called Williston, there were handprints on the window of our motel bathroom. We didn't see them until Adele ran a hot shower. They appeared with the steam. The way those hands had dragged on the glass made the fingers look like claws.

Neither of us sleeps straight till morning anymore.

Sometimes Adele wakes up shouting out names. Her voice a guilty wail. Once in a while it's Snooky's name. But just as often it's Claude's.

I woke tonight to find the bed empty, but I'm used to that. It's two forty-five in the morning, and Adele has snuck off into the bathroom. She sleeps less than me, and when she wakes, she secludes herself for a little while. I've found her in tubs, or if we've rented a cheap suite, rocking on a couch in the living room. She's in our bathroom right now and thinks that by shutting the door she's shielding her thoughts. But I know what they are.

Is this really my life?

Did I choose this?

Maybe I could run away.

I know that's what she's thinking because I'm thinking it too. You're nearly here, and all my daydreams are about escape. Don't be too hard on us. We're just overwhelmed. Unprepared.

Scared.

"You doing all right?" I say to the closed bathroom door.

It's a windy night outside.

Adele stays quiet. Maybe she wants me to fall back asleep. Let her alone. But I'm not asking that question simply out of concern. I admit that hearing her voice, especially in the thinnest minutes of the night, strengthens me.

"I asked you a question," I say.

Finally, Adele clears her throat.

"Blow it out your ass, Mr. Rice."

We're in a town called Ironwood, I remember now. Not too far from Lake Superior. Our car is parked right outside this room. A gust hits and I hear the windows tremble. They don't rattle, they quake.

It's not lost on me that here, thirty years later, I'm following the paths of my parents. Route 2 is the road where my mother had her car accident. Adele and I have been driving all across the United States. Luckily, I remember just about every route there is to know. We'd been farther down, in the Southwest and the South, but then the air-conditioning in the old Mercedes finally conked out so we had to travel north, following the cooler temperatures, and found ourselves here on Route 2.

We actually do all right. Adele and I work temp jobs. We show up in a town and ask around. Usually there's something to be done. But, I must admit, our real moneymaker remains the cabin back in Garland. We cleared it out, cleaned it up, and now we rent it. Ms. Washburn doesn't give us trouble. I don't even know if she ever returned. Maybe Tia Quina and her sisters still occupy the big house. I like to think so.

The lease remains a dollar, though we charge our tenants substantially more. Adele and I pay for these motel rooms with the money we make working, and the money from the cabin is paid directly into a savings account. I'm pretty sure Adele wouldn't be willing to live as frugal as we do if we weren't doing it for you. There's already $9,200 in a Wells Fargo bank, which I think, relatively speaking, is a good start.

Adele just stepped out of the bathroom. She's closing all the windows in the room because we can hear a howl when the strong winds slip inside.

I stopped writing for a moment and watched her move because she's only wearing a top, no panties. I like to see her bare butt bop around the room. Juice Booty, that's what I call her when she jiggles.

"Juice Booty!" I shouted at her, and she wiggled her butt for me, just a bit.

I'm wearing a bathrobe and nothing else, so I pulled the cloth aside and slapped my thigh. It sounded like applause.

Who needs to know this kind of stuff about their parents!

I think some people would say that. But I never did see Carolyn and Sargent so much as kiss during their marriage, and I've got to tell you *that* scarred me.

I've been thinking about my father a lot. Nothing like a baby to make you assess your folks. He hasn't come across too well, but that's why I'm happy to do this. Writing it down is like thinking out loud. It's easier to hold on to a bad idea if you never share it, and it's harder to defend one if you let it out.

Sargent Rice grew up in Syracuse, son of a secretary and a grocery clerk. I never met them because Sargent never allowed a visit. My mother's folks came around here and there, but my father's didn't. I don't even know their names.

Sargent's parents liked to drink so much that they never brought home their paychecks. Instead, on payday, both his mom and dad returned with cases and cases of beer. For thirteen days Sargent would come home to an empty fridge, and on the fourteenth evening it was stocked with Labatts. It got so bad that eventually he petitioned both their jobs to make his parents' paychecks out to him, and when he turned sixteen, the employers actually complied. His parents went along with it because they were embarrassed. That was the start of Sargent Rice's thrifty ways.

But well before that, when he was younger, his parents would make a sandwich he could have for dinner, then head out to drink until last call. Leaving Sargent alone in a house that often didn't have heat or lights. They were always being shut off for nonpayment. My mother used to tell me this story because my father never would. Sargent Rice, eight years old and sleeping in his winter coat when the Syracuse chills hit. A boy alone in a darkened house. His family an institution that had failed him. In bed he'd make a quiet wish for the power to come on. Something to kill the shadows. A modest wish, really. Grace manifested as a little electricity.

It's good to keep in mind that your parents felt powerless too. You can't forgive them unless you do. And I forgive them now.

WE PAY FOR ROOMS with our work and save money thanks to the cabin, but we tend to eat in other people's homes. Not panhandling, we don't do that. It might be someone we work a day job with or a couple we meet while doing laundry. I can be pretty sociable. Also, people see my arm and want to know what happened. They usually think I lost it in the war. The number of folks who've been kind enough to have us in their homes? I can't tell you exactly, but we rarely eat alone. There are generous people in this world. Less than some might hope, but many more than you can imagine.

Three months ago we found jobs off Interstate 40, cleaning rooms at a Comfort Suites hotel in Oklahoma City. Only three of us were new and non-Spanish speakers, me and Adele and a guy named Ravi Arapurakal. He told us to call him Ronny. He could wiggle his long nose in a way that looked both funny and sexual, and even with the language barrier a couple of the older women on the cleaning staff loved him.

At the end of the shift he, Adele, and I decided to eat dinner there in the hotel break room. Adele and I because we hadn't found a cheap place to sleep yet. We sure weren't going to pay to stay at the Comfort Suites. At worst we'd sleep in the car. I suspected Ronny hadn't lined up a place to crash either. The break room was warm, a place for the three of us to rest.

So we ate, and then Adele broke out the Old Grand-Dad. She always has some in her big green purse. Ronny was happy to imbibe. We poured shots into our plastic cups discreetly. Ronny liked to joke around when he was sober, but he gave confession once drunk.

He had a brother named Ranjit who was a heart specialist in Milwaukee. Ranjit had done well and took good care of the parents, that kind of thing. But Ronny, the youngest boy, had less interest in caretaking. He felt a greater devotion to gambling than graduate school exams. He'd worked managing a parking garage in Gary, Indiana, but he couldn't save a quarter. Not with the Majestic Star and Casino Aztar and the Blue Chip within driving distance. Ronny even borrowed money from the heart specialist when his home threatened to go into foreclosure. Blew it in three days. Ronny's wife left him and returned to her family in Toronto. The heart specialist actually bought Ronny's house before the bank could seize it, then kicked Ronny out so some cousins could move in. Ronny didn't fight the arrangement. By then he knew he was a bad bet.

By the time Ronny told us this much, he was blubbering. He snorted, trying to hold in his cries, which only made his nose run. His round chin quivered and he could hardly breathe.

"My brother threw me out," Ronny said. "Everyone just tossed me away."

I don't know how I would've reacted to Ronny's stories a few years earlier. Not too sympathetically. We all got troubles, as Peach Tree once said to me. But by that time, in that break room, I wasn't the same man I used to be. I'd never shaken the image of that nut standing on the side of the highway after we'd kicked him off our Greyhound bus. We'd sacrificed him. And there, sitting with Ronny, I felt I was on the verge of that choice again. Sacrifice this guy, or . . . And just like that, snap, the Voice's commandment made sense to me.

Invite them back in.

How long would it be before Ronny told this story again, in another break room or a run-down bar, and after he was done, the folks listening would commiserate, pat his shoulder, lean in close, and ask if he'd ever heard about a man, a martyr, named Solomon Clay.

Or who knew if the Dean might not become less of a race man in the future, and sometime soon Ravi Arapurakal gets a mysterious invitation in the mail.

This was our moment.

But what to do? How to invite Ronny back in? It's not like we were going to have him move in with us. Or, even if we did, what would we do for the next Ronny? The next woman or man we found teetering at the edge. Even the Washburn estate couldn't house them all. Maybe what Ronny needed right then, in the depths of his own turmoil, was just the possibility of relief. The hope that he might climb out rather than keep falling. In his warped way that's all Solomon had been offering his followers. I wondered if we could redeem the best aspects of his message.

When Judah heard the Voice, he couldn't really be asked to do more than survive. A black man, back then—who could really demand much more of him? But Adele and I weren't Judah and it wasn't 1778. Maybe the Voice knew it could, it should, demand more of us than mere self-preservation. We were strong enough to lift others.

So I told Ronny what had happened to Adele and me. Everything. Me getting the note, the work at the Library, and how we ended up there in a break room in Oklahoma with an Angel on my shoulders. It was the first time anyone had ever heard it. Adele seemed to figure out why I was telling it pretty quickly, and we told the tale together. At the end neither Adele or I knew how Ronny would react.

But you can't predict people. He swallowed the wildest stuff as easy as aspirin. He accepted the existence of the Library, of the Voice, of both Judah and Adele hearing it down in the Devils' Well, Solomon Clay, his ragged army, he even accepted my pregnancy. In the end it wasn't the events that left him skeptical. It was the idea.

He was distraught. "Can people really change like that?" he asked.

I grabbed one of his hands there in the break room, under the humming fluorescent light.

"Yes," I said.

"I mean people like me," he clarified.

"Yes," I said again.

Ravi Arapurakal looked at me, still clutching his hand, and shook his head. Between Adele and me it was clear who was the believer. So he turned to Adele Henry, the pragmatist, the working person.

"This is crazy, Ms. Henry. Right? Second chances . . . People like us don't even deserve them! Do we? *You* tell me. Yes or no?"

Adele's palms were flat on the orange break room table. She looked down at her fingers. She shut her eyes and breathed in deeply. She slid her palms across the surface. The wall clock ticked and ticked. Adele took Ravi Arapurakal's trembling hand in both of hers. She held him steady. She looked him directly in the eye.

Guess what she said.

WHEN WE TELL PEOPLE about our four days in Garland over plates and bowls, most people seem happy for the tale. Even when they don't believe us, they say it's worth a meal. And it's not one-sided. All these folks have reminded me of something I knew as a boy, tapping maps in the Washerwomen's living room. My country is my family. I like America.

I'm not going to say *love*. Forget about love, not because I don't feel it but because love's easy. Lots of people say they love their families, but still treat their families terribly. So I'm purposeful when I say this. I like America, where believers eddy around one another like currents of air. Even our atheists are devout! To be an American is to be a believer. I don't have much faith in institutions, but I still believe in people.

THE TREES BEHIND OUR MOTEL are groaning. I can hear their bark twist and stretch. A storm is cracking their branches. There's a madness in the woods tonight.

One story that people like to retell a lot is the story of Jesus Christ. I can understand why, but the retellings never have much impact on me.

A guy is born divine and grows up to be diviner. I might admire him, but how can I really aspire to that?

The story that actually moves me, as a grown man, is the story of Joseph and Mary. And it's because, for all this talk of them being holy and righteous, they were just human beings. No matter how many visions and dreams and visitations, they were still just folks at first. They didn't *know* if they were right. They could only hope. I can try and aspire to that.

The hardest part of faith is the silence. It's difficult to face that quiet and remain patient. Waiting on your child seems like the same test. Each day, each hour, you don't know if you're passing the exam. You can only hope.

The wind outside has reached our door.

It hacks with so much force I swear the wood bends. I wonder if it'll break.

In case I don't survive, I want you to know this is *my* voice. Ricky Rice. Your father.

Look at all this business I've been through. There are times when I feel like I survived because I've been blessed or chosen or preordained. That kind of messianic hoo-hah. Other times, when the days are terrible, I think that no one's ever had it worse than me. I'm doomed. I'm cursed. I'm wretched. It's easy to become vain. And, for me, this is why my faith has always been valuable. Strip away all the magic and what does religion teach? There's something greater than you in this world. I don't know about other people, but I need to be reminded of this. And when I get too puffed up, when I invest too much in my own powers, I rely on what the Washerwomen taught me. Doubt grinds up my delusion. It makes me humble. And that's a gift.

I've got these words written on legal pads that we keep in a small yellow suitcase under the bed. It's about as bright as an egg yolk. We bought it from a Salvation Army branch in Philadelphia. It's a little heavy by now, too cumbersome for me to get at with my right hand alone. So Adele creeps over when I ask and pulls it out. She opens the top. The wind outside turned into a storm long ago.

It's battering our windows. Even the roof is shaking.

I'm going to set this pad down soon. Put it with the others hidden safe under the bed.

The ruckus outside sounds like rough company. A battle on the rise.

Adele is humming a tune for courage, and before I get up, I'm going to take a sip of something strong. I guess we could lock ourselves in the bathroom and hide. Let someone else face the fight. But we're not going to do that.

ACKNOWLEDGMENTS

Caitlin Grace McDonnell, my dear friend, who survived some serious trials. You deserve every good thing in your life. And more.

Chris Jackson, ass kicker. You wouldn't let me get away with anything in this book! And that's why you're a truly great editor. And friend.

Mya Spalter, thanks for every assistance and great idea. I appreciate it.

Jamie Keenan and Christopher Zucker, for the design of this beautiful book.

Bara MacNeill, for such thorough and invaluable copyediting.

To Mills College, Elmaz Abinader and Cornelia Nixon in particular, for bringing me out to Oakland, one of the best experiences of my life.

Thank you to the Mrs. Giles Whiting Foundation for their generous support.

And thank you to the United States Artists Foundation for believing that artists matter.

Emily Raboteau, my confidante, my peer, my team. I love you.

Jennie Smith, Mat Johnson, and Gloria Loomis for reading (and rereading!) this book over the years. I can't explain how valuable you've been to me.

Albert Lucientes, for the honesty and the insights. Thank you, my friend.

Thanks Charlie Raboteau for the term "spiritual X-Men"!

I grew up reading horror. This novel was influenced greatly by the writers I loved, and still love, in the field: Shirley Jackson, T.E.D. Klein, Stephen King, and my man Ambrose Bierce.

Being a weird black kid can turn you a little crazy unless you have some role models. So I'd like to thank the following for setting great examples. The Black Eccentrics (partial list): Bad Brains, Gayl Jones, Ishmael Reed, Armond White, Michelle Wallace, David Keith, Fishbone, Phil Lynott, Charles Burnett, Octavia Butler, Kim Thayil, Thomas Paine, and Darth Vader.

Last, I'd like to thank the folks who rescued me more than ten years ago now. The real-world basis for the Washburn Library. You invited me out and cleaned me up. I was a mess but you had faith. I'm still grateful. Your secret is safe with me.

VICTOR LAVALLE is the author of seven works of fiction: four novels, two novellas, and a collection of short stories. His novels have been included in best-of-the-year lists by *The New York Times Book Review, Los Angeles Times, The Washington Post, Chicago Tribune, The Nation,* and *Publishers Weekly,* among others. He has been the recipient of a Guggenheim Fellowship, an American Book Award, the Shirley Jackson Award, and the Key to Southeast Queens. He lives in New York City with his wife and kids and teaches at Columbia University.

victorlavalle.com
Twitter: @victorlavalle